Praise for *Daughter of the Goddess Lands:*

"… Kalie is neither a warrior princess waving a sword or a beautiful seductress dressed in shimmering gowns. Instead she's someone who must overcome her own terrors, even as she finds herself assuming the role of a reluctant heroine…So if you want to 'hear' a story that will challenge both your thinking and expectation, (and you will hear the many stories Kalie tells), Sandra Saidak's well-written debut novel of raw courage is waiting for you." — Sam Barone, author of *Dawn of Empire*

"…A masterful epic journey about trauma, healing, love, hate, and the loss of a prehistoric world we can never find again. Debut author Sandra Saidak mesmerizes with clear vivid prose and heartfelt emotion." — Valerie Frankel, author of *From Girl to Goddess: The Heroine's Journey in Myth and Legend*

Books By Sandra Saidak

Kalie's Journey
Daughter of the Goddess Lands
Shadow of the Horsemen

Short Fiction
In The Balance, including a story set in the lands of
Kalie's Journey (Coming in 2012)

Shadow of the Horsemen

Book 2 of Kalie's Journey

By Sandra Saidak

Published by Uffington Horse Press
San Jose, California

CreateSpace Edition

Published by Uffington Horse Press, San Jose, California, USA

This book contains an excerpt from the forthcoming collection of short fiction In the Balance by Sandra Saidak. The excerpt has been set for this edition only and may not reflect the final content of the forthcoming edition.

ISBN: 978-0-9846991-3-1

Learn more at: www.sandrasaidak.com

Acknowledgements

Thanks go first to everyone I already mentioned in "Daughter of the Goddess Lands". Thank you all again!

Those who have added their wonderful help to this second novel (or who I forgot to mention last time) include my high school English teacher Dr. Philip Fisher, for inspiration and mentoring, To Donji Columbine, thanks for the terrific cover art (both times). And to the wonderful ladies of Broad Universe, thank you for showing how to spread the word about the book after it's published.

And, although I've said it before, thank you George for making this novel happen, Tom, for making it possible, and Heather and Melissa — just for being you.

Chapter 1

Grasslands of southern Russia, circa 4000 BC

Somewhere near the front of the line, the lead warrior called a halt. Kalie sank gratefully down in the soft grass and waited for the water skin. She had lost count of the days they had traveled from the winter camp, and didn't know how many they had left to walk. But for now, she didn't care. She was too busy marveling at the transformation in the world around her.

The barren steppes which had so oppressed Kalie since her arrival had turned into a vast garden. Wildflowers of every hue stretched as far as she could see. Even the grass, so hard and brittle the rest of the year, was fresh and green and filled with the scents of earth coming alive.

"Here, Mother. I brought you water—and some more flowers!" Varena gave Kalie the leather-wrapped sheep's bladder of cool water. She took it and smiled at the tug she felt at her heart every time Varena called her that.

Varena, the daughter of a slave woman, had been orphaned as a young child, and left to the abusive care of jealous wives. When Kalie had arrived here as a slave the previous summer, it was with a plan to bring down the cursed beastmen who had killed so many of her kin, and harmed her in ways from which she had never recovered. Creating a family was not part of that plan. Yet, quite against her will, Varena's loneliness and innocence had awoken things in Kalie she had thought to be long dead. So she had adopted

Varena—not that anyone in the clan acknowledged the relationship.

Kalie drank, and handed the bag to the next woman. Irisa took the bag, daggers in her eyes for the humiliation that a slave was served before herself. As concubine to Maalke, Irisa should have been served just after Maalke's two wives, Altia and Cassia. But Kalie's healing magic had caused Maalke's barren second wife to conceive a child for him. So, for the moment, Kalie's status eclipsed Irisa's.

"What are these called?" Kalie asked, examining a cluster of delicate white blossoms clinging to a stick-like stem.

Any answer Varena might have given was lost in the cruel blow Altia struck from behind. "Others still wait for water, slave!" she roared. "Finish your task, then, check on the animals." She seated herself in what little shade the tall grass and westerly sun provided and began fanning herself with a scrap of leather.

"They're called lady's slippers," said Brenia, drawing Kalie away from her rage at Altia. To show it would only encourage Maalke's senior wife to mistreat Varena further.

"How about these?" Kalie pointed to tiny yellow clusters growing on a low bush near where they rested. While Brenia was high ranking woman of the tribe, and the wife of a warrior, she had always been kind to Kalie—an anomaly in this land.

"Mustard. We should pick as much we can. It has uses in healing, as well as cooking," said Brenia, whose interest in healing matched Kalie's. Perhaps another reason a wife of rank dared to be friends with a slave.

There were now two clans traveling to the spring pasture together. Chief Kahlar's clan—Kalie's home since she had come here as a slave last summer — had met up with another of the Twenty Clans of the Tribe of Aahk about five days ago. Led by a low-ranked chief named Boraak, this clan was seriously depleted after a harsh winter and a brutal pestilence. Boraak had only a handful of seasoned warriors to contribute to the tribe's protection on the slow march to their summer gathering.

In addition to being the most beautiful time of year, spring was also the most dangerous. Sheep and goats, weakened by the harsh winter, could travel but slowly, and needed all the rich grass and flowers they could consume if they were to continue to feed the masses of humans who depended upon them. It was important for clans to avoid competing for the same grazing lands until the strengthened herds met at the wide summer pastures, when many would be slaughtered for the feasting, trading and rituals that characterized the summer.

But until all Twenty Clans of Aahk were reunited in their full strength, they were vulnerable to attack. Outlaw gangs, hoping to establish themselves as tribes in their own right, with horses, flocks and women taken from lone clans unlucky enough to cross their paths, were a constant threat. So were other tribes, eager to increase their wealth. Each day, Kahlar and Boraak sent their swiftest warriors riding in search of news of their fellow clans, and any signs of danger lurking on the empty grasslands. So far, no other Clans of Aahk had been spotted. Tension grew, and spoiled the mood of more than just Altia.

Kalie refused to let anything ruin her

enjoyment of this wonderland. She gathered flowers as she walked, asking after their names and uses, just as if she had been back among her own people.

During the next stop, she sat with Cassia, Brenia and several other ranking women, telling a story as she wove a garland into Varena's honey colored hair. While the girl was still thin and pinched with want, the spring air had brought color to her cheeks and a sparkle to her eyes. Even her hair, a dull blonde all winter, was shining. The flowers further enhanced her beauty.

"Enjoy them while you can, Kalie," said Brenia, passing around a skin of water. "The flowers last less than the turning of one moon. Long before we reach the summer lands, the grass will be brown, the sun hot, and the flowers long gone."

"Like in your story about Shara and the Bird," said Varena, fingering the necklace Kalie had given her the time she first told it. How she loved being the special slave of a special slave, Kalie thought with bitter humor. It was not what Kalie had wanted for Varena when she had adopted her, but at least it made her happy. And in this, Varena was better off than her half- sisters.

Many of the women and girls mingled more freely on the march than they had while confined to their tents all winter, visiting with friends from Boraak's clan whom they hadn't seen since the summer. But Altia kept her two daughters marching demurely behind their mother. While they walked haughtily in front of the slaves, Kalie could see they would have preferred to be off on their own, seeking out their friends. Varena, no less Maalke's daughter than the other two girls, was a slave, because her mother had been one. Ironically, in some ways this gave Varena more freedom than her half-sisters. No one worried about a slave-girl's reputation or how demurely she carried herself. Varena could speak with whomever she chose, although she spoke with few people besides Kalie. A slave like Varena did not wish to call herself to the attention of anyone who could hurt her.

Which was nearly everyone.

Kahlar gave the order to resume moving. As always, the women were quickly on their feet and the men on their horses, moving at the speed of their slowest animals within moments. Everything they owned was carried on the backs of the women or walked on four legs beside them. Kalie adjusted her pack, bending beneath its weight like the others, but still intent on the scenery around her. She wove another garland as she walked, thinking to offer it to Cassia, but knowing Maalke's wife would never do something so frivolous as wearing flowers. Fine, thought Kalie, deciding to keep it for herself. She didn't care how she looked to the beastmen, and it would remind her of home.

As if her thought had conjured her, Cassia dropped back from her place behind Altia to walk beside Kalie. "You don't seem like the same woman who arrived in my tent last summer," she said with a smile, her hands clasped protectively over her belly. The gentle curve beneath them was just beginning to speak of life.

"What do you mean?" Kalie twisted a delicate pink flower into her garland. "Oh, by the way, what do you call these?" She held up a bunch of impossibly blue flowers.

Cassia laughed. "That! When you first came here, you'd have eaten dung before you said one good thing about this land! Now, you can't stop talking about the flowers! You don't even complain about how heavy your pack is, or that the men don't help us carry anything."

"Oh, I still find all that as vile as ever," said Kalie. "But this transformation of the landscape has given me so much to think about."

Cassia looked interested, so Kalie continued. "When we first came here, we talked among ourselves about what could make people so brutal. Alessa thought—"

"Is that the healer you've mentioned? The one who was given to Nelek of the Wolf Tribe?"

"Healer, yes. She was Maris's apprentice." Kalie laughed at herself. As if the name of Maris meant anything here! "She thought that the harsh environment was the main cause of the ... difficulties...people have in working together or sharing resources equally.

"But when I see this..." Kalie swept her hand to encompass the whole landscape. "I can't believe it doesn't have some impact! How could anyone experience such beauty; such proof of the Goddess's love, and still behave as inhuman monsters—"

Cassia laughed. "I guess you are still the same woman," she said.

Kalie laughed as well. Then she noticed Brenia walking nearby, listening intently. The older woman was still beautiful, Kalie thought, but her age was showing more clearly in the harsh light of day than in the dimness of her well-kept felt tent. She carried her two-year-old son, Barak, on her hip, between his bouts of proving he could walk like a man on the march. Behind Brenia walked Elka, carrying Yarik, whose first tentative steps with the leg braces Kalie had made for him had been interrupted by the demands of the journey to the summer camp.

Like Tasine, the old slave woman Kalie had come to love, Brenia's slave, Mara, had died early in the journey to the summer pastures, leaving only Brenia and her husband's concubine to manage his tent and serve his needs. But Elka walked brazenly beside Brenia as though she were as much a wife to Hysaak as Brenia. And while custom demanded that Hysaak provide his first wife with at least one new slave before taking a second wife, he showed no signs of doing so.

Instead, speculation ran high as to how long it would take the comely blonde woman—so much younger than Brenia—to replace her altogether. Already, people said, Hysaak was completely besotted with her. There was also much speculation about when her brother Riyik would take a wife and reclaim his crippled son from his brother-in-law's tent.

"Do you really think the presence or absence of flowers can change the way people are?" Brenia asked, seemingly unconcerned about the gossip.

Kalie paused to appreciate the question, which was probably the most thoughtful one she had heard so far in this place. "I don't think it's any one thing, but, yes. I think small things like that can make a big difference. And if you add up enough small things…"

Cassia rolled her eyes. "You think too much, Kalie! When you talk about the People of Aahk, you act like…like a warrior examining a horse he is thinking of buying—but you're not buying something!

You're here! This is your home for the rest of your life! What good does all this examination and comparing it with your old home do?"

Brenia nodded. "I'm surprised you still have such fond memories of that place. If your men couldn't protect you, what use were they? Here you are among the greatest warriors the gods have made. Surely, that is a better thing, is it not?"

Kalie smiled. Brenia, though kinder and more intelligent than most of the nomads Kalie had met, was still a woman of Aahk. She accepted violence, warfare and slavery as facts of life. As such, she would always be a puzzle to Kalie. Yet in her heart, Kalie never gave up hope that someone like Brenia might actually understand her answer—if she could come up with the right one. She was thinking so hard that it took longer than it should have for the signs that something was wrong to reach her thoughts.

Altia's two daughters returned from drawing water from one of the small springs they had passed. But Varena had been with them as well. Now there was no sign of her, and while her two half-sisters giggled over some secret with their heads together, Kalie noticed a flash of blue fire from something they held between them: it was the beaded necklace Kalie had given Varena.

"Where is Varena?" Kalie demanded, looming over the two children. They looked at her, then at their mother, clearly expecting her to come and take charge of this unruly slave. Already at their young age, they knew to disregard anything a slave might require, but Kalie was not acting like a slave. And a large, angry woman was something they were used to obeying.

When Kalie moved closer to the girls, her

manner clearly threatening, they scurried ahead and grabbed hold of Altia's robe, finally pulling her attention away from the woman with whom she was gossiping.

"What is it?" Altia demanded impatiently, as their entire part of the line began to slow.

"I am looking for Varena," Kalie said simply.

Altia bristled at Kalie's lack of "mistress" in her words. It was one of the few retaliations Kalie's new status afforded her, and she couldn't force herself to give it up, even during times—like now—when she probably should.

"I sent all three of you for water," Altia said, glaring at her daughters. "Where is the other one?"

The girls shrugged and looked away, as they fell in place behind their mother.

"They have the necklace I gave her," Kalie said, noting that the bauble had disappeared.

"Slaves do not own jewelry," said Altia. "Or anything else."

Kalie looked down at the two girls. "How did you come by that blood on your hands?" she asked the elder. "Are you hurt?"

Altia began to look concerned. "Go look for her!" she ordered Kalie. "If she's wandered off, or gotten too lazy to keep up, you can be sure she'll get a proper beating!"

Kalie headed off for the spring.

She found Varena in the grass, not far from the faint whisper of coolness that was the tiny spring. She was curled into a tight ball, lying on her side, and only faint, pathetic whimpers reached Kalie's ears, though she was by then only a few steps away. Even when alone, it seemed, a good slave knew how to keep silent.

"Varena, what happened?" Kalie turned her over carefully, searching for injuries. One eye was swollen shut, and she had scratches on her face, and on her arms, where her robe had been torn. Kalie began to breathe again when she realized that none of the marks were serious.

For a frustratingly long time, the girl was silent. Only after Kalie began to gather up chamomile and some tiny healing flowers that grew in the shadows of the grass, and then pound them into a paste did Varena throw herself into Kalie's arms and wail, "They took my necklace! The one that you gave me!"

"Shh, I know," said Kalie. "Here, hold still." She removed her veil and dipped it into the spring, then washed Varena's injuries and applied the soothing, antiseptic paste. Varena's sobs slowly abated into hiccups. "Why did they beat you so?"

Varena's good eye opened wide. "I wouldn't let it go without a fight!"

"That was silly," said Kalie, marveling at the brutality that even children were capable of in this place.

Varena looked away. "I never owned anything like it before. And…I was afraid you'd be angry at me for losing it."

"You thought I'd blame you for being robbed?" Kalie hugged the girl, careful not to hurt her further. "Why do people here always blame the victim?"

Varena didn't answer, nor did Kalie expect her to. Finally, after making sure they both drank their fill from the spring she stood. "Come," she said. "We must hurry to catch up with the others."

"Do we have to go back?" Varena's voice was barely a whisper. "Can't we just leave? And go live among your people? You said we would!"

Kalie's breath caught in her throat. Why had she promised such a thing? She was lucky to still be alive after such careless speech! She looked at Varena, noticing yet again how she stood on the brink of womanhood. And if her life as a slave girl was bad, the life of a slave woman was infinitely worse.

Kalie had been only a few years older than Varena when she had first been captured by this tribe and made a slave. She still didn't know how she escaped; much of her memory was still a darkness lit by occasional nightmares. A few years after her escape, the tribe of Aahk had begun to invade her home to the west, with an interest in staying. Kalie, who had never fully recovered from her ordeal as their captive, knew only that she had to find a way to stop them. So she and group of women, possibly as mad as she no doubt was, had volunteered to be part of the tribute the warriors had demanded in exchange for sparing their town.

Kalie had believed herself safe behind her wall of hatred, and capable of doing anything she had to if it meant destroying these monsters. But then she had met Varena. It hadn't taken the girl long to break down Kalie's defenses, and now Varena was her daughter. There were days when all Kalie wanted to do was to take the girl and run back home to the Land of the Goddess, where she would never know the pain of rape, and slavery could someday be a distant memory.

But Kalie had come here to find a way to destroy this tribe. And already, with the coming of spring, there were rumors that she had to trace to their source: rumors of the king's illness, and of a clan that had gone west on its own, seeking treasure and glory —without much concern that such actions without the king's consent was treason.

Kalie knelt beside Varena and stroked her pale blonde hair. "I would have taken you and left when the rains stopped," she said sadly. "And maybe I should have. But I have important work to do first, Daughter. Secret work. Then, we will leave together."

"Do you really mean that?" asked Varena. "Or is it just another story? It's fine if it's just a story. I just want to know."

This is dangerous! Kalie reminded herself. "If you'll come back with me, and promise to keep it a secret, and promise me that you won't strangle those horrible little brats in their sleep, then I promise we will leave this land before winter comes again."

Varena giggled. "Did you really just call Maalke's trueborn daughters horrible little brats?"

"Well," said Kalie, helping Varena adjust her robe and straighten her veil. "Aren't they?"

"I guess." Varena looked around nervously, as if expecting lightening to strike. "But I never would have dared called them that. Even in my dreams."

"Now you can," Kalie said as they followed the dust trail raised by the large procession. "Just make sure you don't say it out loud."

They reached the caravan late that afternoon, during the last rest stop of the day. No one said anything, and Kalie wondered if two slaves might be unimportant enough to just slip away during such a time. Water and even food were plentiful in this season.

She wondered if that was how she had escaped

the first time.

Kalie had learned so little of any use in her time with the beastmen. For three full seasons she had lived as a slave, seeking a way to prevent the nomads of the steppes from ravaging the peaceful Goddess-lands to the west. She had no idea if the other women who had volunteered to come with her on this mad mission were even alive. But Varena was. Kalie had promised her they would leave before winter. And with or without the secret to her people's salvation, they would.

When the band set up camp for the night, Kalie decided to pursue the discussion that had been interrupted by Varena's disappearance.

Tents were not raised during this journey. Rather, each family set up a hearth or a brazier for cooking, and the women and children slept beside it, rolled in their blankets. The men stood watch around the perimeter, sleeping in shifts on the grass beside their horses.

After helping with the meal and the clean up afterward, Kalie brewed a tea from the mint and chamomile that seemed to be growing everywhere. She added lemonbalm and willow bark to what she gave Varena and Cassia, for their calming effect, and the easing of aches and pains. This time, Cassia sang the praises of the tea, rather than complaining it tasted like horse piss, and claimed it made her morning sickness disappear. This brought several women over to sample it, including Brenia. Elka came as well, resentfully watching the two boys as they played in the grass with the other children.

She noticed Riyik nearby. He appeared to be the only warrior who was neither on guard duty nor engaged in what passed for socialization among the beastmen: dicing, drinking or weapon practice. He was, Kalie realized, trying to carve something from a piece of bone. He was watching his son as well, although trying not to be obvious.

"I wanted to ask you about what you said earlier," she said to Brenia. "About why I don't prefer this...new home over my old one?"

Brenia blushed slightly, but it was strongly evident in her winter pallor. "I meant no offense to your people, Kalie. You were obviously someone of high status among them, and would never insult their memories. But they sound like a weak people. Your men..." Brenia seemed to be searching for a polite way to say what she wanted.

None of the other women shared her compunction. "They were all a bunch of cowards!" said a burly woman with a huge pregnant belly and a son of four or five years playing nearby. "My husband told me about them!"

Kalie's interest sharpened. "And what did he tell you...Kara?" she asked.

Pleased to be the center of attention, Kara spoke loud and fast. "That they know nothing of fighting! That they bow to women! That when our men fell upon them, they shit their pants and tried to flee!"

Many of the women were laughing or staring in shock, especially those from Boraak's clan, who'd had no contact with any of the westerners over the winter. "That could never be, could it, slave?" shouted a young woman Kalie didn't know. Her veil was thrown back to reveal golden hair, oiled with sheep's fat. Jewelry hung heavily from her neck, arms and ears.

"Kara is correct," Kalie said calmly. "And that is just one of the ways my people and yours are different." The laughter and hooting grew loud and crude, but Kalie waited it out, pitching her voice to carry when she continued. "We value generosity and cooperation, not hatred and killing. We take pride in hard work and skill—not in stealing from others. If you were to visit my people, you would see women who walk without fear—"

"I walk without fear," said Leja, the chief's wife in a menacing tone.

Kalie met her gaze without flinching. "In my land, you could do so without needing to terrify those around you. And you could own more than you could possibly imagine—without having to fight and kill to get it."

"Then how could it be worth having?"

Kalie smiled. "That, I suppose is another difference between our peoples."

"This woman spins tales!" said another. "Everyone says she's a gifted storyteller. But I think she's just crazy!"

The woman beside Leja shifted her feet to better show off her beaded slippers and shot Brenia a malicious glare. "So much for your thought that this slave once held high status. People such as hers don't even know what status is! If I came from such as they, I would certainly never speak of it."

Kalie turned her smile upon the new speaker. "Yet another difference. You expect me to be ashamed of honor and decency. Just as I keep expecting you to feel shame for beating a twelve year old girl whose only crime was being raped by your monster of a husband—while she weeps for the family he has murdered!"

There was the hiss of indrawn breath. Kalie kept her gaze steadily on her opponent, and didn't dare look at Cassia.

But the woman appeared more puzzled than offended. "What would you have us do?" she asked. "Roll over and let her have her way with our husbands? Hand her our tents and everything in them?"

"Oh? Is she having her way with your husband? I'd have thought it was the other way around. Or is it your custom to interpret shrieks of pain and terror as cries of victory?"

"Not all women are as unwilling as you were," said Cassia.

"True," said Kalie. "Yet many are. And many are children when they are taken, still reeling from the loss of everyone they loved. So tell me, women of Aahk: where is the honor in brutalizing a terrified child, whom your husband has just finished brutalizing? If she were your daughter, would you not at least hope she would find kindness and compassion from someone in her new life?"

"She really is crazy!" laughed Kara.

"Insults are easy, Kara!" said Kalie. "Especially when you lack the wit to answer my question! Or is it the ability to care for your children that you lack?"

There was hissing, but giggling as well, as Kara's face turned an angry red.

"What would you have us do?" demanded Leja. "Beat our husbands instead?"

"That would be an excellent place to start—"

Kalie began

Brutal laughter and a child's scream put a stop to the discussion and caused the women to look to see what was happening.

Kara's son stood over a fallen Yarik. "Cripple!" he shouted. "You'll never be a warrior!"

"You'll never even be a man!" shouted an older boy joining into the fun. "We'll have to geld you, like one of the—"

Brenia was on him in an instant, slapping the boy hard enough to knock him over. The other boy jumped out of her range, just as she turned to pick up Yarik.

Elka reached to help her, but Brenia slapped her as well. "It was your job to watch him!" she hissed at the negligent girl.

"Brenia shouldn't have done that," Cassia whispered to Kalie.

"Done what? Slapped the concubine or slapped the boy?"

"Both! Her husband is wild for Elka, who will try to supplant her as first wife as soon as she bears a son. She should not make such an enemy of her in public. And no mother will tolerate seeing her son slapped by another woman."

"Even an older boy who harms a baby?" Kalie asked in disbelief.

"Boys of Aahk must fight their own battles."

Kalie noticed Riyik watching the scene. He had made no move to intervene, nor did he follow Brenia and Elka as they hurried his son and his nephew back to their campsite. But blood dripped down from where his hand clenched the knife that moments before had been carving sheep's bone. Riyik didn't seem to notice.

Chapter 2

Kalie lay in her furs in the darkness, wondering why she was suddenly awake. The stars told her that it was nearly dawn, but it would be some time before Altia declared the day begun with her usual round of curses and blows. All was quiet, but for the lowing of the sheep and goats, and the soft cawing of a crow.

Kalie sat up. It was too close to dawn for a crow...

A shriek split the night, and horsemen spilled into the camp. They carried torches. Suddenly, everything was burning.

Kalie sat in the middle of it all, as warriors shook off sleep and grabbed their weapons, while women and children ran screaming into the night. Some of the men who had been on sentry duty were already mounting an effective defense, but there were clearly more attackers than defenders. The battle seemed to be as chaotic as the women's attempt to flee, and Kalie could see no safe place to hide.

Then she saw Varena running straight into the path of a charging horse, and her own safety didn't matter. She wasn't aware of moving; wasn't aware of anything until the moment she landed on the hard earth with Varena under her and a horse leaping over her back.

"Are you all right?" she shouted over the noise, while the girl screamed hysterically. Varena seemed unharmed, but before Kalie could even begin to examine her, something tightened around her neck, stopping her breath.

She landed on the back of a horse, just as she

realized it was her own felt robe that was strangling her. The pressure eased as her captor released her, the better to heave a spear with the hand he had used to snatch up Kalie, blocking an attack with his other.

"Not again!" Kalie moaned while the battle raged around them. She was aware that the stench emanating from this new beastman's body was different from Maalke and the others, whom she had apparently gotten used to. She tried to sit up and figure out how she was going to get off this horse, but her captor only laughed and struck her hard enough to keep her slumped over the horse's withers.

Kalie watched as the ground moved beneath her, back and forth for a while, and murky with smoke, then more quickly as the beastman urged his horse away from the ruined camp. This new group apparently had what they came for and now were leaving—taking Kalie and who knew how many others with them.

The smoke was gone, allowing Kalie to take a gulp of clean air. She had just decided to attempt a rolling leap from the horse, when the clatter of another horse chasing, then gaining on hers reached her ears. The horse beneath her slowed, turned, then reared up with an angry squeal. Kalie hung on, trying to choose the best moment to leap free, while the sounds of weapons clashing and men shouting filled the air around her.

Then there was the meaty thud of a spear striking flesh, and Kalie's captor fell to the ground. The horse slowed to a stop, and Kalie slid indecorously down the other side of it—only to catch her foot in the stirrup, and find herself hanging upside down, her head just inches from the earth.

"Let me help you the rest of the way off," said a man's voice, rich with laughter. "You're safe now. He won't be bothering you anymore."

Back on her feet, Kalie looked down at the dead man. He was smaller and darker than the men of Aahk—and dirtier, if that were possible. He wore a combination of badly made felt and uncured animal skins.

She turned to the other man, and found herself staring into Riyik's laughing gray eyes. He stood beside his horse looking proud and smug; he seemed to be waiting for something. For the woman he rescued to fall at his feet in gratitude, perhaps? Kalie felt a bubble of laughter at that. Then she realized how far they were from the camp.

"If you're going to rape me, just get it over with!" she snapped hoarsely.

Riyik's expression changed abruptly, and Kalie could have sworn he actually got smaller.

"I thought I just rescued you from that fate," he said quietly.

"Yes, and from what I've seen of you beastmen," she spat the word, "that makes me your prize."

"You belong to Maalke. He may choose to reward me for saving you—although why he would want to is beyond me at the moment. But I don't assume any liberties beforehand."

"Well, aren't you just the noblest beastman!" Somewhere inside, Kalie knew she had lost her last connection to sanity—but she couldn't have stopped herself if the Goddess Herself commanded it.

Riyik seemed more puzzled than angry. "Actually, I think I am. Most women would show some gratitude after such a rescue—and few men would have this much patience for your reaction."

"Gratitude!" Kalie was more than spitting—she was nearly foaming at the mouth. Maybe she could pass off her behavior as rabies. "You think being beaten, raped and enslaved by your people is somehow better than being beaten, raped and enslaved by his?" She gave the corpse a vicious kick. It felt wonderful.

Riyik took a step back. "You were putting up an impressive fight. I thought you didn't want to go with him."

"And since when does what any woman wants matter to one of you sick, Motherless bastards?" she demanded.

The renewed sounds of battle drew their attention. Riyik mounted his horse in a graceful leap. "Others may be more needful of my help. It seems clear you can get back to camp safely by yourself— although I pity any enemy warriors you meet on the way." He wheeled his horse and raced back to the battle.

Kalie returned to camp just as the battle was winding down.

The enemy—of her enemies, anyway—was apparently one of the outlaw bands who had decided to take a chance on a pair of small, diminished clans. As she wandered through the ruined camp, past bodies strewn on the ground with little ceremony, and the booty of very poor horses, weapons and women gathered and guarded in a more organized manner, Kalie could see what a prize the Aahken clans must have seemed to the outlaws.

It was only later, as she noticed that there were more Aahken warriors rather than less, that Kalie discovered the cause of such a decisive victory: the arrival of a third clan. Zavan and his warriors had arrived in the midst of the battle, turning the tide, if not exactly saving the day. Kalie could almost hear the stories that would be told around the fires tonight: the savage attack; the heroic stand of the badly outnumbered Aahken clans against the ruthless enemy; the divinely timed arrival Zavan's clan....Perhaps she should throw together a story herself, now that she knew what the men liked to hear.

If she survived whatever retaliation Riyik was planning.

She took in the devastated camp-site, the wailing women, the grinning and shouting men, the piles of bodies, the stench of smoke and blood and death, and for a moment, felt invisible. As if she could just disappear into the smoke and find her way to someplace else.

The feeling was shattered as Varena came running through the trampled grass. Kalie barely had time to brace herself before the girl came barreling into her arms, laughing and sobbing. "Irisa said she saw you taken! I was afraid I'd never see you again! I…"

"Shh, it's all right." Kalie murmured reassurances to the one person she realized did care what happened to her. It struck her then just what it would have meant for Varena to have lost Kalie today. Strange, how a simple act of kindness, hardly noticeable in her own world, could become so complicated in a place like this. She could pretend to Riyik that it made no difference to her which tribe made her a slave, but as she stood comforting Varena, and belatedly wondering at the fates of Cassia and

Brenia—two women who had been kind to her against all need and custom—she knew it wasn't true.

And then Cassia was there, shouting her gratitude to the gods that Kalie had been rescued, but there was work to be done, and she'd better start rounding up their scattered flocks. Then Altia joined them, ordering Kalie to check their gear for damage, with no shouts of gratitude but quite a lot of cursing. Just when it seemed things couldn't get any more chaotic, the women, children and flocks of Zavon's clan—who had been left to make their own way here after their warriors had ridden a break-neck pace to reach their beleaguered brothers—arrived, ready to fight with the women who were already established for a good place to camp and access to fresh water.

Suddenly Kalie began to laugh. She didn't know why, and she didn't care. It was just that everything—even her great mission to save her people —seemed...silly. Unreal. As invisible as she herself had felt earlier.

The men, busy dividing up the spoils of battle, left the women to the job of rebuilding the camp. As evening fell, the three clan-leaders called for a feast to celebrate their great victory. A few skinny goats were killed, and what kumis remained was opened and shared.

This night, the men and women ate separately. Kalie was about to ask Cassia if this was because of the battle, or some other reason, when she heard her name called from the men's side of the fires.

"A woman? Telling the tale of a battle?" she heard some warrior demanding as she reached their gathering

"You haven't heard her," Kahlar was saying.

"Ah, Kalie! Come show these fools that in Kahlar's clan, even the women are better storytellers than they!"

Grateful that she had given some thought to that very subject, Kalie moved to the center of the gathering and surveyed her audience. Most were drunk, or working on getting that way, but were still in the early stages. Not ugly yet, at least. Then she noticed a low, animal-like moaning coming from just beyond the firelight punctuated by even more animal-like laughter, and revised her opinion. The only survivors of the outlaw band—four or five half starved women—were providing entertainment for the victorious warriors.

Then Kalie turned away, willing herself not to think about it. These men were waiting for entertainment from her as well, and she ought to be grateful it was of another kind. If she was lucky, they might settle for stories.

Wetting dry lips with a dry tongue, for no one offered her a drink, Kalie began, pitching her voice to carry over the festivities. "It was on a day in early spring, when the two mightiest of the clans of Aahk were on their way to the great summer gathering that they were set upon by savage men who knew no honor…"

Chapter 3

Kalie watched the flowers fade and die as they walked. The grass was turning brown. And the sun's warmth, so welcome just days ago, was beginning to feel oppressive. In her homeland, it would be the second full moon of spring. They would be celebrating the planting of grain and the harvesting of the first fruits.

It had been five days since "The Battle of Spring Trail" as Kalie had named her story. The name had stuck—further proof of her growing status. She had been called to tell the story every night since the battle, and in all that time, had not been raped. Nor had there been any repercussions of her words to Riyik. She thought perhaps that Brenia was avoiding her, but that might just have been a result of the many women she knew in Zavan's clan who were now filling her time.

Kalie also spent time with the women of Zavan's clan. From them she learned that Dara, who had been living with that clan when Kalie had last seen her, was no longer living at all.

"She was a strange one," said one of the women, making a sign against evil. "Never did learn how to talk properly."

"Never learned how to do anything," said another. "But she had stopped fighting like a madwoman, and seemed like she was going to adjust. Then, on the night of Midwinter, she just walked into the snow and froze to death."

"She was trying to escape?" said Kalie.

"Escape?" the woman looked baffled. "Why

would she attempt such a thing? And in the dead of winter, no less!"

"She took nothing with her," said another woman, more helpfully. "No food; not even her blanket."

"Which direction was she walking?" Kalie asked, but she already knew.

"West," said the first woman.

Kalie nodded. "Toward her home."

One of them shot Kalie an evil glare. "Those women from the west are unnatural beings! They should be put to death before they curse us all!"

"Hush, Tilka," said the oldest of them. "It was only one of them, and evil spirits can attack anyone."

"What happened?" Kalie whispered, almost forgetting to breathe.

"Nothing!" snapped the one who told her about Dara, but the one named Tilka shook off her hand and spoke up.

"It was the one called Traea. Just before we left our winter camp, she went mad and killed everyone in her tent. Her good master, his wife—"

"You mean Gorik?" Kalie cried. "And Goat-Dung?"

The women turned on her, horrified, but Kalie could only laugh, though tears leaked from her eyes. "That's what she called his wife. And I'm surprised any of you know her name, since no one in that tent bothered to learn it."

"She killed their son as well!" cried Tilka. "Their only surviving child! He was to be married this summer to Salia's niece." She nodded toward the first speaker. "Traea was to go with him as his concubine, and slave to his new wife! To show such kindness to a worthless barbarian and be repaid with death—"

"Kindness?" Kalie cried. "If such treatment as she received is called kindness, I'd say she repaid it very well indeed. But then, she had excellent teachers." She met Tilka's gaze with a look of hate that equaled that of the horsewoman.

"We must not speak of such things!" said Salia, stepping between them just as Tilka seemed ready to strike. "We dare not invite something so evil back by speaking its name. There have been ill omens enough already."

Tilka turned away from Kalie and nodded slowly. "A two headed goat born among Boraak's flocks, and ravens circling healthy animals. And who's to say that the madness that seized that horrible slave isn't still loose."

"The priests cut up her body and scattered the pieces to the four winds," said the third woman in a soothing voice. "Whatever spirit claimed her is long gone."

"Perhaps not," Kalie taunted. "Perhaps she was simply bitten by a rabid animal, and he still lives to attack again."

"You mean a dog?" asked Salia.

"No, I mean one of your men!" Kalie turned on her heel and walked away to begin her mourning.

She never again spoke to those three women, but she spoke with others from Zavan's clan. She learned that Alessa had been sold to a warrior from another tribe, and knew she would probably never see her again. Kestra was expecting a child they told her. The women claimed she rarely spoke and that she was sullen and withdrawn. She made no attempt to make friends, but was at least trying to be a good wife, utterly devoted to her fine husband.

Kalie shuddered, grateful that she could put off seeing Kestra. Her clan had traveled briefly with Zavan's clan, until grazing became poor and they decided to make their separate ways to the summer pastures.

She learned nothing else about her friends, but heard other, important news. The most interesting was a confirmation of a rumor Kalie had heard a few moonspans ago on the night of the winter solstice: the disappearance of one of the Twenty Clans of Aahk. Chief Yuraak had indeed, taken his clan west in search of the riches that Haraak had spoken of when he brought Kalie and the other women to the grasslands.

Some warriors whispered fierce denials that Yuraak was capable of such treachery—others denied that he was capable of that much independent thought or planning. Kalie thought of those she had left behind in Riverford: farmers who had seen firsthand what the warriors of Aahk were capable of, and had learned the hard way the need to slay a beast who threatened flocks—or their own children. Craftsmen who were designing defenses for villages when she had left the previous year. If Yuraak and his band of twenty or so warriors survived the winter and reached the Goddess-lands at all, they would receive a very different welcome than Haraak and his men had. Kalie hid her smile as she continued walking. "One gone, nineteen to go," she thought.

"We will arrive at the summer campsite in just a few more days," Cassia's words broke into Kalie's musings as they walked together behind Altia. The dust was becoming a problem, and Cassia had warned Kalie it would get worse. That justified the women's veils, she thought, but not the heavy layers of felt clothing.

"How are you feeling?" Kalie asked.

"I'm fine," said Cassia, a little too quickly. She covered her belly with both hands. "I'm going to make it. He is going to make it, this time."

"Have you felt any more movement?"

"Not since yesterday but..." Cassia stopped walking. Her fingers tightened over her womb, and her face lit up with wonder. "There!" She grabbed Kalie's hand and put it over her belly. "Can you feel it? Like a butterfly!"

Kalie smiled. She had missed the big moment, but didn't doubt that it had happened.

"I've never carried one this far," Cassia whispered. "Never to where I could feel him move."

"You've still a long way to go—with little enough chance of bearing a living child!" snapped Irisa, walking by with her four-year-old son riding on her back, her four month old baby wrapped in a shawl beneath her breasts. She looked exhausted. Yet what choice did she have but to carry on—and make life unpleasant for everyone else?

"Perhaps if you spoke of hope, rather than curses," said Kalie, "others might help you with your own brood, Irisa."

"I need no help with my sons." Irisa grinned as she emphasized the last word. "Not from a barren slave, nor a barren wife." Cassia's face lit up with rage this time. Kalie grabbed her hand to distract her, and shook her head. Sparring with Irisa now was the worst thing she could do for her baby—as Irisa well knew. "But perhaps, if you do manage to carry that baby a little farther, your breasts might begin to flow with milk. Then you can be wet nurse to Maalke's youngest son after yours dies—and finally be of some use to us!"

Cassia gasped, and Kalie caught her other hand to prevent her from physically attacking Irisa. It was an unbelievably bold thing for a concubine to say to a wife. Even Altia's eyes went wide with shock. But she said nothing. Her son was growing towards manhood, and she would likely have no others. Better for her if the two women who still might steal her husband's affections fought each other.

"Think of your son," Kalie whispered urgently to Cassia. "Irisa doesn't matter—and never will!"

"Goat dung!" Cassia spat as she passed Irisa with her head high, affecting not to notice her.

That evening, while Kalie and Varena took on extra chores so that Cassia could rest, Riyik strode into Maalke's camp and spoke with him. She did not hear what transpired, but a few moments later, Maalke approached her with a satisfied grin. "Kalie, you are this warrior's for the night. He must truly enjoy your stories." The whole household roared with laughter at his jest, but Riyik looked away, almost as if he were… embarrassed?

"Come, let us walk," he said, leading her through the cool grass, to a low hill well beyond the camp. Riyik crested the hill, then sat down on the gentle slope on the far side which faced away from the camp. He motioned for Kalie to do the same. Privacy, Kalie thought as she stared into the empty shadows falling across the still green steppes beyond. Not something most of the men cared about when it came to taking women.

"I just wanted to talk to you," Riyik said. Then

he actually moved away from her, and turned so he could face her.

"Why?" she asked in stunned disbelief.

"I have been…bothered about what you said when I…rescued you… during the raid." Kalie said nothing, only stared hard into Riyik's eyes. He looked away.

After a long silence, he said, "Not all men here take women against their will. I do not."

Kalie laughed. "I think perhaps my kinswomen from Riverford might disagree."

Riyik looked as though she had slapped him. "I took no one on that journey! Although, I can see how you might not remember. We thought Haraak had killed you that first night."

"It would have been better if he had," Kalie said, although, as she struggled to remember, it seemed Riyik had acted as a guard the whole time, not indulging himself as the others had—a fact that had seemed strange to her, even then. But was that really any better?

"I wanted you to know that."

"How do you know?" Kalie asked quietly.

Riyik, who was about to speak again, stopped short. "What?"

"How do you know that you've never taken a woman against her will?" Kalie asked, knowing she should be treading carefully. But she was very interested in Riyik's answer.

"I…think that is something a man would know, don't you?"

Kalie shook her head. "No, I do not. You live in a world where a woman's life may be snuffed out at a man's whim. How, then, can you ever know what a woman wants or feels? If she doesn't scream and fight you, might it not be because she's too afraid? Or thinks it's her duty? Or that it simply never occurred to her that she was human enough to have feelings or desires of her own?"

"You seem to think as little of our women as of our men!"

"Less!" said Kalie. "For they labor to maintain their own enslavement..." She broke off, shaking her head as if to clear it.

"Perhaps you only see your own unhappiness, and are angry at them for not sharing it."

Kalie smiled. Finally, someone worth talking to—and it had to be a man!

"Unhappiness is one thing this land always has plenty of. And the women here share it very well." She rubbed the scar on her chin, where Altia had struck her with a sharp bone during her first days in Maalke's tent.

Riyik looked away. "Life is harsh everywhere."

"Not like this. Did my world seem so harsh to you?"

Riyik laughed. "Your world seemed...insane to me! Such wealth! Yet no one to manage it! People with more possessions than I could imagine, yet acting...almost unaware of what they had!"

"With that last part, I agree," said Kalie. "I have journeyed the length and breadth of that world— farther than your fastest horse could travel in twenty days!" Riyik's brows rose in disbelief, but he did not interrupt. "And throughout it all, no one ever really... thought about it. Oh, we thanked the Goddess for all Her gifts, we honored the Earth and everything that came from it…but no one ever realized how precious it all was, because no one knew that it could be any different. That just a little to the east, were monsters who created nothing of their own, and lived only to steal and to maim and to destroy what others had."

"Is that how you see us?" Riyik seemed truly shocked.

Kalie smiled, showing her teeth. "Please, master, tell me how else I might see you."

Riyik was silent for a long time. Then he said, "I suppose, knowing what I do now, there is no other way you can see it. And for that I am truly sorry. Living as a slave to a man like Maalke—a wife like Altia ordering you about." Riyik yanked out a handful of grass from the hillside and flung it into the wind. "You deserve better than that."

Kalie felt as if the universe had suddenly shifted, and for a moment she did not know where she was. "Everyone deserves better than that!" she whispered hoarsely.

"I can't speak for everyone, and I can't say I agree. But there is much that is good in our world. And much that is beautiful. I would like to show it to you. Perhaps…perhaps we could help each other."

"How?" She was on her guard again.

"You could…" Riyik seemed to experience a coughing fit. Then, taking a deep breath, he said quickly, "You could live in the tent I must soon establish. You could care for my son." He paused. "You could be my wife."

Kalie just stared at him.

"I must take a wife. Yarik needs a mother and you have done so much for him already. I owe you a great deal; much more than Brenia has given you in payment." His rain gray eyes seemed genuinely troubled, and for all her cynicism, Kalie could see no guile in them. "I cannot give back what you have lost, Kalie. But I can give you this: you will have your freedom, and status here in my world."

"Freedom?" Kalie tasted the word on her tongue. "That means... what? That you would buy me from Maalke?" Riyik nodded. "Then marry me according to the customs of your people?"

Again Riyik nodded. "I cannot promise you love, as Aahken women are so fond of hearing a man speak of. I still love Yalina, my wi—Yarik's mother. Yet you do not seem interested in love as our women do. Is that yet another difference between our women and yours? You do not dream of love in marriage?"

Kalie smiled. "No. Strangely, both our worlds speak a great deal of love, in stories and songs. But here, women dream that a man's love that will save them from the misery that is a woman's life. Among my people...it is very different. I can't explain it. We have love—it is your notion of marriage we do not have."

To her further amazement, Riyik laughed. "I might have known! And whatever your notions of love, you, I think, will never love anything in this land. Although, perhaps, over time, you may come to. Perhaps, if we had children of our own..."

Kalie wanted to spit in his face for those last words, yet to her surprise, found she could not. This man, and yes, she had to see him as a man, not a beast, was opening up to her and, of all strange things, trying to be kind and helpful. To pay him back with cruelty would be of this world, not her own.

"I cannot marry you, Riyik." The words were

out before she knew it, but as soon as she said them, she knew they were right.

Riyik stared at her in shock, as Kalie had stared at him just moments before. "Why not?"

"Because you are my enemy!" This was not the right way to explain. Strangely, it might not even be true.

An image danced before her eyes: Kestra lying with her "husband"; welcoming his embrace, despite all she had seen and endured. Is that how it happened in this world? Would she, herself, strike such a bargain with Riyik?

In that moment, Kalie was certain of one thing: if she ran to this man for protection, like some princess in one of their tales; if she let herself be lulled by his kindness into accepting his people's ideas of marriage and family, she would lose her way forever. And one day, years from now, while she was busy trying to convince herself she hadn't betrayed her people or herself—her world would fall to these conquerors.

She had to find a way to explain.

"Riyik." If he was offended by her familiar use of his name, he didn't show it. Even her habit of looking directly into his eyes brought no anger. "You offered me my freedom?"

"Yes!" He nodded emphatically.

"Do you mean that once you buy me from Maalke, I will be free to return to my people in the west if I choose? That you will give me provisions—and let me go?"

"No, of course not! You would die out there! Or be taken as a slave by one of the other tribes! Look what happened just a few days ago…"

"Then what you offer is just another kind of

slavery." Even now, he did not seem angry, so much as exasperated. Kalie held up a hand for silence and pressed on. "I know you see a world of difference between being a slave and being a wife. I know Yalina did as well, and so do most of the women here.

"But for me—for all of the women of my land —the difference is slight. Being a wife might mean freedom from Altia and her beatings and curses. It might mean better food and, within your tent, at least, a little bit of power—especially if you brought me slaves to rule over." Her face twisted angrily as she spat out the last words.

Riyik cocked his head at her expression. "You hate the thought of owning slaves. Why? Most women dream of having slaves to help them with the work of the tent."

"Most women here also enjoy beating them. I pray I shall never sink to that level! I think the wives of this land enjoy hurting those beneath them much more than they enjoy getting help with the endless drudgery they live with."

Riyik shrugged uncomfortably. "That's just the way women are!"

"It's the way you have made them! Don't you ever wonder about these things?"

Riyik laughed. "I am beginning to. I'm also beginning to see that you are right that we are unsuited to be man and wife. But there might yet be some use in having a woman who is both healer and storyteller in my tent. Please, Woman From the West, tell me more about the women of my own tribe, since you know so much more than I."

If it had been anyone else, Kalie realized later, she would have given up right there. But she sensed something beneath Riyik's sarcasm that made her push forward. If nothing else, she would give voice to things that had been burning inside her for nearly a whole turn of the seasons!

Kalie twisted her hands into the long, cool grass, as if to make sure she spoke only with her mouth and not her fists. "In this place, what does a woman do when a man hurts her, or does things that make her unhappy?"

Riyik shrugged. "It depends on who she is. And on what he has done, and on what she did to deserve it."

"Ah, yes. Always assume it's somehow the woman's fault. And if it isn't blame her anyway, right?" She grinned at Riyik's expression, but didn't give him time to respond. "I'll tell you what she does: she takes it out on whoever she can! A junior wife, a slave, even her own children! And the only real difference between your women and me is that I want revenge against the real enemy: the men! But the pain we feel inside, the rage at being so helpless—that's the same for them as for me!"

"No!" Riyik was shaking his head. "It's not like that for everyone! There are women here who have no fear of their husbands—and more than a few husbands who fear their wives." He snorted. "Watch Kahlar with his Leja someday if you don't believe me. The women of Aahk are as strong and wild as a rutting stallion! My own Yalina never hesitated to tell me when I was wrong."

Kalie took a deep breath and gazed into the deepening twilight, wondering how to respond to that. She had no doubt Riyik was right about the examples he gave. And, amazingly enough, he was willing to listen. If there was just some way to make him imagine himself living as women were made to live here…

She shook her head. That approach had failed often enough with the women. It would surely have no effect on a man who could just leap on his horse and ride to the ends of the earth the moment he tired of listening.

Then, lightning struck.

Kalie sat up, and faced Riyik as if for battle. "I have seen you riding by yourself often since we left the winter camp."

Surprised by the change in subject, Riyik nodded. "I have always been…different in that way. Oh, I like the company of my brother warriors well enough, but to me, the greatest joy is found beneath a clear blue sky, feeling the sun on my back, the wind in my hair, and a mount who is one with my body." Riyik gazed into the distance, and Kalie knew he was longing even now, to be doing what he spoke of.

For a strange moment, she wanted to be there with him, feeling the things he described. Then resolve flooded her, for she had what she wanted.

"But your oath to your king is greater to you than all of that, isn't it? Even dearer to you than your favorite horse?"

Riyik snapped back to the present. "Yes, of course! It is so for all warriors, and I am a warrior before all else, even if I may prefer the hunting trail."

"What if your king demanded your favorite horse, as a sacrifice to the gods?"

Riyik smiled sadly, as if he knew where she was going. "His name is Thunder. And yes, of course, it would grieve me, but I would do it."

"And what if, because of some crisis, the king

needed his best minds in council in his tent for many days—and he named you his chief advisor." Kalie knew such things happened, but was surprised to see the effect it had on Riyik. A shadow crossed his face, as if he feared that very thing, and had for some time.

"How would it feel, trapped inside a stuffy tent, filled with men who sought only power and advantage? Never again to ride free on Thunder's back? Never even to ride any horse across your grasslands, for as long as the king had need of you?"

Riyik slapped away a wasp buzzing near his face. "I would hate it! But I would do as my king commanded—and count the days until I was free to ride away from the stench of politics."

Kalie met his gaze. "Now imagine this: that day will never come. Through some twist of fate, your king's need of you stretched on and on, and the last day of your life came while you were still in that tent."

"Do you seek to curse me, woman?" Riyik spat in the grass between them and made a sign against evil with his right hand.

Kalie said quietly, "I seek to show you what life is like for the women of this land. Those tents that you so easily avoid whenever you choose to stink of things far worse than politics. Perhaps you have noticed that few adults can stand upright inside most of them? Yet the women here live out their lives in them, without ever once knowing the freedom and joy you feel every time you're on Thunder's back."

"But women don't want to ride horses! They're safe inside those tents! It's what they want!"

"Do you know that? Or have you always just assumed it? And how safe did their tents turn out for the poor women you took from that band who attacked you?" Riyik looked away. "Tell me Riyik? Where are they now?"

"They were too weak! They could never have kept up with the pace the chiefs had set!"

"So after every man who wanted to had his turn with them, you slit their throats and left them to rot! And now you can't understand why I don't long for such a fate myself?"

"Theirs was the fate of women who have weak men! It would never happen to you, Kalie! I will always protect you!"

"Until you meet a glorious death in battle! Isn't that what you warriors dream of? Then my fate is whatever the victor chooses! Do you think your women enjoy living with that knowledge, Riyik?" Her voice rose. "They live in terror of it!"

"I…have never met anyone like you, Kalie. If you were any other woman, I would just buy you to keep you safe from Maalke and Altia, and dismiss your words as some kind of game. But you…Looking at you is like looking at a fellow warrior!"

"I think you are a good man, Riyik. And you have no idea how much it cost me to say that. But I will never give myself willingly to any man who lives as you do. And you will not take a woman against her will. I do not see any future for us."

"You are a warrior!" he whispered. "A warrior who fights with no weapon but courage. I have never met your like." He rose to his feet. "Come. You can sleep beside Brenia's fire tonight." He reached down to help Kalie to her feet, and then stopped, as if understanding what an action, so casual in his world, might mean to her. He straightened, offering his hand if she would take it, but nothing more.

Kalie rose gracefully to her feet without accepting the hand and followed Riyik to where his sister was camped.

Chapter 4

Once again, Kalie found herself awake in the dark. This time, however, she sensed no danger. All was as it should be, shortly before midnight during the trek to the summer pastures.

It was the voices that had awakened her: a man and a woman speaking softly on the other side of the banked coals from where Kalie lay rolled in soft sheepskin of Brenia's making. Brenia had been a gracious hostess, although she had not been inclined to talk as the two women lay down beside the two already sleeping boys. Kalie was grateful for the silence, not trusting herself to speak to anyone just then.

Now she lay as if still asleep, straining to hear the whispered words that had awakened her.

"It's been nearly two years since she died," Riyik was saying. "There are days I can barely summon up a memory of her face. But tonight, after I talked to Kalie…do you remember the day Father presented me with my first horse?"

"Of course," Brenia whispered, but Kalie could hear the laughter in her voice. "You were fairly glowing with pride. None of your friends had yet earned their first mount."

"I stopped to show off in front of a group of girls taking their father's goats to the summer pastures."

"Several groups, as I recall."

Riyik chuckled softly. "I suppose I was rather full of myself. I remember how impressed they all seemed, and of course, a little afraid of the horse's sharp hooves. But Yalina, she must have been about eight years old, strode boldly forward and pet my horse's nose, and announced to me that if I wanted to marry her, I would have to teach her to ride, and present her with her own horse as a wedding gift."

"I can imagine how her sisters laughed at that!"

"Oh, they did, and I rode away with manly disdain for the silly creatures. But I think that was the moment I decided I was going to marry her."

"And you did—without having to pay her father any horses at all."

"But I gave him one, remember? The first colt that Thunder ever sired. And I promised him horses every year, until I had given him the fifty he had originally asked."

"I had forgotten that," Brenia said after a pause. "I suppose because you had so few years in which to keep that promise."

"But I never gave her one. Nor did I ever teach her to ride."

"She did not expect you to, Brother. It was a childish fancy, nothing more."

"So I told myself. But there were times I caught her looking at the horses with a kind of longing that I can't pretend I didn't recognize. Brenia, do other women feel that way?"

Kalie expected a laughing dismissal of the notion and guessed that Riyik did too. But Brenia was silent for just a moment too long.

"I think all of us do, at one time or another," she said slowly.

Riyik's indrawn breath spoke eloquently. "But...why?"

"The horse is the symbol of our tribe, Brother.

Every day of our lives we see and hear them; we survive because of them. What child wouldn't desire the power and speed and…well, beauty…that horses afford men? I remember one summer, when you were still at mother's breast—the heat was beyond bearable —and all the men went shirtless, and were on horseback, for hunting or training or just exercise. I remember thinking how fine it must be to outrun the heat! To have a wind cool your whole body, for as long as you and your horse moved as one."

"Why did you never tell me?"

"What would you have done if I had? Taught me to ride?"

Riyik's silence was answer enough.

"It was nothing, Riyik. Childish fancy, as I've said. The gods made men and women to be different and no one can change that. A girl has to grow up. I did; so did Yalina."

"Perhaps Yalina's short life might have been happier if I had cared less for tradition and more for her dreams."

"Yalina lived in happiness every day she was your wife! Most women would gladly trade all their years and more for a husband as good as you! Never forget that."

There was a long silence. Kalie thought perhaps the conversations was over. Then Riyik asked. "You deserve happiness as well, Sister. And you've always deserved a better husband than Hysaak."

"Brother, don't…"

"I'm sorry; I know I shouldn't interfere, but no warrior of Aahk lets a man mistreat his sister—even if he's her husband."

"It is a matter between myself and Hysaak, and

no one—not even a brother—may interfere without causing greater shame. And it's my duty to see that he treats me well, not yours. For a long time, it was a joy, not a duty."

"You were happy together at first; I could see that. Hysaak is a fool, but he was smart enough to know his good fortune when he won your hand."

"It could be like that again!" Brenia's voice broke. "If it wasn't for her…"

"A man can only think with his balls for so long," Riyik said, but didn't sound convinced. "You're the mother of his son…"

"But I have given him only one that still lives, and cannot give him any more! She will give him many…"

"And Yarik's presence is making it worse for you." Brenia gasped. "Don't you think I can see it? How Elka manipulates Hysaak with whispers of tainted blood when anyone with half a brain should take his walking for a miracle? Why didn't you tell me?"

"You have enough to worry about."

"That does not excuse making things worse for you. I can do nothing about Elka, but I can at least keep my own son from being used as a weapon against you!"

"You will finally marry again?"

"It's time for me to put aside my own childish fancies and remember my duty." Kalie felt Riyik's eyes on her in the dark. When he turned back to his sister, she began to breathe again.

"I wish you joy in your duty," said Brenia. "Have you chosen a bride?"

Riyik laughed mirthlessly. "I certainly have

many to choose from—except for the one I want!" He sighed. "Probably Levak's daughter. Just this morning he named a dowry of a fine new tent and the furnishings as well."

"Yasha will make you a fine wife, and a good mother for Yarik."

"I want her also to be a friend to you, Brenia. And if Hysaak ever again beats you without cause, I want you to come to my tent…"

"You would have me shame myself and our family?"

"I would have you well-treated and cared for! As your husband vowed to do! Why has he not replaced Mara? He owes you a slave at least! More than one, if he marries that witch…"

"His flocks were badly depleted this past winter…"

"So were everyone's!"

"Calm yourself, Brother. He is waiting, like so many of the warriors, for the journey West that everyone is talking about. He says that once we reach this new land, there will be slaves for the taking, and Elka and I shall each have—what troubles you, Riyik?"

"Nothing. Only that I hope your fool of a husband is wise enough to speak so only to his women! There are many rumors about, Brenia. Dangerous ones. I'm told that Ahnaak is very ill. And I've heard that one of his sons was killed during a winter raid."

"Which son?"

"That's the problem. First I heard it was Melaak—then Trobraak. Dear gods, what if it should turn out to be both?"

"Then Kariik might be king before winter. With Haraak whispering in his ear of the glories to be had in the west."

In the dark, Riyik dropped his face into his hands. "Gods help us all," he muttered.

"But is that not what you wanted?" asked his sister. "When you returned home last summer, it was all you could speak of! The man who taught you to carve, the woman who cured you of lung-fever when you should have died, all the wonders that defied explanation..."

Riyik was silent for a long time. "I don't know, Brenia. I just...have a bad feeling about it now." There was a shuffling sound as he stood. "It is time for my shift. And you should get some sleep before Hysaak stumbles over you in a drunken haze."

Brenia laughed bitterly. "There's little chance of that. He's probably in some field right now, asleep in Elka's arms after riding both her and his horse to exhaustion."

"You mean in the saddle? Like a pair of newlyweds?" Riyik sounded disgusted.

"Promise me you will say nothing to him if you see him tonight."

"As you wish, Brenia. But if he shames you any further, he's going to have an accident the next time he hunts alone."

Kalie listened as the sound of Riyik's footsteps faded and disappeared. Brenia was soon asleep, but Kalie knew that for herself, sleep would be long in coming. And it wasn't just the new information about the king she had gained that kept her awake.

Chapter 5

In the torchlit night, Kalie slipped away from the crowd of warriors, and another storyteller took her place. Her tale of a traitor who murdered his king in the hope of ruling through the king's foolish heir had not gone over well. Probably because anyone with half a brain could see that that was precisely what was happening within the tribe. She really had to stop viewing her enemies as stupid.

They would reach the summer gathering the next day. Nights now brought little relief to the heat—and the dust. Kalie stared into the sable sky, awash with stars in a way the sky above her home never was. It was beautiful, she thought, trying to loose herself in its endless depths.

A coughing fit forced her back into the dry brown grass, burning dung and press of more than three hundred unwashed bodies. She sighed. Even the constant steppe wind couldn't make that smell good.

Looking around, Kalie relished another moment of invisibility, as the nightlife of the travelers swirled around her. Not all the warriors were listening to the storyteller. There were dice games and wrestling matches occurring by the light of the stars and the various braziers that marked individual family territory. Across the camp, Kalie could see a pair of talented slave girls dancing for one of the chiefs and his guests, while men who did not rate an invitation looked on enviously from a distance. Wives and daughters were about as well, finishing chores and settling down to sleep. Odd, she thought, how even without tents they were somehow still invisible; as hidden from sight as ever.

Kalie sighed. She had to get back to Maalke's campsite before the dust choked her. She'd had nothing to drink since the evening meal, and the story had been a long one, for all that it was unsuccessful. She was thirsty enough to drink whatever she could get her hands on.

A man stepped into her path. Kalie flinched, then steadied herself. It was Riyik.

"A sad story," he said. "Sadder still, that it might be prophetic. But you told it well."

"Thank you," Kalie said warily.

"I would think it difficult to speak so long without a drink."

At once, Kalie's thirst intensified, as did her fear. What kind of game was this beastman playing? "I am on my way back to my master and his wife. I'm sure one of them will give me something to drink if I plead hard enough. Although what that will be…"

"Then please accept this, and have no fear of their cruelty." Riyik held out a water skin. It was a thing of beauty: softly tooled leather with sun symbols and stars worked through it. The tanned hide would keep the sheep's bladder inside it cool, while absorbing any water that might leak out. Although it was so well made that Kalie doubted any would.

"And if I accept this…?" Kalie hated how much she wanted it.

"You owe me nothing. I merely hope that one day, you will look upon me with favor." Then, clearly reading the alarm in Kalie's eyes, "And if you do not, the gift is still yours to keep."

To cover her consternation, she took a drink. The water was sweet and cool and felt wonderful on her parched throat.

"Thank you," she said, offering Riyik a sip, relieved when he accepted. "Did you work the leather yourself?"

Riyik nodded. "Not as good as the craftsmen from your world, of course, but I enjoyed making it. It is perhaps time for me to give up carving wooden horses and return to more practical applications."

"It's very good," said Kalie. "Uh, what about the bladder inside?"

Riyik laughed. "Don't worry, Brenia helped me with that part! It's perfectly safe."

Kalie laughed too, although she refrained from saying aloud what they both knew: preparing an animal bladder for transporting water was a woman's job. While she found it touching that he sought to make her something with his own hands, she would not have liked drinking from a bladder than might not have been thoroughly cleaned.

Before she could think of anything else to say, Riyik turned and disappeared into the night.

"We praise wise Aahk for a safe deliverance at our journey's end..." The singing of the women continued all day. But if it meant they could stop walking in this stifling heat, Kalie thought, they could praise whomever they wanted.

She smelled, before she saw, the reason for the rejoicing. The beastmen's summer camp was on the shores of a small lake. It was nothing like the lakes back home, where often one could not even see the other side, and strong swimming ability was a necessity. This lake was shallow and brown, choked with reeds and barely a stone's throw across at its widest point.

Still, Kalie found she was picking up her pace, hurrying towards it like the others. She wanted to tear off her sweaty, stifling garments and plunge into the water's cool embrace; to feel clean and free and unencumbered. It was all she could do to restrain herself.

A noisy flock of waterfowl took wing as the even noisier people invaded their territory. Fools! Kalie wanted to shout. That's food flying away, and no one's in position to bring it down! If you keep scaring the birds, they won't come back!

Then she realized: of course they would. This was probably the only water of any size for miles, and it was the time for ducks to fly north. There was no place else to rest and feed. And Kalie's captors knew it.

The camps of many of the clans were already established. As Kalie followed Altia and Cassia into the deafening chaos, she realized how much she had changed since the clans had last been together. She could easily recognize the king's tent, in the center of the long stretch of ugly black tents. She could see how Kahlar, and the two chiefs with him fell to jockeying for the best remaining places to set up their own clan's tents. She could see connections as people eagerly sought familiar faces, even as they fell to the work of establishing a permanent camp. As permanent as beastmen could imagine, at any rate.

As soon as Kalie and the other women had Maalke's tent set up, she asked Cassia for permission to seek out the women who had come with her from the west. Cassia, who was looking well and feeling stronger than she had in many days agreed, and even wished Kalie luck.

Kalie first went to the lake to fill her water bag. Other women were there on the same errand of course, but none had their own private water source. Funny, what a difference that made. She lingered a moment, washing her hands and face in the cool water, then giving in to the temptation to push up her sleeves and wash her arms as well. Finally, the disapproving stares of the other women drove her away. She fell in step with the chaos, dodging mounted horses, shrieking children, and harried women with practiced ease. With her covered head, small steps and demurely lowered eyes, she was just another Aahken slave girl.

Since she had not had the time, or admittedly, the inclination to get to know very many people before they separated for winter, Kalie headed for the royal compound, guessing that would be the place to find Maylene. And perhaps Maylene would have news of Larren and Kestra. Maybe even Alessa.

Outside the king's tent, a guard stopped Kalie and demanded to know her business. "I seek my kinswoman, Maylene, concubine to Prince Kariik," she said, forgetting to be meek and demure.

"The prince's barbarian whores are none of my concern," spat the guard. "Go away."

So Kalie circled the compound until she spotted a slave girl leaving the tent to get water. This time, she was ready with a string of beads to offer in exchange for common courtesy.

"Can you tell me if Maylene still lives with the king's household?" Kalie asked, after the girl had secured the bauble inside her robe.

Her eyes widened. "The stranger from the West? You mean to say you haven't heard the story of how the prince has mourned her this whole season?"

"She is dead?" Kalie asked, trying to sound unconcerned, but it came out a choked whisper.

"She died giving the prince a son," the girl said haughtily. "Just as well she didn't survive, I suppose. She was weak, and never even so much as learned to make kumis or shear a sheep. She could never have been a woman of Aahk! Still, Kariik forgave her for all that when she gave him his first son. Who knows? Maybe he even would have married her. It would have been quite the scandal, a barbarian for a queen, but…"

"Queen?" Kalie shook aside her grief to garner information. "What of Kariik's brothers?"

"You really have been living inside a sheep's ass! Haven't you heard of how Melaak was slain in a battle with the Hansi at the start of winter? And how Trobaak was struck down by a fever during the journey here just this last moon span?" The slave lowered her voice. "Although some say it was poison, not fever."

"But either way, it leaves Kariik next in line."

The girl nodded, and then lifted her heavy water skins. "I must get back now."

"Let me help you," said Kalie, taking two of the bulky containers and arranging them on her shoulders.

The slave looked doubtful. "Why would you want to help?"

"I had hoped for a look at the new prince. He's my kinsman, after all."

The girl seemed convinced, even impressed by Kalie's claim. She followed the nomad girl back to the tent, this time passing easily inside with no attention from the guards. The king's tent had looked big from the outside: at least eight wooden poles, all of them longer and straighter than the usual five held it up. Inside, it was like a shadowy city. Long sheets of felt had been cleverly draped to form private rooms for the king's wives. There was even what could be called an actual kitchen, with at least a dozen women laboring to prepare the feast with which the twenty clans would celebrate the beginning of summer.

Kalie thought at first to ask after Maylene's baby, but instead took the opportunity to slip in beside two scrawny girls, struggling with the carcass of an enormous sheep. She righted it before it tipped one of them over, then helped them with the butchering. No one questioned her presence.

On the other side of the tent, carefully guarded by warriors, a screened off area lay enshrouded by heavy smoke. The incense could not quite cover the stench of illness and decay. Somewhere in there, the king lay dying.

She tried to learn who was who among the women, especially the wives. She thought about offering to tell a story, but the women were busy enough with stories of their own. One in particular, caught her attention.

"Will the king really agree to the alliance?" someone asked. "Embrace the king of the Wolf tribe as a brother? Ride to battle by his side?"

"Shouldn't you be asking if Kariik will agree to it?" asked another. She was about Varena's age, but sleek and well fed; probably a woman already, or would be soon. One of the king's daughters? "After all, he's the one who will have to marry an animal princess to seal the bargain!" There was general laughter at her jibe at the Wolf tribe.

"It's also Kariik who will be riding to battle—as king." There were angry whispers and furtive looks towards the king's quarters, as women made signs against evil. Still, no one disputed the claim, or suggested that the king might live to lead another battle.

"The new king may keep some of the old king's women." Kalie turned from her work, and saw a small group of younger women lounging on felt cushions and applying the now familiar cleansing paste made from ceder and frankencense to their naked bodies. In a land with little water, the paste at least kept the women clean. Kalie wished the men would use it.

The speaker was about sixteen summers, blonde, and her flat unlined stomach suggested she hadn't borne any children. Women of power, or they would not be so idle. Across from them, two ancient crones supervised the work of the others.

"He must agree to marry only the Wolf princess," said Kalie's guide. "And take no other wives until she has borne him a son." Her eyes raked the naked concubines. "Of course, he can keep as many slaves in his bed as he wants."

Kalie was so busy watching the interplay she nearly missed what followed. "Kariik will do what is best for his people," said one of Ahnaak's ancient wives. Kariik's mother, perhaps?

A younger wife, closing her eyes as a slave applied cypress paste to her face snorted. "He'll do what Haraak tells him to. I am to be given to him as a gift."

Several women looked at her in confusion. "To Prince Kariik?" asked one.

The woman snorted again. "To Haraak! Who do you think will rule this place when Kariik becomes king?"

Kalie finished sewing up a bag of meaty bones and hung it over one of several smoky braziers, then wiped the sweat from her face. She approached the smug young gossip. "And what is your name, lady?" she asked sweetly.

Leaving the tent was not so easy as getting in. Kalie had to wait until she could collect enough garbage to look natural taking it to the long trench dug along the edge of the camp. When that chore was done, she strode purposefully back towards the area where Kahlar was camped. She was nearly there when she realized she had not seen Maylene's son.

How had it been for Maylene in her last moon spans? She had been a girl of fourteen when she set out to bring salvation to the savages. Had she been able to keep her faith in the Goddess, as Kalie had not? Had her faith sustained her in the end? Or was her mind, like Kestra's, already broken and empty before her body breathed its last? Was her death even the result of childbirth, or had one of that horde of competing women helped her along?

Kalie knew she would never have the answers. If she asked any of the women who had lived beside Maylene, she would hear only how honored Maylene had been to bear the prince's child, or how romantic it was that the prince had loved a useless barbarian, and raised her up to ride by his side.

Lost in thought, Kalie nearly collided with a woman from one of the other camps. "Sorry—" she began, and then stopped.

"Kalie?" The woman pulled aside her veil, and

Kalie found herself gazing into the face of someone who might be the last of her comrades still living among the Aahk.

"Larren!" Kalie flung out her arms and moved forward to embrace her. Larren hesitated a moment, then stepped into the embrace. Kalie felt the bulge in Larren's middle, and realized she was pregnant.

"You're alive!" said Kalie.

"Yes, and so are you," said Larren. They laughed together over the absurdity of the exchange, then fell into an uneasy silence.

"I just came from Kariik's tent," Kalie said. "Are we all that's left?"

"Other than Kestra, you mean? Yes, I fear we are."

"How has it been for you?"

"So much harder than I ever expected. But that wasn't your fault, Kalie. I just didn't really understand that life could be like this for anyone. Or, that if I came here, I wouldn't be able to change it."

The bleak resignation in her voice frightened Kalie. "You're not in it alone anymore. Maybe, now that the two of us are together—"

"We're not going to change anything! Haven't you figured that out yet?"

"You've given up?"

"Haven't you?" Kalie did not know how to answer. After a moment, Larren continued. "Only those who've died have shown any real courage. Dara chose to die quietly, but with dignity. Traea chose to take some of those bastards with her when she left. And me..." Larren put a hand on her stomach and looked away.

"You do what you have to do to keep your

child safe," Kalie said softly, trying to show that she didn't judge Larren for it.

But the younger woman only laughed bitterly. "I'd rid myself of this thing, if I had the right herbs! When we first came here, I swore I'd never bring a child into a world such as this. Now, I can't even keep that vow! What about you?"

"It appears the healers back home were correct: I can't conceive. At least I haven't yet."

"Praise the Goddess—" Larren broke off. "That's something I haven't said in longer than I can remember. There are days when I think that I dreamed the life we used to have; that this—" She swept an arm to indicate the grassland stretching to the horizon—"is all that's ever been, and ever will be."

Kalie was trying desperately to think of something to say to that, when Varena came running through the crowd that swirled around them. "Kalie! Thank the gods I found you! You must come quickly!"

"What is it?" Kalie hurried over to the panting girl.

"Cassia!" Varena gasped. "She's lost the baby."

Chapter 6

Kalie raced back to the tent nearly as panicked as the girl behind her, her mind leaping from her encounter with Larren to this new crisis. What could have happened? Was Cassia in danger as well? Could she do anything to save her if she was?

Inside the tent, the air was subdued. Irisa sat smirking in one corner, combing wool while she nursed her new son. Altia's two daughters sat silently by the pot that held the evening meal, stirring occasionally, and looking frightened. Altia herself sat beside Cassia, in the second wife's sleeping cubicle, with the curtain drawn back to admit light. Cassia lay rigid, her face pinched and white, her mouth a tight line. As Kalie approached, Altia reached toward the stained rags between Cassia' legs. Cassia glared at the senior wife, and Kalie saw she held a knife.

Altia backed away, and then noticed Kalie. "She won't let anyone near her but you! Foolish, since this all of this is your fault, but there you are. See what you can do for her." Altia moved away.

Kalie knelt beside Cassia and called for Varena to bring her a lamp. With the extra light in place, she gently removed Cassia's clothing, trying not to let her hands shake. Cassia relaxed noticeably, but her face only shifted to bleak acceptance. "What happened?" Kalie asked.

"Nothing! I was sewing. I felt a cramp. Then, the bleeding started."

"Just one cramp? Try to relax; I have to see between your legs." Cassia lay rigid, as if by not moving she could keep the baby from slipping from her body.

"Only one bad one. There may have been some other small ones."

The first thing Kalie noticed was that there was very little blood. It was a frightening amount, of course, but at nearly six moon spans, there should be more. Was this a sign of even worse trouble, with a dead child trapped within Cassia's body? Or could it mean, just possibly, that the child still lived?

Kalie's fingers gently probed Cassia's abdomen. It was still the size one would expect this far along. Maybe this would be a slow loss, or... something moved under Kalie's fingers. Cassia gasped, her hands flying to her belly. "Kalie?" she whispered.

"Lie still! Breathe slowly." Kalie went limp with relief as she realized the child was not dead. For a moment she wanted to strangle Varena for frightening her, then forgot that thought as she struggled to remember what might be done to help Cassia hang on to this tenuous bit of life.

Kalie bundled up furs and cushions, and used them to prop up Cassia legs. "Stay like you are, on your back, but keep your legs up, and keep breathing like I showed you. You've had some bleeding, but the baby still lives. I'm going to make you some tea." And anything else I can think of!

Cassia fixed Kalie with a desperate gaze. "Can you save my baby?" she whispered.

For a moment, Kalie was filled with avaricious thoughts of how good life might become for herself and Varena if, against all odds, this baby survived. Just as quickly, she remembered the healers of Hot Springs, forgotten for nearly a year, and a memory of what it meant to be a healer. "I don't know," she told Cassia. "But I will do everything in my power to do so."

By then, the rest of the household realized something had changed. "What are you doing?" demanded Altia.

"She didn't miscarry," said Kalie, as she rummaged around for what she needed. "At least, not yet. If I can find the right herbs, she might yet deliver a living child."

"What?" cried Irisa, leaping up. The baby, dislodged from her breast, began to howl. "Her baby's dead! I saw the blood!"

Kalie paused, her hand clasping a piece of snakeroot. "Saw it, Irisa? Or caused it? You seem rather upset at what should be happy news. After all, a good concubine rejoices at her master's children."

Altia turned on Irisa. "You were the first to rush to her side, when she cried out. And you declared the baby lost just moments later. Is there something you want to tell us?"

Irisa clutched her baby before her like a shield. "I have done nothing!" she shrieked, but Kalie saw that the younger woman was sweating. Of course, the tent was stifling hot. "Nothing but say what everyone here already knows: Cassia is barren! It is Kalie's fault for putting her through all this again; keeping a doomed child alive inside her, until it dooms the mother as well!" She turned to Kalie with venomous eyes. "Keep plying her with your foul potions and black arts and both will die—then Maalke will kill you as well!"

Kalie thought furiously. Had Irisa been in the household for both of Cassia's other miscarriages?

There might be no connection at all. But if there was…
Kalie shuddered. How could anyone live like this?

She met Irisa's gaze with a deadly look of her own. "Irisa, if you gave her anything, I need to know what it was!" The other woman stared back, her face suffused with hatred, but said nothing. Kalie thought desperately for some way to bargain. "Just tell me, and I promise, Maalke will never know." Foolish, she chided herself. She could hold her own tongue, but couldn't speak for anyone else in this cursed tent! Besides what store would Irisa set in promises?

"If you don't tell us, and she loses the baby," said Altia, "we will tell my husband it was your doing."

Kalie stared at the woman. Was Altia actually trying to help? Or was the old goat just grabbing a chance to do in an annoying competitor? This seemed to be a day for questions.

Irisa turned back to her work without another word. Altia shrugged and did the same. Kalie set about doing a job for which she lacked training, resources and information, and told herself to be grateful for the silence.

She remained trapped in the tent, by Cassia's side for the next two days. There was no further threat of miscarriage, but Kalie insisted that Cassia must remain in her blankets until the baby was born. This pronouncement had the effect of reconciling Altia and Irisa.

"Women of Aahk do not laze around in bed for three moon spans!" Altia had spat.

"Besides, what warrior would want a wife or a baby who were so weak they needed such measures to do what all others can do normally?" Irisa had demanded.

Kalie said nothing, only waited for Maalke's return, where she had no choice but to present the situation to him.

To everyone's surprise, Maalke had agreed to Kalie's suggestions. Then Altia had flown into a rage and demanded more slaves, claiming she couldn't run a household without them, what with Tasine gone, Cassia useless, and Kalie busy tending to Cassia. They fought most of the night, but by morning, Maalke had agreed to purchase at least one new slave before the men left for the summer sacrifices. Kalie didn't like the way he looked at Varena when he said it.

Cassia finally permitted Kalie to leave the tent the day before the men left. There was to be a great feast that night and Kalie's labor was needed. Varena had already collected the day's fuel supply. Now she helped Kalie dig a pit that would be used that night to roast the goat that Altia had butchered. The pit would be lined with stones, heated by a fire above it, and the goat stuffed with vegetables, all of which Kalie and Varena were to gather.

As they scoured the area around the camp for wild foods that hadn't already been stripped by other women on the same errand, Kalie noticed a number of women busy with nets near the lake. She asked Varena about it.

"Most of the nets belong to Leja," said Varena, delighted as always to be the one Kalie turned to for information. "The rest to the other chief's wives. Men sometimes hunt ducks and geese with spears, but that's mostly for target practice. With those nets, Leja can sometimes bring down..." Varena apparently couldn't count that high.

"Mmm, sounds delicious." Kalie tried to remember the last time she'd eaten roasted duck with fruit sauce or goose stuffed with oysters. "Will that be part of the feast?"

Varena shrugged. "Maybe. Some of the women will make a special dish, if their men like birds. Most men prefer deer or boar—game they hunt themselves. But Leja and the other chief's wives will feast while the men are away."

While Kalie liked the sound of celebrating the time away from the men, she wasn't happy with the ever-present hierarchy. The chief's wives owned the nets; the chief's wives decided who got to eat bounty that should be shared by everyone.

"Varena, is there any rule against individual women hunting for ducks and geese?"

"I don't think so. But only chief's wives have nets—and they don't share." Varena looked pointedly at Kalie, as if fearing another speech about the weird customs of her people. "How could anyone hunt birds without a net?"

"Come with me," said Kalie, a smile sliding across her face. "I'll show you."

Kalie led Varena to the huge waste trench that was, mercifully, dug downwind of the crowded camp. While each camp had its own privy for human wastes, this trench was for all the garbage accumulated in the course of nearly two thousand people gathered in one place for an entire season. As much as she hated the endless traveling, Kalie had to admit that even this tough corner of the earth couldn't survive the abuse of beastmen living in one place year round.

As smelly as the trench was, it held a wealth of useful objects, if one knew how to look. Kalie noticed that she was not the only forager here today. Ragged women sought scraps of food and pieces of hide to patch shoes, clothing and other necessities. Shadow women, they were called. Women without protection.

Kalie recalled what she had learned of them before winter set in, when they had to find a tent to stay in, or die. They were women who had been cast out of their tents and families for various reasons, and had to live as best they could, begging and selling their bodies. There were never more than a few at any one time. Cassia had said it was because most Aahken women were honorable, and unlikely to merit such punishment. Kalie suspected it was because most who did were quickly killed, and that allowing a few to linger this way provided entertainment for the men and a warning to the women.

She finally found what she was looking for: a section of sheep skeleton with several ribs still attached. Two of them had the right shape, so Kalie took them both.

It was a busy day, and only Cassia's long nap that afternoon afforded Kalie the time to shape the curved bones into throwing sticks. As Varena watched in fascination, Kalie turned the discarded ribs into simple weapons of deadly efficiency.

That evening, with preparations completed and the warriors of the tribe busy with some esoteric business of their own, Leja and the other chief's wives set their nets and waited for the birds to return to the lake for the night. Many women watched with envy; others with bleak and hungry resignation.

Savory blue smoke hung over the entire camp as meat roasted slowly in pit ovens, or turned on spits above fires. Then, above the noise of camp, came the honking of geese. Kalie had shed as much of her clothing as she thought she could get away with. Now she hitched up her skirts for greater freedom of movement. The nets were ready, and soon the sounds changed to squawks of anger and fear. Those not snared sought to flee. Kalie knew the geese that escaped would not soon return; this was her only chance.

She flung her first stick into the midst of a confused gaggle of birds. As she watched in wonder, not one, but two birds fell into the shallows at the edge of the lake. She followed with the second, but it fell into the water without catching anything.

"Hurry!" she cried to Varena. They raced to the spot. Varena, still dressed properly, was far behind Kalie, who was more interested in finding her weapons than retrieving the geese.

"Here!" said Varena, spotting the stick and grabbing it.

"Good work!" said Kalie. "Get the geese, while I try to get one more." She knew she'd have only one more chance. The ragged remains of the flock were flying east, struggling to gain altitude. She cast her stick again, watching the tiny perfection of the disappearing birds; the deep blue of the evening sky. Then one figure fell from the flock, like a star from the skies. The rest disappeared into the darkening sky.

Kalie pushed through the noisy crowd of women who were excitedly collecting the prizes of the hunt, avoiding sharp beaks as they wrung necks with quick efficiency. She had to travel beyond the edge of the lake to find the last goose. She found her stick as well.

It was only when she had her prize safely in

her arms, reciting the familiar words of thanks to the dead creature, and savoring the quiet solitude of the night that Kalie noticed Varena had not followed her. She was alone. How long had it been since she enjoyed the luxury of solitude among the fresh smells of summer, watching the stars slowly fill the sky? How long since she had felt the exultation of a successful hunter?

But to leave Varena alone with valuable food was like tying a rock around her neck and telling her to go for a swim. Kalie headed back to the to the torch lit camp where a buzzing like angry bees was centered on the place she had just left.

Varena was fighting to hold onto the two geese, stoically ignoring the blows to her body, as a shrieking, red-faced Leja demanded she release them. At least three other women—probably Leja's slaves—sought to take them from her, but only succeeded in getting in each other's way, and making it easier for Varena to hang on.

Kalie flung herself between Leja and Varena in time to catch the next blow—on her chest, because of her height difference—and face the chief's wife ready for battle. Every woman in the camp was looking on, delighted.

"Why are you beating my daughter, Chief's Wife?" she demanded.

"Daughter?" sputtered Leja. "Her whore of a mother is long dead, as she will be soon, for trying to steal my birds!"

"Those birds are mine," said Kalie. "As is this one I've just retrieved." She glanced at the pile of geese, jealously guarded by the other wives and their slaves. "But if all that is not enough for you, then take this!" She offered the goose in her hand. "If stealing from hungry slaves makes you feel more like a woman, by all means, do so!"

There was a deadly silence. Even the fires seemed to stop crackling.

Leja's red face went white. "You will die for those words, slave! But first, amuse me by telling us all why you would send this girl to steal from me in plain sight—then call me a thief!"

Kalie realized that Leja hadn't been trying to take what wasn't hers; she had simply been too busy with her nets to see that a new hunter with a new method had been at work. Leja had assumed, as she had for years, that all birds killed at this lake were hers. Of course, explaining the situation didn't make Kalie and Varena any less likely to die.

"I killed three geese with this." Kalie proffered the throwing stick.

Most of the chiefs' wives laughed derisively. Those who had seen Kalie's demonstration of skill did not laugh, but neither did they speak up in her defense. "Check the marks on my three," she pressed forward. "Here, you can see where the stick struck this one on the wing; this one here in the belly. Then, too you can see how it was actually striking the ground that killed them. Yours have none of this kind of damage; they died only when you broke their necks…"

"She's right," said one of the other wives, examining the geese. "It's amazing! Can you show me how to hunt like…?" Then she glanced up at Leja and went silent.

"Of course she's right!" said an old woman. Kalie didn't know her, but guessed she was one of the oldest women alive in this place. "Everyone here saw her using that stick to knock birds from the sky. Everyone except you greedy bitches who every year flaunt your power to have what others cannot."

Emboldened by Kalie's unknown champion, some of the other women began to press forward timidly, asking if they could learn to use such sticks.

"I don't believe it!" shouted Leja. "It's nothing but a sheep's rib! How could anyone…?"

"Like this!" Kalie flung the stick skyward, hoping her audience would get the idea, since there was no target to aim at.

Or so she thought.

The stick left the torchlight, flew through the night sky in a graceful arc—struck a tiny moving form —and fell down nearly at Kalie's feet.

Just beyond it was a small brown duck.

Kalie thought she heard girlish laughter: bold and gentle and fearless. Not the sort of laughter that was ever heard around here. I won't deny it's You, she prayed to her Goddess. Especially if You help me get out of this alive!

One of the women ran and got the bird. Kalie set a restraining hand on Varena's shoulders, in case the girl was going to fight for it, but Varena was grinning through her battered face. The woman brought the duck to Kalie with a deference usually reserved for first wives.

Leja sputtered. "If something so simple could make hunting so easy, we would have known about it!"

More than one woman bit her lips to avoid laughing out loud. Kalie grinned. "Which is why my people eat well, while so many of yours remain hungry."

Then, they saw the men returning from the practice field and everyone scurried to prepare the evening meal.

Chapter 7

Kalie carefully wrapped the geese and duck in grass and hung them from one of the tent poles. Despite the heat of the day, nights on the steppes were still cool enough to keep meat fresh. Tomorrow Kalie would learn if the birds truly belonged to her. Tonight, she was as close to free as she had ever been since coming to this land.

For tonight was the Summer Festival, where even slaves were—to a limited degree—free to eat and drink and sing and dance, while wives proudly served their husbands. Kalie found Altia's pride in such servitude funny, in a sad way. There was the fierce wife that ruled the tent with a stone first, kneeling before her husband, holding a plate of food within his easy reach while he laughed and joked with his fellow warriors, and ignored her.

If this was how a wife enjoyed a feast, Kalie was glad to be a slave.

It was Cassia who would be staying inside to tend the fire tonight. She had insisted on making a brief appearance when the holy men of the tribe had performed their mercifully short ritual, declaring summer and, more importantly, the feast, begun. Then she returned to the tent, promising Kalie she would rest.

Kalie had tried to treat Varena's bruises, but the girl had impatiently reminded her that a warrior's daughter didn't need to be coddled just because a woman slapped her face a few times. She drank some of the willow bark tea Kalie gave her, but it seemed excitement over the feast she would be participating in was all the analgesic Varena needed.

Kalie stayed to make sure Cassia was safely tucked back into bed, with a nourishing broth and some choice bits of meat, before going back outside to attend the feast herself.

This one far surpassed the winter feast. Here was a beautiful summer night, with meat rich from spring grazing, and even some of the fruits and vegetables she had for so long craved.

As Kalie wandered through the crowds, tasting food from this or that spit or basket, she looked for some of the women who had shown an interest in her hunting success. Varena had disappeared with a group of girls like herself: daughters of warriors and slave women. Kalie wished her well.

Before Kalie could find any of the women she sought, two of them approached her. They were both younger than she by at least ten summers: both wives, but not yet mothers, although she suspected one of them was pregnant.

"Can we see that strange…killing stick?" asked one, who said her name was Tiza. Her companion was Kiska.

Kalie took the weapon from the thong where it hung at her waist, next her water bag. "Perhaps while the men are away, we can arrange a demonstration; maybe even a group hunt."

The women exchanged a startled look, as though such a thought had never occurred to them.

"Is it true that Riyik asked you to marry him?" asked Kiska. "And that you turned him down?"

Kalie knew she shouldn't be surprised that word had spread. Still, she wanted tonight to be about things the horsewomen could do for themselves, and each other—not another round of gossip. "Yes, it's true," she said finally.

"How could any woman turn down a man like that?" demanded Tiza. "Especially a slave!"

Rather than answering, Kalie peered closer at the woman, and realized where she had seen her before. "Are you from the same clan as my kinswomen, Alessa?"

"Alessa? Oh, yes, she was Tarnaak's woman for a time." Tiza lowered her voice. "The fool lost her in a game of knucklebones with that envoy from the Wolf Tribe! Our chief was furious, for she was clever with potions and charms. There was scarcely a one in the camp who she hadn't helped."

"She was the greater fool!" snapped Kiska, a hand on her belly. "Our chief might have made her his own concubine, if she hadn't given away all her magic for free! He never saw any reason to buy her until it was too late. Now she won't be here to help with my baby, and everyone knows she's more skilled than that fool Navia!"

Kalie thought about pointing out that if Alessa had behaved like a woman of Aahk, she probably wouldn't bother helping Kiska in the first place, but decided to drop it. The important thing was that Alessa might still be alive.

She wandered around awhile longer, finally slipping into the fringes of the crowd that ringed the king's tent.

There were games and contests taking place in the open area in front of the tent. They mostly involved mock fights—and some that looked pretty real. The king himself was making one of his rare appearances. Reclining on a bed of pillows, swaddled in blankets despite the mild weather, there was no question he was dying. His eyes were sunk in his gray face and his body shook like a bundle of sticks beneath the richly embroidered linen robes and gaudy gold ornaments.

Kalie could hardly believe this was the same man who had given her to Maalke less than a year ago. Strange, she thought. He's really not that old, even by beastmen standards. Here, when men died young, it was usually in battle. She thought about which illnesses could strike a healthy man so quickly.

Pushing her way through the crowd, Kalie strained to get a closer look, and now her healer's eye began to take in what she was seeing. While she desperately wished for Alessa, or better yet, Maris, to confirm it, Kalie suspected Ahnaak was being poisoned.

Many thoughts occurred to Kalie as she stared. Could she learn to make some poison of her own? How many could she kill at one time? Could she somehow expose the would-be killer and save the king, thus gaining access to the inner circles of power? Kalie took another look at the king. It was most likely too late for that.

That left learning all she could of the power who would soon replace Ahnaak, and from what she could see, that wasn't Kariik. Kalie smiled. It seemed all paths led back to the man who had begun it all.

At length, the king's retainers insisted he go inside to rest. His senior wife, somehow dignified, rather than pathetic in her servitude, followed behind as his men carried him inside the tent. There would be no feasting or dancing or visiting with friends for her tonight. And when he died, there would be no more

life for her either. And, most likely, she would think it
a great honor to follow him to the next life. Perhaps
that was better for her, than if she had screamed and
fought and clung to life, as Kalie would have. But she
still found tears welling up when she thought about it.

Women roamed freer than usual tonight, many
of them allowing a veil to slip or a robe to swing open
as they walked past a certain man, or danced in groups
with other women. Kalie had little trouble placing
herself near a group of warriors who were more
interested in discussion than debauchery. And sure
enough, Haraak was there, at the center of it all.

It had been more than half a year's turning
since Kalie had last seen him. She was surprised at the
rage and ashamed of the fear that swept through her
like a wildfire at that first glance. He was the same: the
scarred and tattooed face, the wild red hair, now
caught up in elaborate braids and studded with gold,
the sheer menacing size. Kalie told herself to keep still
and listen, and one day he would be crawling at her
feet, spitting blood. She tried to smile at the thought,
but could only shrink down into her robe and hide
behind her veil, afraid he would recognize her.

She saw that Yessenia, the king's woman who
had boasted about being given to Haraak, was there as
well. She was trying to draw Haraak's attention as
surely as Kalie was trying to avoid it. So far, Kalie's
attempts to ingratiate herself with the simpering fool
had gone nowhere. She was beginning to think the
woman was too stupid to know anything of value.
Still, everything Kalie could learn about Haraak's
habits, likes or dislikes was valuable. And more
importantly, with Yessenia, she didn't have to get
close to him herself.

The warriors were discussing chiefs and war
leaders from various neighboring tribes, weighing the
merits and liabilities of bargains and treaties with each
one. Kalie tried to remember names, and as much
about each one as possible.

"A treaty with the Wolf Tribe might work," the
scarred old man beside Haraak was saying. "At least
until it's time to divide up the spoils. If these lands to
the west are as rich as you claim."

Kalie inched closer, barely breathing.

"You have no idea," said a familiar voice
slurred with much drink. Gault, Kalie remembered,
brushing aside the memories his voice brought back.
"It's not a place a man could believe existed, until he
saw it."

There was muttered discussion. Kalie strained
to hear it, keeping her head down.

"Alliances never last for long," another man
said. "And usually aren't worth the blood you have to
spill when they end. But you want more than that!" He
pointed an accusing finger at Haraak. "You want a
federation! You think you can bring all the western
tribes together—"

"It will be necessary," said the man on
Haraak's other side. "If we're to be masters of the
lands of the west—"

"The Sons of Aahk live in the grasslands!"
shouted the man across from him. "Leave our home,
and we'll lose the favor of the gods."

"If we haven't already lost their favor,"
muttered an old man, staring morosely into the fire.
Others glared at him, and made protective signs
against evil.

Haraak, Kalie noticed, had said nothing the

entire time she had been listening. Now he cleared his throat, and everyone fell silent.

"We need this alliance because our future lies in the west." Haraak's gruff voice was quiet, yet it carried easily to the far edge of the crowd.

"We're already in the west," muttered a petulant voice. It's owner was richly dressed, but more boy than man. Yutiik, the king's nephew. "We're about as far west as the grasslands go!"

"And that," said Haraak, with an ingratiating smile at the young prince, "is exactly my point. Our enemies are many; yet the grasslands grow smaller and poorer each year. As bad as recent winters have been for us, they have been worse to the east. So men push west out of desperation."

"And always we have defeated them!" shouted Yutiik. "As we always will!" There was thunderous agreement from the assembled warriors.

"But only a little further west," said Haraak, "there is a land like no other. Hills where water gushes down all year, without drying! Rich pastures for our animals, fields of grain, forests of fruit trees." They were spellbound. For all that they had heard it before, the warriors listened like children at a favorite bedtime story.

"And don't forget the game that waits to be hunted," said Gault with a leer.

Haraak grinned. "Yes, the best part. The land is empty of men. Real men, anyway. But filled with women who think the gods gave them the land to rule!" The men exploded with laughter. "Women longing for the touch of real men. Women waiting for us to be their masters!"

"Then why tell anyone else of this marvel?"

cried a young man. "If these men are as weak as you say? If they really are ruled by women—"

"We can take them all ourselves!" shouted another. "Why share the spoils with anyone?"

"Or worry about a knife in the back when settling our shaft into a nice juicy cunt?"

"They are weak, but they are many," said Haraak. "They are more numerous than rabbits in a warren. Their smallest settlements are larger than the clan of the king himself. The place where I…stayed… had more people than our entire tribe." The men stared at each other in disbelief. "Even rabbits could prove dangerous in such numbers."

The prince snorted. "I might risk an army of rabbits, if it meant keeping such a prize for myself."

"And that would be enough," said Haraak, "If all we wanted was to grab treasure and slaves, and return home. But we could have more! With an alliance of the mightiest tribes of the steppes, we could take that land—and hold it!"

Kalie stopped breathing.

"Give up the land of our gods and our ancestors? Forever?"

Haraak shook his head violently. "Bring our gods to the west! Burn those obscene walls, smoke out their warrens, tear down those boxes they live in until only good pastureland remains, and our tents cover the land! Sacrifice nine of every ten people to the spirits of our ancestors—and I think they will like their new home."

The other men were beginning to understand. "Leave only the comeliest women for our beds, and the skilled men to work our gold and silver!" cried one.

"And when the land is ours," said Haraak patiently. "And we prosper there, what happens here, in the east, when the winters get worse, and the summers parch the water from the land?"

They understood, and so did Kalie. Only great numbers could hold the stolen land from the next wave of thieves.

"The king will not support such a venture," said a grizzled veteran, probably older than the king himself.

And that, Kalie saw, was why the king must die. Had his two oldest sons been of a similar mind? Or were they simply too strong to become Haraak's puppets?

Finally remembering to breathe again, Kalie slipped away from the meeting.

She had known this would happen; it was why she had returned to this cursed place as a slave. But now that it was here, all laid out before her, Kalie suddenly wasn't sure what to do.

When? She had to find out when the invasion was to occur.

Kalie was glad that Haraak was her chief enemy here. She already hated him with a passion that felt old and familiar. But she would have to learn who the leaders of the other tribes were. The beastmen had said it themselves: alliances were not something they were good at. She would see to it this one did not last.

Her stories had yielded some results, although admittedly not what she had hoped for. If she could craft a tale that whispered the dangers of trusting outsiders; that promised great rewards to men who acted alone...If she could cause this alliance to fall apart spectacularly enough, she just might be able to convince them to wipe each other out. Or at least reduce their numbers to the point where they wouldn't be a threat to her people for many years.

Kalie was briefly angry that she hadn't learned the arts of seduction: that seemed the surest way to get two men to kill each other in this place, and it was something a slave could do, without corrupting something she valued as much as her stories.

Walking through the camp, she shook her head. She could never be that good an actress.

Maalke's tent was dark when she returned. Only the faint glow from the banked fire let Kalie see her way through the disorderly tent, with Cassia asleep in her corner and Irisa's two sons curled up together like a pair of puppies. Everyone else was still out celebrating.

Kalie was about to seek out her own sheepskin, more to think than with any hope of sleeping, when a faint noise brought her outside again.

Varena was huddled between the shadow of the tent and the spill of starlight on the flattened grass beside it, sobbing as if her heart had been rent in two.

"What's wrong?" cried Kalie, rushing to her side.

Varena looked up at her through dead eyes. "I am a woman now," she said.

Chapter 8

It took Kalie a moment to understand. "Do you mean…is it your first bleeding?"

Varena glared at her. "I know the women are different where you come from, but don't they at least get moon times?"

Kalie sat beside the girl, who was still just a girl as far as she could see. She reached out a hand carefully, as with a wounded animal. "Yes, a girl's first bleeding is what marks the beginning of the transition to womanhood. But where I come from, it's a joyous event; a cause for celebration."

Varena looked puzzled. "Why?"

Kalie sighed. "Another difference between our peoples, I suppose." From across the years, Kalie remembered her own womanhood ceremony. She had been frightened, too, she now recalled. But it was the fear of change; the nervous excitement of the unknown. Perhaps even some discomfort at all the attention: all those people hugging and kissing her; all the gifts and well wishing. Was she thanking everyone properly? Showing enough dignity and decorum? Would she make a fool of herself during the dancing, when everyone was watching her?

Not this blank eyed terror, warring only with a sense of final doom. "I know being a woman isn't a wonderful thing in this land, but what has you so terrified?"

"Maalke is going to sell me. I heard him promise Altia a few days ago. They were arguing; she was accusing me of seducing him; saying I wouldn't be worth anything if he gave in to my wiles. Maalke said he hadn't; that he'd already made a bargain with a warrior from Griiv's clan to trade me for two old women slaves as soon as I was a woman—or sooner, if I took too long about it. I guess they won't have to wait now."

Kalie tried to speak twice, and finally managed, "Could we hide it from the rest of the tent? At least until your next moon time?"

Varena looked surprised. "I thought about trying that! I didn't think anyone would help me with such a deception, not even you, Kalie." Surprising, how much it hurt that she had stopped saying mother. "But Altia already knows. I came back to the tent to look for you; I needed the rags that the women use. Altia was here, getting more kumis for Maalke. She knew right away. I think she smelled it."

"Yet another way in which wives resemble dogs," said Kalie. That won her a nervous smile from Varena. "Did you get the rags, at least?" Varena shook her head. "All right, let's take care of that first. Then we'll worry about the rest of it." Kalie led Varena inside the tent, to the place where she kept her supplies, grateful that she had recently made some new pads of absorbent felt. She didn't want to give Varena something used for her first time.

"The men will leave at dawn for their summer horse sacrifice," Kalie said, as she showed Varena what to do. "They'll be gone four whole days. And when they come back, you'll probably still be bleeding, so they'll avoid you until you're done. That gives us time."

"For what?" asked Varena, hope creeping back into her voice.

"I'm not sure yet," Kalie said with more

confidence than she felt. "But we'll think of something."

The sun was just rising on the eastern plains, when the men rode out of camp.

Kalie, who had barely slept that short night, was dragged from her bedroll by the bleary-eyed women of Maalke's tent, to join in the singing as the women bid farewell to the warriors.

Kalie stumbled out of the tent with a curse, and then froze in awe at the sight before her. The pearly glow of dawn kissed the grass and tents with dew, while a gorgeous display of pink and gold lit the sky in the east. Of course, the most beautiful sight of all was that of the men leaving.

Unlike times of war, when a small group of older or less favored warriors were left behind to guard the women and herds, the summer horse sacrifice was a time when all men—and all boys old enough to leave their mothers for a few days—would be away from the camp. They would be near enough to hear if an alarm was sounded, but Kalie had heard that this was a sacred time for all the people of the steppes, and that not even the worst of enemies would risk the wrath of the gods by violating the solemn ceremony with fighting.

When she had asked what ceremonies the women would perform to welcome in the summer, she received blank looks. Wives apparently performed some kind of short ritual, but slaves and concubines did not attend. Mostly, it seemed, the women went quietly about their work, anxiously awaiting the return of the men.

Kalie took her place with the others slaves, chanting the appropriate responses while the wives made two columns for the men to ride between, singing of the glory of men of honor who served the great god Aahk. She saw Cassia, one of the few who looked well rested, her hands demurely crossed over her swollen belly. Just one more moon span, thought Kalie, and the baby could be born safely.

Cassia's pregnancy, Varena's womanhood, Riyik's interest in her, the planned conquest of her world—thoughts raced through Kalie's mind, giving her no peace. She had the sense of things about to change. And if she wasn't watching the right thing at the right moment, everything would be lost.

As the men disappeared from view beyond a low hill, a change came over the women, but unlike Kalie, most did not become giddy with relief. Rather, they seemed to sag, as if some vital life force had deserted them. Altia, who had obviously drunk too much kumis the night before, staggered back to her bed, clearly intending to sleep the rest of the day. Cassia, fearing she had pushed herself too hard by taking her place in the farewell ceremony, also returned to her bed. Irisa took advantage of the absence of both master and wives to go visit friends. Who knew she had any? Kalie thought.

She turned to Varena who looked lost and sad. Somewhere deep inside, the beauty of new womanhood sparkled in her and mirrored the beauty of this summer day. Kalie ached to give to Varena all that she had been given at this time in her own life.

Then it hit her: perhaps she could.

Hurrying to the tent, Kalie found the three geese and the little brown duck she had killed the day before where she had left them, still unspoiled. But they would need to be cooked soon: the lovely dawn was promising to turn into a hot day. Hurrying to the pit in which last night's feast had cooked, Kalie found it still warm. Little effort would be required to have it ready for the birds.

"Varena, come help me pluck these! Then I will show you how we prepare them in my homeland."

Sullen, but curious, Varena approached. "What are we doing?"

"You're a woman. Tonight is Midsummer. And it's a full moon besides! We're going to have a proper celebration of all of that—but most especially we're going to welcome you into this glorious new phase of your life! And we're going to do it with a feast worthy of you, my beautiful daughter." Kalie embraced Varena, who stared at her as if she had truly gone mad. Kalie didn't care. On fire with a purpose for the first time since coming here, Kalie set about preparing a feast.

Looking back later, Kalie would see the hand of the Goddess in all that happened that day: in the way she found a patch of berries that all the other women had somehow overlooked. In the way fish filled the simple weir she had woven from grass while she went about her foraging. Even in the way that both of Maalke's wives slept all day.

But the most important thing of all happened when Kalie finally made contact with the Shadow Women.

She had been trying, since discovering their existence, to get to know them, offering bits of food and a kind word whenever she could. But while scavenging the midden for bones that might still have enough marrow to produce soup, Kalie recognized one of the outcast women, bent upon the same errand, not twenty paces from herself—and realized she finally had something to offer them.

"Would you like some of these?" Kalie held out a handful of precious berries.

The woman approached her warily, eyed her suspiciously, then grabbed the food from her hand, jumping back and crouching as she stuffed it in her mouth.

Something in the way she moved, some remnant of grace beneath the stiffness and pain, made Kalie blurt out, "You were a dancer, weren't you!"

The woman stared at her for a long time. "No," she said at last, rising painfully to her full height. "I was the greatest dancer of them all. Chief Vorik's fairest treasure. Ahnaak himself tried to buy me from him." As she traveled backward in her memory, her eyes became clearer and her voice, raspy from long disuse, grew stronger.

"What happened?" Kalie asked.

"What always happens. My beauty faded and my limbs grew stiff. Vorik took a new wife who had long despised me, and she persuaded him to cast me into the shadows. He told me he couldn't bear to sell me to another, but if he had any love left for me, he'd have killed me, rather than this." Her gaze narrowed on Kalie's face. "I know you! You are the new storyteller who's hoping for a place like mine." Her hollow cheeks split with a nearly toothless grin and she held out her skeletal arms. "Take a good look at me girl, and see your own future."

Kalie looked. Then she stepped forward and held out her hands in a gesture of friendship. "My name is Kalie. What is yours?"

"Agafa," said the woman, after a moment's

surprise. She did not take Kalie's hands. "Why do you waste your time with me?"

"I want to learn about this place where I now find myself. I want to learn all I can about becoming the favored entertainer of a chief. And I want to tell you about the place I come from. Tonight, I'm going to celebrate the coming of age of my adopted daughter, as we would in my home. There will be food. I invite you—and all the other women who have been wrongly cast out this way—to join us."

Then she turned and walked away without waiting for Agafa's response. And without the soup bones, she realized later.

Word spread throughout the half empty camp that something was to happen tonight; something that involved slaves and barbaric rituals. No one stopped her, but as the sun began its descent, many women hid in their tents with their children. But many more stood at a wary distance, curious as to what Kalie was up to.

The day had been as brutally hot as Kalie had feared, but now, as evening fell, a deliciously cool breeze wafted through the camp. She took it as another good sign as she surveyed the feast spread before Maalke's tent. Geese stuffed with all manner of roots and seeds, fish roasted on a bed of sweet grass, and hard cakes of flat bread Kalie had somehow managed to coax from the wild rye that grew here. They might not taste like much, but they would be filling, and with the syrup she had made from the berries, they might just become a new taste sensation. Beside the food was a basket of dried flowers Kalie had carefully saved from the spring profusion.

When Kalie went inside to fetch Varena, she stopped short at what she saw. All day, Varena had followed Kalie like a shadow, sometimes watching the preparations, sometimes helping. Now, like the moon peeking out from behind a cloud, Varena's face showed a glimpse of the woman she might one day become. Her gray eyes danced with excitement and curiosity. Her skin, though reddened from the merciless sun of this land, was fresh and vital. Her wheat colored hair held a golden sheen.

Forgetting the decorum that had been so important to her on this day in her own life Kalie flung her arms around Varena and kissed both her cheeks.

"What was that for?" Varena looked shocked, but not at all displeased, as Kalie would have been at her age.

"I'll tell you later! Come now; it's time to begin!"

"Where are we going?"

"I found a beautiful spot by the lake," Kalie said as she led Varena outside and watched her gawk at all the food assembled there. She didn't mention that by "beautiful" she meant the cleanest, least trampled and mud-churned place that contained both water and a dry, level stretch of beach for dancing.

Still, the setting sun was glorious. With no trees to block the sky, no mountains to cut off the brilliant show a moment before it played itself out, the feast would have a fine backdrop. Kalie turned and looked toward the east, and nearly dropped her pilfered sacks of kumis. The moon, fat and golden, lay upon the horizon like a tunnel through which one might escape this world and travel to one altogether new and magical.

"How did you get so much food?" Varena asked. "Is it all for us?"

Kalie looked at the feast, hoping again it would be enough for what she had in mind, and then forced a laugh. "I suppose we might be able to eat it all. But a feast is better when shared. Besides, we could never carry it all by ourselves." Kalie nodded to the skeletal, frightened-looking women who hovered nearby, and prayed it all didn't fall apart right now.

"Shadow Women?" cried Varena. "This is how you plan to honor me?"

Kalie faced Varena and her look of betrayal. "Listen to me, daughter," she said gently, yet with an edge that commanded the new woman's attention. "They are women, just like us—"

"They are not like us! They are less than us. The only women in this camp who are! Do you want me to think I'm even less than Altia and Irisa think I am—"?

"I want you to see that you—and they—are so much more than Altia and Irisa think! I want to show you that women—all women—are greater than the men who rule over you have ever let any of you know." Kalie sighed. "Varena, I wanted to invite all of your friends and family—" And Larren, too, if she had bothered to find out where she lived…

"But I haven't got any, except you. I know, Kalie. And I thank you for trying to have enough people to make it a real feast, but—"

"I tried to find some of the girls you were with last night, but none were allowed to speak with me when I went to their tents. Perhaps, if we make enough noise and have enough fun, their mistresses might come see what's going on, and allow them as well." Of course, if that happened, there wouldn't be enough food for everyone. Kalie wasn't sure which one to hope for.

She knelt and lifted the platter holding the largest of the geese. Varena picked up the basket of flat bread. Hesitantly, as if fearing it was all some kind of cruel joke, Agafa and the other five half-starved, Shadow Women came forward to carry the rest.

She had always assumed that they worked together for foraging and mutual protection—or at least warmth, when the nights were cold. But only a single pair of women were together. Mother and daughter? Kalie wondered. Sisters? Perhaps lovers. For women to love each other in that way was yet another "abomination" to these people. Still, any sign of closeness or caring was hopeful. Agafa and the other three moved separately, like solitary animals forced into a herd.

"Come, Varena. Walk beside me." Kalie led them through the silent camp. With the men away, there were no bonfires, no boisterous gatherings. Only the faint light of braziers shone through the quiet tents. Entry flaps were closed, but here and there, Kalie saw veiled faces peeking out at them. The shadow women dared tiny bites of food when they thought Kalie wasn't looking, as fear warred with hunger and lost. Kalie didn't mind. It appeared it would only be the eight of them, and all that food. Yet as the sky deepened to violet and the sun slid below the western rim of the world in a bed of orange and crimson, Kalie found she didn't mind that either. Power swirled around her, palpable in the warm sweet air of summer. She walked toward the sunset, keeping her back to the rising moon, almost afraid to face the aspect of the Goddess at Her most powerful.

Chapter 9

They reached the spot Kalie had chosen. As the moonlight gilded the lake, and cast a silver sheen over the endless stretch of dry grass, the ugliness of the place receded into the twilight. As soon as they began arranging the food, however, Kalie realized that any rituals would have to wait. Otherwise, they would all be too distracted by the feast to hear a word Kalie said.

Still, anything done in joy was an act of worship. Kalie decided to put that teaching to the test. "We have gathered here, in the light of the Goddess, to welcome a new woman into our midst!" Kalie intoned the ancient words. "Let us welcome her with music and dance; with instruction into the women's mysteries. But first, in the oldest way remembered: with feasting! Varena will begin it," she added as two of the shadow women reached forward eagerly. Kalie heaped a plate with the best pieces of goose and stuffing, fish and hard bread soaked in berry syrup.

Varena may not have understood any of what Kalie said about women's mysteries, but she understood good food in plenty, and what it meant to be the first one served. For the others, it was cruder, more basic: food enough to fill their shrunken bellies, without shouts or blows to drive them away as they gorged themselves. Kalie had to physically force some of them so slow down, to chew more fully, to keep them from becoming sick from the very thing that should be helping to restore their health.

Kalie ate sparingly, more for the joy of eating the fruits of her own labor at her own pace than from any real hunger. As the moon rose, a sense of excitement filled her, driving out any lingering despair that this job was too much for her. She sipped some kumis, and thought about how nice summer wine made from those berries would have been, if she'd only had time to let them ferment. Then she wondered how she would begin.

There were ritual words that the priestess would be saying now, but Kalie couldn't remember them all, despite the number of these she had attended, and Varena wouldn't know the correct responses. She could try a story, but translating so many alien concepts into the beastmen's harsh tongue was beyond her right now.

She watched Varena savoring her last bites of food, eyes dancing as she looked eagerly at Kalie, wondering what was next, all her fears forgotten, and suddenly a voice rose up inside Kalie and burst from her mouth.

Kalie began to sing an old song often sung at these festivals. It told of the ancient Earth, lonely and barren, and the spark that began the miracle of life. How the Goddess gave birth to all that now lived upon her body. Kalie sang in her own tongue, with no thought of translation. Yet as she looked at the faces of the women around her, she knew that no translation was needed. The passion and the power that flowed from Kalie reached them just fine.

Women began to emerge from their tents. Most stood and watched from the door flaps, but a few came closer, watching and listening. Kalie beckoned them closer, then began another song; one that went with a circle dance. She grabbed Varena's hand, then the hand of one of the Shadow Women, urging them into a circle. For a moment, Varena seemed willing to try, but the Shadow Woman pulled away, and none of the others would join. Kalie gave up and finished the song, just as a small group of women approached.

She looked anxiously at the remains of the feast, hoping she could offer them something, then saw it would not be necessary. Arriving before the others, despite her slow gate was the old woman who had taken Kalie's side against Leja during the dispute over the geese the day before. Behind her a slave woman carried a tray of food nearly as fine as what Kalie herself had prepared. "If you're going to invite everyone, better make sure you have enough food," the ancient one was saying, and for a moment, Kalie felt she was listening to a priestess.

That was not all. Brenia and one of the other wives Kalie remembered from a storytelling party carried offerings as well, though not as impressive as the crone's. She put an arm around Varena and urged her forward.

"I and my daughter am honored by your presence at her Womanhood Ceremony, and thank you for your gifts," she said.

Some of the women giggled behind their veils, while others grinned with expectation of a new farce. But some seemed genuinely interested.

"I would like to know of this strange custom you speak of," said the old woman.

"And I would like to know who it is I must thank, not once, but twice," Kalie answered.

Brenia came forward quickly to make introductions, looking rather shocked that Kalie did not already know. "This is Danica, mother of Chief Zavan."

Kalie was impressed. A chief's mother was

probably the highest ranked woman in this society, though few lived long enough to attain such status.

"What is this that you do here tonight?" Danica asked.

Kalie felt a strange stirring, as if it was a priestess who had asked a ritual question that would allow everything to begin.

She replied in kind. "We are here to welcome a new woman into our midst, and celebrate the power of the Goddess."

"This slave girl?" Rather than breaking the mood, Danica's mocking question felt to Kalie like an opportunity.

"In this place, for this night, when the moon is at her fullest power, there are no slaves. There are no wives or concubines. There are only women, daughters of Mother Earth, chosen at birth to be Her mortal incarnation."

There was a ripple of whispered exclamations, but Kalie's attention was focused on Danica, whose gaze grew very far away.

"My grandmother spoke as you do," the old woman said. "Perhaps only to me. She came as a slave from a distant land, but when she gave my grandfather his only son—my father—he made her his wife. But when I was a child, she told me she had once been a priestess of the Great Goddess. That in her land, all women were as the wives of kings."

"She spoke the truth," Kalie said, striving to keep her voice steady, while her heart soared at the prospect of meeting a distant kinswoman. "Come, join our celebration, and find out what your grandmother tried so hard to teach to you."

She began another song; more like a chant. The

cadence was similar to the singing the beastmen did in their own rituals. And while Kalie's song was only a simple welcome of the harvest, more appropriate for later in the summer, and rarely sung at initiations such as these, she could feel it weave its web of power among the gathered women.

"Come Varena," Kalie called when the song ended. "Let us make you ready to be presented to the Goddess." She uncovered the basket of dried flowers, taking out a comb and a tiny leather bottle of oil that she had distilled from the rose-like flowers that grew here. When she removed Varena's veil, members of the crowd looked around nervously, but there were only women here, so most of them settled down to watch.

"In my land, there would be fresh flowers for your hair, but dried ones will have to do for tonight, as if you had come into your womanhood in winter."

As Kalie combed the sweet oil into Varena's hair and wove the flowers into a garland for her, everyone saw Varena transform from despised slave girl to an incarnation of the Goddess in Her form as Maiden. Only her ragged felt clothing bound her to the role her world had thrust upon her. One of the women commented on that.

"Well that is because she is here," said Kalie. "In my land, she would be naked. We all would be."

"Abomination!" cried one of the women.

"No!" Kalie rose to her full height. "Abomination is a world where the power to kill is revered, and the power to bring forth life is shunned! Abomination is taking pleasure in hurting others or stealing what they would gladly share if you but asked! Abomination is women who have forgotten their own power while they cower before men who should have been drowned at birth!"

The shocked silence that greeted her words was absolute. All at once, Kalie ran out of words. She had been talking, explaining, arguing and preaching since she came to this land nearly a year ago, and she was sick of it. This was not a night for politics. Kalie felt a rush power inside her more primal than anything she had ever experienced. If she didn't find a way to release it, it would burn its way out.

Closing her eyes, she drew a deep, steadying breath of the summer night air. She kicked off her leather shoes, and felt the earth beneath her feet, as her toes curled into the tough grass. For a moment, she felt the Goddess she had abandoned reaching out to embrace her, and then something suffocating came between them. It was the clothes; the heavy, scratchy felt.

Her eyes still closed, Kalie pulled the stifling garments from her body one by one, until she stood naked beneath the moon, and felt its power coursing through her.

Then she began to dance.

The power of the Earth rose up through the soles of her feet: ancient and unchanging. Older and wiser than any of Her creations could hope to be. And Kalie had feared the beastmen would destroy this? She laughed at her own foolishness, her dance taking on a merry, childlike gait as she wove playfully among the women, tugging at their garments, and beckoning them to join her.

Yet she didn't stop to see if they did; rather she spun and leapt with eyes focused only on the moon whose monthly cycle mirrored her own, and who now commanded that Kalie's dance change. She slowed her steps, stretching her arms overhead. The dance was as joyous as before, but deeper and more sedate; the dance of a woman's power to bring forth life from her own body, even if that meant dying in the process. Yet when she survived the process of giving birth, joys and sorrows multiplied, and a woman discovered the awesome responsibility of nurturing a child.

Finally, the dance drew itself in, and Kalie became an old woman, not bent and slowed by bitterness or pain, but reaching outward, offering her wisdom to her people as they sought the best path. And so her legs gyrated slowly, as her arms and head swung gracefully, supply, as only a lifetime of practice could allow.

Finally, still in step, Kalie slid gracefully to the ground, content to melt into the Earth and never open her eyes to the mortal world again. But steady, irregular vibrations beneath her were breaking the mood, and when Kalie looked up, she found the field was filled with dancing women. Many were awkward and uncertain, but some were moving as if the Goddess Herself directed them. Some were as naked as Kalie, though most wore at least a shift. All had cast aside their veils, and their long hair flowed freely.

Agafa danced, as she once must have danced to please her masters. Now, however, her movements— stiffened and slowed by arthritis, but still retaining an element of their past glory—seemed to blend the seductive dance of a horsewoman with the power and freedom of Kalie's dance.

Larren was there as well, her slave garments cast onto the ground beside where she gyrated, showing her pregnant belly to the moon as if beseeching a blessing. Turning slowly, she saw Kalie, and flashed a smile—perhaps her first genuine one in a long time. Two women stood near Larren, both staring. The older one, probably a wife, looked horrified, but perhaps a little pleased, as if by the knowledge she now had the means to do away with her rival. The other, younger and with a foreign cast to her somewhat slanted eyes and long black hair, moved forward, and was soon dancing with Larren.

But among them all, the loveliest was Varena, her hair a golden halo, her naked flesh glowing with the promise of life and strength, her eyes wide but seeing nothing of the brutal land in which she had been raised.

Kalie wanted to join them, lead them, but they were dancing to their own internal rhythms, and didn't need her. So she watched in wonder and gratitude, until one by one, they spent themselves, and fell gracefully to the grass beside her.

The moon was setting by the time the ecstasy faded, and the disapproving stares of the women who had not joined the dance finally roused them. Some were shaking as they struggled into their stifling garments, but whether from shame, fear or cold, Kalie could not say.

She embraced Varena, who still stood naked, though looking rather confused. "Welcome," Kalie said to her adopted daughter.

"Must we dress, too, mother?" Varena asked, clearly hoping they would not have to.

"You are a woman, now, Varena, and you must make that decision yourself. May it be the first of many." Kalie's smile faded as she realized how unlikely that was. "But for myself...tonight, I will sleep in the arms of my Goddess, under the light of her little sister." To the crowd she called out, "Tonight is only the first night of the full moon. There are two more."

Then, without waiting to see if anyone responded or followed her, Kalie strode forth until she found the right place in the grass to make her bed, though she had no intention of sleeping. Midsummer's night was the shortest of the year, and Kalie and her Goddess had a lot of catching up to do.

Chapter 10

"But why would women choose to lie with men if they didn't have to?" asked the girl next to Varena. Like Varena, she was the daughter of a warrior and a slave woman, and while she was probably a little younger than Kalie's adopted daughter, and not yet a woman, she likely spoke from experience.

"They wouldn't!" laughed Yessenia. "The people would die out! Is that why your tribe is so weak? They let women decide when to breed—and now there's no one left!"

A few women laughed, but most glared at Yessenia. It was the second night of the full moon, and this time, they were sitting on the gentle slope of one of the camp's few hills. The lake was now far enough away to look like a gilded mirror, and the moon was directly overhead. Many women who had been present last night had not returned, but others, hearing about it, had taken their place. Even Cassia, who should have been resting, had come.

"I told you that tonight, I would not complain about your way of life, but rather tell you of mine," said Kalie. "So all I can say is that when women—and men—are both permitted to choose their partners, the population increases, and everyone seems to have a good time."

There was muttering, and Kalie definitely heard the word "whore", but most were intrigued. The moonlight glistened on unbound hair of yellow and red and brown.

"And it's really like that everywhere?" asked

Brenia. "Not just in one isolated tribe?"

"It was like that everywhere I traveled, and I journeyed from the Black Sea to the Mountains Beyond the West—about as far as a fast horse could run in two moon spans." Kalie wasn't sure if that was true, but she enjoyed the effect it had on the audience.

"What was it like, traveling by yourself?" asked Brenia.

"I wasn't usually by myself. When I traveled by boat—"

"Of course she wasn't by herself," sneered a richly dressed young woman. "Didn't you hear her? Wherever she went, she just grabbed the handsomest man and forced him to service her! After that, he took her wherever she wanted to go!"

"Close your mouth, Yasha!" Brenia ordered. "This is a sacred time for her. If you can't listen with reverence, then leave!"

"Reverence?" cried Leja, who sat dressed in her finest robes, surrounded by other rich wives, and slaves far more intent on pleasing their mistresses than listening to Kalie. "We came here for entertainment!" She fixed a frightening smile on Kalie. "And you have provided much, my dear, with your vile talk of things no decent woman could even imagine. But even more enjoyable will be to watch your death when the men return and learn of your behavior."

"And who is going to tell them?" Danica's voice was like ice. Kalie smiled as the mother of one chief met the gaze of the wife of another. Leja's face fell.

"What do you mean, Danica? Do you think talk such as this can be kept from them?"

Danica's voice dropped another degree.

"Perhaps not, but remember dear, it's only the chattering of women. Would a real man ever lower himself to care about such things? He'd be a laughing stock if he did."

"Why would you seek to protect her?" Kahlar's wife seemed truly baffled. But the women around her displayed no such confusion. Rather, they looked eagerly at the two women as if hoping for more entertainment. Kalie smiled in the darkness, and for once, found herself more interested in listening than talking.

"What difference could my motives possibly make to you, Leja? All that matters is that—while I live—when I speak, those who are wise obey. Or do you wish to challenge me tonight?"

Leja's face was whiter than the moon. "I think we have all had enough entertainment," she said, rising slowly to her feet. There was a moment of silently held breath, as those around her waited to see if a weapon would be drawn or an attack launched, but Leja only turned with a wave of hand and walked slowly toward the tents. Her slaves scrambled after her, and several of her fellow wives followed at a more sedate pace

But at least four of the wives remained where they were.

"I would like to know," said one who Kalie remembered as snaring almost as many geese as Leja, "what the men of your people are doing when the women gather for these rituals."

"Most rituals involve both men and women," said Kalie. "It's only these three nights, the time of the full moon, when women conduct their own. Even then, it's only the first night that the women separate themselves for Sacred Mysteries. The one place I visited where the women's rituals lasted all three nights, the men were gathered in another grove, conducting rituals of their own."

"So the men were not excluded," mused Danica. "Not like…"

"Not like women are here? You brought it up!" Kalie said quickly as several eyebrows went up. "That wasn't a complaint, it was an observation." But she couldn't quite keep the laughter out of her voice.

Before she could say anything more about religion, the women brought the subject back to sex.

"But how can you speak so openly about this shameless behavior?" asked a woman, genuinely puzzled. "Oh, perhaps for a slave such as yourself, with no family to concern yourself with—"

"Kalie was not a slave in her land!" Varena's voice carried to the farthest end of the crowd and she looked the woman in the eye as she spoke.

"And my family was large and prosperous, before your men came and murdered them," Kalie said, feeling the elation of just moments ago slowly drain out of her. "How is it that you speak to me of honor when you have none of your own? When your men murder those who have saved their lives, or would gladly give as gifts that which they must take by force—"

"Perhaps we should just accept that each side shall remain a puzzle to the other?" Kalie, as surprised as everyone else, saw it was Larren who spoke.

"Perhaps," said Kalie, wondering if she should invite Larren to take her place. Her fellow Westerner, however, showed no inclination to say anything else, and then another woman spoke up.

"But surely…no one with any honor at all could behave as you claim to! That much is the same everywhere! To throw yourself from one man to another like a common whore—"

"She is a common whore!" shouted Elka. "Haven't you been listening?"

"Even without that part," said another wife. "To go where you pleased without an escort? Where's the joy in that? What of your reputation? What of your father—"

"I think," Kalie said slowly, "that we simply value different things. In your world, it is strength; the ability to control others or make them suffer that is valued. In mine, we value the well-being of the community. Those held in greatest regard are the people who contribute the most. People skilled with their hands create things that make the lives of those around them more comfortable. Healers can give the gift of life itself. Those who bring in food so that winter becomes a time of feasting and plenty rather than a hungry—"

"But it is that way here as well!" cried Yessenia. "We value those things just as much. A man who slays many enemies and feeds his tribe with their flocks is counted a hero!"

"And the status of his wife grows with his own," said Elka. "A good wife gains respect as a woman should—through duty and obedience. Not running wild, making a spectacle of herself. And when she bears her husband's children, daughters as well as sons, their nobility is beyond question, and cannot be taken from them." She glared at Brenia, as if daring her to argue.

"You mean, until he is slain in battle, and his

highborn daughters are made slaves?" Kalie asked with sudden insight. "Is that what happened to you, Elka?"

Elka froze, while laughter and whispers swirled around her. Then, like Leja, she stood and left the gathering. Unlike Leja, no one followed her.

"So both worlds value those who contribute to the greater good," mused Danica. "Perhaps the difference has more to do with the land itself. Here, there is always someone a man must fight. If he wins, his family prospers. If he loses..." Danica shrugged.

"Yes, the men of your world must protect their families and the animals which are your livelihood," Kalie said. "But who is it who feeds, clothes and shelters everyone who lives here? It is you." She swept her hand, to indicate all of the women gathered before her.

"Yes, of course," said a woman, impatiently. "What of it?"

Kalie sighed, and searched the eyes she saw in the moonlight for some sign of understanding. "You carry the life of your tribe—and with more than just your power to give birth, though that is surely important. You also make the tents your men sleep in during winter, the clothes they wear, the food they eat —but none of it belongs to you! Don't you ever wish for the right to enjoy the fruits of your own labor? Or at least some respect for it?"

"I have all the respect I need," said a wife who had thrown back her veil to reveal a thinning mane of dark brown hair. At a gesture from Kalie, Varena leaned over and whispered her name. "My husband knows he wears the finest clothes of any warrior, and he throws many feasts to show his brother warriors what a fine tent I keep for him. He tells me how often men try to buy my slaves for the fine work I get from them!"

Kalie sighed. "Then it is the work of the slaves that is valued, Gallia, as your yourself have just said! While they receive nothing for their skill and efforts but—perhaps—the right to live another day."

The wives were staring at her in confusion, but many of the slaves were showing more interest. Kalie was at a loss for how to explain, and was considering giving up on discussion all together, when she noticed Larren trying to get her attention. Following Larren's demurely lowered gaze, Kalie saw she was looking at the ermine cushion on which one of the wives was sitting.

"Tell me, Gallia, do you snare fur animals in the winter?"

"Every year!" said Gallia proudly. "And my husband wears the mantle of fox fur that matches his beard, which I made for him with my own two hands!" She sat back, smugly.

Now Kalie addressed the crowd. "Has anyone else here snared animals? Used their meat to feed your family in winter? Worked their fur until it was soft and warm, and made something beautiful from it?" All around her, women nodded their heads, some even holding up examples of their work. "Has any one of you made something very special, perhaps for yourself, perhaps for another—and then had it snatched from you by your husband, who then presented it as a gift to his new concubine? Or used it to pay off a gambling debt—" Kalie saw she did not need to continue. The reactions of the women around her told her she had hit her mark.

"My husband did exactly that," said the woman beside Gallia. "Took a fur I had worked to give my mother in her final illness, and gave it to his concubine."

"What did you do?" asked Yasha.

"Filled the fur with stinging nettles while he was busy with her!"

When the raucous laughter that followed subsided, Kalie spoke quietly. "But would it not be better if that fur was simply yours to use as you chose? Better for you—and better for the poor woman whose only crime was catching the eye of a heartless man?"

At that moment Cassia stood and caught Kalie's eye. "I shall retire now," she said quietly, but the message was clear.

Kalie stood quickly, and helped Cassia back to Malke's tent, then got her ready for bed. She set skins of tea within easy reach, to help with the nausea that continued to plague the pregnant woman. Kalie hoped Cassia would fall asleep quickly, so Kalie could return to the gathering.

But Cassia wasn't quite ready to sleep.

"That was…interesting," said Cassia. "I am glad to know more about your people. I never understood how different they were from ours. Perhaps knowing this will allow us to better help them adjust when the warriors of Aahk conquer them and show them the right way to live."

"Uh…thank you," said Kalie.

Cassia yawned and began to drift off. "Do not speak in public anymore, Kalie, even when the men are gone. It is…unseemly."

"Yes, mistress," said Kalie.

Once Cassia was asleep, Kalie hurried back to

the hillside where the women were gathered. Some had returned to their tents, but many were still speaking quietly in small groups. Kalie made no attempt to address the crowd again, or direct the course of the evening. She just walked among them, taking in bits and pieces, almost dizzy with the dream that one day, they might truly understand each other. She stopped where Larren sat, her black-haired companion from the night before by her side.

"Thank you for the suggestion," Kalie said, embracing her old friend, and was rewarded with a smile in a face that almost seemed to have forgotten how.

"And thank you, for doing with it what I never could," said Larren. "This is Mavra," she said, turning to the foreign woman next her. "She is one of the reasons I am still alive—and the only woman I have met in this land who dares to speak of revenge against the warriors who wiped out her tribe."

"But only to crazy slave girls like myself," said Mavra, whose eyes did indeed seem to shine with more than just normal excitement. "I hope you will speak more of these strange ideas. Larren used to, but not anymore—and never as you have."

Kalie grinned. "There is still one more night of the full moon."

She wandered on, listening and learning. Two slave girls spoke in whispers about what it might be like to live as Kalie had. Further on, a wife was loudly telling some friends that the next time her husband took something of hers without asking, he was in for an unpleasant surprise. Kalie hoped to learn what the woman had in mind, but her voice was drowned out by raucous laughter from the next group over.

"Yasha is angry because she would rather have Kariik," one of the women was shrieking. "Better to be a king's concubine than a warrior's wife, is that it Yasha?"

"She is angry because she'll have for a husband a man turned down by a slave girl!" laughed another. "That would cheapen even the finest groom."

Yasha ignored the second woman and spoke to the first. "I could have had Kariik! And as his wife, not his concubine! He wants me; I can see it in his eyes when he looks upon me. But my father would rather have horses from Riyik's herd, than a marriage tie with a future king!" She spat in disgust.

"And did Kariik ever ask for you in marriage?" Gallia asked sweetly.

"He would have! Given time." Yasha was close to tears. "But Riyik offered my father twin foals of his finest horses get." Thunder, thought Kalie. "And he's already given Riyik a tent as part of my dowry. We'll be married right after the men return!"

Kalie didn't like the distracted way she was feeling. And she didn't like the knowing way Brenia was looking at her. She shook her head angrily to clear it. This was supposed to be a time sacred to the Goddess. Perhaps her only opportunity to worship freely in this place. Yet all she could think about now was finding Riyik, and telling him what a mistake it would be to marry Yasha; what a terrible mother she would make Yarik…

"Too bad you don't live with Kalie's people," giggled a woman tipsy from the kumis that had been flowing freely. "Then you could have whatever man you wanted, and your father be damned!"

"And then you'd be no better than a whore!"

Yessenia snapped with a glare at Yasha. "Not that you're much better than one anyway."

Kalie decided she'd heard enough. She should find Varena and make sure they both got home safely. As she turned to go, a shadow stepped in her path, and Kalie saw Brenia's pale face framed by wild red curls, her veil cast aside. "I wanted to speak with you," she said.

Kalie did not want to end a night like this with an argument over Riyik.

"I just wanted to say that…I think I understand now."

"Understand what?" This was not what Kalie had been expecting.

"Why you can't marry my brother. It's just that I was so happy when I saw how he looked at you; he has not loved a woman since Yalina died. And when Cassia told me you could not have children, and I saw how good you were with Yarik—it seemed like such a perfect arrangement. I wanted to have you for a sister."

Kalie was stunned. "I didn't know that," was all she could think to say. Brenia wanted her for a sister? Riyik thought he loved her? She had discussed this with Cassia? Kalie didn't know which news to consider first.

Brenia rushed on. "I couldn't understand how you could possibly turn him down! But after tonight… I think I can. When you stood there on that hill…you were like a warrior after a great victory. No…" Brenia shook her head. "Like a king, standing before his people." She shrugged, giving up. "Perhaps there is simply nothing like it here. Certainly no woman could live as you did…have what you had, there in the moonlight. But I can see now, why you wouldn't give

it up to marry any man. Not even my brother. Even
though I know you love him."

Brenia was gone before Kalie could respond—
which was probably just as well. She found Varena,
and together they walked back to Malke's tent. Varena
seemed to sense Kalie's need for quiet thought, and for
a time, said nothing. But Kalie could tell that, like
everyone else this night, Varena too, had something to
say.

"What is it, Daughter?" Kalie asked, just
before they reached the tent.

Varena looked down, then steeled herself and
met Kalie's eyes. "Only that, oh, Mother you've
brought so much to this place! So much to me! It's not
my place to tell you—"

"Yes it is," Kalie said firmly.

Varena struggled to keep meeting Kalie's gaze,
and Kalie encouraged her as best she could with her
mind and heart already so full of other things. "I think
more people would listen to you if you did not tell
them how bad they were and how stupid our way of
life is." As Kalie stared speechless, wondering how
many more surprises might be in store for her, Varena
pushed on. "I know you're only saying back to them
what most of them have said to you! I know they've
been mean to you, and you have every right to do the
same to them. But, if your home is such a nice place,
maybe you can show the others that by being nice to
them—like you are with me."

Varena stopped and looked down, afraid she
had gone too far. But Kalie kissed the top of her head,
and gently lifted her chin. "My daughter is a very wise
woman," she said.

They stepped inside the tent without another word.

Chapter 11

The next night was the final night of the full moon. It would also be the final night of worship and discussion among the women with whom Kalie was at last forging the kind of relationship Alessa had dreamed of. The next day, the men would conclude their rituals and return to their tents after the sun had set. The women would be busy preparing for their return by cooking some kind of traditional meal, and waiting anxiously for word of the omens.

On this last night, only a small group gathered around Kalie on a rocky outcrop that held them suspended over the lake. The fall of moonlight combined with the lapping of the waves gave the place the most otherworldly feel yet. Kalie had been a fool to think there was nothing holy in this land.

Those who disapproved, or who came only to laugh, had at last been weeded out. Tonight, most of the women were in their tents, getting their last good night's sleep for many nights to come. Only nine women sat with Kalie. Danica was there with her slave Sarika, who, for tonight, was just another woman, and an equal to all there. Larren sat with Mavra on one side of Kalie and Agafa on the other.

Varena had brought a friend, a frightened looking girl named Katya who was risking a severe beating by sneaking out tonight. Brenia had come, bringing Yarik and Barak with her, since Elka had made it clear that chores like childcare (and everything else, it seemed) was beneath her. Two women Kalie had never met before two nights ago, Nika and her slave Basha were there as well. Basha had brought some sewing to work on while she listened. Nika brought her four-year-old daughter, who played happily with the boys, while the women spoke.

To her dismay, Kalie had a headache that had been growing all day. She had slept poorly last night, with Verena's words—and Brenia's and Cassia's as well—keeping her awake. And, she had to admit to herself, thoughts of Riyik had plagued what little sleep she got.

Tonight's discussion had mostly focused on the difference between the work done in a farming community and that which was necessary in a nomadic one.

"But who actually owns what you have?" Nika asked. "My husband was one of those who followed Karik on his great expedition to the west. He spoke of large houses, some filled entirely with grain! And jewelry and cloth and things for which he had no name! Who owns it all? And who assigns the various tasks that must be done?"

"Personal wealth is just that," said Kalie, wishing her headache would go away so she could enjoy this moment. "Clothing, tools, ornaments…all are made or traded by each person—or given as gifts. It is primarily food, or that which becomes food, that belongs to the community as a whole.

"As to who decides who does what, most communities have some kind of governing body—a council of elders, an elected leader, or, in very small villages, just a priest or priestess—who help settle disputes and organize the work that needs to be done."

They still couldn't grasp it. Finally Brenia asked, "What if I wanted to eat meat tonight? Could I just go to the pasture, kill a sheep and cook it for dinner?"

"In most places, yes," said Kalie. "As I said last night, everyone contributes labor, and everyone shares in the results. Even merchants, who travel most of the year, don't leave their homes until the spring planting is done. If they don't make it home by harvest, they help with the harvest wherever they happen to be. But the rest of the time, people pursue their individual talents or interests: crafts, learning, travel, what have you.

"In places where animals are owned individually, and you wanted mutton for dinner, you might trade fish you had caught, or game you snared, or something you made with your hands, like a basket or knife or pot for the sheep." She smiled as understanding dawned several faces.

"I can't do anything like that," said Katya. "Would I starve, then?"

"Of course not—" Kalie began.

But for the first time, Larren jumped in to help. "I think you'd find that you could learn to do many things you've never even imagined, given the chance."

"Yes!" said Kalie. "Anyone who could do the work you do here, every day, could learn to weave a basket or forge metal or anything else you wanted to learn."

Katya looked doubtful. "She's just a slave!" said Mavra. "She doesn't do anything!"

"She's a slave, so she does everything!" snapped Kalie.

"But no one who does that work owns any of it!" said Sarika.

"That's interesting," said Kalie. "Why do you suppose that is?"

"Because everything is owned by those who have the strength to keep it—or take it," said Danica.

"True," said Kalie. "In this land, those who kill, hold the power—in other words, the men."

"The strong men," Brenia corrected.

"But all the necessities of life—food, clothing, shelter—are provided by the women. There are also more of you than there are of them. So a good question might be: why have you never risen up, and taken back from the men what they have stolen from you? Your power, your dignity, the fruits of your labor, even you own children…"

"You expect us to kill our own husbands and brothers?" cried Nika. "Our own fathers?" Her eyes were wide with horror.

"Is killing the only solution you have in this place?" Kalie demanded angrily. "Couldn't you just unite and demand justice from the men? If no work was done by anyone, what could they do? Kill you all?"

Then again, perhaps they would, Kalie thought looking from one confused face to another. She cursed her headache, while reminding herself of Varena's good advice the night before.

"Tell us more about the different work women may choose in your land," Danica, said, changing the subject with the diplomacy Kalie lacked. "My slave Sarika is a skilled healer. Do you mean to say in your world, she could do that all the time, with no other tasks given her?"

Kalie nodded gratefully to Danica, but she addressed her words to Sarika, explaining a little about the temples of healing, and those who traveled her land sharing their knowledge and developing their gifts.

"I'm told I make fine leather," said Basha, avoiding her mistress's eyes.

Nika spoke up anyway. "Every slave does that!" she said derisively.

"Not so fine as hers," said Brenia. "I've seen it." Turning to Kalie she asked, "And could she do that, and nothing else, in your land? People would trade food and other necessities for the leather Basha made?"

"Yes," said Kalie. "Just as you could make a good living by making superior kumis, and Cassia could do well with her beautiful blankets and cushions." Their eyes were lighting up now, as each woman began to speak of things she did well; tasks she enjoyed above others.

"Your dancing would be highly regarded," she said to Agafa, who had remained silent throughout the discussion. "And it would not have been taken as an offer of sex by those who watched."

"Then I don't see how she could hold an audience," said Mavra. Kalie glared at her, but the younger woman did not flinch. "Oh, come now! Surely you're not saying that people were given all they needed to live just for dancing!"

"I knew few people who made their living solely as entertainers—until I myself did so as a storyteller. For five years." Kalie turned her back on Mavra and found Agafa gazing at her with dreamy eyes. "If you had a desire to travel as well as dance, you might join a group of merchants. They're always happy to have more to offer than the goods they carry. With your dancing to attract the locals—"

"I would not earn my living by dancing,"

Agafa said firmly. "I never enjoyed it, even when I was praised for it. But I could wish…could you tell us more about those gardens? Where people grow food and flowers and herbs that heal? They sound like eternal springtime. A place to rest in after this life is done. Could I live in such a place? Is the weather so fair there is no need for shelter?"

Nika gagged. "Have you not slept enough of your life outside, Shadow Woman?"

With a clear effort, Agafa met Nika's gaze. "One night this winter, while I hid from a storm behind old Graf's tent, I fell asleep, though I fought it, for I knew it meant my death. I dreamed of a place like Kalie described. Mala took pity on me, and brought me inside to keep her goat of a husband off her for a time. But that night, a part of me wished she hadn't, for the dream was that pleasant. Now I think that if I could live in such a place, I'd never sleep in a tent again."

The talk turned to matters of family and how the different ways of reckoning lineage and ties. Kalie's headache grew worse, and she finally asked Varena to go back to Maalke's tent for some willow bark tea, although she hated for her daughter to miss any of the discussion. Varena, however, was happy to go.

"But where does a woman's true loyalty lie?" Danica asked. "Her husband or her mother?" Varena returned with a steaming cup. Kalie thanked her profusely, and began sipping the still too hot brew, while Danica waited impatiently for an answer.

"That would depend," Kalie said as she set the cup down to cool. "But I suppose when it comes down to it, blood is the greatest bond, in my world or this one."

The women exchanged puzzled glances. "Blood ties are strong, of course," said Brenia. "The bond between brothers or the duty of a son to his father. But when a woman marries, her duty is to her husband. That's more powerful than any tie, even mother and child."

Kalie knew she wasn't up for another lecture on the virtues of the perfect wife. She sipped more tea and wondered when it would begin to work, growing more and more irritated. "Then perhaps we should ask Basha why she has lived as a slave to her own daughter for all these years!" she snapped.

There was a strangled cry, as Basha jabbed herself with her bone needle, then dropped her sewing into a heap, all color draining from her face.

My, this tea works quickly, thought Kalie, as her headache disappeared in the horrified realization of what she had just done.

Chapter 12

"Basha raised me since my mother died," Nika said loudly into the silence. "She even nursed me. Of course I value her, but she's still only a slave. My father was a chief and my mother his favorite wife."

They don't know, Kalie marveled. None of them. Can't they see when they look at the two women next to each other? She murmured, "Of course. I'm sorry. I don't know why I…"

But it was too late. Now everyone saw, and Basha's fear-filled eyes, her face bone white in the moon's glow, only confirmed it.

"Perhaps if we all take a vow that whatever is said in this place, stays in this place, Basha will tell us her story," said Sarika.

Danica nodded. "Promises made beneath the full moon are binding to our people. I can only imagine the curse breaking a moon oath would bring among Kalie's people."

"Worse than anything you could imagine," Kalie said quickly.

"Basha?" asked Nika, her eyes begging the slave to deny it.

But Basha shook her head. Some of her color had returned as she gazed proudly at her daughter. Then she faced the curious onlookers.

"My tribe was destroyed by the Warriors of Aahk before I was a woman. My older sister and I were the only of our family to survive. She had been married and was pregnant with her first child. She died a few days later, when the man she was given to struck her stomach so she would lose the child. I was alone, you see." Basha's eyes begged Nika to understand.

"I was given as slave to the chief of my new people. An honor, of course, but it did little to ease my fears, or the loneliness that I ached with every night. I became pregnant before I even knew I was a woman. My master's favorite wife was with child as well, though for all the fine food and easy work she was allowed, it seemed to go far harder for her than for me. I gave birth to a beautiful daughter, but few who lived in our tent took a good look at her, for my mistress began her labor at the same time—and hers was a long and terrible ordeal, lasting four days.

"I remember that the midwife belonging to the king himself came to help with her birth. And as I lay ignored, nursing my precious child in peace, I wondered what life lay in store for her. If she had been a boy and found favor in my master's eyes, I might have gained status; perhaps even become a wife. But a daughter..." Basha shook her head and once again sought the eyes of her audience. "She could well be my only child, since my master had already grown tired of me. And even if I could give him a son, what of it? He already had three by his first wife! For all the joy that any new mother feels when she nurses a healthy baby, I sorrowed at our future.

"After four days of labor, my mistress died, leaving behind a weak and sickly daughter. The women of the tent were exhausted, and collapsed into a deep sleep as soon as my master left to drown his sorrow in kumis. When the dead woman had been borne away by her sisters to be prepared for burial, I found myself left to care for the chief's new daughter."

It was clear enough to everyone listening what had happened next, but no one spoke. "I sat there,"

Basha continued. "Thinking of what a waste it all was —and then the thought came to me that it didn't have to be. So I wrapped my daughter in the ermine blankets that lay waiting for the chief's daughter, and covered the other baby in the felt rags that were to have been your destiny." For the first time, Basha looked directly at Nika, who sat mute, as white as her mother had been just moments before. Nika's young daughter froze in her play with Yarik and Barak, all three staring in wonder at the sudden seriousness of the adults.

"My dead mistress's baby died that night, and her body was thrown in the midden, as would be with any slave's bastard. And while no one spoke of it aloud, there was relief at how things worked out: a wet nurse was now available to give not just milk, but undivided attention to the motherless girl. So my lot improved more than if I had given the chief another son: I was nurse to his only daughter, freed from his demands on my body, and eventually, the highest ranked slave in the household!"

"And no one suspected?" Mavra asked. "No one thought it strange that a sickly newborn was suddenly healthy?"

"Or that a healthy baby suddenly died?" Kalie asked.

"That last happens often enough," said Basha, while several of the other women nodded. "Besides, no one had ever asked after my baby's health."

Sarika nodded. "I have attended many births like Amara's—that was her name, wasn't it? When a woman dies after such a long labor, no one has energy to spare for the baby. They were probably so glad to have something to rejoice over, they didn't ask questions."

"Was it hard for you?" Kalie asked suddenly. "Being a slave to your own child? Watching her grow into an arrogant princess who ordered you about?"

Nika's white face flushed a sudden angry red at Kalie's words, but Basha jumped in before she could speak. "I loved every moment of her life. To see her grow strong and tall...petted and spoiled by her father as few girls are! And it was to me she ran with her sorrows and joys, as any daughter does. And she was never taken from me! Even when she married, and moved to a different clan, I went with her. How many mothers are granted that?"

"But it was all a lie!" cried Nika, finding her voice at last. "All my life, I've believed I was royal! Chief Gorrik's only daughter! His sole link to his beloved Amara! People even say I look just like her!"

"People see what they want to see," said Sarika.

Nika shook her head furiously. "No! It cannot be! I am not the bastard of some worthless slave girl..."

"And you are not," Kalie said softly, but with an edge that silenced the younger woman. "You are the daughter of a courageous woman who took a grave risk to give her child a better life. You have the blood of heroes in your veins, Nika. And that is a great legacy to pass to your own daughter. And the child you now carry."

At the mention of her own children, Nika went still. Her hand flew to the gentle mound on her belly. "My husband!" she whispered. "If he were to learn of this..."

"He won't," Kalie said, even more softly.

She met the gaze of each woman present. Each acknowledged, in some small way, the pledge of silence.

But Kalie wondered how long such a promise could hold in this place where gossip and scandal were the only outlets for women confined to dark tents and the capricious rule of men.

She felt a little better, later that night, when Basha and Nika slipped away from the camp to talk, for the first time, as mother and daughter. But they would be in danger from now on. It seemed like one more piece in a great puzzle; a reminder to Kalie that she had to do more than find the weapon that would save her people.

She had to take half the tribe with her when she left.

Chapter 13

The next morning, the women were startled out of their routine by the early return of the men.

King Ahnaak was dead.

As word spread throughout the camp, the women began to wail, tearing their clothing and smearing their faces with ashes. Kalie followed their lead and tried to ascertain what had happened. It was hours before any solid news reached the women, who seemed far too busy with funeral preparations to care.

The king had collapsed the previous night while conducting the sunset rituals. His spirit had departed soon after, finally ending his journey through a long and wasting illness. All that remained was to determine whether his death during such a sacred ceremony boded well or ill for his people, and to send him to the next life with ceremony befitting his rank.

Kariik seemed in shock as he was rushed from place to place, bathed, dressed, asked what his commands were—and then told what they were by Haraak or one of Kariik's new advisors, all loyal to Haraak. Kalie could almost feel sorry for him.

She needed to learn what Haraak's plans were and what this change in leadership would mean for her people, but Maalke's tent was as busy as all the others, what with Maalke needing an entirely new set of fine clothes and the best food and kumis his women could provide as his funeral offerings. Altia bellowed orders every other moment. It was especially hard with only Irisa, Kalie, and Varena able to do most of the work, and for once, Altia drafted her daughters to work beside the slaves.

The only good thing to come out of all this, Kalie reflected as she and Varena worked the sheepskin for Maalke's new cloak, was that mundane business—like the trading of slaves—was suspended for a time. There would be four days of fasting and purification while the old king was prepared for burial, then four days of feasting and celebrations as the new king was raised. Varena would not be going anywhere until all of that was over.

The burial, when it finally arrived, was nearly anti-climactic after all the stress of preparations.

First, a litter bearing Ahnaak was carried through the camp by the high priest and his assistants. While the king's gray and wasted body surely added little weight to the litter, the gold ornaments and jewelry he was decked in certainly did. The royal household followed behind, and behind them, ten of his horses. The warriors stood in two long lines, creating a broad avenue for the litter to travel between. The women stood behind the men, keening their grief. As the king's body passed, each warrior, hair hacked short for mourning, cut his arm or his face, spilling blood onto the path of his king's last journey. While the women wailed, the men remained eerily silent.

Not until late in the afternoon were the people of Aahk summoned to the gravesite of their king.

Kalie watched with detachment as Ahnaak's senior wife, dressed in her finest robe and veil, covered in jewelry and disdaining the offer of assistance from a young concubine, walked proudly to the stone cairn where the king's body now rested. There she was strangled by the high priest and laid in the place of honor beside her husband. The king's three favorite concubines were dispatched with far less ceremony and laid at his feet

Kalie couldn't help wondering, as she realized they were probably the oldest and ugliest of the concubines, who had decided they were Ahnaak's favorite. When she caught sight of Kariik gazing at the dozen or so of the king's women who now belonged to him, she knew the answer. At least some decisions were being made by the new king, rather than Haraak.

Last of all, the ten horses were sacrificed on top of the human bodies, sealing the grave for all time.

The funeral over, it was time for the coronation —and feasting—to begin. Kariik looked pale and small inside his splendid robes of red and blue linen, and the heavy gold crown seemed far too big for his head.

Not everyone agreed, however, given the number of women who gazed longingly at the young king. Kalie noticed Yasha among them, pushing boldly forward through the crowd, allowing her veil to slip just a little when the king's gaze fell her way, until her mother dragged her back to her tent. Riyik stood speaking with a group of warriors near the royal tent. If he noticed his betrothed's behavior, he gave no sign.

The next day, Kalie sat in the shade of the awning Altia had raised beside Maalke's tent. Most of the other tents sported something of the kind. It made the searing summer heat more bearable, and allowed the women to watch the celebrations of the men in relative comfort. Kalie gnawed a goat rib and reflected that food had been unusually plentiful lately. She wondered how much would be left for the coming winter if it turned out to be as bad—or worse—than the previous one.

"He will be born early, but he will live."

Cassia's words brought Kalie back to the present.

"What do you mean?" Kalie asked. Cassia had been quiet lately. Or perhaps, Kalie thought, she herself had been too busy mingling with powerful women, trying to convert the female population of the steppes and planning the rescue of her people to pay much attention to Cassia. She felt guilty for that; a normal reaction, she realized, for a slave raised in this world. Cassia was her mistress; therefore her reason for being.

"I had a dream last night," said Cassia. "I saw my mother." Kalie nodded. She knew from her own experience that funerals often brought dreams of deceased loved ones. "She told me the baby would be here soon. When I grew afraid, thinking she had come to tell me he would be born too early and die, she said that he would live." Cassia glanced around warily and lowered her voice. "She said he would be grow to be a great warrior—a great hero, even! That he will be remembered in song and legend."

"That's…wonderful," Kalie said, trying to sound sincere. When she sensed Cassia was waiting for something more she asked, "Did your mother's spirit tell you the child will be a boy?"

"No." Cassia's gaze traveled to her belly. She stroked it gently. "I've known since the beginning that I carry Maalke's son. And that he will be the only child I bear." She paused. "My mother said he would be remembered in song and story. Long after Maalke's other sons were forgotten."

Kalie nodded, wondering why Cassia was repeating herself. Then she understood. "You want me to be the one who tells his story?"

Cassia blushed. "I know it will be many years.

Who knows if either of us will live to see my little warrior grow up? But if you do, I hope you will tell his story. You tell stories so well, and, whatever his great deeds turn out to be, your words could make him live forever."

Kalie wanted nothing more than to tell Cassia that she would be happy to tell of her son's "great deeds"—like how many women he raped, how many people he murdered and how many friends he betrayed —just as soon as her people were safe from him. But Cassia was not finished.

"You're a good storyteller, Kalie," she repeated. "But I think it would be best if, from now on, you told only the stories of this land. Stories of your home are…interesting. But I fear some of the women here might take them the wrong way."

"Like believing them to be true?" Kalie asked innocently. "Or perhaps, even believing that the freedom I once enjoyed could be theirs as well?"

Cassia jerked her gaze away from her unborn child and sought Kalie's own. "No decent woman would desire such…freedom," she said. "Any woman who did would bring shame to her family. Such a woman would be better off dead. Do you understand?"

Kalie certainly did, but she was spared the need to answer when an older boy—or perhaps young warrior, he was about thirteen or fourteen summers— ran up to the tent shouting, "Maalke has commanded his slave girl Kalie to come and tell stories for the men! Which one is she?"

He waited impatiently for Kalie to rise to her feet then set off, clearly anxious to return to the festivities. As Kalie hurried to keep up, she grew excited. Everything was in play now: Haraak's puppet now wore the crown of the Twenty Clans of Aahk. Events could begin moving very quickly, and at last, Kalie was in a position to learn about them.

She watched the men engaged as they were in bouts of eating drinking, dicing and boasting. They looked strange with their suddenly short and ragged hair. Most had rubbed a noxious smelling paste into the cuts they had made on their arms and faces. Soon, each would have another fearsome scar to frighten their enemies, and proclaim the strength of their love for their dead king. Kalie decided she would look at Haraak's whenever she needed a good laugh.

Although it was only the second day of Kariik's coronation feast, nearly every man she saw was already drunk, or working hard to get that way. This would certainly be an ideal time for another tribe to attack. While an attack on a tribe in mourning for the death of a king was universally forbidden in this land, Kalie knew how easily such conventions could be overlooked when someone like Haraak was in charge. She half hoped an attack would come. If another tribe could wipe out this one, the plan to invade the West might well die with them.

Unfortunately, Kalie's storytelling went poorly, and she learned nothing of any value. The men were too drunk to pay attention to anything she said, and a fight broke out in the middle of her first story. While her audience hurried to surround the two combatants, and begin betting on the outcome, Kalie slipped away before she could become a prize for the winner or consolation for the loser.

She moved slowly through quieter crowds, unwilling to give up after her first try at seeking information. There were groups of men everywhere.

Some of them had to be speaking of the future. Or perhaps she should simply risk assault and spy on some of the drunks. Drunken men often spilled secrets that sober ones would not. And if they did attack her… it wasn't anything she hadn't endured many times before.

Kalie had just attached herself to such a group, when she noticed Riyik walking away from the festivities, wandering aimlessly toward the tents. For no rational reason, she decided her time might be better spent seeing what he was up to instead.

Chapter 14

Kalie followed Riyik past tents where women prepared food for the feasting, or sat at their leisure beneath awnings. He seemed not to notice them as he traveled through the warren of dwellings, stopping at last before one that had not been there just days ago.

Riyik's tent. His new home. She knew Yarik already lived there, and—temporarily—so did Brenia, who was making things ready, while Hysaak enjoyed time with Elka, his new bride, as well as with the slave girl he had purchased for her. But he had not yet provided his first wife with a new slave, shaming her further before the tribe, and fueling the gossips who thrived on such scandals.

As Riyik threw aside the door flap without scratching and crawled inside, Kalie found a spot on the other side of the tent, where two layers of new felt did not quite join, creating a tiny slit for her to peer through. Praying that the dark night and her dull clothing would hide her from view, she settled down to observe.

Riyik sat alone in the middle of a tent that smelled of new felt and herbs that Kalie remembered from her visits to Brenia's tent. A fire danced in the brazier, illuminating clean new rugs and cushions. Bed furs were neatly rolled, awaiting use. Riyik was examining a bright copper cooking pot, as if unsure what it was.

The sounds of childish laughter and a woman's gentle voice pulled them both from their examinations. The tent flap was flung aside and Yarik and Barak tumbled into the tent, followed more demurely by

Brenia.

"Riyik!" Brenia was clearly surprised to see him. Then she grew concerned. "You shouldn't stay away from the feasting for long. It might be noticed."

He appeared not to hear her.

"Riyik... Is anything wrong?"

"Is anything not wrong?" he cried suddenly. The raw pain in his voice startled Kalie. "I may have just sworn loyalty to a fool of a boy who lives solely to do the bidding of a man who slew his own king! How could anything be right?"

Brenia, her face pale, shot him a warning look, and hurried to the open door flap to peek outside. Crouching in the shadows, Kalie held her breath.

"I do not think anyone heard," Brenia whispered when she returned. "But you must never say that again!"

Riyik lowered his voice to a matching whisper. "You seem more surprised by my outburst than my words."

"It was clear enough that the king was poisoned. Anyone who has nursed a man through an illness could see what ailed the king. And what did not."

"'Anyone who has nursed a man through an illness?' Meaning what? That every woman in the camp knows the king was murdered?"

"Only those with eyes," said Brenia, her mouth twisting into a grimace. "Few enough of them in this camp to worry Haraak. Not that he would ever concern himself with what we think."

Riyik smiled. "You sound as though you've been listening to Kalie."

It was Brenia's turn to sound startled. "I guess

I have at that. Sometimes it's hard not to. She's...not like anyone I've ever met."

"I have been saying that to myself a great deal lately."

Brenia smiled. "Yet if either of us told her that, she would ask us how we knew. She'd say we've rarely actually met anyone. You've simply killed or enslaved anyone you've come across, and I've lived my life in a felt tent, meeting only those people my men have allowed me to meet."

"When you put it like that, I suppose I'm a fool to pursue her. She's obviously mad."

For an instant, Kalie saw fire blaze in Brenia's placid eyes. Then it was gone. "You have seen her world, Brother. You know she is not mad. Though how a woman could go from living as she did to living as we do and not go mad...that is the true puzzle."

"And how did she live before?"

"You know the answer. She lived like a man. And that is why you cannot have her. And perhaps also why you so desire her."

For a moment, Kalie feared Riyik was about to strike Brenia—and she didn't know what she would do if he did. But to her immense relief, he ground his fists into the rug beneath him instead. When he had control of himself he glared at his sister. "Are you saying that I prefer men?" he asked softly. "That she..."

"I am saying," Brenia said calmly, "that Kalie lived as proud and free as any warrior. Of course she didn't live the same way as our men; they have no horses. They're farmers, not warriors. But I've listened to her stories. Even if none of them are true, she didn't learn them by sitting in a tent and waiting for some traveler to come in and tell her. She sailed boats up and down her rivers the way you ride a horse. She walked across a land wider than our steppes. For learning, for healing, for adventure, Kalie's done all the things you dream of, Riyik. Even those dreams you've never told to me. And she never even thought of being afraid while she did it. Could such a woman as that exist among our people?"

Brenia paused while that sank in. Riyik seemed about to deny it, but paused. It was as if memories of his time in the city whispered the truth of his sister's words.

"And I helped take all that from her."

"Yes," said Brenia. "Which is why she cannot marry you, although I believe she loves you as much as you love her."

Riyik was about to speak, when he heard the last part.

"Loves me? You think she loves me? Then why won't she…"

Brenia sighed. "Riyik, could you marry a woman who broke both your legs, then healed them in such a way that you could never ride a horse again? Even if she swore she would take care of you all your life so you wouldn't need to ride again?"

Riyik was silent, while Kalie's heart soared within her. And while she still wasn't certain what she felt for Riyik, she knew at that moment that she loved his sister.

"Is it really like that for her here?" Riyik asked sometime later.

Instead of answering, Brenia reached inside a basket of clothing and showed Riyik a pair of shoes. "She brought these by for Yarik."

Riyik looked over the special shoes that might

someday allow his son to walk like other boys. Except that he would never be like other boys, because they needed no special help for something as simple as walking. And they would never let him forget that. And if he could not run? Would they leave him alone, as someone not even worth tormenting, or would they beat him until they finally killed him? And which would be worse? Kalie could read the play of thoughts on his face as clearly as if he had spoken.

"Do they help?" he asked hoarsely.

"See for yourself. He's been watching and listening while pretending to sleep this whole time."

His secret out, Yarik leapt from the furs, crying, "Dada!" He rose to his feet, pushing off with his good leg, and ran to his father.

Riyik caught the boy, just as his twisted foot gave out beneath him, and tossed him lightly into the air. Yarik squealed with delight. "More!" he cried. Riyik tossed him again.

"Dada go riding? Take me riding?"

"Dada is busy now," said Brenia, moving to take Yarik from his father.

"We can go riding now," said Riyik.

Brenia opened her mouth to protest, then closed it and smiled.

Kalie slid back into the shadows, and hurried back to Maalke's tent. She sensed another sleepless night, with much to think about, lay ahead.

Chapter 15

"Haraak is planning a feast for Wolf tribe," whispered the Shadow Woman. "There will be gifts exchanged, and many marriages made."

Kalie handed her another morsel of food. "When we reach the gathering?"

"Before," said the woman, with a hint of pride.

"How is that? We haven't left yet. The Wolf warriors are already at the gathering place." Kalie gazed at the endless brown grass, nearly as tall as a man, while shimmering waves of heat danced above. Not a breath of wind stirred anything. Kalie thought that if they did not leave soon she would go mad, though whether from heat or boredom she wasn't sure.

"There is to be a secret meeting of select warriors of the two tribes when we are halfway to the gathering. Haraak and his Wolf spy spoke of it while they took turns having me last night. It seemed to excite them. One of the Wolf warriors is to be killed there."

"Do you know which? Or why?"

The Shadow Woman shifted nervously, and shot a quick look at Kalie's basket. Kalie sighed. She wished the woman had the confidence to simply tell her that her that big news cost extra.

Kalie took out the wedge of cheese that was supposed to be her midday meal. She broke it nearly in half, and offered the larger piece to her informant.

The woman's eyes grew wide. "They did not mention a name—I think both men already knew. But it is to be Haraak who does the killing, to prove he can be trusted."

Kalie dropped the cheese into the starving woman's hand and watched her gobble it down and then skulk away. She started to return to Maalke's tent, but couldn't bear the thought of the tension inside, even worse than the heat.

The new power structure of the tribe seemed to hold no place for Kalie's master, who had done poorly in the latest jockeying for position. Then the warrior from Griiv's clan had pulled out of their bargain to exchange Varena for two of his slave women. Kalie and Varena were both thrilled to remain together, but tension lay heavy in the tent. When Altia had berated Maalke about his promise to her for new slaves, he had beaten her nearly senseless. Both her eyes were swollen shut, and her daughters had to lead her around her own tent. Maalke spent most days riding and hunting with other disgruntled warriors, or brooding in the tent drinking kumis.

Kalie went to the lake instead. She wanted to be near water, even if it was nearly as hot as the air above. They had stayed overlong in this place and the water was stagnant and foul. If they stayed much longer, pestilence would rage through the camp. Already many were ill. Yet still Kariik waited, closeted in meetings with Haraak and messengers from the other tribes.

Something big was going to happen; Kalie didn't need a network of spies to tell her that. But whether or not it was the invasion of her homeland by a well-organized federation of tribes? That fact still eluded her.

As well as what to do about it.

There were fewer people about, and no one ordered Kalie out of the water when she slipped off her shoes and waded in, careful not to raise her skirt above her knees. Many remained in the shelter of their tents, too wilted by the heat to move if they didn't have to. Others, mostly older boys and slave women, had been sent with the flocks to better grazing lands to fatten them up for the late summer Gathering.

That, at least, was normal for this time of year, but then again, it also suited Haraak's purposes. Since the boys had charge of the bulk of the tribe's wealth, each group had two or three seasoned warriors for protection. Haraak had made sure that anyone who could be a threat to his plans was sent on that mission. Kalie settled into the relative shade of the tall grass, listening to the soothing trill of brown grasshoppers as she wondered again what she might do.

She was nearly asleep when someone called her name. Jerking awake, Kalie found Tilla, another of her spies, shaking her. Tilla had been a Shadow Woman until Kalie had convinced the wife of Daliik, a rising young warrior, to take her as a slave. Daliik was a favorite of the new king, but too stingy to buy his wife more slaves. In fact, he had given the younger of the two she owned as a gift to Kariik, leaving his sick and pregnant wife to fend for herself. Kalie had convinced her that Tilla was skilled Healer, and then quietly taught Tilla everything she could about midwifery. So far, it was working, and in gratitude, Tilla came to Kalie with every bit of gossip she heard —useful or not.

"The wife of Gault now sneaks out at night to lie with my master," Tilla said, as they filled her water bags.

"How is this done in a camp so full of bored and watchful eyes?" Kalie asked. "And why would she risk death for such limited pleasure?"

Tilla shrugged. "It is whispered that Gault cannot father a child. A childless woman in this land is..."

Kalie nodded. "Yes, I know. So she hopes to get pregnant and pass the child off as Gault's?"

"Or perhaps she hopes Gault and my master will fight over her. If Dariik wins, he could choose to claim her as a second wife."

They left the lake and headed back to camp. Kalie thanked Tilla for the information and went slowly toward her own dwelling place, wondering what use she might make of this latest bit of gossip. She had come to this Goddess forsaken land to learn about her enemy, and now she probably knew more than anyone in the Western world about the beastmen. If only she knew what to do with the knowledge!

She was just passing a neighboring tent, well within sight of Maalke's, when a loud altercation erupted from within. Kalie froze in time to see Maalke drag Varena from the tent. "Break my goblet, will you?" Maalke roared while he shook Varena like a young tree. "I'll teach you!" He began dragging her into the empty grass beyond the camp.

Kalie watched them disappear into the tall grass.

If Maalke wanted to beat Varena for some transgression, he would do it in the tent. Which meant he had another purpose for seeking privacy.

Kalie was barely aware of following them into the grass; barely aware of pausing at the waste trench at the edge of camp to grab the leg bone of a horse. The bone was nearly picked clean by tiny scavengers, some of whom continued their feast as Kalie walked.

Its solid weight felt good in her hand.

The rustling of grass in the still air told her where her quarry had gone. Kalie followed.

She lost track of them when a stray breeze set all the grass to moving. It was gone a moment later, but by then she could find no sign of Maalke and Varena.

A sharp cry of pain, followed by a roar of anger told Kalie where they had stopped.

"Please, father, don't..." Varena begged.

Maalke cut her pleas short with a blow from his fist. "Don't you dare call me that, you little slut! You think anyone knows who your father is? Your mother was a whore and you're just like her! You think I haven't seen the way you move your ass for every passing man? If some dirty cunt calls herself my daughter and eats my food, I've damned well got the right to some use of her! Gods know, everyone else has!"

When Kalie came within sight of them, Maalke had Varena on the ground with her robe torn nearly off. His trousers were down and he was working on prying her legs apart. Kalie was impressed by the strength of Varena's struggle: she never thought the timid slave girl had that much fight in her. Maalke must find the struggle amusing; there was no other reason for him to allow it to continue so long.

Finally, with a brutal twist of his knee, Maalke got her legs apart.

Kalie stepped forward and raised her club. She watched it travel downward in a smooth, slow arc that made her think of a beautiful waterfall.

The jarring crunch that traveled up her arm as it struck the back of Maalke's head was the most satisfying thing she had ever felt.

Kalie had seen many men struck in the head in her time with the beastmen, but having never done it herself, she wasn't sure what to expect. So, she was rather concerned when Maalke slowly turned to face her, rather than simply falling over. Kalie raised the bone again, ready to dash it into his face.

That proved to be unnecessary, as Maalke blinked once, then slowly folded to the ground.

Kalie stood over his still form, and felt an urge to roar with triumph.

Varena's labored breathing brought her out of it. "Are you hurt?" she cried, kneeling by the girl. Varena's face seemed wiped of all humanity, as she struggled only to breathe. By the time Kalie had determined she was not physically injured, the girl regained enough of herself to whisper, "He was going to...I never led him on, I swear it! I was a good girl!"

Kalie gathered her daughter into her arms, rocking them both for the comfort it gave. "Shh. It wasn't your fault."

"He said I was..."

"And he knew he was lying even as he said it." Kalie gazed at Maalke's unconscious form. "Strange, that he had to convince himself that you were asking for it. As if even filth like Maalke has a sense of right and wrong. You wouldn't know it the rest of the time."

Varena finally recovered enough to look at Maalke's body, then at Kalie. "What have you done?" she shrieked.

Kalie followed her gaze, and said dispassionately: "Something I should have done a very long time ago."

"But we'll be killed for it! As soon as he wakes

up, or someone finds him…"

"Then we'd better make certain he has good cause to keep this a secret."

As one, Kalie and Varena gasped and turned to see who spoke.

Riyik stood in the grass behind them, a rather curious smile on his face.

Chapter 16

Kalie moved between a shrieking Varena, who was trying to cover herself, and this new threat. Yet somehow she knew, though she told herself otherwise, that Riyik was not a threat. "What do you want?" she demanded.

"To help you if I can."

Kalie snorted with contempt, and searched for a scathing remark, but once again, her tongue betrayed her. "Why? And what did you have in mind?"

Riyik shook his head. "I've been trying to explain the answer to your first question for longer than I can remember, so I won't bother anymore. But as to the second—we'd better act quickly. Give me that bone." Kalie surrendered it reluctantly, and set herself to comforting Varena. Riyik pushed the bone into the dry earth by Maalke's head.

"Take her to my sister," he told Kalie. "See if she can fix the girl's clothes. If not, borrow something of Brenia's for her. When Maalke wakes, I'll tell him he fell and hit his head on that old bone."

"And you think he's going to believe that? He wasn't that drunk!"

Riyik shrugged, took a skin of kumis from his belt and poured the contents liberally about the face and clothes of the unconscious man. "The important thing is that we make him believe that he was. He'll wake up with the same symptoms as a hangover. Nice shot by the way."

"And later? If he remembers what really happened?"

"By then you and your daughter will be safely

in my tent, under my protection."

"We'll be what?" For once, Kalie and Varena shared the same reaction.

"It's simple, really. Your actions will mean your death if Maalke remembers. I can't change the law, but I can offer Maalke enough horses for you and the girl to buy himself ten comely slaves. I might even be able to get Maalke invited to one of the feasts reserved for the new king's inner circle. Wealth and opportunity of that magnitude will make him eager to forget anything that would jeopardize it."

Kalie looked at her daughter. Varena, at least, looked happy.

She felt her face close about her like a mask. "So we would be your slaves then?" She looked down at Maalke, and laughed. "Very well. It seems I have outmaneuvered myself once again."

Riyik sighed. "Will I never be able to do anything right in your eyes, Kalie?" The pain on his face was like a slap to hers.

"I'm sorry, Riyik. It's just that I don't know what to make of all this."

"You may be my slaves if you wish. But if you recall, I did ask you to marry me. The offer is still open."

Kalie's head spun. "I thought you were to marry Yasha," she said faintly.

"I am." The words were bitter. "I wish I were not. But you could still be a second wife. I would make you first, but I dare not offer such an insult to Yasha and her family."

"What of Varena?"

"She will be my daughter."

"You would do that?" Kalie felt that a faint

breeze might knock her over.

"A man who marries a widow will often adopt her sons as his. There are fewer formalities with daughters, but they do exist. I will declare her my daughter, and name a dowry. Before the year ends, no one will remember she was ever anyone else." Varena seemed caught somewhere between ecstasy and fear that it was all a cruel trick.

Kalie stared Riyik in the eye. He calmly returned her gaze. "I have rejected every effort you have made to win me over—"

"Save one." Riyik glanced down at the water skin she wore at her waist, and then returned his gaze to hers.

"Yes," Kalie said, the ghost of a smile on her lips. "For which I thank you again. It has been very useful. But what you speak of now involves a bit more of a commitment—from both of us. I have never been nice to you, or behaved as a good Aahken woman. Why then do you still pursue me? Why offer to help a girl you don't even know?"

"Perhaps to convince you that not all men of Aahk are evil. Or perhaps out of the debt I owe to your people for sparing my life and showing me there is more to live for than battle and conquest."

Kalie grabbed Varena for support—something that would strike her as funny later on. They both stumbled, and Riyik reached forward to steady them. This time, Kalie accepted his hand. She opened her mouth to speak, but whatever she might have said was cut short by the sounds of shrieking women and shouting men.

At once, the three who were conscious hurried to see what was going on. Riyik's face showed regret that he would never know what Kalie would have said. Then he put a hand on his dagger, and hurried in front of the women to whatever danger awaited.

Chapter 17

Pausing at Riyik's tent only long enough to hand Varena over to Brenia with a few whispered instructions, Kalie and Riyik raced to join the crowd gathering in front of the king's tent. While Varena was happy enough for the sanctuary of a dark felt tent, Kalie could tell Brenia would have preferred to follow the crowd and see for herself what was happening. But, like a good Aahken woman, she did as her brother commanded.

Before the king's tent, a half naked woman was being tossed between three guards while she tried desperately to cover herself. Behind them, a slave girl with demurely lowered eyes quietly answered questions put to her by two other guards. Kalie strained to hear, cursing the fact that these women never spoke at a normal volume. Those nearest, however, were happy to repeat everything the girl said to those around them.

As the story of a slave girl interrupting an afternoon tryst in the king's tent slowly unfolded, a rumpled, but fully dressed Kariik emerged from the tent and began barking orders to his guards. Just then, an older man arrived, greatly agitated and out of breath, demanding to know who had dishonored his daughter. It was then, when the woman broke free of her tormentors and rushed to her father that Kalie and Riyik saw finally saw her face.

Riyik's intended, Yasha.

"He is my king, father!" Yasha shrieked. "I could not disobey him!"

The warrior turned to Kariik, but seemed

suddenly at a loss on how to demand satisfaction for his daughter's honor from his king. "My liege..." he began. "Yasha was promised to another, but if you wish her for your own, I of course will gladly..." Whatever else he might have said was swallowed by ugly laughter and ribald comments from those around him.

Kalie and Riyik looked at each other in the same moment. "It seems a solution had been handed to us, Kalie," Riyik said. She could not hear him over the noise of the crowd, but she could read his lips well enough. "Whose work, do you think? My gods or your goddess?"

"Must be your gods," she replied. "My Goddess is as confused as I am over this mess!"

Before she could say anything else, Riyik began wading through the crowd, trying to catch Kariik's attention. "My king! My brother Levik! I would gladly renounce my claim on this woman out of loyalty to our new king..." Kariik did not seem to hear him, for he was still shaking his head in answer to Levik's offer.

"I do not want this woman," Kariik said, as though he was being offered a plate of fruit. His voice was soft, but it silenced the crowd, but for a single shared indrawn breath, and a strangled cry of horror from Yasha.

Levik shook his head as though he misheard, and managed a confused, "My king?"

Riyik, a black cloud of anger masking his face, surged forward even more desperately. "Brothers, please!" he shouted. "This is not the time or place for such talk. Privately, within your tent, my king..."

"I was enjoying a well deserved nap when

she," Kariik jerked his head toward Yasha, "pushed her way into my sleeping chamber. She had already shed her clothing, and made it plain what her intentions were. Of course I accepted the offer. What man wouldn't?"

If the crowd had been wild before, they were frenzied now. Most only laughed and jeered, but others, sounding genuinely outraged, began gathering stones and pieces of bone from the hard ground.

Levik turned on his daughter, disbelief warring with rage. "Father, no!" she screamed.

A large, breathless woman, whom Kalie knew to be Yahsa's mother pushed her way through the crowd. "It isn't her fault!" she beseeched whoever would listen. "It's those foreign slaves! They fill a young girl's head full of ideas…"

Yasha was nodding desperately. "It was Kalie! She told me that among her people, if a woman wants a man, she just goes to him and…"

"Silence!" Levik roared over the voice of the mob.

Kalie pulled her veil tight around her, terrified she had already been recognized. Her eyes sought Riyik, who was making a last desperate attempt to reason with the king. "Kariik!" he whispered harshly. "That was not well done! Tell Levik you want his daughter, and offer him a few horses for her! He'll sell her cheap in her present condition, and he'll accept this stain on his honor if it means grandsons with royal blood. Everyone can still win!"

Kariik shot an annoyed glance at Riyik, then a more worried one at the still growing mob. "What do I need with another woman?" he demanded. "I have more than I can use already! And why should I waste good horses on one who throws herself at a man like a harlot? Doubtless she'd make me a laughing stock before winter! Besides," Kariik eyed the mob. "Their blood is up. They'll have their entertainment one way or another. It might as well be her."

But there was more shouting than those demanding the blood of a dishonored woman. Men came to stand by Levik, calling for just compensation for the loss of his daughter. It was, after all, the king himself who had taken her. No true king would behave in this way they muttered, while others shouted that Riyik, too, was owed compensation. No one, they cried, not even a king, could just help himself to a warrior's betrothed and walk away as if it were nothing.

Then Haraak arrived, out of breath and angry. No, Kalie realized. Not angry. Frightened. He had made Kariik king, and assumed he could control him. Kariik's blatant incompetence at the job, demonstrated today by alienating so many of his men, threatened to destroy everything Haraak had worked for.

Kariik saw the look on Haraak's face, and looked frightened himself. Then, gathering his composure, he turned to Levik and the noise of the crowd dropped off sharply. For a moment, Kalie thought he might take Riyik's advice, and salvage the situation. "Take her home!" the king told Levik. "Find her a husband if you still can."

Fury boiled in Levik's face, and Kalie did not think all of it was directed at Yasha. But she was the only one he could strike at.

Riyik now fought to reach Levik, but the crowd would not let him pass. "Wait!" he shouted at his brother warrior. "I will still honor our agreement…"

Kalie never knew if Levik had heard Riyik's offer. Taking his daughter by the shoulders, he flung her onto the hard, hot ground. Then he turned and walked away. His frightened wife rushed after him, trying to catch hold of him, and the protection she hoped to find for herself, now that her daughter was lost. Kalie guessed that her husband would keep her— after beating her for raising such a wanton daughter.

Then the mob closed in around Yasha's sobbing form. Kalie sought to back away, as raised arms flung stones, bones and even their own filth at their victim, but found herself trapped by the press of bodies. She noticed the women flung their missiles even more viciously than did the men, and yelled even more outraged epithets.

Then Riyik was by her side, leading her through the crazed mob. They reached his tent, and were at once enveloped by an oasis of calm and quiet. Brenia brought kumis for Riyik and tea for Kalie— without being asked. Dressed in better clothes than she had ever owned, Varena shadowed her, quietly assisting Brenia in all she did.

"Did she die quickly, at least?" Varena asked, pulling Kalie's thoughts back to the horror she had witnessed.

"I don't know. I couldn't see." Kalie looked at Riyik, surprised to see anger and grief and something more…guilt, perhaps? No, she realized: she wasn't surprised at all.

Hesitantly, Kalie reached out. "It wasn't your fault, Riyik. Yasha knew the risks when she went into the king's tent."

"She didn't have to die!" he said, tossing back

the skin of kumis. "It would have cost Kariik nothing to save her life, and he'd have gained her father's loyalty for all time. Instead he threw away a young girl's life and made an enemy of her father. What kind of king does that?"

Having no answer, Kalie asked, "Would you have really married her after what happened?"

"Yes."

Brenia gasped. "Brother! You could not have!"

"Do you care for her so much?" Kalie asked. That hadn't been how it seemed to her. Or was she simply jealous?

"I don't care for her at all! I was thrilled when I saw her with the king, for I thought it meant a way to honorably get out of the agreement and marry you!" Brenia's head was whipping back and forth between them as she sought to catch up with recent events. "But I care about what is right! What happened to Yasha was not right."

"According to your people it was," Kalie breathed.

"Of course, I didn't think to ask you." Riyik now looked uncertain. "Would you have been willing to share a tent with her?"

"Of course!" Kalie realized Brenia wasn't the only one having trouble keeping up with recent events. "I doubt very much Yasha would have liked it, but I think she might have preferred it to death."

"Are you two really going to marry?" Brenia asked. Crouched in the shadows, Varena awaited the answer with bated breath.

Kalie opened her mouth to speak but found she could not. Riyik looked up from the leather scroll, which held the tally of all his horses and met her gaze.

"Let us go for a ride," he suggested.

Chapter 18

They walked through the camp to where the horses grazed under the watchful eyes of many guards. The camp had settled down by then, Yasha's body dumped beyond the borders of the tribe's territory and left for the scavengers. As they walked, Riyik made a point of asking if anyone had seen Maalke, and to direct him to Riyik's tent when they did, as he was anxious to conclude their business.

The horse camp was different from the beastman camp. If there was anything in this world Kalie could call beautiful, it was this. The grass was only knee high and more green than brown, especially by the one of the small springs that fed the lake. Reserved for the horses, the water was still sweet, the land around it fresh and green.

The horses, too, were beautiful. In the early days of her captivity, Kalie had speculated that it was the horses that had shaped the beastmen into monsters. Astride the mighty beasts, men looked down on the earth and those who spent their lives upon Her, as something less than themselves. They tasted power, and the speed at which they could now travel seemed only to inflame their desire for more. As if increased speed actually decreased their ability to think through their actions. It certainly brought them more rapidly into conflict with others like themselves.

Now, as Riyik stopped beside Thunder, preparing him for riding, she could only marvel and the grace and nobility of such animals. Surely there could be no evil in them. Surely they were no more to blame for their rider's behavior than the women who were held equally captive.

Perhaps, Kalie thought as she watched Riyik calling to a second horse, it was that horses were like mirrors: it was what each individual human brought to them that determined what they did. Evil men used the horses for evil purposes. But Kalie could imagine many positive uses as well. Improved travel and communication; Healers brought where they were needed at lightning speed. And imagine how much more productive farms could become if horses could be taught to pull hoes...

"Well, do you want to ride or not?" Kalie came out of her reverie to find Riyik in front of her, holding out the reigns of a placid gray mare.

Kalie stared. "Women do not ride, or so I am told," she said coldly.

"True," said Riyik. "But you once said you wanted to. Do you still?"

"Yes, of course!" To her great embarrassment, Kalie found she could not keep the enthusiasm from her voice. Then to her greater embarrassment, she found she had no idea how to mount the animal Riyik held out to her. Rather than admit that, she demurred. "I had thought we would ride on one horse. It is a part of your marriage ceremonies, is it not?"

"Yes, but if you and I are to marry, it would not be as any marriage among my people. We would have to find a way to live as equals. I thought we might start by riding as equals—side by side, each on our own horse. Unless you are offended by the notion of riding on animals, and thus treating them as less than each of us ourselves would wish to be treated..."

Kalie shook her head, unable to believe what Riyik was saying. Yet with all her being, she knew he spoke the truth. Or rather, from his heart. How this new truth of his would stand when met by reality—that was something neither of them could know.

But she wanted to be part of it, for as long as it lasted.

"I would like to ride," she said, petting the nose of the lovely gray mare, who rasped a tongue across Kalie's palm, searching for treats. "But I don't even know how to get on her back, let alone guide her."

Riyik smiled. "If you could allow me to pick you up without breaking any of my bones, I could set you on her back. She's a gentle creature; I've used her to teach many boys how to ride, and I think you will take to it quickly. Would you like to try?"

For a moment, Kalie stiffened, at war with herself. Later, she was never sure if it was desire to learn to ride, or desire to learn more about the man beside her that made the decision. Perhaps it was both, but she let Riyik pick her up and put her astride the horse. His touch was strong and confident, and not at all threatening. Kalie was surprised by what a simple thing like a man touching her for purposes other than torment and control could mean to her. Once, it had been an unquestioned part of her life.

For the next space of time, Kalie had no thoughts to spare for anything save riding. Once she had learned to move with her mount in a gentle walk, the rest was easy. Riyik showed her how to stay seated until a bone-jarring trot passed into a smooth canter.

And then the world changed.

Kalie was flying! The world passed beneath her, as it must for the birds she had watched with such envy as a child. The horse's muscles bunched and stretched beneath her body with a power she had never before imagined—and now it was a part of her!

They rode through the tall grass with nothing but the vivid blue sky to stop them. As the wind cooled the sweat from her body, Kalie finally saw just how beautiful the summer sky was. How could she have ever seen that endless blue glory as cruel or oppressive?

Finally, however, the horses slowed, the heat returned, and Kalie began to feel aches in places she didn't know she had. Riyik led them to a nearly dry watercourse. Three skeletal trees stood guard on the hill above it, providing enough shade to make the place welcoming. Then he showed Kalie how to rub down their tired mounts, who were soon contently drinking water from what looked to Kalie like nothing but mud. Grinning, she saluted their patient ingenuity, and went to join Riyik on the grass beneath the trees.

He had brought bread and cheese and full skin of water. Kalie's own water bag was only half full, and not nearly as cool, but she offered it to Riyik after drinking from his. He accepted with thanks, and made no complaint when he tasted it. And for just a moment, Kalie found herself admiring him without reservation.

They ate in silence. Kalie, who had been eating less than she might have in order to pay her spies, nearly devoured her share. She could have eaten Riyik's as well. He was clearly willing to give her all of it, but by then, Kalie had regained a measure of control.

"Is it strange for you," Riyik asked at last, "to enjoy a picnic, so soon after seeing a woman stoned to death?"

Kalie thought about it. "Yes. And no. Maybe I've lived here long enough to grow used to such things." She glanced at him curiously. "Is it strange for you?"

"Yes. But not for the same reasons it would have been a year ago. Back then, I would have felt as any man of tribe—dishonored by her actions, partially mollified by her death, but still angry; perhaps angry enough to begin a blood feud with her family."

"And what do you feel now?"

"Guilt. Confusion. Perhaps not grief. I didn't want Yasha. I suppose I agreed to the marriage precisely because I cared as little for her as she did for me. But now…I feel I failed her. Every boy who grows to manhood among my people is taught about honor. It's the most important thing a man has. But somehow…I'm starting to think that its real meaning has been lost. Most of the men in that crowd today could see only that Yasha had betrayed me. They could not imagine honor demanding that I still remember my duty to her."

"I suppose they felt your duty to her ended when she failed in her duty to you."

"I'm sure they did. But where's the honor in that? I gave my promise to protect her; in this place, that's a man's most sacred obligation. And yet, they find it so easy to shed."

Kalie was intrigued. "Perhaps they felt your obligation only extended until honor was restored by her death."

"I'm sure that is true," he said sadly. He looked off in the distance. "Of course, it's not just a woman who can regain honor in death. Sometimes, it's the only way for a man as well."

Kalie felt a cold knot of fear in the pit of her stomach. Instinctively, she looked for any sign that she was in danger and found none. It took a long time for her to realize that the fear she felt was for another human being.

It was Riyik who was in danger. He was being swallowed by despair. And Kalie had nearly forgotten how to deal with such things. Had, in fact, forgotten that she had once been a person who had cared about the pain of strangers.

And suddenly, more than anything, she wanted to be that person again.

"Riyik?" she said finally. "Are you all right?" Oh, brilliant! Anyone can see he's not all right! Goddess, if you're there, help me out here!

Riyik shook himself, as if surprised to find himself here. "Yes, of course—"

"Of course you're not all right. What I meant was, is there anything I can do to help?"

Riyik's eyes widened. He seemed about to speak, then shook his head.

Kalie sighed. "Tell me, please. I promise, no matter what it is, I won't break any of your bones. Even if I'm tempted."

She had hoped he would laugh. Instead, he looked at her sadly. "You could want me as much as I want you. You could marry me with joy instead of a sense of duty. But that's the problem: you can't. Not because you choose to deny me, but because you just…can't."

And for once in her life, Kalie had no idea what to say.

Then, as if it was part of the same conversation, Riyik asked, "How did it feel, hitting Maalke?"

Kalie cut short the laughter that bubbled up inside her, for fear it would never stop. "Wonderful," she said at last.

"I imagine it did." Riyik was smiling now and seemed at ease with Kalie. More surprising was the ease she felt with him. "I've never seen a woman do that before! It was incredible."

Kalie wanted to savor the moment, but there were serious matters to discuss. "Riyik, you should know that if you marry me, you could be taking on a lot of trouble, and getting very little value in return. Yasha and her mother both denounced me before..." She could not finish.

"You have nothing to fear from that. For all that you hate our customs, you'll find that our habit of dismissing what a woman might say—especially at a time like that—will work in your favor." Riyik hesitated, and then pressed forward. "And you have nothing to fear from me. When I offered to marry you, and adopt Varena, it was because I wanted to help you; to be a hero in your eyes. I hope someday I can be that, but until then...until then, we do not have to...lie together as man and wife. Not if you don't want to."

To her horror, Kalie began to cry. She tried to summon up anger at Riyik for breaking down her defenses, for making her feel things that should be long dead—but it would not come.

"Why are you being so nice to me?" she wailed.

Riyik looked away and did not answer.

"Riyik, please! You are offering me so much more than I can ever repay! Maybe it doesn't make sense to you but my code of honor won't allow that! You're offering protection not just to me but to Varena, you're saying you won't force me to have sex with you...what do you want in return?"

"For you to keep my tent and raise my son, and do whatever you can to help him walk."

"You know that I'll do whatever I can for Yarik whether I live in your tent or not, and—wait, what tent? The one you live in was part of Yasha's dowry. Won't you be returning it to her father?"

Riyik shook his head. "It is the custom, when something like this happens, for the man to keep the dowry. I will, of course, insist that Levik take back some of it, as a peace offering, but he will probably refuse, for the same reason. We can, at least avoid a blood feud, if we try."

"Haraak was angry with Kariik," Kalie observed.

"Many men will be angry with Kariik," said Riyik. "He has shown himself to be a fool and unfit to rule—and over a woman, no less!" He glanced at Kalie and looked embarrassed, then continued. "I doubt this will be his last poor showing. That is what Haraak fears."

Pushing a wild lock of hair behind her ear, Kalie discovered that she had cast aside her veil. When had she done that? And why was she just noticing it now? She turned her attention back to her own situation.

Riyik was offering her the chance of a lifetime. More than just a life free of drudgery and beatings and forced sex. More, even, than the best life this world could offer Varena.

He just didn't know about that part of it.

As the wife of a high-ranking warrior, Kalie would have access to more information than she would ever have as Maalke's slave. Her resources for buying knowledge from shadow women and slaves would be virtually unlimited. And what about a few feasts in her husband's tent? If she could persuade him to invite Haraak and some of his lackeys...? Her skin crawled at the notion of being in the same tent with Haraak, but what an opportunity! She might even be able to poison Haraak, which might, in the end, be enough to make the alliance fall apart...

So why did she feel as if she were betraying a friend?

Kalie looked up suddenly, afraid Riyik had seen everything she had been thinking. But he was lost in thoughts of his own. "There is another possibility," he said slowly, measuring his words. "I have never spoken it aloud."

Kalie smiled. "Look around you, Riyik. There's no one to hear except me. And I promise whatever it is, I won't laugh. I won't even use it in a story."

The pain and love mixed in Riyik's gaze made her want to weep again, but she held his gaze. She would hear what this man had to say with the same kindness and support he had offered her.

"We could go west, Kalie. We could go and live with your people."

"What?"

"Would they accept me? And Yarik? If you spoke for us...that is, if you'd be willing to?"

Kalie shook her head, trying to stop the buzzing in her ears. "Yes, of course they'd accept you, whether I spoke for you or not. Or, at least they would have a few seasons ago. Now, perhaps, I would have to speak for you..."

"But would you?" Riyik seemed so earnest he looked like a boy.

"Yes, of course I would. But why would you want to?"

"Because...my people are not who I once thought they were. And I am not the man I once was."

"Because of me?" Oh, Goddess, that was all she needed! Riyik as a hero out of one the women's so-called "romantic" tales, where the man gave up everything he had for love of a woman. Their stories always ended before the man grew bored, and woke up to the reality of what he'd lost, then had to kill the woman to regain his honor, although some of the men's stories included that part.

But Riyik surprised her again.

"I cannot serve a weak and selfish king! A king who cares nothing for the good of his people! Who cannot think for himself—and lacks the wit to even see there's something wrong with that! And..." Riyik's voice dropped to a whisper. "I cannot serve the man who rules my king...who I suspect murdered the true king to gain power."

"So you know that Haraak poisoned Ahnaak? And murdered Kariik's brothers as well?"

Riyik's head shot up, then he sighed. "I don't know why I'm surprised you know such things. Perhaps I'm just the last to know. No, no, that cannot be! They don't see...or they don't want to see..."

"I thought such things were common among your people." Kalie was truly puzzled. "Is that not the usual path to power? Killing and taking...?"

"In battle perhaps! But not...this! Not the slaying of the king one has given his oath to! I see Haraak leading my people to ruin, and not a warrior among my so-called 'brothers' with enough sense or honor to stop him."

Kalie considered what she knew about these men and their beliefs. "But doesn't honor demand that you stay and fight it? By yourself, if necessary?"

Riyik raked his hands through his deep brown hair and gazed at Kalie with troubled eyes. "Yes, it does. But I don't want it badly enough anymore. Not when there exists another world where I might regain my honor in new ways; where my son might grow up whole, as he could never do here."

For the first time, Kalie realized just how long Riyik had been thinking about what life for his son would be in this place. But who would have thought that a beastman could care so much about his child? Or be capable of seeing a different path for his future? For both their futures?

Sadly, Kalie shook her head. "I'm sorry Riyik, but the life you dream of is not possible. Not yet, anyway."

Stunned, Riyik could only gape at her.

"Haraak's ambitions range much farther than simply ruling this tribe through a puppet king. He means to forge a federation of tribes, and conquer my homeland. Not just raid it and return here. He means to take all your people, and all your ways, far to the west, and set himself up as king. If we left tomorrow, you would have at most one year to live your new life, and see Yarik grow whole and accepted. Then your people will come. And you would die along with all the others."

"You know this for a fact?"

Kalie hesitated, unsure how far she could trust him. *The fact that you can think of trust and one of them in the same sentence should tell you you've already lost what little sense you had,* Kalie berated herself.

"I have heard whispers. And I believe they are true."

Riyik smiled with relief. "Indeed you miss nothing, Kalie! But I have heard these whispers as well. More than that, I have watched it play out among the warriors, and those knaves from among the Wolf and even the Hansi, who Haraak thinks will do his bidding. But rest easy: for as long as the tribes have existed, in every generation a man arises who thinks he can create a federation of tribes and conquer all the lands to the ends of the earth. Nothing ever comes of it. Haraak's federation will collapse just like all the others."

Kalie was thrilled with Riyik's words, but not for the reasons she knew he hoped. This was the first sign she had received that her hopes might actually have some basis in reality! If alliances broke apart so easily, as she had long supposed, there was a chance she could make this one fall apart as well! The weaknesses, the tools, were already there.

But what could she say to Riyik now?

"You're afraid to trust me, aren't you?" Riyik asked.

"You read me too well," she replied. "Very little has been asked of my mind in this place. Now, suddenly, there is much to think about. I can tell you that I am grateful for all you've done, Riyik. And all you're willing to give up. If I could trust anyone in this land, it would be you." And she realized as she said it that she spoke the truth.

She took a pull from the water skin and continued. "Even if Haraak's federation collapses, my people will not be safe. There will be raids—not just your tribe, but all who hear of the easy wealth to be had in the west. There will be those, considered weak and unimportant here, who will find that a rich land, whose people know nothing of fighting, offers them place to settle and grow strong—after they've killed or enslaved all of its inhabitants. Then, they will find they must defend their stolen land against those who will come later, in greater numbers."

"All the more reason for us to leave now!" Riyik insisted. "With enough horses, and even one seasoned warrior, we can teach your people to defend themselves when this invasion you fear comes! If I am right, we will have many seasons to prepare, but if you are right, we have little time. Either way, we should leave at once!"

"Can you do that?" Kalie asked, truly curious. "Just take your horses and flocks and just...leave? Without permission from your king?"

Riyik looked away. "It is true, I must have permission from my king—and my chief as well. But Kariik knows what I think of Haraak's schemes, and may well be happy to see me go. If not...the people of Aahk prize honor above all, but we cherish freedom as well." At Kalie's strangled laughter, he smiled wryly. "Perhaps I never saw the hypocrisy in that before, but if it gives us a chance to leave here without fighting our way out, I'll take it!"

"Varena, too?"

"I may take whatever belongs to me. Women, children, slaves, horses. The one necessity I might have to leave behind would be my flocks, or at least most of them. But a few sheep will feed us until we reach your land." His gaze grew hard. "But I could not take Brenia from her lawful husband. And I can't just leave her…" His voice trailed off.

"Could you convince her to take Barak and come with us in secret?"

"Then we would risk pursuit. Hysaak and all who consider themselves his spear brothers would be required to hunt down his wife and son, and kill whoever stole them from him."

They sat in silence, mulling that over. Kalie wanted Brenia with her when she left. But she knew her proper and dignified friend would never endanger those she loved by going along with such a scheme.

"Of course, if Hysaak were to die, Brenia could return to her family."

"Which would be you. Excellent. But, wouldn't she be expected to follow her husband into the next life?"

"Expected, yes. But no one would give chase if she went with her brother instead. Especially since Hysaak has shamed her before all eyes by flaunting his preference for his new wife."

"Then perhaps the honor of accompanying her husband to the next life should fall to her," Kalie said with a breezy smile. Privately, though, she was in awe of the thought Riyik had put into this, and the lengths to which he was willing to go. And the most amazing thing was that it could possibly work. With Riyik and Varena and Brenia—and perhaps a few others whom she might persuade Riyik to buy and bring with them —she would finally have what she needed to make her people see what kind of threat they faced. With horses, and an experienced teacher of the ways of war, they might—given enough time—learn to defend themselves.

"Kalie?" So gently, Riyik took her hand, and

gazed into her eyes. "What say you? Might it work? Could you consider a life with me, in your own home, on your own terms?"

A voice inside Kalie shouted for her to say yes. You've suffered enough, it told her. Leave this waking nightmare and go home with the one man who might someday teach you how to love again! Show your daughter what joy a woman's life can be. Let go of the arrogance that makes you think you alone can save your people, and give them some say in the matter! And if they fail to act wisely—again—take your family all the way west to Hot Springs, where the beastmen will not reach for many years!

Then, even more loudly, another voice demanded her attention. Stay here for just awhile longer it urged her. Marry Riyik according to the customs of his people, and use him as he and his people have used you. Learn every weakness they have, destroy these tribes so thoroughly that a thousand seasons must pass before they are strong enough to again threaten the People of the Goddess. And if Riyik still wants you then…let him come with you.

Riyik was still waiting for an answer. Kalie opened her mouth to stall for time. "I can't leave yet," she heard herself say. "I can't leave until I have destroyed your people's ability to wage war, killed Haraak, and freed every woman and girl who are willing to be free. Then, if you still want to, we can try to make a life together."

Chapter 19

Kalie didn't realize what she had said until she saw the dawning comprehension in Riyik's face. *Oh, brilliant!* Shouted an angry voice inside. *It's a fine plan—but you weren't supposed to tell it to the enemy!*

But Riyik wasn't her enemy, and as dangerous —as foolhardy—as it seemed, Kalie knew she had to be honest with him. *Otherwise, I'm just like them!* She told the voices.

Still, even Kalie wasn't prepared for what came next.

"That has been your plan since the beginning." Riyik was nodding slowly to himself, not looking at Kalie. "That was how you came to be part of the tribute."

"Yes," Kalie said simply.

"The scars on your back. You lived among one of the tribes before, didn't you?"

Kalie nodded. "Eight summers ago, I had a thirst for adventure; a common enough thing among my people. Or at least it used to be. I joined a band of merchants who were heading east into the grasslands. Little was known of that part of the world. I suppose that made it more exciting to us."

Riyik looked ill. "You were captured? And your master returned you to your people?"

Kalie gave him a withering glare. "Of course he didn't return me! I escaped!"

"Escaped? By yourself?" Riyik asked, as if he had never heard of such a thing. Then again, Kalie thought, he probably hadn't. "How?"

"I'm afraid I still don't know the answer to that. The Goddess, in Her Mercy, took my memories. I was found, half starved and raving, at the edge of the grasslands. The Healers who cared for me eventually brought back some of my memory. A bitter kindness that turned out to be, for no one believed me when I told them what happened, and no one did anything to prepare for the invasion that I knew would come."

"So you took the battle to your enemy? Alone? Without so much as a dagger?"

Kalie smiled. "I didn't plan on it at the time. In fact, for seven years, I ran in the opposite direction. I kept heading west. But it didn't help. I was…broken. And nothing anyone could do seemed likely to fix me."

"Why not? Your people don't seem the kind to hold with our notions that a woman is dishonored if she's…er…no longer a virgin. You said they tried to help."

"Yes, they tried very hard to help. And, no, of course they didn't blame me for being raped. But the fact of it made most of them very uncomfortable. Try to understand, Riyik, no one among my people knew what rape was." Kalie sighed. "Perhaps you can't imagine something like that."

"I can. But not easily." He seemed about to say more, then shook his head and waited for Kalie to continue.

"I couldn't function. When I slept, I woke up screaming from nightmares. I spent every waking hour haunted by fear: fear it would happen again, fear it was still happening, sometimes fear of my own shadow. Physical joining became impossible."

At Riyik's confused look, she tried to explain.

"Among my people, the physical joining of a man and a woman is meant to be a joyous thing for both parties; almost an act of worship. It can't happen unless both parties want it. When I tried to take up my old life, that was a part of it. But there was no longer any joy in it for me. All it did was bring back horrid memories. My partners were…uncomfortable, to say the least. Some of them tried to help, but all I could do was run.

"I learned I could not have children. The damage done to body during the rapes—or perhaps during my escape—was too great. I settled in a mountain town with a temple famous for Healing, and decided to remain."

"And then we came." It was not a question.

"And then you came. I was sent for." Kalie looked at the horses. "If we'd had horses, I think I could have made the journey to Riverford in just a few days, and you would not have remained prisoners so long."

Riyik smiled sadly. "Then I would not have had time to learn to carve. I would not have seen enough of your world to know such wonders truly existed."

The play of emotions across Riyik's face had been growing easier to read as he spoke. She should not have been surprised that his first words had nothing to do with her plans or his duty, or the gulf that now separated them. "I had suspected you could not have children. It did not matter to me. It still doesn't. Except that now I know the reason. I am deeply sorry…no…I am ashamed that it was my people who did that to you."

"Truly? Even if it wasn't Aahken warriors who did it."

"As you once said, we practice the same customs. What was done to you has doubtless happened to many women in this camp. How I ever believed there to be honor it…"

"What will you do now?"

"I find myself in a rather difficult situation," he said.

"I'd say that's an understatement," she said.

"When I became a warrior, I swore an oath to be loyal unto death to my king and to my spear brothers. Haraak is my spear brother, but he has murdered my king. Kariik may be my king, but he got that way through tainted means, and is unfit to rule. That both must die seems clear."

"Both? What if Kariik knew nothing of the murders?"

Riyik looked at her curiously. "How else do you expect him to give up the kingship? We just ask him to step down?"

"Oh, of course," said Kalie with a bark of laughter. "I forgot where I was. I don't suppose there are many options for a former king."

"I don't even think we have a word for it." Riyik sighed. "But at least for that part, we want the same things. Am I right?"

"About Haraak yes. Preferably, in a way that destroys any trust he has built among the other tribes." A glimmer of an idea teased her, but was gone before she could grasp it. "As for Kariik…a weak king might well suit my purposes, but not yours. Ahnaak left no other sons. Who will be king after Kariik?"

"If his son was older, perhaps he."

"Son?" Then she remembered. Maylene's child.

"Now there's a solution that might have worked for both of us. A king with the blood of both our people!" Riyik shook his head sadly. "But he's still a baby, and whatever is to happen will happen soon. Most likely, each of the chiefs, or one whom they support, will fight. The winner will be the new king."

"If only they could keep fighting until all were dead!" At Riyik's expression, Kalie dampened her enthusiasm. "Er, sorry. It's just that, with a system like that, there's no way to influence the outcome."

"That's why we use it. When someone can influence the outcome, we get men like Haraak."

Kalie shook her head. "I'm sorry, Riyik. I just don't see any way we can work together on this. We both have duties to our own people. Yours may demand that you kill Haraak to avenge your king, even that you kill Kariik for the common good, but after that, you must continue to raid and fight—and kill your tribe's enemies. Even if that enemy is the woman you want to marry."

Riyik took her hand and squeezed it, stopping just when it became painful. He looked into her eyes. "A warrior risks death for his people, but rarely more than that. You have come unarmed into the camp of your enemy and endured degradation, hunger and abuse on the nearly impossible chance that you can single handedly save your people. You are a nobler warrior than any I have ever heard of. I will never kill you Kalie, but I swear that I long as live, I will kill anyone who tries to."

"Riyik, please, don't make such a promise!"

The hardness was gone from his eyes. "It's too late," he said mildly. "I have sworn an oath, and unlike other men here, for me it is binding."

"But what can I promise you that will not violate my oath to save my people?"

Riyik thought hard. At last he said, "Promise that when the threat my people pose to yours has been destroyed, you will take Yarik, and as many of my tribe who prove worthy—whether they be men or women—back to your home, to live by your ways."

Kalie's breath caught in her throat. She knew it was no accident that Riyik had not included himself in this new future. "How will I know who is worthy? Only you can judge that, Riyik. And to do that, you must live."

"I would like to Kalie. I would like to build a life with you. I would like to see what kind of place we could create blending the best of both our worlds."

"You just swore to protect me! You can't do that if you're dead!"

"Then we must pray for a miracle. But in my world, a man who slays his brothers has no future. And a man who slays his king must die."

"Even if he is a false king who deserves to die?"

"That doesn't matter—"

"Maybe not in your world, but in my world it does. And you told me yourself you want to live there! So do what you must here and come with me!" The voice Kalie was learning to hate was back, telling her to stop arguing and accept Riyik's sacrifice. Everything she had worked for was finally going to happen!

All she had to do, the voice told her, was let Riyik die for her.

Kalie struck at that voice so hard it hurt.

When she could see again, Kalie realized she had the answer.

"There is a story I heard once during the winter," she said. "About a warrior, who, on the eve of battle came across a man of his own tribe in a secret meeting with an enemy warrior—"

Riyik nodded. "The Tale of Amon. Yes. He caught a traitor showing the enemy where they might set up an ambush, and thus win the day. All to win the daughter of the enemy king."

"Yes, there's always a woman involved. But when Amon slew them both, who did he discover the traitor to be?"

"His own brother. And when the battle began, he flew into a frenzy and sought his own death at the hands of the enemy, for not only had he slain his own brother, he now knew that the blood of a traitor flowed through his own veins as well. And since their father was dead, and neither had any sons, their tainted line would be ended once and for all."

"But the gods intervened, and kept him from dying. And when the battle was won, Amon emerged as the greatest hero of all. And when the men sang his name, and the king offered him riches, he chose instead to leave, vowing to return whenever his people were in peril."

Riyik's dark gaze pieced Kalie's. "And is that how you see me?"

She smiled. "Perhaps. I think you should at least consider that following your conscience doesn't have to lead to your death."

"Did you come here expecting to return alive, Kalie?"

She tried to look away so she could lie, but

Riyik would not let her. "No," she said at last.

"Do you see me as having less honor than you yourself possess?"

"No," she said, more certain of herself this time. "But now I find I very much want to live. So let us devise a plan in which honor is served, villains are punished, good people are saved, and a future exists for you and I."

The beginnings of a smile pulled at Riyik's mouth. "You know you're insane, don't you?"

"Yes." Quite against her will, an answering smile was playing on Kalie's. Suddenly serious, she asked Riyik for his dagger. He gave it to her without a word. "Blood is sacred to both our peoples, although we use it differently." She drew the blade across the palm of her hand, staring at the blood that welled up as if it belonged to someone else. Then she felt the sting, and knew it was really herself doing this. "So let us make a pact as warriors do."

Riyik nodded and took the knife, mirroring Kalie's gesture in his own flesh. He placed his bleeding palm against hers, an act she knew he had performed before, though never with a woman.

"We are one," Riyik said solemnly. "In life and death; in all we do, we are one."

If Riyik found it strange that he was swearing a sacred oath between brothers with the woman he intended to marry, he gave no sign of it.

And if Kalie found it strange to swear an oath in the manner of the people she had come to destroy, or bind her life and soul with a man she loved but had no intention of sleeping with, she was equally silent.

They rode back to camp lost in thought.

Chapter 20

Maalke was waiting in the tent when they returned.

Brenia was calmly applying a compress to his head where Kalie had struck him, and trying to coax him into drinking willow bark tea, while Maalke grumbled and demanded kumis. Varena hid in the shadows.

"Greetings, Maalke," Riyik said, sliding onto a cushion opposite his guest. Brenia brought him tea and the tally of animals he had been studying earlier.

Maalke's gaze slid from Riyik to Kalie, who had gone to help Brenia prepare the evening meal. "A bit presumptuous, isn't it?" he said. "Enjoying my slaves before we've reached an agreement? I don't even remember that we discussed it!"

"You were perhaps too deeply inside the kumis skin for any kind of fair bargain," Riyik said calmly. "Perhaps now is a better time?"

Maalke grunted. "I believe you offered twenty horses for the both of them."

"I believe I offered ten. It was you who said twenty, which I can well understand. Both are the kind of women men lose their heads over. Shall we agree on fifteen?"

Maalke hid his pleasure by gulping down his tea. Then, he shouted as if offended, "My daughter alone is worth fifteen!"

Kalie gagged so loudly that Brenia clapped a hand over her mouth to keep her quiet. By the time Kalie was done imagining Maalke staked to the ground by his balls, the haggling was finished and she and Varena both belonged to Riyik.

"I will go to his tent to collect your things tomorrow," Riyik told Kalie and Varena as they gazed outside the open tent flap, watching the deepening twilight.

"There's little enough there that's ours," said Kalie. "But I would like to continue treating Cassia during her pregnancy. Will that be allowed?"

Riyik smiled at her. There was no trace of ownership in it. "Tomorrow you will be the wife of a warrior. Of course you may call on a fellow wife." He smiled at Varena as well. "And you," he said, lifting a small wooden chest from among his bundles of belongings. "You will have this for your dowry." Riyik lifted the carved lid and revealed pieces of gold and silver jewelry. "You can tell everyone it came down the family from your mother's side."

Varena gasped. In that small box was enough wealth to win her a chief's son for a husband. The box alone was probably worth more than what Maalke had paid for her birth mother. With a future like that, Kalie thought sadly, Varena might well decide to remain with the tribe, rather than going with her to live among strangers.

"May I see?" she asked. Varena pushed the box to her, and Kalie looked in, seeing her past reflected in the lustrous metal.

"My share of the spoils from the west," Riyik said, not meeting her eyes. "I never did know what to do with it. Maybe now, it can serve a higher purpose than the one that brought it here."

Kalie hadn't been in Riverford very long, but she thought she recognized some of the work. Varena could not take her eyes off of the treasure. "May I wear some of it now?" she asked Riyik.

He hesitated. "Inside this tent, yes. Outside, only at festivals, and only when you are with Kalie or me." Riyik grimaced. "I've never had to worry about a daughter, and now, suddenly, I have a grown one!"

"Oh, thank you so much, mas...father!" Varena grabbed Riyik's hands and kissed them, then bowed and placed them on her forehead.

Kalie smiled at him. "You've made her very happy," she said as Varena arranged the bedding for the night. "And...me as well." She took both his hands in hers, and while she wanted to do more, found she could not.

"My pleasure," said Riyik. He kissed her hands, and then released them.

That night, Brenia and her son returned to Hysaak's tent, as custom demanded, now that her brother had taken a wife. Kalie wished she could have stayed. She slept beside Varena and Yarik on one side of the tent, Riyik on the other. Varena seemed upset by the arrangement, but said nothing. I'll have to find a quiet moment to explain things to her, Kalie thought as she drifted off. Soon.

Kariik's announcement that the tribe would, at last, be leaving the next day for the second and final gathering of the summer was greeted with enthusiasm from most of the camp. Riyik, however, was angry.

"I wanted to give you a wedding fit for a king's daughter!" he told Kalie. "Now we will have to throw together something for tonight! And everyone's mind will be on an early departure for tomorrow!"

"Could we not wait and be married at the new gathering site?" Kalie asked. "Many others will be married then."

Riyik shook his head. "If we are not married, you will be seen, at best, as my concubine. Varena's status as my daughter can't be established either without a marriage. It's best for both of you if we do it now." He went to fetch Brenia, to show Kalie where his sheep were, and told them to slaughter four of them for the feast.

After that, everything was chaos, as people began preparing to break camp, and Brenia called into service anyone she could to prepare the wedding. Kalie was whisked away to the tent of some woman she didn't know, but which stank worse than Maalke's, and bathed with the now familiar paste of cypress, cedar and frankincense. Her hair was then combed with sheep's fat. Brenia donated a heavy black veil sown with tiny jet beads. Kalie would apparently be wearing her old clothes, which would not matter, she was told, since the veil went nearly to her feet, and was completely opaque.

"How am I to see where I'm going?" she demanded when the women had her arranged to their satisfaction.

"You won't need to," one of them called over a chorus of raucous laughter. "We will lead you to the place you must wait for your groom."

"The rest is up to him!" said another, provoking more laughter.

What followed was a round of crude advice for the wedding night, followed by horror stories of first time sexual experiences that these women seemed to find funny. Kalie's status seemed to have magically been raised to that of a virgin bride, despite the fact that everyone present knew she had been Maalke's slave for the past year.

When Kalie asked if Varena might be allowed to keep her company, she was told that only married women could be in the tent with her. She thought about asking for Cassia, but her ignorance of their customs made it too awkward. Would it be improper for a slave to request the company of her former mistress at a time like this? Or was it expected? .

So she asked for Larren instead, expecting to be refused on the grounds that Larren wasn't a wife. To Kalie's surprise, however, her captors agreed.

"She'll be a wife soon enough," said the one who seemed to be in charge.

"Only if she births a son," argued another.

"She will," said the third in a haughty voice. "I can tell these things."

"Then she'll be as much a wife as their kind can ever be," said the first.

But they seemed to be as happy to leave Kalie as she was to have them gone, and as Larren's presence would maintain a minimum of propriety, they brought her.

As soon as the horsewomen departed, Kalie removed the stifling veil—carefully, as it belonged to Brenia—but determined to see her old friend. The younger woman seemed hesitant, seating herself carefully around her swollen midsection.

"I'll bet you miss furniture more than almost anything," Kalie said.

Larren looked as though the thought had never occurred to her. "When I think of my old life, it's the food I miss the most. That, and not being afraid all the time."

Kalie regretted her first attempt at conversation. "I'd offer you something to eat, but as you can see, I haven't got any. I guess fasting is part of the ritual." When Larren said nothing, Kalie tried again. "I hear you'll be a wife soon, too, if your baby's a boy."

Larren nodded dully. "Itaak has promised it. And, Zolia, his first wife, hasn't tried to make me lose it. Of course, she could just be waiting until it's born."

"Would she really harm a living child? From what I've seen, they fear their husband's wrath too much for that."

Larren shrugged. "At least you'll never have to worry about it! Yet I heard you've adopted one of their slave girls."

Kalie nodded. "Her name's Varena. She's wonderful. She's helping me reach the women of this world."

Some of Laren's anger fell away, leaving curiosity in its place. "You seemed to be doing a fine job already. What could one of their bastard slave girls do?"

"Basically, she told me that I can win more of them over with honey than with vinegar," Kalie said, using one of their own people's sayings.

Larren nearly smiled at that. "That must be hard for you, considering how most of them treat us."

"But that's just it, Larren!" Kalie said with excitement. "Not all of women here are monsters like I first thought. Even you've seen that! I saw how you were with Mavra. And she's not the only one. There are women who've helped me; shown me kindness. Some, I hope will even come with us when we go home!"

Larren met Kalie's gaze, letting her veil fall away. The pain and despair that ravaged her once beautiful face made Kalie look away. "Do you really believe that's going to happen? Tell me, Kalie, I need to know!"

"Tell you what? That we're going home? I hang on to the dream of it. If I didn't I'd end up—"

"Like me?"

"I wasn't going to say that!"

"It doesn't matter. It's true. I've given up. And in doing so, I've damned us all." Only when Larren said "damned", a word from the beastmen's language, did Kalie realize they had been speaking in their mother tongue.

"You don't have the power to damn us all," said Kalie. "And it's not over yet."

"It is for me!" Larren began to cry. "Kalie, please! Get us out of here! When I thought I was the only one left, it didn't matter what I did, so I prayed for a son, just like a cursed beastwoman! But now... Now that I know you're alive, and still fighting..." Larren looked up, and eerie calm taking her. "Zolia is no threat to my baby—but I am. I won't allow a child of mine to grow up in a place like this! If I can't get out of here before it's born—"

"How long have you got?" Kalie asked, grabbing both of Larren's hands in her own and holding on tight.

"Three moonspans."

"Then we'll leave before then, I promise." Larren collapsed, sobbing, against Kalie, who held her, whispering soothing words that neither of them heard. It was just another promise, she told herself. One of many she might not be able to keep. But she would try. The woman she had been two years ago couldn't have dreamed of even that much.

The women returned at sunset, furious at Kalie for removing her veil. When it was once again in place, Kalie was led from the stifling tent to the hot, but breathable, air outside. She could see nothing through the veil, and had to depend on the chattering women who surrounded her to reach the ceremonial site.

As soon as they stopped, the women began singing. It was a long song, about the joys of marriage and the happy bride awaiting her groom. Kalie could hear, but not see, the crowd who joined in for the chorus, clapping their hands at intervals.

She couldn't tell how many people were attending the wedding, but it sounded like most of the camp. Finally, there was the thunderous sound of hooves, and the women surrounding her scattered, shrieking in mock terror at the bride's impending abduction. At least she hoped it was mock.

The noise grew louder, and she could smell the horses. Then a hand grabbed her and pulled her neatly up onto the horse.

Kalie hoped it was Riyik.

Other riders followed as they rode onto the steppes, slowly falling behind, and eventually "losing" their quarry, and the now married couple continued on alone.

Finally they stopped. Riyik helped Kalie slide from Thunder's back, and carefully removed her veil. She saw he had brought them to the hillside where they had made their pact the day before. The deepening twilight and cool breezes made the place even more inviting now.

"So that was an Aahken wedding?" Kalie asked. She had seen a few, but had paid little attention.

Riyik nodded. "Now I am supposed to take you violently on the grass, with only the sky god for a witness."

Kalie shook her head. "How did your people get this way?"

"This is a harsh land. What else could it breed but harsh people?" Riyik seemed lost in thought, as if intrigued by his own insight. Then he asked, "How is it done among your people? I know men and women mate as they choose, but surely some of them choose to spend their lives together. Is there not a ceremony marking that event?"

"Oh, yes. We have Joinings. When two people —well, it's usually two people—announce their intention to form a union. A priestess blesses them in the name of the Mother, and the couple exchange vows, and recite poetry that they have composed themselves. And course there's a feast."

"That much our traditions have in common. The feast is already beginning. When we return, we will be expected to sit together for a time, while men drink to our health and future, and women bring us choice morsels of food."

"How long will we have to be there?" Kalie stifled a yawn.

"Not long. For you anyway. The women who attended you will bear you to the tent, while I am expected to drink for most of the night."

"Sounds about right," Kalie sighed. After all, the man had already gotten what he wanted. And if he wanted more, after carousing with his friends all night, he had only to wake his sleeping wife and demand it.

"It will likely be a short feast. No one wants to face an early start and a long ride while sick from too much kumis. We can go back now." Riyik stood and reached to pull Kalie to her feet.

"We'd be done already?" Kalie blurted, recalling some of her own sweet nights in the fields. In the time she and Riyik had been here, Kalie and her partners would have barely begun.

Riyik looked at her curiously, and Kalie felt herself blush crimson. "Sorry," she said. "It's just... another of our differences."

"Someday," said Riyik. "I hope you will decide to show me just how different."

Riyik had spoken lightly, as if in jest, but Kalie sensed he was serious. And she could think of nothing to say in answer. The ride back was uncomfortable for both of them.

Once they reached the camp, however, they were quickly swept into the loud and wild feast, already in full swing. Kalie was able to enjoy some of the food, and ignore most of the warriors' toasts, which all seemed to involve advice for Riyik about beatings or sex—or both together.

None to soon, Kalie was again whisked away by a gaggle of women, this time to the tent of which she was now the mistress. She lay on her fine new sheepskin blankets, not sleeping as the sounds of celebrations grew less noisy and finally died; not even when Riyik crawled quietly into the tent, and lay down in its far side.

As his breathing slowed and he began to snore, Kalie wondered: was that what she was waiting for. Proof that he would keep his word, even after the wedding? Fine then, she should be asleep now. But she remained stubbornly awake.

A new thought struck, but perhaps not so new

after all. Was she hoping Riyik would break his word? Cross the barrier between them, and do what she wanted, but no longer possessed the ability to ask for on her own?

The thought appalled her, but there in the darkness, with no one to hear her thoughts, Kalie could finally admit that she did want Riyik. That was nothing to be ashamed of, she told herself. Strange as it seemed, Riyik was a good man. There were probably others here who were as well. Kalie should be pleased to learn the damage done to her might not be permanent after all. To trust a man again, to take pleasure in his touch…that would be a fine thing.

If it were possible. If she wasn't here on mission to save her people, which would probably require her to kill indiscriminately, or somehow induce these people to kill each other. Without regard for who was good and who was bad.

Not the best time to be thinking about romance.

Besides, Kalie was not completely certain she was barren. She couldn't risk becoming pregnant now.

At last she drifted into a peaceful sleep, and dreamed of the Goddess in her maiden form, who whispered to Kalie erotic suggestions that no maiden had any right to know about.

Chapter 21

They began the journey to the site of the final gathering of summer the next day.

In the course of that journey, Kalie became mistress of an Aahken household, which consisted of her daughter, her stepson, her husband, Agafa and the only two shadow women left alive who had not found anyplace else to live. While others might whisper that Riyik must be a poor warrior indeed to provide only the lowest order of slaves for his wife, at least he finally had a proper household, which, everyone agreed, Kalie managed quite well for a barbarian.

Managing Riyik's household turned out to be easy for her, in part because she wanted to pay him back for his many kindnesses to her. But also because she left most of the actual work to the other women—far more skilled at it than she—while she concentrated on the work that brought her to this land.

She watched Haraak, spying on his meetings when she could, and receiving information from a growing network when she could not. Three tribes were to join with the Aahken at the Gathering, and form Haraak's mighty federation: the Wolf, the Hansi, and the Spears of Malquor. No assassinations occurred on the journey, but both Kalie and Riyik heard whispers of several such plans.

She took pleasure in watching Varena walk with her head high, sometimes in the company of highborn girls who had snubbed her before, but more often with the few friends she had had when she was Maalke's slave: daughters of slave women, with little hope of being more than slaves themselves. To them,

Varena was a fairy tale made flesh and blood; they seemed to gain strength just by touching her. And when other women in the camp shook their heads at Varena's bizarre habit of sharing food and friendship with those who were now her inferiors, Kalie beamed with pride.

Varena was not the only one whose status had risen. Kalie tried to follow Varena's good advice when women whose previous behavior towards her had ranged from indifference to outright cruelty, now greeted her politely or sought to include her in their gossip. She smiled, and listened, and whenever possible, asked them questions about why they did things a certain way, or how a particular custom had come about.

But inevitably, someone would make a remark so casual in its cruelty, or show pride in something so appalling, that Kalie would lose her tight rein on her temper, and tell them that this wasn't a good time to talk, she had to go boil a baby like a good Ahken woman, or that she preferred the company of human beings not animals.

Not surprisingly, most of them walked away as angry as Kalie herself was. A few, however seemed genuinely confused, and stayed to ask Kalie what she was talking out.

And perhaps because now her time and labor belonged to her, or perhaps because she was finally free of some of the rage she had carried for so long, Kalie took the time and made the effort to explain to these women exactly what she meant. She finally found the words that could convey her own confusion at the behavior that she saw among the people of Aahk, and how different it might be if the women—all the women—worked together, rather than against each other.

Kalie wasn't surprised when most of them shook their heads and walked away, but she was when the rest stayed to hear more. There were other changes afoot as well; so subtle Kalie could almost believe she was imagining them—yet they were there.

Children always occupied themselves on the seasonal treks with games of make believe, and as long as they kept moving and did their required chores, the adults never stopped them. But from the first day of this late summer journey, Kalie saw little girls playing at being goddesses and priestesses. They weren't getting it right: the goddesses they played were all consorts to male gods, and the priestesses acted like haughty first wives. But blended into those games were enough elements of Kalie's recent teachings that she worried for their safety. Yet she couldn't bring herself to stop them.

Older girls and several women approached her in all seriousness, asking for more stories of her homeland, medicines to prevent conception, or just a sympathetic ear. Kalie treated every question, every confidence as the fragile treasure that it was, and prayed more than she had in her life that the Goddess would guide her answers.

One thing Kalie could not do, however, was follow her Goddess's advice about Riyik.

It should have been easy: they got along well during the journey, telling each other stories of their childhoods, working together to help Yarik walk, teasing Varena about possible suitors, and even speculating about what life would be like for them when they journeyed west to Kalie's home.

Best of all, whenever there was time after setting up camp for the night, Riyik continued teaching Kalie to ride. Blossom became her horse, as much as Thunder was Riyik's. Riding together, Kalie decided, brought them closer than even sharing a bed would have.

Yet whenever Riyik grew silent and brooding, Kalie found all she could do for him was give him space to think. She couldn't even ask him what was wrong. Perhaps it had been trained out of her, although she had no fear he would beat her, as Maalke would have beaten Altia for disturbing him in such a mood.

Kalie suspected Riyik's concerns had more to do with his own loss of status than about what sacrifices he might have to make when leaving his people. He had clearly fallen from Haraak's favor, and while speculation ran high as to why, no one seemed certain. Riyik was not invited to Haraak's meetings, and warriors who had once offered him their daughters no longer sought him out for anything. Kahlar, his own tribal chief, still sought his advice, but now he did so in secret, never inviting Riyik to his tent.

Kalie had feared this was because of his marriage to her, but Brenia laughed when she brought it up. If anything, the opposite was assumed: highborn women who disapproved of a slave marrying so far above herself seemed to find it amusing that the upstart foreigner had not gained what she hoped; had not married so well after all.

And she had to admit, Riyik seemed happy enough. He spent most of their travel time in the company of lower ranked warriors or men who, like himself, preferred riding alone. Some of the latter group were highly ranked, and might have had a place in Kariik's council, but to a man, they scorned the company of the puppet king or Haraak's dreams of conquest. The rest were viewed as misfits, just a step away from a mysterious "accident" any time they rode out with the others.

With these men, Riyik now talked and joked and practiced his skill at hunting and fighting. On the fourth night of the journey, Riyik invited them—and their wives and children, for those who were married —to share a meal together. Kalie was nervous at first, but soon found herself enjoying the company of this small group of women. And when Riyik asked her to tell tales from her own world, she realized who they were: the people whom Riyik was considering bringing to the west.

Taking a deep breath, Kalie began to tell stories she had never before told in this land: tales of courageous women who braved impossible odds, and compassionate men who wept tears of magical power. And tales of the Goddess.

Some of the men laughed at things that were not meant to be funny. Others grew bored and made excuses to leave early. But some listened with interest. And some, after thanking both Kalie and Riyik for a fine evening, left in thoughtful discussion with their wives.

"Very clever," Kalie whispered later that night, when Riyik returned from walking the perimeter of the camp.

"What was?" Riyik asked.

"Suggesting that I tell stories from my home. Already I can see that some of them might be able to make a life there."

"Not all of them, though," said Riyik. "I'm

looking for men who won't try to set themselves up as kings the moment they see how your world is run, and it's a dizzying feat. It's not that the men who were here tonight are greedy or ambitious, it's just that it's been bred into their bones to take anything that another man isn't strong enough to keep."

"Some of them were listening to what their wives had to say about the stories. Those might be the ones to start with. Men who can do that might have an easier time in a world where all women speak their minds."

Riyik nodded, but seemed unconvinced. "I won't bring anyone to your home who might harm it. You know that, don't you Kalie?"

Kalie felt a rush of tenderness to this man: her enemy; her friend. "I do know that, Riyik," she began haltingly. "Just as I would never ask you to kill those you are oath bound to serve, to protect me. If you are troubled..." She had no idea how to say the rest, and was relieved when the whisper of bare feet on hard ground alerted them to the presence of a veiled woman who dropped to her knees on the ground where they lay.

"Forgive me, lord," she whispered, clearly expecting to be beaten for disturbing a man and wife in bed, yet just as clearly puzzled by their separate bedrolls. "My master has sent me to ask that Kalie attend to his wife in her labor."

"Cassia?" Kalie asked, sitting up.

The timid slave nodded. Kalie realized she was one of the new ones Maalke had bought with the horses Riyik had given him in exchange for herself and Varena. "How far along is she?" Kalie asked, pulling on her robe and searching for her veil.

The girl only shook her head, trying to hurry Kalie along without actually touching her.

Cursing herself in the language of the beastmen, Kalie followed the slave to where Maalke's household camped. She had barely spoken to Cassia since the start of the trek. Every day, she had intended to find her, ask how she was, and brew her new medicine. Yet every day, it seemed, she was distracted by some new question about how things were done in the West, some new rumor of Haraak's plans, or the chance to learn more of the art of horseback riding.

Cassia lay between two braziers, breathing deeply between contractions. Her panicked face relaxed when she saw Kalie. Maalke's other slaves— all young and pretty—fluttered around uselessly, while Altia looked on dispassionately. Irisa, Kalie noticed, lay beside Maalke, feigning sleep. Apparently, the woman who had once wished miscarriage or death on her rival was hoping to avoid any participation in the birth.

Maalke stood up from his place next to Irisa and loomed menacingly over Kalie. "She has waited a long time to give me son," he said, glaring haughtily at his former slave. "See that she does so. And see that she lives through it, to bear me another."

Kalie stared across the brazier at the man who had once filled her nights with anguish and shame. A strength she had never known filled her being as she saw only a pathetic old man who could not even voice what little feeling he had for his wife without veiling it behind threats. Though less than two hands of years separated them in age, Kalie knew that Maalke would not live to see another son after this one. His color, his breathing, and the kumis on his breath all spoke of a disease eating him from the inside.

"I come here out of love for Cassia, and no other reason," Kalie said, meeting his gaze with cold contempt. "You no longer tell me what to do, Maalke. Don't ever try to again." Then she turned her back on the gaping warrior, and set about making Cassia more comfortable. But not before she enjoyed seeing Maalke blanche, and hearing the gasps of the slave women.

"Get me a torch," Kalie told one of the slaves as she rearranged the cushions and blankets that Cassia had tangled. Hesitantly, the woman did so.

"When did the pains begin?" Kalie asked as she adjusted the light and began to examine Cassia.

"This afternoon." Cassia teeth clenched as another contraction gripped her.

"Why didn't you call me then?" Kalie asked in disbelief.

Between contractions, Cassia had time to grow confused and hesitant. "I could not simply…send for you, Kalie. You are a free woman of high standing. Having once been my slave—and I knew how you felt about that—I did not know how you would feel about me now."

"And I never bothered to see how you were," Kalie sighed. "Cassia, I hated being a slave, but I never hated you." Not entirely true, at least not at first. But that hardly mattered now.

"I was hoping I could hold it off. We'll arrive at the gathering place in two or three days—" Cassia broke off as another spasm took her.

They were coming very close together. It might not be so long. But how much harm had the grueling journey done to Cassia? Could Kalie have found a way to keep labor at bay until they arrived? She shook the thoughts away. "Have you sent for Brenia?"

Cassia shook her head. "You were the first person I thought of." She gripped Kalie's hand, looking frightened and much younger than her twenty years.

Kalie squeezed back reassuringly. "Let us ask her to join us. I have assisted in many births, but I would like the help of one who has been through it herself." One of the slaves hurried off to get Brenia.

"It's a moon early," Cassia whispered.

"But far enough along for the babe to be born strong and healthy," Kalie said. She knew many babies born this early were fine, but in this land, with their beliefs that the weak should die, even simple techniques that could help a premature baby through the first critical days might not be available.

But it was the mother that concerned Kalie more. She didn't think that Cassia would be able to just drop the baby and get up with the dawn to resume the journey, as a nomad woman was expected to do. And if she could not, what then?

Brenia arrived, and things got better. She seemed to know just what to say to calm the laboring woman, and how to distract her while Kalie slid her hand inside Cassia to determine the baby's position, and learn how much the birth canal had widened.

"Soon," she said with a confident smile.

When the baby finally came, after much pain for the writhing mother, and very little screaming, for that would have disgraced her, everything was blessedly simple. Cassia bore down as instructed, and Kalie saw the baby's head. There was one bad moment, as Cassia pushed, and nothing happened besides more pain. But then the head popped out in a rush, and Kalie barely had time to catch it before the rest of the body followed. The baby was small, but perfectly formed and squirming silently in her grasp. She thumped its feet, and was rewarded by the high, thin wail of new life.

"It's a boy!" Brenia shouted. Kalie laughed. So concerned was she with getting the child to breathe, she had forgotten to look. Cassia would be so happy, she thought, as exhaustion crept upon her.

"Kalie, she is bleeding too much!" Brenia cried in alarm. "I can't stop it!"

Kalie leapt back from the stupor to which she had been about to surrender. "Yes you can!" she shouted before she could even see what was happening.

"Give me my son," Cassia whispered. Fear clutched Kalie's heart at the weakness of the sound.

Brenia set the boy gently on his mother's chest while she struggled to pack her birth canal with absorbent wool, applying as much pressure as she dared.

"Raise her legs! Raise the whole lower part of her body!" Kalie shouted. She pulled the blankets and cushions from under Cassia's back and head, and set them under her legs.

"What? Why?" Brenia stared at her, baffled.

Kalie struggled to find the words to explain something she half remembered from Hot Springs, but Brenia seemed to grasp it.

"I don't think it will work for this much bleeding, but we can try."

"More pressure!" Kalie cried, then, "Silence!" as the slave girls began the mourning song of a woman who dies giving birth.

"Too much will kill her womb," said Brenia.

"She already has the son she was so willing to die for! Better that Cassia never have another than that the living one lose his mother!"

Finally, the bleeding slowed to a normal level for after childbirth. Cassia was weak, and frighteningly pale, but she lived—and so did the child. It was a miracle all around.

Maalke came to see his new son, just as the sky began to lighten in the east. "He shall be named Enak," he said. With that, Cassia stirred, though Kalie hoped she would sleep through it, and begin to regain her strength. "I feared you would never give me a child, Beloved. Now that you have, I will give you new slippers and the richest of furs. And when we plunder the cities of the west, I will bring you jewels for your hair, and a dozen new slaves who will wait on you alone." Cassia smiled and drifted back to sleep.

Maalke turned to Kalie. "Make sure she's ready to travel when the sun is up."

"Go to hell, Little Prick," Kalie told him, then went to find her bedroll.

Chapter 22

Kalie awoke to the gentle pressure of Riyik's hand on her shoulder. The sun was high above the eastern plains, and most of the camp was already moving in that direction. Cassia had been judged strong enough to be carried on a blanket slung between two slow moving horses, while her husband paced angrily, mortified that his wife was responsible for the delayed departure of the entire clan. Worse than that, Maalke was now last in line, the others already far ahead of his family.

Kalie stayed near Cassia for the last two days of their journey to the big gathering. From what she had gleaned from the women around her, Cassia was recovering more slowly than a woman of Aahk was expected to after childbirth. Given the difficulties she had experienced, no one was surprised.

Since Kalie had lost a night's sleep to help Cassia, Riyik insisted she ride pillion with him on Thunder so she could doze if she needed to. She was riding with him that way when they reached the gathering.

The sight spread out before her took her breath away. Black tents stretched to the far horizon. Three tribes were camped together, something unheard of in this part of the world. Kalie had come here to make the tribes turn on each other; to kill until there was no one left to threaten her world. But at the sight of them, doubt filled her: how could she fight this?

Then, a strange kind of resolve filled her. Not an otherworldly power; just the detached certainty that whatever was to happen—not just this year but for centuries to come—was going to be decided here, on this plain in the next moon span. It would be, as the beastmen would say, a glorious battle.

"Kalie?" Riyik was gazing up at her from the ground. "Are you ready to get down, now? Thunder needs to be fed and rubbed down."

While Kalie had been lost in whatever vision had seized her, the tribe had arrived at their destination. Suddenly overwhelmed by the noise and stench of what must have been at least three thousand people, and who knew how many animals, Kalie slid from the horse.

"Are you all right?" Riyik asked, steadying her.

"Yes, fine." She looked around. "There's just…so many of you."

"But remember, fewer than half the folk here are warriors."

Kalie looked up in surprise. Had Riyik been reading her mind? Or was he, too, calculating the strength of each side in the upcoming battle?

But he was already leading Thunder to the horse-runs, so she couldn't ask.

There was no lake in this new summer campsite, only a spring, which was reserved for the horses, and a well, which would provide water for everyone else. That was good news for Kalie, for it meant that every morning, women would have to wait in long lines for their turn to get the day's supply of water. And while Kalie now had servants to perform such chores for her, she insisted on doing it herself. There was no better source of information in the camp.

By the time she returned to Riyik's tent on the first morning, she thought her head would explode from the abundance of gossip, slander and quarrels she had overheard. Riyik took one look at her, and suggested they go for a ride.

"Too much noise for you?" he asked her as they mounted their horses.

"Too much everything!"

Riyik laughed. "It's like that for me, too, the first day the whole tribe is together again after a winter of just my clan."

"But now there's three times the number than even you're used to!"

"I wonder if Haraak has at last bitten off more than he can chew. How about a race?"

"Do you think I'm ready?"

"You've taken to riding like you were born to it." Riyik smiled as Kalie blushed at his praise. "Perhaps we should..."

Kalie was never quite sure what happened next.

Blossom reared up with a terrifying scream. Kalie's attempt to do what Riyik had taught her for moments like this only resulted in the horse needing to buck twice to throw her from her back rather than once.

Kalie landed on her back with a bone-jarring thump, so stunned she could only stare at the sight of a flailing hoof just above her face—and moving down until it filled her whole vision.

Riyik pulled her out of the way, just as Blossom's hoof grazed her forehead and took off a clump of hair. With that, the blessed numbness of a moment before gave way in a wash of pain throughout Kalie's whole body that nearly left her senseless.

Sometime later, she became aware of Riyik kneeling beside her. He dropped a dead snake into the grass and began feeling her body for injuries. "I'm all right," she said, and then realized no sound was coming out.

"Lie still," said Riyik as he continued his examination. In some corner of Kalie's mind, the healer she had become assessed Riyik's manner and approved.

"I don't think anything is broken," Riyik said. "But you've got a nasty scalp wound." Kalie's hand flew to her head and came away bloody. "Don't worry, they always bleed like that. Camp isn't far. Do you think you can walk?"

Kalie wasn't sure, but she let Riyik help her stand. "Where are the horses?" she asked, confused. The grassland was blurry, and the horses were nowhere in sight. She thought she could hear them, but it was hard to tell over the buzzing in her ears.

Riyik nodded toward the dead snake. "It leapt up right in front of Blossom. I can't tell if he bit her." He picked up the brown and white serpent and set it gingerly in his pack. "Fortunately, this one's just a karn, not the deadly basilisk which looks nearly the same. But to a horse it doesn't matter: any snake will scare it to near madness, and when that happens, gods help even the best rider."

Everything was spinning and Kalie was having trouble hearing Riyik, but one thing flowed clearly into her muddled brain: snakes frighten horses. Of course, she already knew that. Didn't she? Maybe. She couldn't seem to concentrate. But there was something about snakes and horses that seemed like it should be important.

As they reached the camp, she noticed that Riyik was carrying her. When had that happened?

People swirled around them, exclaiming, asking questions, hurrying to gather up medicines and supplies.

"Has she got the brain swell?" someone asked.

"Now do you see why women shouldn't ride?" demanded another.

"I was watching them," Kalie heard a younger man say—she thought it was one of the men Riyik hoped to bring west. "She kept her seat longer than some warriors I've seen when a snake frightened their horse!"

They went into their tent. Riyik set Kalie gently onto her bedding, and every part of her body screamed in pain. Then someone was efficiently cleaning her head wound with a stinging ointment. She saw that it was Sarika, handmaiden to chief Zavan's mother. Riyik brought her something murky in a bone cup.

"Drink," he told her. "It will dull the pain and help you sleep. But we'll have to wake you up and check your eyes every so often. If you have the brain swell, we can't let you sleep too long—or you might not wake up."

Kalie nodded to let him know she understood —she had done the same thing herself at Hot Springs —and instantly regretted the movement. The drink tasted terrible, but soon after, the pain became more tolerable. She should ask Riyik what was in it. The healers at Hot Springs would want to know about it. That was the last coherent thought she had for a long time.

Kalie was running toward the setting sun. Monsters were chasing her and she had to warn her people. There! A city in the distance; she was almost home. Then horses with men growing from their backs rode between her and safety. There was the sound of harsh, masculine laughter.

She turned to run a different way, but found a row of poles with rotting heads on top. Screaming, Kalie tried to find another way to run, only to find a hundred hissing snakes blocking her path.

Suddenly, the snakes turned to face the horses, and now it was they who screamed, falling on the ground, while the men attached to them fell broken and helpless beneath them.

"Snakes!" Kalie cried, sitting up.

"Shh, it's all right, the snake is dead." Agafa took Kalie's hand and gently eased her back to her blankets. Kalie peered through the open tent flaps at the night sky. The moon told her it was nearly dawn. Had she been asleep since the previous morning?

"There were snakes," Kalie said, trying to hold on to the remnant of the dream. Something in the dream was very important; she had to remember…

"But not here," Agafa whispered so as not to wake the others sleeping in the tent. "Do you want some more of the pain drink?"

The dream faded and Kalie felt slightly nauseous, though whether from the nightmare or the concussion, she wasn't sure. She was still in pain, but it was more of a dull ache than burning fire. "More of the drink, please," she whispered.

She meant to tell Agafa to get some sleep; that she didn't need to be watched, or if she did, get someone else to take a turn, but sleep crept over her before she could form the words. All Kalie remembered as darkness took her was that horses were afraid of snakes, and even the deadliest warrior couldn't kill anyone if he was trapped beneath a horse.

By the next morning, Kalie was feeling better, although she still doubted she could get out of bed. Riyik made her, however, and insisted she walk in a large circle around Chief Kahlar's section of the camp. While the aching was now confined to her back and neck, each step made them hurt more, and despite her healer's training that told her that exercise was a necessary part of recovery, she still complained bitterly to Riyik.

Her gentle husband had become tyrant, much to the amusement of the rest of the clan. When Kalie was ready to stop after one circuit and refuse to take another step, Cassia appeared beside her, quietly offering to keep Kalie company, as she needed exercise as well.

Kalie could hardly admit she couldn't keep up with a woman who had nearly died giving birth just days before. Cassia was nearly as white as a bleached bone, but she walked slowly, with purposeful measured steps, breathing deeply as Kalie had taught her.

"My milk came in yesterday, did you know?" Cassia asked.

"No, I didn't," said Kalie, trying to muster enthusiasm. "I don't remember much after the horse threw me."

Cassia shook her head to Kalie's offer of an arm for support, and shot her a sideways glance. "I hope you'll take that fall as a warning to stay away from matters best left to men."

Kalie nodded cautiously. "Perhaps I don't need any more riding lessons."

Cassia sighed; a sound of great relief. "My

milk took so long! I was afraid I would have to ask another woman to nurse my son. Now I can do it myself."

"I was afraid your milk wouldn't come at all," said Kalie. "As difficult as the birth was."

Cassia moved her fingers in the sign against evil. "That would truly be a curse! Waiting all my life to bear a child, then not being able to feed him when he finally gets here."

"It would be sad, of course. But surely, with so many nursing mothers in your tribe…"

Cassia shook her head. "What good is a woman who can't nurse her own child?"

Kalie sighed. "So many things make a woman useless in this place!" she said.

At last the circuit was completed, and both women returned to Riyik's tent and sank gratefully to the soft cushions that had been wedding gifts from both Brenia and Cassia. Riyik approached Kalie with a steaming pitch-lined basket. Kalie glared at him. "What new torture are you going to attempt?" she asked, emphasizing the last word.

"Something you'll like a lot more than walking." Riyik set the basket beside Kalie, and she recognized oil from rendered sheep's fat mixed with herbs she couldn't quiet identify. "It's something we use after riding accidents like yours. When rubbed into the skin it soothes sore muscles. I'll rub some on you if you'll let me."

Kalie was about to exclaim in shock that the people in this place had actually developed the art of massage, but decided not to risk the good humor surrounding her. Besides, she hadn't had a good massage in more than a year—nor truly enjoyed one in more than seven. Even an unskilled masseuse would be better than trying it herself in her current state.

To Kalie's delight, Riyik worked her sore muscles with a skill that rivaled the best Healers in Hot Springs. The oil soaked deep into her skin and swept her away in utter bliss.

With slow, deep pressure, Riyik's hands traveled down the length of her back, then up again, drawing the pain from her aching shoulders. Even her tense neck muscles relaxed beneath his hands.

Kalie nearly fell asleep, but to fall asleep meant missing out on this moment, and that she was not willing to do. She heard the others leave the tent, so now she and Riyik were alone. It occurred to Kalie that Riyik might choose to push this encounter into something beyond a backrub. Or that she could roll over and invite him to do so.

But she did not, and the rhythmic motions of his hands continued exactly as they had, with variations to give her greater pleasure and nothing more. And for the first time since coming to this land, Kalie relaxed completely, knowing she was safe.

Just before she drifted off into an exquisite sleep, Kalie decided that if they both lived long enough, she would one day indeed invite Riyik to do more.

Chapter 23

Kalie was several days in recovering. But Agafa managed the household well enough and Varena drew the water, and reported to Kalie all she heard each day at the well. Others came to visit, and Kalie was truly surprised at how many friends she had in this land. That hadn't been part of her original plan, any more than getting married here was, but she found herself deeply moved nonetheless.

They came in groups to keep her company, and offer advice and herbal teas to speed her recovery. And they came alone, to ask advice on personal matters, or questions about the west, and what life would be like for them if the king actually decided to lead them all there. They came with news and gossip, often with hope of a reward, but sometimes, just because they knew Kalie was interested in such things.

On the fourth morning after the accident, when Kalie had decided she was getting up and resuming her duties no matter how bad she felt, Agafa opened the tent flap to admit Danica, mother of Chief Zavan, who requested a private audience.

Agafa and the other servants fled before Kalie had the chance to tell them to. Varena scooped up Yarik and hurried after them. Kalie was alone in the tent with one of the most powerful women in the tribe, who, she noticed, had not even brought Sarika with her.

Interesting.

"I have wanted to speak with you alone for some time," the old woman began.

"I would gladly have attended you any time

you summoned me," Kalie answered, in the careful tones one used in addressing a woman of high status.

Danica shook her head dismissively. "Too many listening ears; too many wagging tongues. I had to wait for a pretext…"

"Such as visiting an invalid?"

Danica nodded. "Not that I would wish such a thing upon you. But it happened, and I knew I had to act soon—before you were up and about, stirring every pot and holding court among your followers."

Kalie felt a sudden chill. "Perhaps I have grown fond of resting all day while others do the work, and will simply linger in my tent all season."

Danica's wrinkled face split in a grin of surprisingly strong, yellowed teeth, worn low into blackened gums. "You could no more lay about your tent all day than I could, Kalie. I have been thinking a great deal on the things you said at the Summer Festival." She snorted. "Strange, how for the women of this land, there wasn't such a thing until you gave it to us. And I have been listening to what others have said of you since then as well."

"Surely the wild stories of a mad foreigner are of no concern to so lofty a person as yourself."

"Ah, but I am greatly fond of stories," said Danica. "I especially love tales of greedy men whose own actions bring about their downfall. One in particular, but I can't recall the ending. I thought perhaps, with all the stories you know, you could help me. It's about a man who prizes women above even his horses. But he is faithless to them, always acquiring more, then cruelly tossing them aside when he tires of them."

"That sounds more like everyday life in your

tribe than a story," said Kalie.

"True. But what's strange about this story is how he met his end. You see, while many men wished him dead, and plotted how they would accomplish it, this man was slain in his bed by one of his own women! But I can't seem to remember what happened after that."

"Surely she was put to death in a most gruesome fashion," said Kalie.

"Perhaps," said Danica, her brow even more wrinkled than usual as she sought to remember. "Yet, strange as it sounds, I think she escaped. One would assume she was merely a tool, doing the bidding of one of this man's many enemies, but what made this story so different is that she acted on her own. Why would she do such a thing? Was she jealous of his many other loves, perhaps? Or did she love another man, whom she fled with in the night...?"

"Perhaps she loved a woman, and they fled together to place where they could love openly, with no men at all."

"Yes! That was it!" Danica was enjoying herself.

Kalie was not. Fearful that someone would come to the tent and ruin her chance to learn what the crafty old woman's game was, she spoke in a rush. "What have you truly come for, Danica?"

"I want to know if your people—my grandmother's people—are as wise as I have begun to dream they are. For I think it was no accident that you came to be among the tribute that Haraak brought home from the west. I think perhaps that you wanted to save your people from mine—just as Basha wanted to save her daughter. Our customs—our peculiar blindness—gave her the means, just as Haraak's greed gave you the means. And the greatest joke of all is that, even now, he cannot see it."

"But are there others who can?" Kalie asked.

"None that I know of. And my thoughts are just the ramblings of an old woman. But it seems to me that if a people who had neither horses nor warriors wanted to save themselves from an invasion, the surest way to do it would be to insert weapons directly inside their enemy's camp. Weapons no would recognize as such."

"That is an interesting idea. For a story, I mean. It is certainly wild enough."

"Yes. It could, of course, be nothing more than that. But you are so gifted, Kalie. Perhaps you could craft it into something worth listening to on a long winter's night."

"I have actually been hoping to create a new story, but could find no inspiration. I think you have just provided me with much. What can I offer you in return?"

"Oh…simply the chance to see for myself how the story ends. My time on this earth grows short, but if I could see the land of my grandmother just once before I die—just to see for myself what is true and what is not—I would count it a life well lived."

"And if I could live to bring you there," said Kalie, "I, too, would have lived a worthy life."

Danica stayed a while longer, speaking of Chief Kahlar's wife, the dreaded Leja, and how a wasting illness kept her within her tent, while Kahlar fretted desperately, and sent for all the best healers, but Kalie heard little of it. Then Danica rose gracefully to her feet and ducked out of the tent.

And while Kalie had planned to get up and go out herself, she found herself seated in the tent for the rest of the day, with much to think about.

The next morning, Kalie woke late, which surprised her, for by now she was quite sick of sleeping, and desperately afraid she had missed something important. Just as she had finished dressing herself to leave the tent—now in soft linen, rather than scratchy felt—yet another visitor came to the door flap.

Varena hurried to open it, while Kalie planned to invite whomever it was to walk with her through the camp, for she was not staying inside another day.

But the voice she heard offering deferential greetings to the daughter of the tent drove all such thoughts away, for she spoke in the lilting accents of the west.

"Alessa?" she barely whispered, as Varena barely got out of the way as the other woman leapt into the tent and caught Kalie in a fierce embrace.

Chapter 24

"Where have been? What are you doing here?" Kalie held Alessa by both arms, afraid to let go lest this vision of her past vanish into smoke.

"I'm with the Wolf tribe now," Alessa said, as calm and dignified as ever. As if the Wolf tribe was just another stop on her journey, and she would move on as soon as she was ready.

"Yes, I'd heard that," said Kalie, remembering. "But how did you find me? How do you have the freedom to move about on your own?"

"I can move about on my own, in part, because of you, Kalie. That bag of healing herbs you took from Maris's gear and gave to me helped me establish myself as a healer from the beginning."

"Surely your own skills would have done that..." Kalie began.

"Eventually, perhaps. But this place is so primitive! Those medicines gave me stature that would have taken me years to achieve while I learned the local herbs—and waited for permission to go out and look for them." Alessa grimaced. "I learned you were here the day your tribe arrived. I'm always seeking news on the women from the west—though I think I'd have heard of you anyway. You seem to have made quite an impression on the people out here."

The open admiration on the young priestess's face caused Kalie to turn to see who Alessa was looking at.

There was no one else in the tent.

Kalie shrugged, uncomfortable. "I do what I can. Probably nothing compared to what you've done here." She settled back ready to listen.

"I've made some progress," said Alessa. "But I move slowly. I guess it's Maris's teaching, still at work. My first 'owner' gave me to Nelek, the king of the Wolf Tribe, as a gift to help forge this alliance that Haraak's working on."

Kalie smiled. "I see we've both kept track of the same enemy. Oh, Alessa, it's so good not to be alone in knowing what's going on! Or in trying to stop it."

Alessa looked surprised. "Alone? But what of the others? I heard about poor Maylene of course, and Traea. But surely Larren…"

"Larren has all she can manage with a baby she hates growing inside her. Kestra lives as a horsewoman—if you can call it living—seeming without memory of who she once was. You heard that Dara took her own life last winter?"

Alessa looked stricken. "I had heard she escaped."

"Well, in a manner of speaking, she did."

"But not the way you did, all those years ago." The admiration was back in Alessa's eyes. If others could have seen Kalie that way when she first returned home, all those years ago, how different things might have been…

Kalie shook her head. They had much to discuss and little time.

"I must not stay long," Alessa said, as if sharing Kalie's thoughts. "I have been looking for an excuse to come find you since I discovered where you were in this vast camp. I got it today when Nelek sent me to examine Leja, and see if I could help her."

Kalie remembered Danica's news from the

previous day about Leja's illness, and how frantic Kahlar was to have his beloved wife back to her old ferocious self. "Yes, that would be good for Nelek, if his concubine saved the wife of one of Kariik's chiefs. Kahlar would owe him."

"I'm not sure I can do much for her beyond easing the pain. She has a growth in her breast which is poisoning the rest of her body."

Kalie nodded. She knew of such things from her time at Hot Springs. "Forgive me if I can't sympathize. Leja has been a cruel and vicious enemy to many people here—myself included."

"I know," Alessa said sadly. "I've heard stories about her. Even today, in her pain and weakness, her strength shows through. I've met many like her in my travels through this land. Can you imagine what assets such people could be back in our world, once they learned to use their strength for good, rather than evil?"

"I would first have to believe it was possible," Kalie replied tartly.

"Of course, I may be seeing what I want to see," said Alessa. "That strength will keep Leja alive —and in pain—longer than most others in her condition. And her death, inevitable as it is, will be blamed on me."

Kalie sighed. "More accurately, your inability to defy simple reality will anger Kahlar and reflect badly on Nelek, who will take it out on you."

"I try not to take such things personally, or let them taint my calling and my oath. But it is difficult."

Knowing what such a perversion of the sacred art of healing must be doing to Alessa, Kalie shuddered. Then, inspiration struck. "If you could, I'd like you to examine my step-son Yarik. He was born with a clubfoot. I've done what I can for him, but his problem is just your specialty."

Alessa nodded eagerly. "Step-son? I had heard you were married to one of the warriors who brought us here, but had feared the worst. Does your adoption of his child mean that the marriage was not forced?

Kalie sagged into the cushions. "I don't know how to answer that." She had never formally adopted Yarik as she had Varena, but she had grown fond of him. She was about to try to explain her complicated situation with Riyik, and perhaps seek Alessa's advice, when her friend shook her head.

"Later, when there's time. For now, we must exchange what knowledge we have gained, and decide what is to be done."

Strength and resolve flooded Kalie. "Already three tribes have joined for an assault on the west," she said. "I fear there will be more."

"They mean to occupy our home, not just raid it," Alessa added.

"I have been seeking a weapon. But the closest I've come so far has been being thrown from a horse." Kalie described her dream of snakes and horses to Alessa.

"Interesting," said Alessa. "Dreams of snakes are always considered important, because of their close association with the Goddess; they are often Her messengers."

"I have heard of certain priestesses who work with snakes," said Kalie. "Don't they use snake venom to journey from their bodies?"

Alessa nodded. "They tend to be secretive groups—not even groups, usually. More often hermits who teach their arcane knowledge to a single apprentice. Their temples are in barren places; so remote I doubt they even know of the horsemen. Maris took me to one once."

"Could they be our weapon against the beastmen? Would there be enough of them to assemble along the eastern frontier? Could they teach snakes to attack the horses?"

"I doubt it," said Alessa. "And even if they could, I don't think they would be willing to use their snakes for such a purpose. I think we must look for a more symbolic meaning in your dream."

It was not the answer Kalie had hoped for, but it did not surprise her. "Then I guess we're back to finding a way to make them turn on each other. Or some other way to keep them from moving west."

"Preventing the tribes from moving west might already be impossible," Alessa said.

Kalie's head jerked up. "What do you mean?"

"Things are getting desperate in the east. The water is drying up and the grass is dying. The tribes have to move west."

"Which brings them in conflict with the tribes already here. So they fight for what little water or grazing land there is."

"Exactly. And the sad thing is there simply isn't enough for everyone." Alessa sighed. "When we first made plans to come here, back in Riverford, I was so certain that all we had to do was teach them to grow crops and make more efficient use of scarce resources, so they wouldn't have to fight each other."

Kalie, who had never had any faith in those plans, nevertheless felt sad for Alessa, and what had to have been a rude a wakening. "It turned out to be more complicated than that, didn't it?'"

Alessa sighed again. "Very little of this land could be used for farming, even with the most advanced techniques our people have devised. And while these people could certainly improve things if they'd let us teach them about cooperation and sharing, the fact is that there simply isn't enough water and grazing for all their animals. And the animals are their life! Either they have to kill each other to keep their numbers down, or some of them will have to leave."

"Then we need to work on ways to get them to kill each other more efficiently!" Kalie was growing impatient.

But Alessa looked shocked. "Kalie, you can't really want that!"

"You said yourself there isn't enough land to support them all! And they've developed their own way of solving the problem: they kill each other. All I'm suggesting is that we encourage them to do it on a large enough scale so that they're not a threat to us! It was why we came here."

"I don't think any two of us had exactly the same plan when we left Riverford," said Alessa. "As I recall, your original plan involved killing King Ahnaak. Instead, it was our foe Haraak who did that— and got very different results from what we were hoping for."

Kalie blushed. "That may be true, but we still have to find some way to keep these 'people' as you call them, from murdering and enslaving ours!"

Alessa set a gentle hand on Kalie's shoulder. "I know. And we will. Already you have made a huge difference among the women. And I have been seeing some encouraging results in the Wolf Tribe with both men and women."

Kalie stared. "What do you mean?"

"There are many here who are open to new ideas. It is slow work, and most of them laugh at what I say about the Goddess, but little by little, they are starting to listen. They won't accept a female deity— but some of the men are fascinated by what people can do in the west. Things they can only dream about here."

"I'm sure they find the gold and silver we have appealing. And jars of wine and food in plenty…"

"It's more than that! All right, some of the men can only hear about riches and spoils when I speak, but some are actually interested in what a world without slavery would look like. And there are plenty of men with talents and interests that would know no bounds in the west, but they're stuck being warriors for as long as they stay here! They'd embrace a better way if they had the chance!"

Kalie wanted it believe it. Had not Riyik said nearly the same thing? "If we could find a way to kill the men like Haraak, and spare the ones you speak of," she began slowly. "Or put men like that in charge, then it might work. Alessa, you know more about herbs than I do. Poison slipped into the right kumis…"

Alessa's face grew hard "I'm not going to kill anyone, Kalie. And I can't believe you would either."

"It's what I came here to do! I made that clear from the beginning."

"And Maris was equally clear that if we use the methods of beasts, we will become beasts ourselves. I still believe that."

"Traea believed it once herself. She soon

changed her mind."

"And where is she now?" Alessa's voice was soft, but her gaze thrust into Kalie like a knife. Then she looked away. "But I fear you may be right. Last winter, I saved Zolah, Nelek's first wife from death in childbirth, and delivered her of a healthy son. My status soared. I came to believe that I could make them ready to merge with our people in as little as three years."

"We don't have that long," Kalie said quietly.

"I know. I thought perhaps I could do it sooner, but now…" Alessa's voice trailed away. For the first time, she looked uncertain.

"What? What have you heard?"

The tent flap flew open, and Varena came in with the day's supply of water and gossip. Sula followed with a squirming Yarik in her arms.

Silently, Kalie cursed their timing, but there was nothing to be done. She feared she already knew what Alessa would have said.

They used what time remained to them to examine Yarik, and plan a course of treatment better than any Kalie could have done herself.

Chapter 25

Alessa's unspoken fears were confirmed the next day.

Haraak had decided the news worthy of a feast that even the women and children would attend. Kalie worked alongside all the other wives, with little opportunity to do more than catch a glimpse of Alessa all day.

When at last the sun had set and the bonfires were lit, and all of the men had been served, Kariik rose to address the assembly. Nelek of the Wolf Tribe stood with him, as did the leader of The Spears of Malquor, a scarred, pockmarked young man whose name—or title—was also Malquor.

"My people!" Kariik began. Beside him, Haraak winced. Was Kariik straying from his assigned speech already? The full moon was as bright as the torches that filled the camp. Faces stood out as clearly as if it were day, but with a strange, sinister glow.

"I stand this night, beside by my brother kings…" Here Kariik flung an arm each around Nelek and Malquor. "Evil times have come to the lands of our ancestors. To the east, the grass has withered; the water has begun to disappear.

"The Men of Aahk could struggle for what is left with the tribes who push west—and we would win!" Kariik paused for the cheering and striking of spears on the ground. "But the gods have called us toward another destiny…a greater destiny! Far to the west lies a land of grass and grain; of water flowing from every rock! Best of all, it is a land empty of men. A land ripe for the taking!" The cheering grew in volume, and Kariik had to struggle to be heard.

Finally, the crowd settled down to listen, though Kalie could see that Kariik would soon lose them. "The priests have read the signs for the coming winter. It will be the worst in living memory. Few who remain here will even live to see the spring. Therefore, on the eve of the next full moon, a mighty federation of tribes..." Kariik clasped arms with the two kings who flanked him, "...shall begin the journey west. It will be a long and difficult journey. We will not arrive before winter." Haraak was at Kariik's shoulder now, growling a warning. "But winters are far milder there than here," the young king hastened to reassure his men.

"If we are true to our gods and our ancestors, before the feast of midwinter, every man here will be as a king in that new land! With more gold and slaves than your fathers owned in their lifetimes! You will drink wine as if it were kumis, and your wives will roast whole cows as if they were sheep!"

Since she left Riverford, Kalie had wondered what she would feel when the invasion she foresaw finally became a certainty. Now it had come, and for a long time, as the cheering and dancing nomads swirled around her—she felt nothing. Then she met Alessa's eyes across the crowd. A quiet certainly shone from them, as can only come from someone committed to her beliefs beyond all doubt—or even reason. Alessa would bring the Goddess to these people or die trying. It was simple as that.

And while Kalie longed to share in so beautiful a vision, she knew she could not. She would keep these monsters from her home, even if she had to kill them to do it. And as absurd as both of them would undoubtedly sound to anyone who should happen to overhear, Kalie discovered a warm glow of calm growing inside her. She was ready. Let the battle begin.

Rumors flew over the next few days. News was brought to Kalie by an ever- expanding network of spies. It soon became clear that many small fractures already existed in the three-tribe alliance. The best solution, Kalie decided, would be to exploit those weaknesses so the tribes turned on each other.

The challenge would be convincing Alessa.

Three days had passed before the two women had the chance to speak again. The huge camped swarmed like an angry hive of bees, as they prepared for their longest journey ever.

"We have twenty-four days, not three years!" Kalie had cornered Alessa inside Riyik's tent. "No matter how strong your faith or how great your vision, that is not enough time to turn these savages into civilized people! Or even people ready to consider the concept!"

Alessa was troubled. She would not meet Kalie's eyes—but neither would she back down. "I keep praying for a sign. If the Goddess would just give me the slightest hope that She would perform a miracle along the way…"

"And has She?" Kalie pressed.

"Not yet." Alessa finally looked up, her eyes serene as ever. "Perhaps it is a test of faith."

"Perhaps the Goddess is fading from the world, and what happens next is up to us!" snapped Kalie. She hated to say such things, things that she knew would hurt Alessa, but she had to get her to see reason.

Alessa, however, showed no sign of being

upset by Kalie's words. Perhaps she knew that Kalie herself did not believe them. She was a priestess, after all.

"I did have one dream, that I'm certain was sent by the Goddess," Alessa said. "It was about you."

Kalie could not hide her interest. Alessa seemed pleased by that.

"I saw you, surrounded by warriors and firelight. You were telling a story of things they value: honor, loyalty, glory. It seemed to be one of theirs, but as I listened, I heard it was really a spell of some kind. Their laws and our faith, woven together in a web that trapped them."

"I don't suppose you remember any of the words I was saying?"

"No. But then, I'm not the storyteller, you are."

"Barely!" Kalie stared through the open door of the tent, lost in thought. "It's strange. When I decided to come back here, I planned to gain a reputation as a storyteller in the hopes of being given to the king—then slaying him. I saw early on that wouldn't work, so I began to craft stories that I hoped would cause the men to turn on each other, or do rash things in a wild quest for glory."

"That seems to have worked," said Alessa. "I heard that Yuraak's clan was wiped out by outcasts, trying to get to the Motherlands before anyone else."

Kalie shook her head. "I can't take credit for that one, much as I'd like to. It was Haraak and his endless boasting of his exploits that inspired Yuraak."

Alessa smiled. "And I like it much better that way. There's good in knowing that Haraak himself is helping to bring about the downfall of his people, while your stories are serving a higher purpose than enflaming violent men to greater acts of violence."

"I know you think the Goddess would have been displeased at the corruption of one of Her own beloved art forms, Alessa. But I hardly think failure is the same as a higher purpose."

"I'm talking about where you've succeeded, Kalie. With your stories to the women."

Kalie thought about that, then laughed. "Funny, isn't it? The place where I put all my energy and effort turned out to be a waste of time. But where I was barely paying attention—not even telling stories, but simply the truth—that did have an impact, didn't it?"

"A very big impact."

Kalie shook her head. "It's not going to change anything. For most of the women here, the Goddess is just a passing diversion; perhaps a way to get excitement by partaking in the forbidden. It might even change how the women treat each other. But they're never going to make any real changes in how things are run here."

"But some of them will follow you when you leave. I'd say that's impressive."

"They joke about it. But when the time comes, are there any who actually will?"

Alessa smiled. "When the time comes," she said, "I think you will be surprised. Funny, as you said. In the very thing that all the rest of us failed at, you have succeeded. And you're the one who said it wasn't possible."

For the first time in a long while, Kalie thought about the others who had left Riverford with her, more than a year ago. Many had come to minister to the women, to teach them a better way. Kalie had scoffed, and told them the women would fight them harder than the men. Had she really succeeded in carrying out their work?

"Can we agree to this, at least?" Kalie asked. "Both our purposes would be served by dividing this alliance. If you are right, the smaller their numbers when they reach our homes, the easier they will be to assimilate into our world. And if I am right, there will be fewer of them to fight."

Alessa thought about it for a long time. At last she looked up, her face once again troubled. "I will agree to that. It is the means we use to accomplish it that concerns me."

"Then let us both think about it, and work together for a solution we can both live with." Let's just not take too long, she thought. "And in the meantime, I will work on discovering this story the Goddess wants me to tell."

"I will do all I can," said Alessa, and Kalie knew she would have to leave it at that and wait—and pray.

Haraak sent emissaries to the Hansi, despite earlier promises that he would never sit in the same tent with his ancient enemies. Rumors of yet another tribe—the Axe Men—Kalie found even more intriguing, for they were the only tribe that dwelt in the barren land to the north and west. If those two tribes could be brought here, there would be no one standing between this gathering and her homeland. And if a five-way battle were to occur…

With Agafa and Varena to manage the household and organize their departure and Yarik mastering the art of walking in the greatly improved shoes Alessa had made for him, Kalie had little work to distract her from the task at hand. Riyik was equally busy during this time, looking for men to join them on the journey west—as well as solid evidence that Haraak had murdered the former king. While much was being accomplished, Kalie and Riyik saw little of each other. She was surprised at how much it bothered her—and at how much she looked forward to what time that had together.

A summons to the tent of the king caught Kalie by surprise. She and Varena were preparing stew for supper—meatier and tastier than anything either had eaten in Maalke's tent—when two of the king's own guards appeared at the open door-flap.

"Kalie, wife of Riyik, you are to come with us," called the shorter one.

"What for?" Kalie asked, ducking outside, and looking the speaker in the eye.

Clearly not expecting that reaction, the man stared, then repeated his order.

Kalie smiled, although Varena looked worried. She was about to ask if they wished to speak with her husband, when the second guard spoke. "Nelek's witch-woman said she needed you to assist her in curing the king of a minor illness." He made the sign against evil. "But we can tell her you refused—"

"Let's go!" Kalie said, hurrying past the guards and leaving them to catch up with her as she ran to Kariik's tent.

Kalie had to admit it: the king's tent was much improved since the change of ownership. It was cleaner and better organized. Newer luxury goods were in evidence as well: cushions and furs were tastefully arranged along with treasures from the west: carved wooden boxes and furniture; a golden goblet on a low table. The women working or lounging about were all young and beautiful. Kalie wondered where the older women had gone; she knew they hadn't all been killed to accompany the old king.

As Kalie reached the inner sanctum of the king's private sleeping area, she found Alessa kneeling beside Kariik, who lay upon a bed piled with rich furs. Despite the luxury, the king looked anything but comfortable. He was feverish and clutching his stomach.

"Kalie, good, thank you for coming," said Alessa. "Help me rearrange these furs and get him cleaned up." As Kalie hurried to obey, Alessa called to the women who hovered outside, "Get me something to catch his vomit!"

A moment later, a frightened looking girl came in with a tightly woven basket. She gave it to Alessa, then scurried away. No sooner did Alessa have it than it was needed. "Give us privacy, or face the wrath of Nelek's witch!" she shouted with obvious distaste, but Kalie could hear the whisper of skirts and slippers as the women hurried from the tent.

When Kariik finished retching, Alessa covered the basket and helped the king lie on his side, sponging his face with compress of soft leather. Automatically, his legs curled up, reminding Kalie of a new baby, and telling her that the cramping and soreness inside him remained.

"Grind those herbs," said Alessa, indicating a mortar and pestle. "Two parts chamomile, one part mint." Kalie nodded and set to work. It was exactly the tea she would have prescribed herself. A pot of water steamed on the brazier. Alessa poured half of it into a cup of shredded willow bark, leaving the rest for Kalie. The healer added honey, and, when it reached the right temperature, gave it to Kariik. Kalie followed with her cup a few moments later. Kariik sipped the tea and looked at Kalie, as if noticing her for the first time. "Couldn't you have brought one of the pretty ones?" he asked Alessa.

"All the others from my country who know healing are dead," Alessa said, examining the contents of the basket. "And you can trust Kalie. I think we both know how important that is." Kalie's head jerked up in surprise. What was Alessa doing, speaking to the king this way? Yet Kariik only nodded bleakly, as if this were the continuation of an earlier conversation.

Alessa completed her examination, then set the basket aside. Kalie and Kariik noticed the relief on her face at the same time. "So…?" Kariik asked, his fear and misery palpable.

"Not the poison that killed your father," Alessa said.

Kalie gasped, but Kariik showed no reaction. "But poison still?" he asked in a flat voice.

"Only if you consider bad meat poison. King or slave, all stomachs will behave as yours if meat spoils, or is badly prepared."

"Kings are rarely served spoiled meat," said Kariik, sounding more like his usual self. "One of the few things that makes living with this charade worthwhile."

"But in this weather, it happens quickly." Alessa did not drop her gaze, as would have been proper. "Your father had the finest cook in the tribe. What happened to her?"

"I sent her back to her family. I don't like having old women about." Kalie thought briefly of Kariik's mother, and for the first time, felt a stab of sympathy. "Shayla said she could run the kitchen."

"And how has your food been since Shayla took over?" Alessa asked sweetly.

Kariik seemed about to get angry, then laughed. "I will send for Etria, and anyone else she needs."

"In that case, I think your stomach will soon be much improved," Alessa said.

Kariik gazed intently at Alessa, with more thought than Kalie would have believed him capable of. "If I could buy you from Nelek, could you keep me safe?"

"From poison?"

"Poison, curses, ill-wishes, my own stupidity..." Kariik rolled onto his back and stared morosely at the tent-poles. "The list is endless."

Alessa waited until the king turned his head to see her. Kalie, it seemed, had been forgotten. She didn't care; she only hoped they would continue speaking.

"Haraak will not dispose of you until he has someone to replace you, which he does not have," Alessa said. "Your people are far too afraid of this journey to accept another such change. For now, your wit serves you best—simply continue to act the fool as you have been doing. When the time comes to make a change in your advisors, you will know."

"Playing the fool is my one true talent," Kariik said bitterly. "My father always said so."

Kalie could tell Alessa was searching for the right thing to say, but Kariik was already drifting into sleep.

Alessa carefully gathered up her tools, then led Kalie outside.

They walked quickly, to avoid listening ears. "It seems you know more than I gave you credit for, old friend," Kalie said. "What was all that about?"

"Kariik has it in him to be a great king," Alessa said.

Kalie was certainly surprised by what she had witnessed, but she shook her head. "I saw his greatness when he threw Yasha to the mob to be stoned."

Alessa nodded sadly. "Compared to the men we are used to, he seems like less than an animal. But considering where he came from, and what has been forced on him...Kariik is weak and frightened, but underneath, there is so much more to him..." Alessa stopped as they reached the edge of Nelek's camp. "I did not want to admit it, but you're right," she whispered in Kalie's ears while noisy chaos swirled around them. "I might be able to work with Kariik, but not two other kings, and not while Haraak controls him. Meet me in front of Nelek's tent tomorrow before dawn. Come dressed as a slave."

"I will," Kalie breathed back.

Alessa seemed about to slip away. Then she hesitated. "Take this." She slid a bundle of dull brown plants into Kalie's hand. "Boiled down to a heavy syrup and mixed with any liquid, they bring forth visions—to those with the training."

"And those without the training?"

"Drunkenness, stupor, terrifying nightmares, and if too much is consumed—death."

Kalie's hand closed tight around the plants. "Alessa—I know I have asked for this, but if it is betraying your oath...you don't have to—"

"I wouldn't have done it if I didn't want to," Alessa said, then hurried through the crowded field back to her master's tent.

Chapter 26

The tent seemed to sag in the still air of late summer. Kalie felt a stab of guilt, and something more, as she realized she had barely seen Brenia since they had arrived at the Summer Gathering nearly half a moon span ago. And now she came, not out of friendship, but because this was the one place where she might find more of the plants that the Holy Women of the west called datura. She squatted down and scratched at the door flap.

Kalie could hear muffled sounds from within: angry words, then the crying of a child. Abandoning propriety, Kalie pushed open the flap and crawled inside. As her eyes adjusted to the gloom, she saw nothing to connect this tent with the pleasant, orderly home it had been last winter. Clothing and tent furnishings were strewn about haphazardly, and the remains of several meals were rotting beside the unlit brazier. Over and above it all, the smell spoke of oppression and despair. It was a smell she associated with Altia's tent.

Brenia lay on her bed. Beside her, Barak sat whimpering.

"Brenia, what's wrong?" Kalie asked, hurrying to her side. "Are you sick?"

When the older woman didn't answer, Kalie threw back the tent flap, the fastest way to get light to see by.

"Close the flap!" Brenia shrieked, shielding her eyes with her hands, but careful not to actually touch her face.

As soon as Kalie saw her, she understood why.

Brenia's face was battered almost beyond recognition. Both her eyes were swollen shut. Gently easing Brenia's robe open, Kalie found more bruising, although the greatest damage was to her face.

"Did Hysaak do this?" she asked pointlessly.

"It's Elka," Brenia wailed. "She has turned him against me!"

Kalie went to the water bag that hung from the rafters and found it empty. "How long have you been like this?"

"Since yesterday. After he beat me, he took her and rode off, like some sixteen-year-old with his new bride. My little boy has been guiding me, finding things for me, but…" Brenia's voice trailed off.

"I will take him to my tent," Kalie said. "Varena will feed him, and watch him for as long as you need." She scooped up the crying boy, ignoring his feeble struggle at being taken from his mother, and hurried back to her own tent.

Handing the child to the servants with a few curt instructions, Kalie poured half their supply of water into the bag that Riyik had made for her and hurried back to Brenia's tent.

She got Brenia to drink some of the water, lit the brazier, and used what remained in the bag to make willow bark tea. She then made a poultice by folding some healing herbs that she managed to find in the wreckage into heated felt. Brenia sighed as the poultice took effect.

"Thank you," she said sometime later, while Kalie sat silently, holding her hand. After a while, she spoke again. "I've seen this happen to other women. I never thought it would happen to me. She wants me dead."

"Why?"

Brenia shrugged, and then winced. "Sometimes they just do. For most, it's enough to turn the senior wife into a slave; to goad the man into humiliating her. When Hysaak forbade me to use our tent to prepare you for your marriage to my only brother—to force me to leave you with crude strangers who wanted the job simply as fodder for gossip—I thought things had gone as far as they could. Surely, I told myself, she could devise no greater hurt."

Kalie thought back to her wedding day, the memories already hazy. Suddenly, she saw the strange tent and those women she barely knew in a whole new light. Even in the west, family was a crucial part of the planning and celebrations of joinings. Had it even occurred to her to ask why Brenia wasn't part of her preparations—something obviously important to these people? Or was she too busy trying to endure the barbaric ritual; to survive her own distress, to think of what it all meant to the one person who actually wanted to welcome Kalie into her family?

Had Brenia been in charge of the preparations, Larren would have been an honored guest, along with anyone else Kalie had wished to invite. They would have spent the afternoon painting each other's feet with henna, and styling their hair. Kalie might even have enjoyed it; the others certainly would have. Kalie was mortified by her insensitivity.

"But for some," Brenia continued in a flat voice, "there's a need to be a man's only woman. I suppose I should prefer death. There's no honor in living like this."

"Honor for who?" Kalie squeezed Brenia's hand tightly. It didn't hurt her, since neither her hands nor arms were bruised. "You're the only person in this tent who's behaved with any honor at all—by your standards or mine! Why should you be the one to die?"

"If I die, I may not die alone," Brenia said sadly. "She carries his child now. If it is a boy, she will want him to be her husband's heir. His only heir."

"Riyik will help you—"

"An Aahken woman does not run to her family and complain to them of every marital problem she encounters."

Just the serious ones? Kalie stared into the shadows dancing beyond the light of the brazier. "Brenia?" she said at last. "If you were to become a widow, would you consider allowing Hysaak's second wife—his favorite wife—the honor of accompanying him to the next life?"

Kalie was so surprised to discover that she was serious; that she could actually sanction the killing of a pregnant woman, that she did not at first realize that the noise coming from Brenia was laughter. "You foreign witch!" she cried. "You've been seeing into my thoughts!"

Then the laughter turned to tears, and Kalie hurried to freshen the poultice. "Don't cry, you're eyes are swollen enough!" she said.

Brenia, like any Aahken woman could control her tears, so she did. "Why did you come here?" she asked.

"I came to ask if you had a certain plant called datura," Kalie said.

Brenia's head jerked up and her limited sight sought Kalie. "Datura? What would you want that for?"

Kalie found she couldn't lie to this woman. "It

is time for me to return to my own land, Brenia. And I will take you and your son with me if you will come. But when I leave, I must make sure certain people cannot follow us."

"Does Riyik know?"

"About my leaving? Yes. He plans to come with me. About the drug I plan to make? No. I cannot ask him to be complicit in the killing of his own kind."

Brenia moved aside her bedding. A pile of dried plants identical to the one hidden in Kalie's robe lay exposed in leather wrappings. "I was counting them this morning, just before the dizziness brought me to my bed. Just before you arrived."

Stunned, Kalie looked from the roots to Brenia, then back again. "Were you going to poison Elka?"

"These plants have other uses besides poison," Brenia said, telling Kalie what she already knew. "I was going to make a love potion to win back Hysaak." She snorted, then winced again at the pain it caused. "Foolish thought! It's far too late for that. So I did, briefly, consider poisoning Elka. Then I thought, perhaps, it might be better to poison all three of us: Hysaak, myself and our child, and leave her to die for the crime!"

Quite without her will, Kalie's hand shot out to take the plants. She would not realize until later that it was an act borne of the need to remove dangerous objects from a person who might harm herself, and nothing at all to do with Kalie's need to kill her enemies. And later, she would be proud of that fact.

Brenia set her own hand over Kalie's. "Take them. It's obvious I'm not myself; I shouldn't have such magic around me at a time like this."

"I will take them, and no one will know where

I got them. But when I leave, will you come with me?"

Brenia stared bleakly at Kalie through her swollen lids. "I am a woman of Aahk. I cannot steal my husband's son from him and flee like a thief in the night. Such things are not done."

"But a man beating his wife to death for the pleasure of his new bride is done all the time! And what of a husband's vow to honor and protect his faithful wife? His vow to cherish her for giving him a son? Those remain in effect until the husband finds them inconvenient?" When Brenia said nothing, Kalie pressed further. "And your son? How will he fare once you are dead? Or does his dying with you solve everything?"

"Stop it!" cried Brenia. Strange, Kalie thought, that while she could barely see Brenia's eyes at all, she could easily see the pain in them. "I have wanted to see your world since before I even met you! You don't think I've dreamed about it at night? You think I haven't whispered prayers to your Goddess when no one was around? I have! And what's more, I've even heard Her answer!"

"You have? What did She say?"

"Nothing that makes any sense," Brenia sighed, lying on her bed again. "Then again, nothing in my life makes any sense either."

"Come with me," Kalie pleaded, "and we'll make sense of it together! Brenia, your own brother is going! Isn't your blood tie to him stronger than your marriage vows to a man who has already broken his vows to you?"

"Such foreign thinking! Yet I would love, just once, to breathe the air of a world where everyone thought as you do. And I would love to feel my body sink beneath a pool of water that never dried in summer, and was hot in the winter—and do it with my clothes off and never fear to be beaten for it. But I won't leave Barak, and Hysaak would hunt us to the ends of the earth if I took him. And I won't endanger the rest of you by doing such a thing."

"You let me worry about that," Kalie whispered as she gathered up the datura. She waited until Brenia was asleep, then hurried to find Alessa.

Chapter 27

It was hard to remember to walk behind Alessa with her head meekly bowed.

It was harder to get used to the scratchy, stained robe of a slave, even though Kalie had worn one just like it until barely a moon span ago. But for this plan to work, she had to play the role of a slave flawlessly.

It was a role she had never mastered, even when she was one.

"Remember to let me do the talking," Alessa whispered as they reached the enormous tent of the Wolf Tribe's king. "At least at first."

Kalie nodded, tried to scrunch herself down even smaller, and followed Alessa into the tent. As her eyes adjusted to the gloom, she saw the tent was less crowded than Kariik's, despite its near equal size. A red haired woman played a stringed instrument and sang for Amaar, the king's eldest son as he ate his breakfast. A girl of about twelve crouched naked in the blankets, watching him eat, and looking hopeful for scraps.

They crawled through twisted passageways of felt, and came to a dark alcove. There, as Alessa had promised, Valaan, the king's second son, lay sick from too much drink the night before.

Alessa knelt before him, holding a drinking skull filled with one of the morning after remedies that had made her famous among the king's warriors. Despite his obvious discomfort, Valaan took his time acknowledging her.

He finally sat up and grabbed the cup from her,

gulping down the contents in a single swallow. "Gods! This must be what horse piss tastes like! I told you to find a way to make it taste better!" Valaan muttered. For a moment, Kalie thought he was going to vomit up the medicine, so green did he look. But his stomach must have settled, for soon color began returning to his face, and he seemed to feel better.

Valaan expressed his recovery in the way typical of the men of his people: he slid his hand down Alessa shift and tried to grab her breasts. She moved smoothly out of reach, but did not try to flee. Kalie remained warily behind her.

"Ah, Alessa," said Valaan. "Your considerable charms are wasted on my father!"

"Someday, I shall be yours, Valaan," Alessa said in a seductive voice that sounded nothing like her.

"Why wait?"

"I would never tempt a man to betray his father." Alessa motioned for Kalie to move forward. "But I bring news of another woman who desires your company, and she does not belong to your father and king. Nor any man of your tribe."

Interest gathered in Valaan's eyes, making him appear, Kalie thought, almost intelligent. She slowly drew out the red linen scarf she had hidden in the folds of her robe. "My mistress, Barta, wife of Krul of the tribe of Aahk, desires that you return this scarf to her tonight, while her ancient husband sits in council with his king."

A flicker of suspicion crossed the prince's face. "Barta? Who is that? Was she ever presented to me?"

"She is beautiful and young," said Kalie. "Too much so for such an old man to satisfy. She has longed for the touch of a real man for all these moons that she has been married."

At a nudge from Alessa, Kalie continued. "She has watched you since you arrived with your warriors, and even sent me to discover who you were. My mistress knew at once you were a prince, and was surprised to learn you were a younger son. She has whispered to me that your brother is not nearly so fine a man as you, and surely it is you who shall rule after your father. Barta wants to be part of that future."

Kalie was afraid she had overplayed her hand, but the flattery had worked. "She wishes to deceive her husband inside his own tent?" Valaan tried to look disgusted, but couldn't quite manage it. He took the scarf. "I will, of course, do as the lady asks."

Kalie and Alessa backed slowly out of the tent, letting out long sighs of relief once they were back out in the summer heat.

"It worked!" Kalie whispered, as they walked through the noisy, bustling camp.

"Wait until tomorrow before you start celebrating." Alessa's voice was unusually harsh.

"Barta won't be hurt," Kalie reassured her. "Valaan expects to find an empty tent and a willing woman. When he sneaks in, she will scream and whoever comes in will find her defending her honor against a thief and an enemy. Her slaves—the real ones— will swear that she did not invite him."

"We can hope. Kalie, I never doubted we were on the right path this whole time I've lived in this land. But now, I'm not so sure."

"If we had enough time, Alessa, I know that your way would have worked. Eventually. But we only have days to turn a horde of more than a thousand warriors into groups small enough to be managed. The stakes are just too high."

"Yes, they are," said Alessa. But Kalie didn't think they were talking about the same thing.

They parted company, Alessa, to visit a sick child, Kalie to her tent to render more of the drug from the datura plants, and then to practice the story she was working on.

When Kalie had showed her the plants she had gotten from Brenia, Alessa had stressed that if they drugged the kumis—the logical way to assure that mainly warriors were dosed—there would be no way to control the amount or strength any one man received. Some would undoubtedly die, while others would be only briefly incapacitated.

That sounded fine to Kalie, though she knew Alessa was not happy about it.

The next problem to overcome was taste. Fortunately, Kalie had discovered that the women of Malquor flavored their kumis with a strong spice called nutmeg, which—she hoped—would mask the bitter taste of the drug. Kalie had already mastered the art of brewing kumis as the Spears of Malquor drank it.

She set the latest batch to ferment, then turned her attention to her story.

"…And so at last Marik and the other noble warriors saw how they had been tricked; a dishonorable reign bought with their lives. They had believed their prince and he had led them to their doom—" Kalie broke off, shaking her head. "Why not just hit them over the head with a war club and save everyone the trouble!"

She tried again. "Once there was mighty warrior named Sloak who was strong and true, and high in favor with his king. His only weakness was his lust for his king's wife…"

Late that night, all three camps were awakened by screams and flaring torches from within the tents of Aahk. Running with the others, Kalie reached the tent of Krul, too far behind the others crowding around it to do more than glimpse the bloody spectacle: Valaan, Krul, and Barta all were dead, along with one unlucky slave. The others were all busy telling what had happened, although no two people seemed to have the same story.

Krul had lived long enough to tell those who first arrived on the scene—guards and neighboring warriors—that he had returned to his tent earlier than he planned due to stomach pains. There he had lain beside his wife, only to be awakened by her screams as a dog—not Wolf—entered the tent and attempted to ravish the pure and faithful woman while she slept beside her husband.

At least her reputation survived, Kalie thought bitterly. Perhaps that will be some small comfort to her family. She stayed focused on the scene before her, fearing to find Alessa's accusing eyes in the darkness.

The stories swirled around her: how the two men had fought, Valaan foully slandering Barta, Krul defending his home and his honor, how Barta had been struck an unlucky blow by one of the men. No one seemed to know which.

When everyone had had their say, Kariik faced the grieving king of the Wolf Tribe and tried to look intimidating. "Is this how your people—your sons—honor a treaty?"

Kalie rather hoped Nelek would defend his son's honor by insisting that Valaan would not have been in another man's tent without an invitation, and thus beginning a fight that would not end until the two tribes depleted each other.

But nothing the old man said would remove the stain on his honor, and by extension, that of his tribe. He simply ordered Valaan's body be prepared for travel, and set about breaking camp. He would not wait until morning, although Haraak used all of his considerable skill to hold the alliance together. In this endeavor, Haraak was not alone. There were men in all three camps who claimed that honor had been served: whatever the cause, the fight had been a fair one and was now over. The gods could sort things out in the next world, but here on earth, this federation was needed to secure all of their futures in the west.

Nelek, however, would not be moved. He led his tribe from the camp by the light of the gibbous moon and many torches. Kalie barely had time to find Alessa hurrying with the rest of the women to break camp and load all their possessions onto the horses, or their own backs. They exchanged swift farewells and the Goddess's blessing—then Alessa was gone. For the first time since finding her, Kalie realized that she might never see her friend again.

When the first light of dawn touched the sky, only two tribes remained. The huge camp seemed almost empty to Kalie, as she wandered alone for a few stolen moments. She wanted to revel in the stark evidence of the federation's diminished numbers, and in her first real feeling of power at having made it happen, but could not. She was sorry about Barta, and the slave, whose name she did not even know, but she had witnessed such things every day since coming here. Kalie had reached the point where it was possible to regard such things as these people's own choice.

What bothered Kalie, as she sat beside a tiny spring she discovered, hidden in the tall grass that had been part of Wolf Camp, was how it would affect Alessa. Kalie did not possess the shining faith that her friend had, but she knew well how fragile it was. She could only hope this day's events did not shatter it, even as she prayed they would help secure the safety of her people.

Chapter 28

There were more problems for the alliance in the days that followed.

The envoys from the Hansi tribe turned out to be assassins, who, unfortunately for Kalie, proved to be as lacking in skill as they were in honor. Both Kariik and Malquor escaped without serious injury. Haraak sent the heads of the envoys back to their king by way of response.

The good news was that now, war with the Hansi was a strong possibility.

The weather turned cool, then cold, with no sign of rain. The date of departure drew near, and the beastmen all knew that, weak or strong, their only hope of surviving the coming winter lay in the west.

Haraak spent all his energy trying to hold the two remaining tribes together, and force the leaders to accept his plans for the attack and subjugation of the city dwellers. The strain was beginning to show on him. Kalie learned that he rarely visited his tent or his women, and when he did, he was often impotent. All his energy; all his lust went into his planned conquest.

Eight days before the time of departure, the tension was palpable in the air. Fights were breaking out between the men. But this, it seemed, was normal enough, and nothing threatened the remaining alliance, or the proposed date to bring the tribes of the beastmen to the undefended lands of the west.

The world seemed to be holding its breath. Kalie walked through the still air, through parched grass desperate for rain. It was a wonder the animals could eat this stuff, she thought. The last of them were being brought into camp, and made ready for travel. As Riyik's wife, it was Kalie's duty to check each animal, choose the strongest and best able to make the journey, and mark the rest for slaughter. The meat would sustain the travelers through the winter— whichever way they went.

While Kalie had left most of the managing of the household to the servants, this task was highly visible, and her absence would have been noted. So she worked with the other wives and slaves these last days, herding the sheep and goats into pens made with stakes of precious wood, twined with cord made from the ever-present grass.

Older boys pressed into service looked longingly at the men, all gathered in a huge field beside the campsite, exercising the horses in their own preparations for departure. The boys, deeply resentful, and wishing they could be among the men who spent these last days with the horses, took their anger out on the women and animals, making an already unpleasant job worse.

When the sun slanted to the west, Kalie brought the last of the goats to the pen, and left Varena in charge. She stopped in the tent to see Agafa, whom she had ordered to remain in bed. The old woman's cough was not getting any better, despite all Alessa had done while she had been here.

Agafa was awake, so Kalie stopped to visit. Yarik sat across the tent, playing with the horses his father had carved for him. The other children had rejected him completely now, as their mothers spoke of evil omens and their fathers worried about imperfections angering the gods and endangering their chance for victory in the west. Riyik had told Kalie to keep him inside at all times.

Kalie was seized by a sudden urge to leave now. To take both of these people home with her: one so she could know freedom before she died, the other so he could grow up whole.

As if reading her thoughts, Agafa smiled. "I'm afraid I won't be coming to that good land with you." Her voice was barely a whisper.

"Nonsense," Kalie said, bringing her water. "We have six more days for you to rest. And a horse will carry you if you can't walk the whole way."

At that Agafa smiled. "Always the finest of storytellers, Kalie." Then she began to cough. Kalie tried not to notice the blood that came up. "Fear not," Agafa said after more water. "I'm not going to die yet. I may not make it to your world, but by the Goddess, I'll find the strength to walk out of this one. I won't die in a stinking Aahken tent. That much you've given me, and for that I'll always love you."

Kalie turned away, not knowing why she didn't want Agafa to see how much those words moved her. "Can I get you anything else before I go?"

"Where are you going now?"

"Just…out."

Agafa's filmy eyes grew sharp. "You take too many chances, girl. The alliance will fall apart on its own now. Stay here. Or go to the practice field and lure that man of yours into the tall grass for a time."

"I'll be back soon," Kalie promised.

She chuckled to herself as she threaded her way through the camp, made even nosier than usual by the crowded pens of sheep and goats, and the sweating and cursing women as they struggled through the last of the marking and sorting. Grateful for the now cool

—though still dry—breeze that blew through the tall brown grass, Kalie headed for the small hidden spring she had discovered the day Wolf Tribe left. Now, in these final days, it seemed more important than ever to escape the noise and stink of the camp, just to order her thoughts. Just to take a breath.

But she could never escape the turmoil inside her head.

Kalie had more than twenty skins of kumis hidden in her tent. And nearly that number in Brenia's. If turning the warriors against each other didn't work, she could render at least half of them dead or useless for fighting.

If she could figure out a way to be sure they all drank the right kumis at the same time.

Then all she had to do was figure out how to fight the other half while she led a bunch of women and children across the steppes and against a lifetime of conditioning.

Kalie parted the screen of tall grass and stepped into a hidden glade. The spring was little more than a trickle of water into a muddy ditch. But it was hers.

Far from the camp, and hidden from the disapproving eyes of the tribe, Kalie threw aside her veil and cast off her shoes. Lifting the skirt of her heavy black robe, Kalie stepped into the cool water, sighing with pleasure. With one last look around, she slipped off her outer robe. Then, a prickle on the back of her neck warned her she was not alone.

The man was on her before she turned fully around to face him.

"Haraak!" she gasped.

He looked disappointed. "I thought you were

sneaking off to meet a lover. I had hoped to disgrace Riyik by showing his wife to be a whore." His eyes traveled up and down her body, a look of near desperation on his face, which suddenly turned to hope. "Perhaps I still can." In a single motion he tore her remaining garment from her body.

"Leave here now or I will scream," Kalie hissed.

"Go ahead," said Haraak. "No one will hear you from this distance." He pointed to the screen of grass. "You planned well for privacy."

Kalie feared he was right but screamed anyway. Haraak slammed his hand over her mouth, looking surprised, though whether because of her volume or the fact that she had tested his statement, she didn't know.

"Don't make this harder on you than it has to be," Haraak growled, using the full force of his weight to push her to the ground.

Kalie put all her energy into moving her head until his hand slipped from her mouth. "Riyik will kill you if you go through with this!" If screaming didn't work, she would bargain.

Haraak opened the front of his lower garment and began stroking his partial erection. Where was his supposed impotence? Kalie thought desperately.

"He will try, of course," said Haraak. "He will have to. That is: if you tell him."

"You think I won't?" Kalie twisted on the ground, trying to lock her legs shut.

"You must tell him. Our laws demand it. And then he will have to fight me. If he wins, I die, and you are avenged—although dishonored for the rest of your life. But when have your kind ever cared about honor?"

Kalie's struggles inflamed Haraak's desire to the point he no longer needed his hands. He used them instead to pin Kalie's arms to the ground on either side of her body. "But if I win, your beloved dies—and you and everything else he owns will belong to me. Are you willing to risk that?"

He pried her legs apart with one knee and leaned over her, leering. The breath that whistled between his crooked yellow teeth stank of rotten meat and kumis. "Of course, if you don't tell Riyik, and he finds out later, no one will believe it was rape. Then he will be forced to kill you as an adulteress."

Kalie had to admire the intricacy of the trap Haraak had set, as he shoved his meaty phallus inside her. His face floated above hers with a look of ecstasy and triumph. As he grunted and moaned, she tried to shake her mind free as she had with Maalke, but found herself anchored to the real world by her rage.

When it was over, Haraak stood up and grinned down at Kalie. "I guess you're not much of a witch after all."

"What?" Kalie asked blankly.

"I have eyes and ears everywhere in this camp," Haraak said as he adjusted his clothing. "I know about your attempts to make trouble; to turn the warriors against each other. Some of the weaker men have even whispered that your so-called goddess had cursed our glorious venture in the west. That you and that other slut from your land were witches." He spat on the ground just inches from where Kalie lay.

Suddenly, things began making sense. It seemed her stories of the Goddess had not only circulated among the women, they'd reached the men as well. And frightened them. And then, just days before the start of the great westward conquest; when superstitious warriors looked for omens in every sheep's stomach… "…Their great leader couldn't get it up with a woman!" Kalie stood up and laughed, then spat in his face. "When word of that began to spread…"

Haraak punched her hard in the stomach. She doubled over and vomited into the mud.

"Now that I've shown you and your cursed goddess how much power you really have, I don't expect any more trouble." He spat again, this time in Kalie's face.

Haraak's anger faded and his satisfied grin returned. "I decided to fuck you just to prove to myself you're no witch. And I was right. But the men need to see it as well. I don't have to wait and see what you decide to do. I could just drag you to the middle of camp right now and do it again."

Kalie forced herself back to her feet, not caring how her legs shook. "And I could just cut off your balls and stuff them down your throat while you're trying to raise an audience, Haraak! We both know how many women would happily give me a knife for that purpose. But I'll start by asking Yessenia."

Haraak's eyes went wide, and Kalie thought she was about to die. Then he laughed. "I did what I came here to do: before we leave this place, that cowardly traitor Riyik will be out of my way, and so will his slut of a wife. If you want to scream rape, you'd better do it soon. But we both know you loved it." Then he turned on his heel and left her there.

Kalie turned away from the spring and vomited again.

Then she sat shaking for a long time.

This was no time to lie down and die, she told herself. But it was what she wanted to do. The despair she remembered so well from years ago came welling back up. Even if she killed Haraak; even if she killed them all, it would not change what happened here today. She thought of all her grand plans for escape. They seemed laughable.

Which is exactly what Haraak wants you to think, Kalie told herself as she took inventory. Her outer clothes, though somewhat muddy, were intact. Kalie washed herself and dressed, realizing as she did how well Haraak had planned it all. He had avoided striking her face, as he had avoided damaging her clothing. The only bruises would be on her arms and legs. Places that could be kept covered, even in the confines of a tent.

The choice really was hers.

And that was the terror.

Riyik would believe her, she was certain of that. But then what? Riyik would fight Haraak fairly and in a cold rage, which might dull his judgment. Haraak would never fight fairly: he would do whatever it took to win. Which made it very likely that Kalie— and Varena and Agafa and the other Shadow Women she had rescued, and possibly even Yarik—would soon belong to Haraak.

She began to walk, vaguely aware that she was going farther from camp rather than closer. If she hid what happened, as Haraak clearly expected her to, he would boast about it until everyone in camp knew— Riyik last of all, of course. Or perhaps he hoped her acting ability would desert her one night as she lay beneath her husband, and he would discover the truth of it then.

Of course, if that were the case, Kalie had one advantage. Haraak had no way of knowing that she and Riyik had never slept together. Perhaps, with that factor missing from their marriage, she would be able to explain it to him logically. If Riyik could see how Haraak intended to use him, perhaps he wouldn't fall into the trap. Perhaps they could even work together on a way to turn Haraak's plan against him.

Kalie turned and began walking toward camp, clutching desperately at that one hope, when she stopped, a cold hand gripping her insides. What if Riyik couldn't see what she saw? What if he didn't listen to her? What if…Kalie's mouth went dry and she began to sweat. What if he didn't believe her at all?

She told herself not to be foolish. This was Riyik, after all, not some swaggering bully who thought with his prick; who lashed out first and asked questions later. But try as she might, Kalie could not still the panicked racing of her heart.

She began walking away from camp again. As she walked, she wondered how many other women had been trapped like this. Happily married, confident and secure—all of it taken away in an instant by a man's will. How many other men had done the same thing? For power, or revenge, or simply amusement?

And how many of the women, ready to rush to the husband they had loved and trusted the day before, found they couldn't do it now because they couldn't trust him quite enough? A recent quarrel, a bored look, the lack of a son—all insignificant yesterday, now became signs he was tired of her. Reasons to discard her rather than fight for her. And how could any woman here ever really know how much shame a man would be willing to bear for her sake?

So they kept silent. And fear and shame dogged their steps for the rest of their lives. All their energy went into keeping a secret that grew more dangerous each day. And if years went by without exposure, even if the rapist died, could she ever really feel safe again? And if he did expose her...

"No wonder nothing ever changes here!" Kalie said aloud. "They don't fight to keep themselves enslaved, they fight to keep themselves alive! But they have to do it a cage of secrecy, where they can't even trust their closest friend with the truth." She shook her head, and thought about it some more. "They would lose the power to reach out to anyone, for anything. No wonder they can't feel another woman's pain or work to ease their suffering. It's not about competing for men's favor, it's about making sure no one ever has the means to threaten their existence!"

Kalie had lived with these people for over a year, yet standing here today she realized she had never really understood them. Not like Alessa did. And not like Larren.

Even if what happened to her today only happened rarely—which she doubted—to grow up knowing that it could was probably just as crippling.

The sounds of men's voices raised in cheer caused her to freeze. Her empty stomach began to heave again as Kalie realized she had wandered to the border of the men's practice field.

Crouching down and carefully parting the tall grass, she gazed at the island of flat ground where the grass had been mowed and the stubble pounded smooth by the racing hooves of many horses. The sharp smell of horse nearly covered the stink of the men. Men from both tribes were there, training young horses, racing older ones, and teaching their sons how to ride.

Not a hint of anything female, Kalie mused. It's a world of men. How soon before every shrine of the Goddess became buried beneath place like this?

She looked for Riyik, half hoping, half fearing to see him, but he wasn't there. Kalie knew she should leave before she was seen, yet she remained rooted to the spot, attracted and repelled by the beauty and power of the horses, and the raw energy of the men

She didn't know how long she had stood there, mesmerized, when the accident happened. Kalie had been watching a race between a red-coated stallion and a grey gelding when the grey suddenly screamed and reared, crashing into the red and sending them both to the ground. Shouts from the agitated men nearly drowned out the terrible cries of the horses. The stallion eventually made it to his feet and was led away, shaking and snorting.

The gelding remained on the ground, thrashing about in pain. Kalie watched in awe as a grim circle of men examined the animal, and came to the dreaded conclusion: one of the legs was broken. The horse's young owner, a boy of about sixteen, and only recently admitted to the ranks of warriors, wept uncontrollably until one of the other men slapped him across the face, loudly enough for Kalie to hear it from her hiding place.

The boy turned his grief into curses and shouts of rage. Satisfied by this improvement, one of the other men brought him a long knife. The young owner slit the horse's throat with more sorrow than Kalie had

ever seen expressed in this land. Then, to her
amazement, a group of about twelve men actually
lifted the dead animal and carried it from the field. The
rest of them men followed in respectful silence.

Kalie waited until long after the dust settled
and silence reigned. Then she hurried to the spot
where the horse had fallen. The blood made it easy to
find, but difficult to discover what had made the
animal fall. And Kalie had to know what that was.

Finally she found it: a long piece of bone,
splintered down the middle. A jagged section, like a
serpent's fang, had imbedded itself in the horse's hoof.
Gravity and chance had done the rest.

Kalie's dream of an army of snakes came back
to her with crystal clarity.

Gripping the bone until the sharp edges drew
blood from her hand and mingled it with that of the
horse, Kalie knew that at last, she had found the
weapon she had so long sought. The bone she held
was, she realized, the bone of a horse. Auspicious,
perhaps, but she suspected that any bone would do. It
would take some work: the shape wasn't the most
efficient. And even in a land full of bones, one bone
per…what was she going to call this thing? It didn't
matter. They would have to be small, and spherical.
With splinters of bone in all directions, so whichever
way the thing landed, whichever way a rapidly moving
horse stepped on it…

She set to work. The sun was a fiery ball on the
western horizon by the time Kalie came up with a
rough approximation of what she needed. It was
shaped like a star, but more beautiful than any that
shone in the sky. It had five sharp teeth of varying
length and thickness protruding in different directions.

No bigger than Kalie's hand, it lay lightly in her palm. An average sized leg bone from a sheep could produce four or five of these, once she got the hang of it. Standing up and brushing bone fragments from her thighs, Kalie saw how late it was and hurried back to camp.

Chapter 29

For three days, Kalie sat in her tent made her new weapons.

She had changed her clothes, and gave what she had worn during the rape to one of the servants. But for three days, she did not change the new set, nor did she comb her hair, bathe, or acknowledge anyone in the tent unless she had to.

Kalie knew that people were looking at her strangely. In rare moments of clarity, she even admitted that many were worried about her; that they wanted to help. But she couldn't dwell on that. If she did, she might remember what happened at the spring, and try to confide in one of them. And time was too short for that: already final preparations were underway for breaking camp and moving west.

The Serpent Fangs, as Kalie had named her weapon, had to be ready before that happened.

On the morning of the third day, someone scratched at the tent door. Kalie was alone in the tent, so she ignored it, and continued with her work. A shaft of sunlight, quickly blocked, surprised her. Against all custom and good manners, Brenia was entering a tent without leave from its mistress. Then she turned back, pulled a heavy basket after her, and let the tent flap close behind her.

Kalie started to tell her to go away, but one look at her friend and the words died on her lips. The swelling on Brenia's face had gone down, leaving it a mass of yellow-purple bruises. But she could see, and her eyes shone with a grim determination.

"You would not leave me in my darkest hour,"

the horsewoman said simply. "I will not leave you in yours. So don't bother telling me to leave."

Kalie nodded, trying to find a balance between anger and gratitude. "What have you brought?" she asked, nodding to the basket.

"Some tea to make you feel better. And a bath, which you sorely need." Brenia wrinkled her nose and withdrew from the basket the now familiar packets of cypress, cedar and frankincense that the women of the tribe used for bathing.

Kalie thought about arguing, but found she really didn't want to. So she let Brenia remove her garments, and apply the fragrant paste to Kalie's body. Brenia worked gently and efficiently, and to Kalie's relief, without speaking. Kalie had expected Brenia to ask questions or offer advice, but her sister-by-marriage did neither, and much to her surprise, Kalie found herself feeling better.

Finally, when Brenia was rubbing Kalie down with a piece of rough felt, and Kalie's skin felt clean and tingly, Brenia said, "Riyik will not blame you for what Haraak did. He will not love you any less."

Kalie was about to ask how Brenia knew, or who else might, then decided it didn't matter. She only knew that hearing the words made her feel better, and, more importantly, she believed them.

But still she asked: "How can you know? How can any woman?"

"I know because he is my brother. That is perhaps a stronger bond than most. Certainly more than what most marriages share. But what you have is special. More, I think than what Riyik had with Yalina. Don't let your hatred of this place destroy that."

A tear slid unnoticed down Kalie's face. "I don't hate everything about this place," Kalie said, surprising herself. "I have found more to love here than I ever thought possible. But why risk loving anything when men like Haraak can take it away in a heartbeat?"

"Because to refuse what few good things there are in life is to choose death," Brenia said simply. "But I have known many good things in my life, and I have decided that a few is not enough. And that is why I am coming with you when you leave."

Kalie's heart leapt. "You will steal your son from his father? Against all law and custom?"

"Yes."

"You will give up your fight for Hysaak? Your chance for revenge against Elka?"

Brenia was silent for a long time. Then she lifted her ravaged face to Kalie and said, "I've decided that when a woman steals your husband, sometimes the best revenge of all is to let her keep him." Her lips twisted into a mischievous smile.

And for the first time in three days, Kalie smiled too.

The next day, slaves from Cassia's tent came with tearful pleas and desperate tugs at her clothing. Kalie followed them out, more to stop their whining than out of any interest in what Cassia wanted. After so long inside the tent, the bright sunlight was blinding. As Kalie walked, she felt as if all eyes were on her; as if they could see her shame.

Maalke was away, thankfully, when Kalie and the slaves reached the tent. Cassia was clutching her son and praying softly.

"Help him," she whispered, when Kalie crawled through the low opening into the place that had been her home more than eight moonspans. She had to fight a rising sense of panic that she would not be allowed to leave.

"What's wrong?" Kalie asked, wishing she were anyplace else. Cassia held the baby to her, and Kalie got the answer at once as she took in the baby's bluish color and weak breathing. Since his birth, she had suspected Enak's lungs were not strong enough to keep him alive for long. A twinge of emotion fought free from where she had locked it, as she thought of Cassia's pain at the loss of her only child.

"Please," Cassia said, her voice hoarse with fear. "You must save him. I will give you anything!"

The shield—or possibly madness—that had protected Kalie these last four days crumbled under the baby's plight and the mother's desperation. "Sage," she said. "Do you have any?"

While one of the slave girls hurried to get some, Kalie shifted the baby's position to better encourage breathing and began to massage his chest. "Couldn't Alessa do anything for him while she was here? Her skills are so much greater than mine, I had thought that surely—"

Cassia's lips became a bitter line in her face. "She never even saw him. Maalke quarreled with her master the day she was to come and would allow no one from Nelek's household into our tent."

Kalie sighed but said nothing. When the sage arrived, she crushed it into the coals of the brazier and poured onto them a measure of water. Carefully, she held the infant over the brazier, out of range of the heat, but close enough for the herb-laden steam to reach into his nose.

Almost immediately, his breathing became easier and his color improved.

But she knew it was only temporary.

From the look on Cassia's face, Kalie knew that she knew it too. "I promised you whatever you wanted," she told Kalie. "Yet we both know there's little I can give that you would want. I promise the gods the same thing, but what do they care about the pleadings of a woman? I suppose there's nothing more pathetic than a mother's struggle to save her child."

Kalie laughed bitterly at Cassia last words. "I would have said there's nothing more noble."

"You can't have nobility without power," Cassia said sadly.

"You may have more power than you know," Kalie muttered under her breath.

"What did you say?"

Kalie was already turning to go, but she stopped and looked back at Cassia. Suddenly she asked, "How far would you go to save Enak?"

Cassia only stared at Kalie, as if willing her to explain herself.

"Would you leave all this?" Kalie gestured to the tent and everything in it. "Would you cross the steppes alone? Would you travel all the way to my homeland, where the healing magic exists that could save your son?"

Cassia snorted. "I'm going to do that anyway in a few days' time. Maalke says we'll be there before winter and we shall own all the land before spring. But I fear Enak will not survive the journey." She made the sign against evil as she spoke.

"Even if he did, you might have trouble finding

a healer for him after your men kill them all and burn their medicines!" she said brutally.

"Then why bring it up in the first place?" Cassia demanded angrily.

"I was just wondering…" Kalie shook her head in frustration. What was she wondering? If the suffering of innocent people would ever begin to matter to Cassia? "If you would give up all you've ever known; change who you were and adopt a new way of live, if doing so would save your son."

"As we once thought you would change?" Cassia asked, too shrewdly.

"Keep Enak where he can breathe in the steam until morning. Give him hyssop tea before he sleeps and when he wakes up." She hurried out of the tent without waiting to be dismissed.

It was only on her way back to Riyik's tent that Kalie noticed the small but certain change in the activity of the camp. Tucked into the usual bustle of women and children and even men preparing a camp for departure, were the furtive sights of busy hands splitting bones and twisting the splinters into little sharp stars.

In the doorway of a large tent, where a large woman stood shouting at a cowering slave girl, the slave next to her sat impassively, shaping a sphere of splintered bone.

Another woman sat telling her children a story as she made similar shapes from bones, nodding approvingly when her oldest daughter took a piece and clumsily began to copy her actions. Kalie kept walking, but thought for a moment she heard the word "Goddess" in the woman's tale.

And by the midden, an old woman, recently

cast out by an angry husband to live as a Shadow Woman, knelt in the filth, humming to herself as she arranged the pile of bones she had gathered by length and shape.

"I truly have gone mad," Kalie muttered. "I'm seeing things that cannot be." Then she passed by the grand tent of a clan chief, and saw old Danica standing in the doorway, as straight and proud as any warrior, directing her slaves in the gathering and sorting of bones. Sarika and two others knelt inside where the light was the best, a growing pile of Serpent Fangs beside them. As Kalie passed by, Danica smiled at her, a light of grim determination in her eyes.

And Kalie knew she was not imagining things. But what was going on so defied her imagination she might as well be.

When she reached the tent, Riyik was waiting for her. He was alone.

"Where are the others," Kalie asked seating herself opposite her husband, beside the brazier where the coals were still hot and her cooking knives close at hand in case she should need them.

"Varena has taken Yarik out for exercise, and the serving women have gone to the midden to gather bones. For stew, they said."

Kalie noticed that Riyik no longer referred to them as slaves.

"You have not been yourself these last few days," Riyik said.

"Are you sure?" Kalie countered.

Riyik had been about to speak again, but stopped. Uncertainly creased his handsome features. "What do you mean?"

"Can you honestly say you know who I am

well enough to know when I am not?"

Riyik honored her by considering her words and nothing else for at least one hundred heart beats. Then he said, "No, I cannot say that I do. But I can see that something is wrong. And I am asking you, as your husband—as your friend—to tell me what it is."

If he had left it as husband, Kalie could have assumed the guise of a horsewoman and come up with a convincing lie. But Riyik had asked her as a friend, and he had proved himself one time and again. Even if the truth destroyed their friendship—or their marriage —Kalie knew she had to tell him.

"Before I speak, Riyik, you must give me your word as a warrior of Aahk that you will hear all that I have to say, and not leave this tent until I am finished."

She saw the tension coil the ropes of strong muscle beneath his skin and his eyes darken as though his worst fears had just been confirmed. But he nodded and said, "I swear in the name of Aahk and by my honor as His warrior that I will listen to all you say and not depart this tent until you give me leave."

That was more than she had asked for, but it did not make beginning any easier. Her mouth suddenly dry, Kalie took a drink from the water skin at her waist, stopping to look at it for the first time in a long while. Riyik had made this for her while she still thought of him as her enemy. She took another drink.

"Four days ago I went out from camp to be alone by a spring I know of. Haraak followed me there and raped me." Riyik's hand shot out to grasp his spear. He seemed about to leap up, but stayed where he was, though the effort cost him. Kalie pushed on. "I was foolish; I should have known he would learn of all I was doing to thwart his plans. But I thought I was being so clever, and..." Kalie's breath caught in her throat. She controlled the tears that threatened and continued. "I allowed rumors of his impotence to convince me I was safe from that particular form of revenge."

"Why did you not tell me?" Riyik's voice was barely audible.

Kalie fell silent. She had thought of little else since that day, yet now...

"You already know why, Riyik. I could tell you Haraak's threats word for word, but...you already know." Riyik nodded, but did not seem inclined to speak, so Kalie did. "If I told you, I had to risk losing you in combat with Haraak. And I had to risk the possibility that you would not believe me." Riyik's head shot up, a look of such hurt on his face that she fairly shouted what should have been the truth. "I knew you would believe me! I know you are not like the others of your kind! But I couldn't risk him killing you!"

"Do you think so little of my skill as a warrior?" Riyik demanded.

"I think too highly of your honor, Riyik. You are the better warrior, but you would have fought fairly. Do you believe for an instant that Haraak would have?"

Riyik looked away. Kalie pressed her point. "Had he killed you, I would have been his. For the rest of my life, he could have done to me what he did by the spring, and no one would have called it rape. And he would have done it to Varena too."

Riyik's knuckles shone white where he gripped the spear. "You still should have trusted me," he whispered.

"Yes, I should have," Kalie said sadly, suddenly wishing she could bridge the gap between them.

"I will kill Haraak," Riyik said, more calmly. "And I will do it without putting you or Varena at risk of falling into his hands."

"You will not challenge him, then?"

"As you pointed out, that is what he is counting on."

Kalie began to relax then. Yes, she should have known Riyik would not be like the other men here. With the easing of tension, came a clearing of her mind. "Killing you was always part of Haraak's plan," she said. "Even before he chose to use me as the means. Why?"

Suddenly Riyik looked embarrassed. "I fear he has learned of my plans, as well. Not the part about going west with you, though that is the hardest part. I promised to take you home; to live there with you if your people would accept me. I have come to realize now that I cannot."

Kalie had never expected Riyik to come home with her. Yet now she felt as if her heart had been ripped from her chest. I can't do this without you! she wanted to shout. Instead she took his hand and squeezed it lightly, as one friend offering another support. "What has happened?"

"I found many followers willing to travel west with us. Men who did not fit in to this life; men who were sick of the corruption and dishonor that Haraak and his kind have brought to our land; men who just wanted the adventure of new sights and new ways. Then, as I got to know them better, I saw they were a more diverse mix than I realized. Like spring water contaminated by dirt and sand. If you set the cup down and wait long enough, the pure water rises to the top, and the sand and grit settles on the bottom.

"I began to see them as two camps. One consists of men who want to come, but should not. Oh, they listen well enough when I explain what this new life will entail. They say they are eager to meet women who speak their minds and men who have skills at things other than war. But beneath that I sense…"

"Men of little status on the steppes, who dream of carving out their own kingdoms in a land of easy pickings?"

Riyik looked startled. Then he laughed ruefully. "I guess you saw all that before I did. Before I even chose them."

"I feared it," Kalie said. "But what of the other camp? Those that are the water which rises to the top?"

"They are men who would make your world proud to ally with the warriors of Aahk. They would teach your people to defend themselves, and die in their defense. But they—we—have all agreed that our duty to our own comes first. We cannot travel west until we have cleansed our tribe of the corruption that poisons it and set it once more on the path of honor."

Kalie remembered the day Riyik had offered to go west with her. She had known then that he could not leave his countrymen in the hands of a man like Haraak, and she had been right. That didn't make hearing it any easier.

She found she was still holding Riyik's hand. He lifted hers to his lips. "I love you Kalie. In ways I have never loved anyone. But if I left with you now, I would always know myself for a coward and an oathbreaker. I could never become the kind of man your people could accept, or the husband you deserve."

"I know, Riyik. And that is part of why I love you." With a startled look, they both realized that she had finally said it. She wasn't sorry.

"What of the alliance?" she asked. What was left of it, anyway. "And who will be king of the tribe of Aahk?"

"Reasonable questions. And they create more problems. If we stay on the steppes, and the alliance remains, we will be strong; strong enough, perhaps, to survive the winter, and the hard times beyond.

"If the alliance fails—and many among us think that it should, that the times ahead are a test by our own gods, for us alone—who knows how many of us will survive the winter? But those who do…they will be like a spear, tempered by fire. Like a fine tool, shaved to its core…" Again Riyik stared at things only he could see.

"And the new king?" Kalie prompted.

Riyik brought his full attention back to her. "Some say it should be me." He looked searchingly at Kalie.

She was looking for an appropriate reply when a wave of laughter took her. Riyik seemed more puzzled than angry, and when Kalie could finally speak again, she hastened to explain. "What a system of government you people have! You would indeed make the best of kings, my love, but you fear you are not worthy and that the job will corrupt you. Yet of course, that is why it must be you! In this land, only someone who does not want the job is right for it, while those want it are made unfit by the very qualities that make them seek it in the first place!"

Then Riyik laughed as well. "So I myself have discovered after many sleepless nights. If I had spoken with you sooner, I'd have saved myself much grief."

"But the answer would still be the same," Kalie said sadly.

"Yes it would. And it would still all come down to this: tomorrow night, under the dark of the moon, you must take Yarik and Varena, Brenia and Barak, and leave this camp, with provisions, and those of your followers who are willing. Before the sun has risen the next day, I and my followers will move against Haraak, and let the gods decide all our fates."

So soon? Kalie had worked for this moment since she had arrived over a year ago, yet was now discovered that she wasn't ready.

"Before that happens," Riyik continued, "I would like very much to lie with you as a husband and w—" He stopped. "—As a man and a woman whose souls are one. As a man and woman of your people do. If you will show me how."

And Kalie decided that she wanted it too. She realized as they began, first awkwardly, then with growing skill, that she had never before shown a man how to do it. Teaching a willing partner, she discovered, was more arousing than the practiced skill of her most experienced lover.

And perhaps, knowing that this might be their last—their only—time together, they loved with a passion greater than they would otherwise have. They rolled together in the felt tent, sometimes with Riyik on top, sometimes Kalie. And when at last he entered her, there was no pain, no memories of Haraak or Maalke. Only a sense of rightness, and a longing that it might always be this way.

Chapter 30

Kalie awoke before the first light of dawn. For a moment, she didn't know where she was. She felt warm and rested and something inside her was insisting that she stay this way and not spoil everything by waking up.

Slowly, exquisitely, she became aware of Riyik's body against hers. His heart was beating gently against her side. Close to hers and for a moment, it seemed, in time with hers.

Then, as she came fully awake and he remained asleep, their heartbeats lost synchronicity and Kalie gently disentangled herself from him, more to take a long uninterrupted look at him than from any desire to get up and start the day.

The features of his face, so serious, so often troubled during the day were serene now. A half smile tugged at his full sweet mouth. He rolled over, muttered something, and began moving his hand along the spot Kalie had just left, as if searching for someone.

Riyik opened his eyes. The half smile blossomed into something beyond beautiful when they focused on Kalie. He was about to speak, then suddenly sat up, reaching for the spear that was never far from a horseman's hand. Then Kalie heard what Riyik had: the heavy footfalls of many men. When they stopped before the door flap of the tent, raised angry voices had joined them. Kalie knew from the way the sound filled every part of the tent that they were surrounded.

The flap was jerked open without ceremony.

"Come out, traitor!" yelled a voice Kalie did not recognize. Riyik set down his spear, glancing at Kalie and shaking his head sadly. He kissed her once, hastily pulled on his trousers and made his way to the front of the tent.

"Stay here," he told her. Kalie looked around the tent and saw that everyone was there: Varena held a whimpering Yarik, while the two young serving women struggled awake. Agafa, fully awake sat like a statue, a look of bleak resignation on her face. They must have come in after we fell asleep, Kalie thought. Did anyone get supper?

Riyik slipped from the tent, pushing the flap closed behind him. It was jerked open a moment later, and a booming voice ordered everyone out of the tent.

"What is the meaning of this?" Riyik demanded of the dozen or so warriors gathered outside his tent. Kalie crawled out in time to see a warrior strike Riyik's face by way of an answer, while another was busy tying his hands behind his back. Varena came out, carrying Yarik. Kalie took the boy and put an arm around Varena, holding her close. The girl stood tall and proud beside her adopted mother. If she felt fear, she did not show it. The three servants huddled nearby, fear-filled faces veiled.

"Take them before the king!" shouted one of the men. Two remained behind and entered the tent as the rest began to move. Kalie realized they would be searching it. The Horse-Killers! Had she even bothered to hide them before she went to see Cassia?

They marched through the sleeping camp as dawn slowly brightened the eastern sky.

Soon, everyone was awake and watching the procession. Most of the men followed behind, speculating loudly on what was going on, or raced ahead to the king's tent to be among the first to find out. Women and children peeked out of tents as the prisoners passed, then shrugged and began the mundane labors of the day.

When they reached the open space before the king's tent, most of Kariik's chiefs and high ranking advisors were already gathered, seated on stools and looking more pompous than serious. Kalie automatically looked for Haraak, surprised to find him missing. He arrived just moments later, at the head of another group of prisoners. Kalie recognized many of them as men Riyik hoped to bring west. Haraak searched the crowd, his gaze pausing only briefly on Kalie, then resting on Riyik with a satisfied smirk.

When everyone was assembled, Kariik finally emerged from the tent, adjusting his tunic and tying on his belt, and looking angry at having been awakened.

"What matter is so important it could not wait for a decent hour?" Kariik demanded.

"Treason, my king," said one of the men who had arrested Riyik. "A group of your loyal warriors have uncovered a plot to kill you and all your kin, and make this man—" he pointed at Riyik, "—king in your place."

"That is a lie!" Riyik shouted. Kalie wasn't sure which part he was denying. Based on what Riyik had told her the night before, the accusations might not be far from the truth.

Other men were named. Some were members of Riyik's very real conspiracy. The rest, she suspected, were men whom Haraak, or one of the other power brokers, simply wanted to be rid of.

Kariik at least seemed to be showing more

interest now. "Have you uncovered what means these traitors planned to use to slay their king?" he asked.

Haraak nodded to two younger warriors, and they came forward, carrying a large hide between them, which sagged beneath the load of whatever it carried. Riyik and his friends exchanged puzzled glances, and Kalie leaned forward in sudden dread at what she would see.

Haraak left the king's side and strode forth, lifting a skin of kumis from the pile. "Poison!" he shouted in voice loud enough to carry through the camp. "So vile and unnatural that no warrior would have even suspected it of one of his brothers. Yet it is true. These were taken from Riyik's own tent! And yesterday another batch was found. Not so many, it's true, but just as deadly."

"It's true," said chief Kahlar. "We tested some on a slave, who now lays dying, yet still not able to cross over. A hideous kind of living death is what our so-called brother intended for our king and those loyal to him!"

The crowd was in uproar. Kalie was reminded of the time Yasha was stoned to death. Kariik sat frozen on his costly wooden stool, as though he were carved out of wax.

"Those weren't Riyik's—" Kalie shouted, trying to be heard over the crowd. She surged forward, trying to reach Kariik, only to be stopped by his guards and shoved roughly to the ground. When she gained her feet she saw Riyik waving to her frantically and shaking his head. "NO!" He shouted. Kalie could not hear him over the roaring crowd, but could read his face well enough. Implicating herself would not save Riyik. She would just have to keep silent and watch, and seek an opportunity to free him.

How had Haraak found out about the kumis? And what could she do now? Kalie was prepared to trade her life for victory over her enemies, but she hadn't planned on trading Riyik's. Or anyone else's she thought with sick horror, as the next victim of this farce was brought forward.

A pair of warriors dragged Brenia before the king. "Why is this woman here?" Kariik demanded.

"We believe it was she who brewed this kumis, and had the knowledge and means to create the poison," a nervous looking young warrior blurted out too quickly. Probably promised advancement for pretending to be the one who figured it out, Kalie thought. "The poisoned kumis we found yesterday was in her tent."

"Then where is her husband, who is the owner of the tent and everything in it?" Kariik demanded, nearly rising from his stool.

"Here, my king!" came a breathless voice. Hysaak came forward on his own, rather than being brought by guards. But only because he was moving so fast, Kalie thought.

He stopped at a safe distance from the king and bowed low. "It was I who discovered my wife's treachery! I returned late to my tent the night before last. The kumis skin was empty—typical of my useless wife's housekeeping! I searched the tent for more, thinking she had already packed it with our travel rations, and I found these." Hysaak pointed to the small pile of skins that had been set out by still more warriors as he spoke.

"I knew at once that something was wrong from the taste. Then I began to feel very strange. I am certain that if I had drunk anymore I would now be dead."

"As you will be soon," someone in the crowd called out. At once others took it up as a chant. Hysaak blanched.

"So it is your claim that your wife is behind a plot to murder your king? And that you knew nothing of what was going on within your own tent?"

Hysaak's desperate denial was swallowed by the laughter and jeering of the crowd. When they finally quieted enough for him to be heard Hysaak's voice was barely a squeak. "It is her brother who is behind all of it! Anyone can see that! It was his orders she followed, not mine!"

Members of the crowd began to call out lewd jokes about men who couldn't control their own wives, but Kariik silenced them with a raised hand.

"Why did you not come to me immediately?" Kariik demanded.

"I did!" Hysaak nearly shrieked. "I was stopped from disturbing your rest by your own loyal guard!" He pointed to the nervous young guard who had denounced Brenia, then frantically beckoned him forward. The man did not move, nor did he meet Hysaak's eye. "He said he would take care of the matter!" Kalie could smell his sweat from where she stood. How different he looked from his wife, who stood calmly with her head held high.

"Well?" Kariik demanded, looking for once like a king as he fixed the guard with a black stare. The boy began to squirm, then to search the crowd.

Haraak stepped forward. It's about time you showed your hand, Kalie thought. "My king, as you know, I have been investigating reports of this treachery for some time. When this news was brought to my attention, I knew I had to flush out all the traitors at once, or risk leaving some to begin plotting again. Surely the king can see how dangerous it would be for even one to escape justice, at such a time as this."

Kariik took all this in, as the crowd fell silent, straining to hear every word.

Into this silence, Riyik spoke up calmly. "If those who pretend to be your friends are finished, my king, may I now have my say?"

"Do not allow the traitor to speak!" Chief Zavan shouted, though he sat near enough to Kariik to be heard whispering. There were many in the crowd who echoed his words.

But others wanted to hear what Riyik had to say. He was a warrior, they argued, and any warrior— even an accused traitor—had the right to speak in his own defense.

"I will not coat my words with honey, in the manner of men who seek to curry favor with a king," Riyik began. "And I will speak the truth, though doing so will only hasten my death."

Silence reigned. Riyik spoke into it.

"I was once proud to bear the name of Warrior of Aahk, but no longer. Once, our people valued the freedom to roam the steppes over warfare with all whom we met. We fought to show our might against those who challenged us and to protect what was ours. Now, we seek only to take what others have, and rarely fight anyone who is not weaker than ourselves. Of late, it seems unarmed people who do not fight at all are our targets of choice."

A soft muttering began, like the quiet before a

storm, but Riyik pitched his voice above it, and it carried all the way to the fringes of the crowd. "We have spawned men who have slain their own king and seek to put a puppet in his place." Riyik's gaze finally sought Kalie's. "And, we have spawned men who have made slaves of strangers who dealt honorably with us. People who tended our wounds when we were lost and injured. People who deserved our respect."

Haraak was whispering frantically in Kariik's ears, while others who surrounded the king began shouting for Riyik to be silenced. This time, however, the crowd did not join in. They, it seemed, wanted to hear more.

Riyik, perhaps sensing time was short, raised his voice above the din. "I have only one more thing to say! I freely admit to plotting to bring down those who murdered King Aahnaak and betrayed our people. But my family is innocent!" He took a step closer to Kariik, and held his gaze. "I beg you my king: prove me wrong in thinking you to be only a witless tool of ruthless men! Allow my wife to return to her people, taking my sister and those of my household who wish to accompany her. This once, think for yourself and make a decision which is right…"

The storm broke and the roaring of the crowd closed over Riyik's words.

But Kalie knew that she never loved anyone more than she loved Riyik at that moment. And she wanted desperately to tell him that.

There seemed to be as much shouting going on between the men seated in front of Kalie as in the crowd behind her. She began to move closer to Riyik. Then Kariik stood, and silenced his people with such stony calm that Kalie thought Riyik's words had had some effect. But when order was restored, and everyone waited for their king's judgment, his face clouded, his eyes uncertain again.

He looked toward Haraak, then checked and turned away before their eyes met. Kariik turned instead to Hysaak, who stood in a little cleared area which no one but Elka, hand over her bulging middle, was willing to share with him.

"As king I shall pronounce sentence over the men who broke their oaths to me. But a wife who breaks faith with her husband is a different matter. Hysaak, I find you free of fault in this matter." Hysaak seemed ready to faint with relief. "But what of your wife? Her punishment falls to you; it would be beneath a king's dignity to say otherwise."

Hysaak did not even look at his first wife. He spat upon the ground in Brenia's general direction and said, "I throw her away, my king. Let her die with her brother if it pleases you."

Brenia showed no reaction to her husband's words. Kalie saw she was looking off in the distance, to the west, with a kind of sorrowful longing.

"Nothing pleases me at the moment," Kariik said to Hysaak. "But you, at least are free to return to your tent. As for these others…" Kariik turned to look at each of the prisoners. He tried once again to avoid Haraak's gaze, then gave up. "They shall all die tonight." Haraak gave an audible sigh of relief.

"But surely not as sacrifices to the gods," said the high priest. "To do so would curse this venture not bless it."

"I know little of these matters," said Kariik looking suddenly exhausted. "But I'm sure you do. I leave it in your hands." He turned to an older warrior, one whom Kalie remembered as a close advisor of the previous king. "Bring me an accounting of the property held by each of the traitors. I shall dispose of all of it tonight, before the executions."

Kariik rose and turned back to his tent. Many of his chiefs and advisors tried to follow him, but he waved them away, and went into his tent alone.

It was a long time before the crowd dispersed. Everyone seemed to be waiting for something more. Haraak, Kalie was pleased to see, looked outraged when he was turned away from the king's tent. A group of at least twenty warriors led the prisoners to an empty tent, where six followed them inside and the rest stood guard outside. Brenia, the only woman among them, walked beside her brother.

In the meantime, no one seemed concerned about Kalie standing alone and unfettered. What of the wives of the other prisoners? She searched the crowd for some sign of the few she had met. She saw no one she recognized, but what did that prove?

Kalie took an experimental step. When no one stopped her, she took another, then another. She moved like a ghost through the excited crowd, a destination slowly growing inside her.

She passed Hysaak and Elka, and brushed close to hear their words.

"...Out of the question!" Hysaak was hissing.

"The king will want to purge the blood of traitors from his tribe," Elka argued. "Once Riyik and his slut of a sister are dead, the boy will be all that is left of their tainted bloodline."

"A son takes nothing from his mother, as everyone knows. All that he inherits is from his father!" Hysaak pursed his lips and gazed at his wife.

"Barak is my heir and will remain so even if you give me ten sons! If you hope to see him displaced, it will be because one of his brothers bests him, not because their scheming mother gets him out of their way."

Elka lowered her smoldering eyes demurely. "Of course, husband. I merely sought to protect our family." She paused as if the discussion was over. Then, just as Kalie passed out of earshot, said, "But a boy whose uncle and mother were traitors will have a hard life. Would not an honorable death as a sacrifice to the gods…?"

Kalie had one day. She would find a way to rescue Riyik, and perhaps all his men. But first, she had to ask someone a question she very much wanted not to ask.

Chapter 31

Cassia stood near her tent, respectably robed and veiled, but Kalie knew she was listening carefully; catching every piece of news that flew by. There was much news and many eager mouths to spread it.

"No need to rely on gossips to learn what was said outside the king's tent," Kalie said. "I was there; I can tell you it all."

Cassia regarded her levelly; appraising. Planning defense or attack? Kalie wondered.

"Let us go inside," Cassia said.

"Let us not," Kalie replied.

Cassia raised an imperious eyebrow, clearly surprised by this argument from...a slave? That was, Kalie realized, how Cassia was looking at her.

Kalie bristled, more curious than angry, though that emotion was smoldering inside her. With a toss of her veiled head, Kalie made her tone light. "Oh, come now, Cassia, we are just two women talking." She gestured at the many such pairs and small groups throughout the camp. "And safer from curious ears out here in the light than inside your shadowy tent."

Cassia nodded, casting a concerned look back toward her tent, and then turning to Kalie with less arrogance in her stance than a moment ago.

"It was you, then?" said Kalie. "You who set Haraak on me? How? Why?"

Again, Cassia seemed surprised by the direction of the conversation. "I could see what you were doing to our people, Kalie. Your foreign ways, your shameless words. It was like a poison! I fooled myself into thinking that you meant no harm by it, or at least could do nothing if you did. After all, you were a lone woman and a slave besides!

"But then you married Riyik and your words began to carry weight, and I could see how the women looked at you; how they whispered when there were no men around. I still didn't believe it…how could I? How could anyone believe that the tribe of Aahk could be brought down by a little barbarian slave girl?

"But then I went to visit Brenia, and found the kumis you asked her to hide."

"She told you about it?" Kalie asked, trying to keep her voice level.

"She denied it was poison; in fact, she tried to keep your name out of it all together. She said it was a love potion to bring Hysaak back to her and she couldn't remember who gave her the recipe." Cassia snorted. "From the look of her, and the gossip about his new wife, she would have been wiser to try such a potion. But Brenia's not a good liar. Besides, there were enough bags of the stuff for half the camp!"

"So what did you do then?"

"I put things together. I didn't know exactly what your plans were, or how much Riyik knew about it. But I knew Haraak was looking for a way to pull him down. I knew he would be grateful for the information, and would reward the man who brought it to him. So I told Maalke everything I had seen and guessed."

"Maalke?" Kalie thought back. "He wasn't with Haraak—he wasn't even at the king's tent—"

"I know!" said Cassia, raising her voice for the first time. "The fool didn't believe me! He said the men who ruled the king would pay him in laughter for such wild ravings. He told me to confine my gossip to women's matters and stay out of politics. Then he went to get drunk and fuck the slave girls."

Kalie began to laugh. Nothing about the situation was funny, but the irony of it all had her doubled over, nearly shrieking. How close she had come to winning the day—all because of Maalke's stupidity!

Cassia slapped her hard across the face. That might not have stopped the laughter, but Cassia's next words did. "So I had to go to Haraak myself. My foolish husband threw away a chance for advancement and I had to risk my reputation."

"Why?" taunted Kalie. "You were so afraid of me that you couldn't come to me yourself? You needed a creature like Haraak to fight your battles for you?"

"Battles such as these can only be fought by men! That is something every girl of Aahk learns before her tenth year! I saw there was a danger that had to be stopped, and knew that if I did it right, I might save my son!"

"How?"

Cassia sighed. "Why do you think you're walking free right now, rather than tied up next to your husband? Haraak promised me that you will be returned to your position of slave in this tent in exchange for the information I gave him."

It took Kalie a moment to understand. Of course. Enak. Cassia's sickly child who owed his existence to Kalie's fertility treatments and any future he had to her healing abilities. "That's what this is all about?" she cried. "That's why you betrayed me—"

"Betrayed you?" Cassia's eyes were wide with shock. "You were going to poison half the men in our tribe!"

"Of course I was! What did you expect me to do?" Kalie was nearly shouting. "Sit back and play the helpless woman while your people enslaved all of mine?"

"Well I never expected you to kill anyone! I never expected you to corrupt half the women of this tribe into thinking they could change things!"

Kalie lowered her voice and asked with genuine curiosity, "What did you expect, Cassia? Knowing the stakes for what they were, what did you really expect me to do?"

"To make the best life you could for yourself, here, in your new home! To use what skills you possessed to influence a powerful man, so that when we conquered the land of your birth, you might be in a position to help some of them. It's what any sane woman would do."

"Then I will happily remain insane, for whatever time I have left to live!" Kalie snapped. At Cassia's puzzled look she added, "You don't really think I'd go back to being your slave, do you?"

Cassia's color rose with her temper. "Do you think you will have a choice?"

"Careful, Cassia! Don't use words you don't understand! If you wanted to save your son, you should have asked for my help, not murdered my friends." She peered intently at her former mistress. "And what about Brenia? She was your friend before I ever came to this land. Do you feel nothing for her?"

Cassia lifted her head and looked past Kalie. "If she had remained a dutiful wife, no harm would have befallen her." But her voice shook, and Kalie could see the pain the other woman tried to hide.

"Other than being beaten to death by her husband for the pleasure of his new wife. That would likely have happened sooner rather than later once you helped Haraak kill her brother."

"Why do you taunt me like this?" cried Cassia. "I saved your life! Haraak has promised—"

"And we all know how Haraak keeps his promises." Kalie's voice was low, but so frightening that Cassia went still. "And now that you've brought yourself to that particular rapist's attention, Cassia, I'd suggest you be very careful to never be alone."

"I do that anyway," Cassia said, regaining some of her composure. "So will you, once you finally learn how to be a proper woman of the tribe."

"I will die first."

"Why?" cried Cassia, throwing up her hands in frustration. "Do you think dying with your husband will take you to paradise? It won't! He's a traitor, and to die with him will only mean—"

At that moment the cry went through the camp: "Riders! A small party, carrying the banners of Nelek, King of the Wolf Tribe!"

Discussions of treason and executions were forgotten as everyone who could hurried to the open area outside of the encampment where Kariik and his chiefs were already mounted and riding out to meet the visitors. If speculation had run wild before, it knew no bounds now, as everyone whispered or shouted possible reasons a former ally would be returning without a war party.

Kalie followed along, leaving Cassia torn between curiosity and her wifely duty to remain inside and wait until given permission to leave.

It was strangely thrilling, Kalie thought, as she

lifted her skirts and ran to get as close to the main action as the king's guards would allow. Here she was, about to watch nearly everyone she loved die, while everyone else she loved faced slavery, and she herself became Haraak's pawn—and yet she felt free.

It was as if events had been put into motion—by Kalie, by Haraak, by his gods or her Goddess—who knew? Maybe all of them. And there was nothing to do but ride along with them, and see where they went.

And she wasn't afraid.

Nelek was dismounting, his whole being on fire with a kind of manic energy. He had perhaps twenty men with him. Kalie recognized his brother, and one of his chiefs, but his sons—his remaining sons—appeared to be absent. Crouching behind two fortuitously tall children, she had an excellent view of the drama as Kariik, flanked by guards bristling with weapons, slid from his horse, and strode to meet his rival king.

The king of the Wolf Tribe looked older than he had just days earlier, Kalie thought. He stood with an air of tragic dignity as he held his empty hands out in the beastmen gesture of peace. Kariik halted a few paces before Nelek, and motioned his guards to stand down.

"Kariik, my brother king," Nelek began. "I come to you with news of grave importance."

"I await it eagerly," Kariik said, eyeing his one-time ally warily.

"I left this camp in anger, thinking a grave insult had been offered me, and my son Valaan, whom I knew to be blameless in the matter which led to his death."

Tension filled the air, for Nelek's words seemed more the prelude to a fight than any gesture of peace. Several warriors reached for their weapons, but the stony faced Wolf King held up a hand for patience. "I say this because I now know he was blameless—and so was your warrior, Kariik, my brother. And so, most likely, was his poor wife."

Voice cracking with emotion, Nelek shouted into the now silent crowd. "We were all of us betrayed! All for the petty scheming of one who owed us nothing but loyalty!" Nelek turned and motioned to a hide-wrapped bundle on the ground behind his horse. At his nod, one of the warriors flung it open, none to gently.

Inside it was Alessa.

Chapter 32

Alessa met Kalie's eyes from where she lay, as composed as ever. Kalie sighed with relief. For someone who had been dragged by a horse across considerable distance, Alessa looked surprisingly good. She was bruised and disheveled, and as she sat up shakily, Kalie could see fresh welts on her back, but she was not fatally injured. Kalie's relief faded, however, as Nelek began to speak.

"This woman," Nelek spat the words, "was not even born to our tribe! She came to me as a foreign slave! A worthless outsider—yet I raised her up! I made her my beloved concubine—honored above a dozen who were fairer than she. I entrusted her with the care of my wife when she was sick in childbed! And when this slave delivered my wife of a healthy son, I showered her with gifts, and honored her as if the child were hers!" A low growling arose from the spellbound crowd.

"I have learned that it was she," Nelek pointed to Alessa, "who arranged for my son to be found in your warrior's tent, to brew trouble between our two noble tribes. And it was she who seduced my older son and sought to turn him against me! His own father! All so that she might rise even higher as his favorite! Or perhaps even become his wife!"

Well, thought Kalie, as the crowd grew wild over this new scandal, at least no one's thinking about Riyik. Perhaps she could turn this distraction into an opportunity to rescue Riyik and Brenia. But then what of Alessa?

Kariik glanced at the woman on the ground.

"Why does she still live?" he asked Nelek.

"I was not her only victim," Nelek said. "She cost you a fine warrior. Both of us, therefore, should share in the judgment of her." Then Nelek bowed his head and came as close to abasing himself as a beast king could. "Kariik. Malquor. I have come to humbly beg your aide in cleansing my household of the filth brought by this faithless slave. And that afterwards, let we three great men once again turn our eyes to the west."

Malquor gave only a noncommittal nod, but Kariik stepped forward and embraced Nelek. "Come my brother, let us speak in my tent. I, too, have known the pain of betrayal by those close to me this day. Those who owed me their loyalty; their very lives. It has fallen to me as well to cleanse my house of corruption and deceit. Tonight, let the gods see how kings of this land deal with betrayal, be it from brother warriors or lowborn slave girls."

The kings repaired to Kariik's tent, while two warriors dragged Alessa off in the direction of the tent where Riyik and the others were being held. Kalie followed for a while, to be certain that's where they were taking her, while around her the camp took on the appearance of a huge beehive knocked down by the wind. Kalie felt like she was an island of calm, all to herself. For the moment, she was free, and the first thing to do was find the rest of those who were not under guard.

She found Varena cleverly hidden in the shadows cast by the arrangement of three tents. "Are you all right?" Kalie asked, gathering her adopted daughter into a fierce hug, and praying the girl would not reject her.

Varena's response was to cling to Kalie with no sign she would willingly let go.

"Oh, mother, what are we going to do?" she asked.

Until now, Kalie had managed to keep her emotions under tight control; even the guilt that threatened to tear her apart from within. But Varena's simple faith nearly undid her. "You must continue to hide, as you're already doing so well. Do you know where Agafa and the others are?"

"They went back to Riyik's tent after the warriors left." Kalie nodded. Waiting for the next owner, of course. What else could they do?

"Is Yarik with them?"

"Yes. He would not stop crying"

"What will happen to him after...tonight?" Kalie finished faintly.

"I don't think he'll have any living family. At least, none that will claim him. He probably won't be sacrificed, for fear of offending the gods with an imperfect gift, but they may send him along with his father, as a way to keep Riyik out of paradise."

Kalie's stomach clenched. Would the tally of lives she had ruined ever stop growing? She thought furiously, as Varena waited anxiously.

"All right now, listen to me. Stay here until the kings emerge from Kariik's tent. They will be making speeches and everyone in camp will want to hear them. If I haven't come to you with a plan by then, I want you to sneak back to Riyik's tent, gather up all the supplies you can, and make your way west to my homeland."

She tried to think of a message to send, but feared any words that came from her would only make

things worse. "You will have to be ready to leave as
soon as everyone's attention is on Kariik; he said he
would distribute the condemned men's property before
the executions. Take Yarik if you dare—no," Kalie
shook her head desperately. "He will slow you down.
Just take what you can and go! When you reach the
Land of the Goddess, tell whomever you meet what is
happening here, but then you must keep moving west.
There is a place in the mountains where I once lived. It
will take the tribes many lifetimes to penetrate that far.
Go there, they will take you in."

Varena stared at Kalie. "I could never do that!"

Kalie clutched Varena's shoulders and shook
her. "I know you're afraid! I know you think that you
can't do it! But—"

"That is not what I meant! I mean that I won't
leave here without you, Mother. We go there together
or not at all. And you've come too far to give up
now!"

Kalie stared at the calm, confident woman
before her, and wondered what had happened to the
terrified slave girl whose only goals in life had been
more food, a kinder master, a the safe delivery of a
son. Oh, Goddess, if I have done one good thing in this
land, she stands before me now.

"Varena, I have to stay behind, and try to
salvage some of what I came here to do." Although the
chances of doing anything but dying under a horse's
hooves as the horde rode west were slim.

"Then let me help!" cried the young woman.
"Let all of us help! You have more friends than you
know, Mother."

"Friends?" Kalie sobbed. "Every human being
in this camp who has been kind to me or believed my

words is about to die! Or be reduced to a lower form of slavery, just when they began to believe life might hold something more for them! And it's because of me!"

Now it was Varena who clutched at Kalie's arms. "Is that what you think? You think Riyik regrets standing up for his honor? You think Brenia would have rather have died without a fight? You think I regret one moment of the life you gave me?"

"I don't know! And now I'm afraid I'll never find out." Varena wrapped her arms around Kalie and held her, as Kalie had once held Varena. A long time later, she backed out of the embrace and took a deep breath. "Those stars I've been making from bones. They're for—"

"I know what they're for," Varena said, rising to her feet. "I think we all do. All whom the Goddess gave eyes to see with, at least."

Kalie shook her head, amazed by this woman who had become, in every way, her daughter. "If the warriors didn't take them, I'll take that as a sign that there's still hope. Get Yarik." Then she thought of another child whose life was in danger. "Get Barak as well." Varena nodded. "Wait for me in the grass a spear throw west of here."

"What will you do?"

"Offer my services as a storyteller." Kalie kissed Varena and hurried away without further explanation.

Despite Varena's brave reassurances, Kalie received no welcoming looks from any of the women she passed as she walked through the camp. Everyone, even wives and slaves, stood in plain sight, at the doors of their tents or in the shadows between them, but when Kalie tried a few experimental approaches they turned their backs, or slunk inside their tents. She had thought to beg food from Danica, but the look the old woman shot her sent her moving past at greater speed.

Kalie hadn't eaten all day, and it was clear no one would give her food, but she still wore the finely crafted water bag Riyik had given her. No one stopped her when she went to fill it at the well. Here, the looks were more curious than hostile, as women speculated on Kalie's fate. From what she could glean by listening, it appeared that being the wife of a traitor carried less of a stigma than being the sister of one.

While no one would actually speak to her or make eye contact, they spoke freely about her while she listened. Some insisted she would be Maalke's again, and would do well enough for as long as she could keep his newest son alive. Others cackled that Haraak was so bewitched by her he planned to keep her for himself, and would carry her on his horse, dressed like a princess when he rode in triumph into the city from whence he had long ago plucked her.

"And does that not prove she is a witch?" demanded a well-dressed wife, who had come for water herself rather than sending a slave, in order to join in the gossip. "She connives to turn a good man traitor, and instead of dying for it, earns a place in the tent of the most powerful man in camp?"

"Perhaps it is for her power that Haraak desires her," another said cryptically.

"It's certainly not for her beauty," said a young slave, raking Kalie up and down with her eyes. She was rewarded by raucous laughter.

Kalie laughed along with them, probably

causing speculation that she was mad, but she didn't stay to find out. She had enjoyed listening to their banter, for it had made the old anger sing in her blood. And now, finally, it was time to act on it.

Tell them a story Alessa had said when they had last been together. And Kalie had sought to craft one that would have the warriors of three tribes at each other's throats. She had not practiced enough; had put too much time and energy into dramatic plots involving weapons and poison.

But now she saw what it seemed everyone else from Varena to Alessa to the Goddess who sent her on this journey had seen all along: if she were to defeat the beastmen, it would not be with their own weapons. It would be with the gifts Kalie's own Goddess had given her, from a land that knew nothing of beastmen's power.

Storytelling was the one thing she still had from her old life. She could only take that as an omen, and do her best.

Kalie threaded her way through camp to where the crowd was the thickest: the open space before the kings' tents. There she stood in the shadows and waited with the others for the kings to emerge.

Chapter 33

She didn't have long to wait.

The sun had barely begun its westward journey when Kariik, Malquor and Nelek strode forth, blinking in the bright glare after the dimness of the tent.

Kariik began speaking. Kalie couldn't help noticing how much he had grown, outwardly at least, into the image of a king. "Tomorrow, we will begin a glorious journey of conquest," he told the gathered tribes. "We will, for the first time in memory, leave the grasslands of our ancestors. We will take our gods and our greatness into a land that possesses neither, and make that land our own. But before we do, we will purify ourselves, as in the tales of old."

Kalie bowed her veiled head to hide her grin. There was an opening if ever she heard one.

"Our ancestors knew that the shedding of blood pleased the gods. Tonight we shall give them gifts such as they have never received." Kariik pointed to where the priest stood amidst a gathering of the finest animals Kalie had seen in this land. Sleek goats, fat sheep hidden beneath folds of glossy wool, and most impressive of all, fifty of the best horses. "These are worthy messengers to carry our pleas to the gods.

"But there will be another shedding of blood tonight, not sacrifice, but no less holy." At a signal from one of the warriors behind Kariik, all of the prisoners taken that morning were led out. And, Kalie saw at once, new ones had been added. Men she did not recognize, but who bore the distinctive tattoos and spiked hair of the Spears of Malquor.

Now that was interesting.

Riyik walked in front, with Brenia and Alessa beside him, while the men followed behind. Even more interesting.

"Before we leave," Kariik continued, "it is the will of the gods that we rid ourselves of the weakness and corruption that nearly destroyed this alliance from within. All of our tribes were riddled with traitors. Tonight they shall be purged from our midst, leaving only the strong, the pure and the noble among us to take up the challenge of the new land."

Kariik went on to explain in gory detail how the traitors were to die. The crowd quivered with anticipation. Kalie wondered if eight years ago, the sight of bloody rites like these had unhinged her mind. Today, she barely noticed them, as she listened for what useful information could be found between the king's words.

Kariik spoke of traitors in all three tribes. It seemed the current Malquor had his own version of Haraak, eager to "cleanse" his tribe of possible rivals. Nelek had accused Alessa of seducing his eldest son into betraying his father, and had asked for help in cleaning his household of her filth. Translated into some semblance of reality, that implied a rebellion and attempted patricide. Was the prince dead, and Nelek in need of help weeding out his followers? Or were the twenty warriors with him all the followers he had left, while his son now ruled the Wolf Tribe?

"We shall have entertainment such as the gods envy!" Kariik shouted. Well, he'd mentioned ancient tales and now, entertainment. It was now or never.

Kalie pushed through the tightly packed crowd and strode into the open space before the kings, stopping just before the guards for all three moved to block her path. She pulled off her veil, and let her brown hair tumble to her waist. "My kings!" she cried, her head held high and proud. "On this night of nights, I offer entertainment of my own, to please both gods and men."

She allowed herself a moment's pause to gauge the shocked reactions, then realized she'd better push forward, before they took her offer as an invitation to gang rape. "I am accounted a fine storyteller by the tribe of Aahk. I would offer for tonight, a special story, so ancient it speaks to us from the dawn of time." Kalie faltered, wondering where that had come from. She had intended to say she had created the story herself to honor the noble kings.

There were boos from the crowd, and plenty of vulgar comments about better uses for the wives of traitors. Some seemed genuinely offended that Kalie had spoken at all. But she had supporters in the crowd, even among the chiefs who sat with the kings. When Kariik pointed to her and asked a question, Chief Kahlar leaned forward and began describing with great enthusiasm Kalie's "Battle of Spring Crossing".

Haraak nearly shoved the chief out of the way, as he hurried to his puppet. "This woman is my slave, Kariik, as you promised me earlier. Allow me to remove her before she causes any further disruption."

Kalie locked her suddenly weak knees and held herself erect. Looking coolly past Haraak, she met Kariik's gaze and held it. "As you can see, my king, men will fight to possess me. See how your own loyal advisor seeks to claim me, even while my husband still lives! Listen to my tale, and you may decide to keep me for yourself!"

The crowd roared with delight at Kalie's

audacity. A slow grin spread across Kariik's face, and Malquor leaned toward him. He seemed to be making an offer for her. "This is a day for the unexpected," said the king of the Tribe of Aahk. "We had best enjoy what of it we can. I have not yet made any decisions on the dividing of the traitors property, so for the moment, the woman belongs to no one. You may tell your story, girl." He beckoned her forward.

Kalie slid smoothly through the crowd, as stools were brought for the kings and their chiefs, and felt awnings arranged above them. Kariik called for food and drink, then suddenly called for a stool for Kalie. This was unusual, but when Kalie looked around she discovered that most of the combined tribes were settling down to listen to her as well. The entire cleared area before the royal tent was filled, as well as the spaces between all of the nearby tents. Men were sending their wives for food. In the shadows of the tents, slaves were slipping closer, eager to hear.

This was fast becoming the largest audience Kalie had ever addressed.

She found herself seated on a comfortable stool, lower than the kings, but high enough to be seen by most of the crowd, and more importantly, see them. Someone gave her a skin of kumis. Kalie tasted it gingerly. It was not laced with any drug she could detect, but she didn't know who had sent it, and decided to drink from her water skin instead.

When all was arranged, Kariik nodded for her to begin. Kalie took a deep breath, and called on the Goddess for help. But as she opened her mouth to speak, the story that she had worked on these past days died on her lips. In its place came a new story, fully formed. And in that instant Kalie knew that the

Goddess had truly answered her.

"Long ago, when the tribes of this land were new, there lived two warriors, both grandsons of Saak.

"Tolik was the greatest king of the greatest tribe to dwell in the land. His fist could split a man's skull. He could ride horses that would trample any other man. His herds stretched to the horizon. The greatest warriors in the world were proud to call themselves his men.

"His cousin Rahaak was a weak and cowardly man. Rahaak had prospered well enough as a minor chief in his cousin's tribe, but jealousy and envy twisted him, until he could no longer live in Tolik's shadow. Rahaak's arm was weak but his tongue was clever, and before he left, he persuaded many warriors to follow him. Last of all, he sought to persuade the beautiful Valeska, Tolik's wife, to come with him as well."

Kalie took a sip of water, and surveyed her audience. They seemed interested, men and women both. She tried not to look at Haraak, but her eye was drawn to him like a loadstone to the north. He stared at her with an angry, yet puzzled frown. He clearly did not know what she was doing, but it worried him, as did anything outside his control.

"Loyal Valeska would have none of Rahaak's crude advances, and that angered him. He swore to her she would regret her decision, and fled with those whose loyalty could be bought.

"The years went by, and Tolik continued to prosper. Rahaak scratched out a meager living by preying on weaker bands, and stealing whatever he could. In this manner, his tribe grew in size and strength, and he earned the name 'Hyena'."

There was laughter at this. Kalie had found her stride, and continued with more confidence.

"Tolik had been blessed in all ways but one: he had no children." An angry ripple passed through the audience and Kalie hurried her tale. "When at last Valeska gave birth to a fine, healthy son, Tolik roared with joy. He named the boy Alesaak, and declared that if he had no other, he was still the richest of men, for surely no man had a son as fine as he. Tolik slaughtered one hundred goats and one hundred sheep, and threw such a feast as to be remembered for years to come. He invited all the tribes in the land. All, that is, except his cousin, the Hyena.

"When Rahaak learned of this slight, he went wild. Even worse than the insult of being excluded from the feast were the tales of the splendid boy in whose honor it had occurred. Rahaak had many children, yet none, it seemed, so fine as the only son of his hated cousin. For five years, he plotted his revenge, growing strong and bitter, sitting in his ill-made tent like a spider, spinning his web.

"At last he was ready. Rahaak took his motley band and traveled to Tolik's wide domain, and proposed an alliance, sealed with two marriages: Rahaak's oldest daughter would marry Tolik's greatest chief, and Tolik's sister would marry Rahaak's greatest chief. Tolik was not well disposed to an alliance with such a pack, but he greeted his kinsman warmly, and threw a welcoming feast that only served to enflame Rahaak's envy."

Haraak must have finally realized the name of the story's villain was his own, inverted, for his face flushed an ugly red, and he rose from his place with doubled firsts. The man behind him clouted Haraak on the head, cursed at having his view blocked and focused once again on the story, without even looking to see whom he had struck. Kalie swallowed a grin and continued.

"Rahaak's evil plan was carried out with perfect smoothness. That night, when the drinking and boasting before the king's tent reached its height, each of Rahaak's men slid a knife from his sleeve and slew the man nearest him. Before Tolik's men could react, half of them were dead. Those that were left fought bravely, and made many a Hyena pay with his life, but they were deep into their drink and unprepared for such a vile act under a pledge of friendship.

"When the sun rose the next morning, the largest herds, the finest pastures, and richest treasures in the world belonged to Rahaak the Hyena. But there was one prize above all he would claim first. He ordered Tolik's body carried before him, and then swaggered into the sumptuous tent of his defeated enemy, planning to take Valeska upon the corpse of her husband. Then he would throw her to his men as reward for their loyalty.

"But Valeska had thwarted Rahaak once again, for she had taken her own life at the instant of her husband's death. And beside her body stood her five-year-old son, holding one of his father's spears, and looking ready to take on all of Rahaak's warriors before surrendering any of his father's treasure, or allowing his mother's body to be defiled.

"Rahaak flew into a rage greater than any before, and declared that if he could not have the woman he wanted, then his men would suffer along with him. He ordered the slaughter of every woman in the camp. By the end of the day, the steppes ran red with blood, and no human legacy of Tolik remained save one: the conqueror spared young Alesaak. Rahaak's final revenge against Tolik would be exacted against his son."

Kalie had planned to follow with brutal descriptions of the child's sexual abuse at Rahaak's hands, but one look at her audience caused her to change her mind. The story had clearly marked Alesaak as its hero, and to the beastmen, a hero could never be a victim.

Hastily changing course, Kalie continued, a bit too loudly at first. "Rahaak had planned to keep the boy as a kind of pet, then offer him to the gods at a celebration of the one year anniversary of his kingship. But Alesaak proved so worthy, and such an asset to the tribe, that Rahaak soon forgot such plans. He even began to forget whose son the boy was.

"Now, Tolik's people were not all dead. Many had been away at the time of Rahaak's cowardly attack, hunting or raiding, or in one case, attending a wedding. Those whose families were intact joined other tribes, while those who had lost everything in Rahaak's massacre, wandered the land as near-shadows, dreaming of revenge, yet lacking the direction to carry it out.

"Meanwhile, Alesaak grew toward manhood in Rahaak's tent, outshining every boy in the tribe, whether it be in riding, fighting or endurance. When a small, but well armed band came to attack the tribe, it was Alesaak who heard them in the dead of night when the sentries did not, and Alesaak who met the first on the battlefield, though he was still a boy, and without even his own horse.

"After the battle, when all the warriors sang his

praises, Rahaak offered Alesaak a fine horse from his own herds, but Tolik's son refused. Instead he went out the next day and captured a wild stallion, as black as the night. Everyone said the creature could not be broken. By the next morning, horse and boy rode as one creature.

"Soon Rahaak began comparing Alesaak to his own sons and they did not fare well in the comparison. They were now grown to manhood, and not blind to where their father's favor fell. One day, they decided to rid themselves of this nuisance.

"They invited Alesaak to go hunting with them in the nearby mountains, thinking to kill him, drop his body off a cliff and claim it for an accident. They smirked to one another at how easy it would be, as the reckless boy rode to the very edge of the cliff. But then he turned and taunted them for cowards that they feared to ride as close as he. Rahaak's eldest son spurred his horse in a black fury to slay the arrogant half-blood who dared speak so. With the ease of a god, Alesaak rode the prince—horse and all—off the cliff and to his death."

Kalie sipped her water slowly as the audience roared with delight. She spared a glance at the condemned prisoners. Still bound, and separated from the rest of the audience, they too were listening to her story. Riyik smiled and nodded at her in a knowing way when she caught his gaze. Kalie faltered and turned back to the spellbound kings.

"Soon after, Rahaak's second son hatched a different sort of plan to kill his rival and avenge his brother. He obtained a poison from his mother, which he smeared upon his knife. Then, pretending to be drunk, he met Alesaak by the horse runs and slapped him as one would a woman, and accused him of speaking slander.

"Alesaak calmly drew his own knife while a crowd gathered around them. The prince, now moving with deadly grace, lunged again and again, but could not touch the other with his blade. Enraged, he became careless.

"With a flick of one foot, Alesaak tripped the prince so that he fell upon his own knife. Not a fatal blow—but for the poison on the blade. The young prince howled in terror and ran to his mother, but nothing she did could save him from his own poison.

"Rahaak's youngest son, a half wit too stupid to even make a good puppet king—" Kalie now looked directly at Haraak, who blanched under her gaze, "—decided it was time to seek his fortune in another tribe. And so Alesaak grew even higher in Rahaak's favor.

"He gained a fine reputation as a scout, and was often away for long stretches of time, returning with succulent game and news of other tribes. He returned from one such outing with a beautiful wife, and Rahaak raged and grieved mightily, for he had planned that Alesaak would marry the Hyena Princess, and then become Rahaak's son by marriage, and king after him.

"Well, Alesaak intended to be king after Rahaak, just not the way Rahaak had planned. And his greatest secret was that the woman he married was of his own tribe, daughter one of Tolik's warriors, who had been escorting his sister to her wedding when Rahaak had attacked their home.

"For what no one knew was that when Alesaak rode out alone, he was seeking out the remnants of his father's tribe and planning the day they would rise up against those who thought to murder an entire tribe and rule the land that was not theirs.

"At first, no one would listen to him: Alesaak had been a child of five when his parents were murdered, and now he was high in favor with the new king. Could he have kept the fires of hatred and vengeance alive all these years? Would he truly risk all he had now to avenge his father? And how could any one man, with nothing but the ragged remains of a great tribe lead them in victory against the most ruthless and powerful tribe in the world?"

Kalie paused and one by one, met the eyes of each of the kings, then raked her gaze across the audience. She was silent so long that the chiefs who sat nearest her began to offer her their own skulls of kumis. Kalie smiled and shook her head.

"For each of those questions, the answer is another story. But the hour grows late, so I will tell you only how it ended.

"Slowly and in secret, Alesaak built his father's warriors into a mighty army. With wit and cunning, he devised a plan to take back what was his. And he might have succeeded, had not Rahaak's youngest son, a scheming, and misshapen creature, discovered it. Knowing he could never convince his father to find any fault with his golden rival, the evil prince instead sought to capture one of Alesaak's loyal men, for by now he had followers even within the Hyena's own camp. Men who tired of serving a traitor, and longed for a noble warrior to restore honor to the land so blighted by Rahaak.

"At last the prince was able to find such a man, and had him tortured in the most gruesome fashion. It is said that that Rahaak's son vomited at the sight of what it took to break the man.

"When Rahaak was brought to hear the dying man's confession, he wailed and tore his clothes like a woman, so devastated was he by the betrayal of the man he had loved like a son—to whom he planned to make king after him—"

Laughter and booing erupted all around her. "Well he got what he wanted, didn't he?" shouted a voice from the crowd. "Alesaak's going to be king, right?"

"Got what he deserved his more like it!" chorused other voices. "Black hearted bastard!" "How dare he feel betrayed?" "Did he really think a hero would serve a traitor?"

Kalie waited until the noise died down. "The king ordered Alesaak bound and brought before him. But when Alesaak learned of this from yet another man loyal to him, he did not flee, as everyone expected. Rather, he sent runners to call his men to attack Rahaak's camp itself! Then he went, armed only with his father's spear, to challenge the Hyena himself to single combat.

"Rahaak only spat in the dirt, and turned his back on the man he had once called his son, and ordered his warriors to hang Alesaak upside down from the pole of his own tent, and cut off first his fingers, then his toes, then his legs, and then his man parts, and scatter them into the four winds, so that he might never be whole in the next life, and never admitted to paradise. His arms, Rahaak said, could be left attached, but broken, so they could never hold a spear again."

An angry hissing arose from the listening warriors, many of them shifting uncomfortably, trying to cover their crotches, yet remain inconspicuous.

"But Alesaak surprised them all. With a single spear, he slew twenty of Rahaak's warriors. He kept fighting, even with a dozen spears in his body. He kept fighting with wounds on him that would have killed any other man. He kept fighting until his small army fought its way through all of the warriors of the outlying camps and at last reached the heart of Haraak's territory.

"They were still outnumbered. But Alesaak had so depleted Rahaak's forces, that an army who fought for more than just material gain might have a chance. And when Tolik's warriors—now Alesaak's—saw their ravaged king, that is what they became. So enraged were they to have lost two great kings at the hands of the Hyena, that they fought, not as men, but as gods.

"In Alesaak's final words to his victorious warriors he ordered them to swear loyalty to his son, too young to rule yet, but who would one day redeem both his father and grandfather in the eyes of men and gods. And so they did, and Alesaak died.

"His funeral was the greatest ever held, while Rahaak, who it is said, died not in battle, but from a broken heart, was left for his own namesake, the hyenas to devour."

Then she bowed her head, signifying the end of the story.

Chapter 34

There was shouting and applause, and a buzz of discussion. Kalie surveyed the kings and chiefs beneath demurely lowered eyes. To her amazement, Nelek's face was awash with tears.

"Oh, to have such a son!" he cried.

"Yes," said Kariik. "Such loyalty and courage seem sorely lacking in the world today. But it does my heart good to hear of it, even if it exists only in stories."

"Perhaps in ancient times there were such men," Malquor said sadly. "But not today."

Kalie raised her eyes boldly and met the gaze of each of the kings. "But Great Ones, the story I have told is true, and did not happen in ancient times, but only this very year."

Everyone seemed to be puzzling out her meaning, for the magic of the story still lingered.

"Tell us," ordered Kariik.

"I will," said Kalie. "But first tell me, oh my kings, why was Alesaak a hero, and not a traitor, in your exalted eyes? Did he not betray the man who raised him up? Did he not plot in secret, and steal that which Rahaak had rightfully won in battle?"

"He avenged his murdered father!" Nelek shouted as though that was the end of the matter.

"He made himself king as the son of Tolik," said Malquor. "Not as some hyena's bastard! Did the fool think Alesaak would forget his father and accept his own rightful kingship as a bone from the hand that slew his kin?"

"To fight on as he did, while dying," Kariik

mused, staring morosely into his skull of kumis. "To die for his family and tribe, rather than fleeing when he had the chance. Do any really live who would do such things?"

"Yes," said Kalie, over the pounding of her heart. "And I shall tell you where. But first tell me, each of you, how would you reward a warrior such as Alesaak?"

"I would make him chief of all my warriors," said Malquor. "I would allow him to ride beside me into battle."

"I would give such a warrior horses from my own herds and concubines from my own tent," said Nelek.

"I would grant such a hero whatever he might ask, for I think it would do me good to discover what a hero most desires," said Kariik.

Kalie rose and stood before the seated kings. "And will each of you swear to that before your gods?"

They all nodded, if a bit impatiently. Kalie took a deep breath, knowing full well it might be her last.

"Then I shall tell you now that the hero I spoke of is right here." She walked a few steps closer to the prisoners, and pointed to Alessa, who smiled back at her.

The faces of all three king's grew dark with rage, but none more so than Nelek. "What is the meaning of this?" he demanded.

Kalie whirled on the kings and their chiefs, the rage in her own face matching Nelek's. "Did this woman not come here, as a slave, a pet, through the same act of treachery as my story described? Rahaak greeted Tolik under a banner of truce when he meant to kill him. Haraak took Alessa as a slave when by your own laws, she already owned the blood-debt of Kariik and at least six of his warriors after she, a Healer of Riverford, saved their lives!"

Kalie could feel the rage boil around her, but on the faces of the assembled warriors was the same spellbound look she often saw when telling a story. She felt the voice of the Goddess rise up inside her and knew that, for this moment at least, they would listen.

"Did not King Nelek take a noble priestess, destined for power and status in her own right, and seek to make her his slave, expecting her to feel honored to serve him for the rest of her life? That she would forget her murdered family and her own great destiny, as Rahaak expected of Alesaak?

"Did he not expect her gratitude and loyalty every time he forced his body into hers, or threw her to his men for a night's pleasure? And did he not offer her gifts that any slave girl should love, as Rahaak offered Alesaak horses and women? Both kings should have known such acts would engender hatred and bring about just retribution, yet when justice arrived, both felt betrayed by people whom—they thought—should have loved them!"

She turned from the kings to the vast gathering of common warriors and shouted their own words back at them. "'Got what he deserved' you said. 'Would a hero ever serve a traitor?' 'How dare he feel betrayed?'"

She turned back to the kings. "Your warriors demand to know how a man who murders his own cousin and steals all that he owns dare feel betrayed by an honest warrior seeking revenge. They want to know how any man can expect loyalty and gratitude from one who must surely seek revenge!

"Well I have wondered that since the day I arrived in this accursed place, so I am asking you: How did any of you expect loyalty and gratitude from Alessa after you murdered her people and made her a slave! I want you to explain how she is any less of a hero for using the tools at her disposal to avenge her family and protect those still left in her homeland! And I want to know how you, Kariik, dare to call her a faithless slave, when it was by your own treachery and ingratitude to her people— who saved your life— that she became a slave in the first place!"

Her words were finally lost in a roar of angry shouting as the glamour that held the crowd silent wore off. They surged forward, seeming ready to tear her to pieces. Yet when the first men reached her, they stopped just short of actually touching her, growing confused and looking to their leaders for direction.

Perhaps the Goddess had lent Kalie more than just a voice.

"Kill her!" Nelek shouted.

Kariik probably wanted to do exactly that, but perhaps angered that another king should usurp his authority, he held up his hand, freezing those who would have killed her.

Into the momentary silence, Kalie spoke. "I remind you each of your oaths before your gods. You promised this hero horses, women and her heart's desire."

"We promised 'him' those things, not her," said Kariik in a voice Kalie had never heard from him. For the first time, she could see a king inside the puppet. "A slave girl can never be a warrior."

"And yet you have proof of the opposite. By herself, without even a spear, Alessa nearly succeeded in breaking apart the alliance that seeks to destroy her world. With her knowledge of herbs, she might have poisoned her enemy and escaped alone, yet like Alesaak, she remained to carry out her duty—though it meant her certain death. And she endured torture more bravely than most, for she never named an accomplice. Did she?" Kalie's gaze bore deep into Nelek's eyes.

"She named my son!" he shouted.

"Are you sure?" Kalie had pondered that part all day. She took a chance. "I'll wager she tried to warn you that your son plotted to betray you—on his own! You preferred to blame her instead. Isn't it interesting how you people believe that a slave has no power and no free will—except when you need to shift blame away from someone who clearly has both?"

From the expressions of some of Nelek's men, Kalie could see she'd hit the mark.

"She used deceit and subterfuge," Kariik insisted.

"She used the weapons she had," Kalie countered.

How long this stalemate might have lasted, Kalie would never know, for at that moment, a lathered horse came crashing into the gathering, a badly wounded man slumped over its back. What happened to the sentries? Kalie wondered, then saw them running behind the horse, belatedly trying to clear a path.

Guards caught the rider as he slid to the ground. "Attack!" he wheezed. "They come…"

"Who?" Nelek demanded, pushing his way through the guards, for the dying warrior was his.

"The Wolf tribe; led by your son!"

"They shall be swiftly dealt with," Kariik said easily. "They are few to our many."

"Hansi rides with them and the Axe men as well…"

"The outcast band?" Malquor demanded.

"They have become large and strong…" The messenger began to cough. Blood leaked from his mouth.

"How many?" That from Haraak, pushing his way to stand beside Kariik.

"More than six hundred…" The man coughed once more and died.

Everyone looked east, the direction of the Wolf Tribe. The direction from which the messenger had ridden. The dust raised by a fast riding horde could be seen on the horizon. The distant thunder of the hoofs could be felt, if not yet heard.

"To arms!" Kariik shouted. The scene around Kalie dissolved into chaos as men raced for horses and weapons. Each king gave hurried directions to his chiefs, who gave orders to their men—except for Nelek, who had only the twenty who rode with him.

A final order from Kariik was of great importance to Kalie. "Pulik!" he called to a brawny, much scarred warrior—one of the few of his personal guards to have gray hair. "Take three men and remain behind to dispatch the traitors. I want no ugly surprises when we return."

"I will obey, my king," said Pulik, although it was clear from his expression that he preferred to ride into battle beside his king than remain behind to execute traitors.

"Join us when the job is finished," said Kariik.

With that, he leapt forward to the head of his army and rode out of camp.

Chapter 35

Kalie had never been present for a full scale battle; one which was fought away from the camp, and in which every warrior was called to fight. What she would remember most was the deafening silence, as the pounding hooves of the departing army gradually died away, and over a thousand humans beings remained behind like statues in the dust.

Then the women began a high-pitched wailing. Some remained standing where they were, covering their faces and tearing the hems of the garments. Others hurried inside their tents, where their keening became eerily muffled.

Ignored again, Kalie knew she had to act, for lives depended on it. But for the life of her, she didn't know what she was supposed to do.

Then, slowly, people began to gather around her. Varena, Katya, Larren, Mavra, Basha and even old, bent Agafa, standing as straight and proud as Kalie had ever seen.... All looking to Kalie for direction.

"Four men were sent to kill Riyik and the others," she said. "Does anyone have a knife?"

"For what?" asked Mavra. "Do you think you can kill four warriors by yourself?"

"Do you have a better idea?" Kalie demanded.

"Killing one's own is distasteful work," said a powerful voice. "They will need much drink to make it palatable."

Danica stood, holding two skins of kumis.

"Are those…?"

Danica grinned, showing her strong yellowed

teeth.

"How did you get them? Kariik had them burned." Kalie could still smell the foul odor.

"One of the men who followed your husband is my nephew," the chief's mother explained. "The guards thought nothing strange of a wailing old woman begging to see her kinsmen. Of course, they refused me. So, like any old woman, I fell shrieking to the ground—right on top of their pile of drinking skins. They were so busy cursing and shouting when they dragged me away, they failed to notice the two I slipped in my robe."

"I always knew these awful clothes would be useful someday," Kalie said, but she continued to stare suspiciously at Danica.

"I'm sorry about earlier," the chief's mother said. "I was being watched. If I had shown you any welcome…"

"I understand," Kalie said, hoping she did, but knowing she was out of time either way. "Varena! Katya!" Kalie gazed down at her lovely daughter and the frightened, slip of a girl who cowered behind her. She considered that Katya's fear might be more attractive to the men of this land than Varena's blossoming beauty. But both would be risking a lot.

"I would not ask this of you if there were any other way…"

"There's no time for this, Mother," snapped Varena, taking both skins and thrusting one of them into Katya's hands.

Kalie nodded. "Offer it to the warriors before they reach the prisoners. Show yourselves to them." Varena cast aside her veil and outer robe and was shaking out her lustrous hair, but Katya dropped her kumis skin and fled, pulling her clothing tight around her as she ran.

Mavra shook her head and recovered the skin. "Never send a girl to do a woman's job," she told Kalie. Then she took Varena's arm and the two of them hurried away. "Are you a virgin?" she asked the younger woman. Varena nodded. "All right. Here are some things you need to know…" The rest was lost as they hurried through the now silent camp.

Kalie turned to the others. "I still need a knife," she said. "More than one, if possible."

"Here," said Basha, offering a small cooking knife. Danica gave her a better one.

Kalie flung aside her veil and heavy outer robe, delighting in the sudden coolness she felt. Then she hitched up skirts that could impede her progress and raced off to where Riyik waited.

Woman stared, their faces blurring as she ran past. What could possibly come of this crazy scheme, Kalie asked herself. Would four hardened warriors assigned to kill their own brothers actually stop to ogle young girls and drink drugged kumis just because Kalie wanted them to? It seemed ridiculous.

Yet when she reached the tent where the prisoners still sat, that was precisely what was happening. Mavra had exposed her breasts and was now pouring kumis over them, brazenly inviting one of the warriors to have a drink, while Varena more discretely held the other skin for another warrior. He grabbed it from her and drank noisily, while the man beside him pounded his shoulders good-naturedly, demanding a turn.

That took care of three of them. But Pulik was having none of it as he ordered the prisoners from the tent. He stopped in front of Riyik and raised his blade. Riyik stood motionless and stared at the man, daring him to strike.

Kalie ran toward them, feeling herself move, slowly as in a nightmare, but then Varena saw what was happening and shook herself free of the two men who were now fondling her breasts and ran to Pulik. She snaked around in front of him, smiling an invitation. Pulik, angry at the interruption, shoved her aside. But he stopped and looked around when he realized his men were no longer behind him.

Pulik turned and marched to the man who had, by now, nearly emptied the kumis skin. "The drink and the whores can wait!" he yelled, knocking the man to the ground. Kalie noticed how slowly the man staggered back to his feet, while Pulik roughly interrupted the warrior who was busy with Mavra. But the last man—the one who had first taken the kumis from Varena—was moving strangely, his arms and legs twitching. He stared around him with widened eyes.

Kalie finally reached the prisoners, many of who were struggling against their ropes, unwilling to die like trussed sheep. Riyik stood perfectly still as she cut the cords which bound his hands and gave him the knife.

"Have you got another?" he asked her.

For an answer, she drew the second knife and moved to the next man, slicing through the cords that bound him, and moving on to the next. Kalie could hear the blood pounding in her ears as she cut through the ropes, certain that a knife was even now poised above her neck.

Then she heard the wet sound of combat as

knife met flesh, felt the splatter of blood, and her hand froze on the ropes of the man in front of her.

"Give me that!" the anxious prisoner snapped, pulling the knife from her with his teeth and finishing the job himself.

She couldn't move until Riyik's face swam into her vision. Even then he had to pull her to her feet; Kalie seemed to have forgotten how to do it on her own.

"It's all right," he said. "You did it; you saved us!"

With a gasp she remembered how to breathe; then she looked around. Two of the would-be executioners were lying dead from knife wounds, while former prisoners stripped their bodies of weapons. The other two men were writhing on the ground, eyes rolling. No one was willing to get near them

Kalie looked from Riyik to Alessa to Brenia, not sure who to hug first. Then Riyik caught her in a fierce embrace. "Barak is hidden in your brother's tent," Kalie told Brenia over Riyik's shoulder. Then Brenia was trying to push Riyik out of the way to hug Kalie herself and the three of them nearly fell over rather than let go.

As Brenia ran to get her son, Riyik kissed Kalie firmly on the mouth and released her, turning quickly to organize his men. That finally woke Kalie up to her own responsibilities as the women she had left behind came panting into the clear area around the king's tent.

"Gather supplies," she told the women before they could catch their breath. "Food, water, blankets— only one blanket each. The nights are not so cold yet, and we will have to travel fast. Faster than you have ever traveled in your lives."

They dispersed to their tasks. Danica remained. "We must take a share of the herds," she said, surveying the penned animals. "But only enough to feed us on the journey. There must be enough left behind to satisfy…whichever side wins this fight."

"And you think they will just let us go?"

"If we leave behind enough wealth? Possibly. Herds and women—most of the women will remain, you know?" Kalie nodded. "With all that, and winter coming, they may not feel the need to track down a handful of traitors and madwomen. But if you give them reason to fear us…then they may choose to wait many years before searching for us in the west."

The two women stared at each other. "I made many little stars out of bone…" Kalie began.

"Yes, they were so pretty that I made some as well. So did all the women of my household, and many others besides."

Kalie smiled at the strange twisting of fate. "Perhaps, Danica, you could gather them up, and bring them here?"

Then Riyik was by her side once again. "We will have perhaps thirty horses," he said. "Enough to carry those who would otherwise slow us down. The rest will have to walk."

Kalie nodded. "Can one or two be spared to carry supplies?"

"Possibly." He looked around at the women who stood by their tents, staring open-mouthed at the madness that had taken hold of their camp. "We must hurry. Gather who you will, but get them ready to leave at once!" Then he kissed her again and was gone.

Kalie hurried through the camp, more interested in it than in finding those she sought. Whether or not she would ever again see the land of her birth, this day would be her last in the tribe of Aahk. She tried to see it as the Goddess would: with compassion and sympathy, or perhaps without any judgment at all.

She failed. All she could see was senseless waste: of potential and life and even the fragile beauty that sometimes lived in this endless land of grass.

Altia stepped directly in her path.

Kalie halted suddenly as Maalke's wife caught her wrist. "I am told you are once again my husband's slave," the older woman sneered. "When the men return, we will leave for the west, and then all the worthless whores of your land will learn what it means to live as proper women." She pulled Kalie toward her and slapped her across the face. "Dress yourself and get to back to my tent! After I give you the beating you've earned, you may begin your work."

Kalie looked Altia up and down, and smiled. Then she drew back her free arm and punched Altia in the face with all her strength. The woman released her and fell flat on her back, legs flying up in a scandalous fashion.

Kalie couldn't believe how good it felt. She leaned over the stunned woman, who lay gaping up at her. "You are right about one thing, Goat-Dung: I do have work to do. But I assure you, none of it involves being your slave!"

She looked around, knowing that her future would be determined in the next few moments. Women everywhere were staring at the scene, most too frozen with shock to be any threat to Kalie. Some were giggling behind their veils, but Kalie sensed a note of hysteria.

"Kalie! What have you done?" Cassia was in the crowd, rushing to Altia's side, and potentially very dangerous. Despite her difficult childbirth, Cassia was as physically powerful as Altia, and much more determined to keep Kalie with her.

Strangely, as she looked down at her, all Kalie could feel was sadness. "I'm sorry, Cassia," she said. "I had hoped this would be a joyous day for both of us."

Before Cassia could fully comprehend what she was saying, Kalie turned and ran back to Kariik's tent at the center of the camp. The stool he had occupied that morning stood empty, the only high ground available in this flat, Goddess-forsaken grassland. Kalie leapt on top of it. With her height an added advantage, she could be seen by nearly everyone in camp.

"People of the Horse!" she shouted. "Women of Aahk and woman of Malquor! The time has come for me to leave this place, and return to the land of my birth. I ask all of you who would be free; who would dream of a better life, to come with me!

"Come with me to a land without slavery, where a woman's body belongs to her alone, and if any man were to hit you, he would be driven from the settlement by every member of the community!"

"What about when a woman hits you?" cried a timid blonde slave whom Kalie remembered from Varena's rites of womanhood.

The woman next to her did just that, but the girl did not cower, nor even show she felt any pain, only looked at Kalie with a kind of desperate hope.

"She, too, would be driven from the community," Kalie said. "Although, perhaps, if some of you who are wives choose to come with us, time must be set aside for you to learn not to hit, just as young children must learn. And those of you who were slaves must learn not to strike back, now that you have the chance." She pointed to where Altia was being helped to her feet by two other women. "I just struck the woman who thought she had the right to hit me. I promise all of you, here and now, that—except for when I must do so to protect myself or one of you—I shall never again strike another woman. Although I know I will want to!"

Laughter spread through the crowd that now included most of the tribeswomen.

"Why would any wife give up all she has to follow a shameless whore out into the wilds to die?" demanded a harsh voice. "Our husbands will soon return and hunt you down! Then you will learn what happens to slaves who speak as you do!"

Kalie stared coolly into the fierce eyes of Leja, who with her pain-ravaged face, didn't seem so fierce anymore. "Your husbands may return, victorious over their enemies. Or they may even now lie dead on the battlefield, as food for ravens. If that happens then you and your children will belong to the victors. While you wait to learn your fate, I shall leave here and fight for mine! The choice is yours."

She stepped down from the stool, and found Riyik beside her. He lifted his arms as though to take Kalie into them, then hesitated. It was that hesitation that made it so easy for her to fling herself into his arms and wrap hers tightly around him.

"I believe, my love," he said, gently disentangling himself, "that it is time for us to go."

Chapter 36

Between them, Kalie and Riyik were able to make order out of chaos in a surprisingly short time.

Most of the women making the journey were slaves, and thus good at following orders and doing what needed to be done. The problems occurred when they began taking things out of their tents, such as water bags, food or even a single blanket. And of, course, themselves.

Kalie resented the fact that she had to call on Riyik and his warriors to pry a number of outraged wives off the women they believed to be their property. She had hoped this would be something she and her followers could handle themselves. At least the men were able to settle matters quickly. For, while those staying far outnumbered those leaving, and nomad women possessed impressive strength when it came to beating up other women, none of them would challenge an armed man with anything other than sharp words.

"Stop this!" screamed a desperate wife, as the slaves who were staying behind looked on in wonder. She kicked the departing slave girl viciously in the leg, causing her to stumble, and then launched herself at Kalie with wickedly sharp fingernails. "He will beat me if he finds her gone!"

"Then keep a knife handy and find the strength to use it on him!" Kalie shot back, pushing back a stray lock of hair, which now, freed from its veil blew wildly around her face. "You have two others who choose to stay! Be thankful for them!"

"But she keeps his interest from returning to

me! Another baby will kill me!"

Kalie groaned and waved to one of the warriors to take over. Borik, a muscular giant, came over and lifted the struggling slave girl, carrying her to where a growing line was preparing to leave.

"Come with us!" Kalie said uselessly to the weeping wife, who now sobbed in the arms of her two remaining slaves.

There were bigger problems over supplies. It seemed that no matter how little the runaways were taking with them, it was too much.

"Fine, go, you worthless slut!" a red-faced wife was shouting at a skinny, half naked girl. "But all you're taking with you is your rotted cunt!" She then tried to tear off the rest of the girl's clothes. Kalie was grateful she had clarified the exception about defense of herself or another in her vow to stop hitting women. She had to pummel the woman half unconscious before she would stop.

For those few who were wives in their own right, the departure was easier. There were still disputes when a senior wife wanted to argue, or all of the women of the household united to stop her. But most simply stared in baffled amazement at their good fortune.

"You are his first wife, Nesia!" cried a pockmarked woman with a fussy baby at her breast. "You want to leave all you have to go die of thirst? What about your children?"

Nesia adjusted the strap that kept her infant son securely bound beneath her breast, then took the hand of her five-year-old daughter. "It is for them that I do this," she said. "You know how ill our husband was when he rode to battle. What are the chances he will return alive?"

"But if he does, he will ride for as long as he must to bring back his children," said a young concubine, a malicious grin on her face. "And he will beat you until you plead for death—which you deserve for such a deed!"

Elka watched with a puzzled frown as Brenia packed and walked quietly out of her tent with Barak on her back. Only when they passed the last of the tents, and took their places at the front of the line of refugees did Elka suddenly howl and give chase. "No!" she screamed. "It isn't fair! Hysaak must kill you himself! It's the only way I can be sure he loves me!"

"He will kill her as soon as he catches her!" laughed a woman who stood watching. "Why aren't you happy to see her go? She's taking your son's only rival with her!"

Elka launched herself at Brenia. "I will not be cheated of my prize!"

Kalie pried the younger woman off Riyik's sister and flung her to the ground with more force than was perhaps necessary. Elka kicked at her from the ground, her blond hair tangling around her head like a nest of snakes. "If she leaves, Hysak will remember only that he once loved her, and will want her back! She must stay! Without her to hate, he will begin to hate me!"

"I know this place is crazy," Kalie said to no one in particular. "But I think she'd qualify as insane anywhere."

"You're probably right," said one of the Aahken men in their group. In all, twenty-seven men were going west with them. It seemed to Kalie a good number: enough to provide protection on the journey home, but not enough to threaten a city if they proved less than honorable when the journey was over.

Finally, the camp was divided into two groups: a small group of women, ready to brave the unknown and make new lives, and the rest, who would wait in their tents as they had done for all of theirs.

The most heartbreaking, Kalie thought, were those who wanted to go, but stayed because of their children.

More than half the women leaving were either pregnant, or carried a nursing infant. Some had older children, who followed their mothers without question. But those with older children who understood what was going on and did not support it, faced an agonizing decision.

Most boys over the age of ten had gone with the warriors. But Kalie wept as she watched six women give up their dream of freedom when threatened by their own children.

"I will wait for father!" an angry seven-year old boy shouted with arms crossed over his chest. His mother looked sadly at Kalie, shook her head, and allowed the boy to lead her back into their tent.

"If you try to take me, I will kill you!" a child no older than nine shouted at his concubine mother. "You dishonor my father and all my ancestors."

"I'll show that little brat honor!" Kalie shouted.

Riyik held her back. "I know this is hard, but in these cases, we cannot interfere."

"So we let children dictate to their mothers?" Kalie demanded. "Don't they know that if the Wolf and their allies win this battle, every one of those boys will be killed? Their mothers to follow if they're not desirable enough to merit rape and slavery?"

"Of course they know!" said Riyik. "But to them, it's a better fate than fleeing the protection of a home and clan. Of being branded a coward and a traitor, and losing any chance of reaching paradise in the next life."

Kalie had known how much the women who followed her risked, but until that moment she hadn't realized how much they were giving up—for themselves and their children. It made her more determined than ever to make sure they lived to rejoice in their decision. But the scene before her still stung.

"We could drug the children. Or bind them." Kalie looked pleadingly at Riyik. "Just until they understand it's for their own good. When they reach the west they'll be glad they came!" At Riyik's look, she faltered, but did not give up. "If we could at least convince the mothers to come, they would not have to watch their sons die, or endure a life of slavery knowing every day that didn't have to!"

Riyik's face was lined with pain, but he shook his head. "If those women leave their children, they will come to hate themselves. And if we take those boys with us by force, what do you think will happen?"

Kalie groaned. "They will seek every opportunity to escape, and bring the warriors after us —or destroy us on their own, to avenge what we have done," she said bitterly.

"As you yourself have done to this tribe, my beloved."

"I hate it when you're right," Kalie said, shoulders sagging with defeat.

Riyik flung an arm around her and turned her

until she faced west. "I grieve with you for those who stay behind. But look upon what you have accomplished!"

Before them stood an orderly line of thirty-two women, fifteen children, and twenty-six men. All of the men were mounted. Seven horses served as pack animals, to allow the unencumbered travelers to move at higher speed than they normally did. The old and sick, including Danica and Agafa, rode pillion behind patient warriors. Two horses stood saddled, but without riders: Thunder and Blossom. About fifty sheep and goats milled about, anxiously anticipating the signal to begin walking.

Riyik looked at the sky. "We can travel ten miles before dark. Perhaps twice that each day that follows." He pointed to the full moon rising in the west. "If fate is kind, we will be in your land when next the moon reaches this phase."

Kalie turned to him, memorizing every bit of this beloved face. "Get them started on their journey, Riyik, for that is something only you can do. I will catch up with you before the sun sets. But there is something I must do first."

Chapter 37

Riyik swung on her so suddenly Kalie thought he was going to hit her.

Then she saw the look in his eyes, and knew he would not—only that he was as determined that she not do this thing as she was determined that she would.

"I can't let anyone follow us," she said simply. "You know as well as I that if the men of Aahk are not wiped out to a man, that they will come after us. And if the other side wins, they may well be drunk enough on kumis and victory to hunt us down tonight while we sleep, just for the sport of it."

"Then we shall deal with that tonight," said Riyik. "Together. You know that it's much more likely neither side will have the strength or desire to pursue us at all."

"I can't let their lives depend on what's likely!" Kalie pointed at the group ready to depart. "Please, my love! I've come too far and suffered too much to leave my work unfinished. And you are the only one I can trust to lead these people to my home."

"So what is your plan?" Riyik demanded. "Ride to the battle and take on every warrior who survives?"

"No, only those who ride in this direction. Those who ride east may do so with my blessing!"

"By yourself? With neither training nor experience? And no weapons besides those bone toys?" Riyik pointed to the baskets of Serpent Fangs, which stood ready.

"It's what I have to do!"

"I will not let you die on the very day we begin

our new life together!"

"And I will not let you live with the knowledge that you killed your own spear- brothers while they tried to retreat to safety!"

"That is not your decision to make, Kalie!"

"Neither is how I finish my mission your decision, Riyik!"

"You've done enough! It's time to leave!"

"Excuse me," said a gruff voice. Borik loomed over both of them. "Could we get this group moving, and explore the future of marriage latter? They're getting restless."

Kalie could see the excitement of departure turning to panic. Varena stood with her arm around Katya, waving anxiously for Kalie to join them. Agafa looked like she might lose her resolve and die now if they didn't start. Kalie felt her own resolve weaken.

"These new weapons are a wonder," said another of Riyik's men, carefully touching one of the Serpent Fangs. "Leaving behind a small group while the others begin the journey might be a smart idea. We could find out how well they work, perhaps destroy the tribe's ability to pursue us and with good horses, join up with the others by nightfall."

Danica had dismounted and come to see what was going on. "It would increase our chances of reaching the west safely," she said.

After a swift discussion, about half the men agreed to go with Kalie and Riyik to scout the area of the battle, and make sure no one followed the escapees. The rest would lead the women and children west. If all went well, they would be together again that evening.

Kalie paused long enough to duck into their

tent and change into an old outfit of Riyik's, realizing as she did so that she was probably the only woman here who'd worn pants before.

When she emerged from the tent, Kalie found Alessa, similarly dressed, waiting for her.

"I have to go with you," Alessa said.

Too rushed to argue, Kalie simply asked, "Why?"

"I'm not altogether sure," said Alessa. "I just know that I have to."

"You were brutally beaten and dragged by a horse this morning…" Kalie began, but Alessa merely shook her head. "We will be killing men and horses," she added more firmly, knowing Alessa would want nothing to do with either.

"She can ride with me," said Borik. Kalie saw that it was time to go. Borik lifted Alessa effortlessly —and surprisingly gently—and placed her behind him on his horse.

Then Riyik gave the signal, and the larger group began to move slowly to the west. Kalie and her raiding party moved at a much faster clip in the opposite direction.

"I loved your story," Alessa said to Kalie as their horses ride side by side. "And I loved the way you used it to save my life. But you still should have told them the truth."

"What do you mean?" Kalie asked.

"Alesaak was you, not me. His name should have been Kalaak."

Kalie thought about it, not really surprised to discover it was so. But she wasn't completely convinced. "His anger and determination were mine," she conceded. "But his strength and courage were yours."

Alessa was silent for a moment. Then she said, "I told him, you know. I told Nelek everything we did to Valaan and Barta."

That was, of course, the only way Nelek could have known. Kalie had been too busy to think of it earlier, and did not want to think about it now. "Anyone can break under torture," she told her friend. "Even you. I would never think any less of you—"

"Nelek never tortured me, Kalie. I went to him on my own. These welts on my back are from the beating he gave me afterward."

Kalie did not know what to say, so she waited.

"You were right when you guessed that I learned of Amaar's plot to overthrow is father; that I went to Nelek to warn him. But then, somehow, after that…I just couldn't stop. After Barta was killed, I became so lost…I could no longer hear Her voice. I couldn't find Her anywhere! I needed guidance, and for reasons I'll never understand, I went to Nelek for it!" Alessa shook her head in confusion.

"Alessa, your faith sustained you through so much. Losing it must have been like trying to navigate a boat during a storm: nothing to give you directions. Is it really so surprising that you simply went to the man with all the power? Confusing that, as these people do, with having all the answers?"

Alessa thought about that, then nodded. "I wonder if that's what happened to Kestra?" she said. Kalie lost the rest as Borik urged his horse forward.

They traveled silently; tensely.

Quickly, too quickly it seemed, they heard the sounds of battle. Two scouts rode forward before Kalie realized that Riyik had sent them. The rest dismounted and hid in the tall grass until they returned. The sky above was black with ravens and vultures. The not so distant clang of weapons and the screams of the dying were harsh and unreal in Kalie's ears. Blood and death rode on the wind.

"It is as we hoped," reported the first scout after only a short time had passed. "Each side has inflicted heavy losses on the other. The battle is ending now, and they seem to have fought to a stand-still. The Wolf and Hansi are returning to their camps in the north."

"What remains of 'The Great Federation of Tribes,'" smirked the second scout, "is already limping back toward camp. They shall pass this way very soon."

"We should set up there," said the first scout, pointing to a stand of grass a short distance to the east.

"A good thing we have so many of these new weapons," remarked Borik. "The warriors will travel singly or in small groups. They'll cover a wide area over an unknown length of time. We will need all of these."

"Maybe not," said Riyik. "I fear they will become useless once the horses begin falling and the men become alert to what is going on."

Kalie surveyed the endless stretches of grass. Some had been beaten down by the army, which had passed through earlier in the day. Most stood waving, eternally indifferent to the creatures that lived upon it. "I hadn't thought of that. It is the perfect weapon for forests, where riders must travel down a single trail."

"All the more reason you must return to your people to show them," said Riyik.

Kalie waited, then smiled when Riyik said

nothing more. She knew he wanted to her head for safety; to leave this fight to the men, but he didn't argue. And she loved him all the more for that.

But not enough for her to run from this fight.

She had exchanged the knife Basha had given her for a larger, more deadly knife from one of the warriors. Riyik had given her a spear, but they both knew she had never cast one before. Kalie wore it strapped to her back as the warriors did with their spares. In her hands she held a basket of Serpent Fangs: a weapon no one had any experience with.

At least in that they were all equal.

Each of the raiders took a basket of the new weapons and spread out among the places where they hoped the retreating warriors of Aahk and Wolf and Malquor would have to pass. Kalie had wanted to scatter the stars and retreat, but the others had insisted there weren't enough of them to take such a risk. For today, her new weapon would have to be used at close quarters and flung directly in the path of fast-moving horses.

She sensed Riyik's presence nearby, even though she couldn't see him. Kalie wished the warriors would arrive soon so she wouldn't have to brood about what had she gotten him into. If he killed a kinsman or a childhood friend this day, would he ever forgive himself? Would he ever forgive her?

Then she heard it: the sound of pounding hooves riding for the camp just behind them. Everyone was in position. Kalie peered through the grass and saw exhausted men riding lathered horses. Many were in injured. Some, from the way they slumped in their saddles, were either dead or dying. She saw men she recognized. And although she hated every one of them, the cost of war sickened her.

Suddenly, Kalie knew this was not why the Goddess had shown her this weapon. And more importantly, that she could not simply spring an attack on defeated men who only sought the safety of their own tents.

With a quick birdcall to Riyik, she motioned to him her intentions. Not waiting to for a response, Kalie slid forward in the grass. Kariik was just coming into view, riding a once fine black stallion. Both man and horse were covered with blood and grime, Kariik with a hastily dressed wound on his spear arm. The largest group of warriors clustered around him, while stragglers followed.

Kalie rose to her full height, allowing her head and shoulders to show above the grass. She raised her empty hands. "Kariik, stop!" she shouted. "You are not in danger yet, and you needn't be, but pause and listen." Kariik stopped, more puzzled than alarmed. Not so the men around him. Kalie knew she would have only moments before they began scouring the grass, and discovering her companions.

"A small number of your people have chosen to leave your tribe. Some of them are men you have condemned—however unfairly—while others are women held against their will. I ask only that you let them leave in peace. You have survived this battle; take that as a sign of favor from your gods. Go in peace to your winter camps, and you may continue as you always have. But seek to follow us, or threaten the lands of the Goddess, and all of you will die. The choice is yours!" And although she couldn't see her, Kalie sensed Alessa's approving gaze.

Kariik's pallid face grew red. "A horse to the

man who brings me her head!" he shouted.

The survivors of the battle formed a perfect column, all heading straight for Kalie. As if, she realized, they were on a road through a forest. Those of Kariik's men who rode away from the column to search the surrounding area were the first to fall.

The shrieking of injured horses was the first indication of the effectiveness of the new weapon. To her right, Kalie watched as two horses reared and stumbled. One managed to remain upright but threw its rider, who hit the ground with a curse. The other horse went down, pinning its rider beneath. The screams of the dying man mixed with those of his terrified horse.

The nearby commotion caused some of the warriors with Kariik to swerve or slow, but most continued straight on to where Kalie stood. She never flinched. As the lead horses came so close she could feel their hot and winded breath and smell the stench of blood mixed with their sweat, she flung half her stars straight into the faces of the startled riders, then flung herself hard to the left.

Kalie rolled, tangling herself in the tall grass. Even before she found her feet and began crawling to safety, the thunderous sounds of chaos behind her told her the attack was successful.

Only a few horses had stepped directly on the stars, but each of those fell into one or more other horses. Kalie watched in amazement as a falling horse knocked the one beside it into the one behind that. All three horses fell in a tangled heap, thrashing and writhing, two men pinned beneath. Two more horses could not stop in time and fell full length into the melee. The warriors behind those five, Kariik among them, were able to swerve in time, parting around the pile of bodies like a river around a boulder. But by then, everyone else had gone to work.

Some of the men had already exhausted their supply of Horse- Killers, and had left the cover of the grass to engage in hand-to-hand fighting with the fallen warriors. Others were chasing those who had avoided the bone stars. There were, Kalie saw in amazement, quite few of the latter. They just might be able to fight until everyone left alive from the previous battle was cut down in this one.

Riyik paused to cut a suffering horse's throat, and then did battle with its crazed rider. Kalie feared that rage might make their enemies more dangerous, but panic engendered by the new weapon seemed to be clouding their judgment. Riyik dispatched his opponent with a thrust of this spear, then turned to leap on a warrior who had discovered Alessa in the grass and was poised to run her through.

Kalie spared only a moment to make certain they were both all right, then raced to where the men protecting Kariik were making a last stand. She flung the last of her sharpened bone fragments up into the men's faces and down to where the horses were stepping, dodging both deadly hooves and flying spears. Somehow, she always stayed a step ahead of them.

Men she knew as allies came to her aid, just as Kalie realized she was out of weapons. Riyik was shouting for her to fall back; that the rest of them could handle things, when a voice shouted, "Hey! We could use some help over here!"

Not far away, Borik stood holding Kariik at knifepoint. Literally holding, Kalie saw, for the king's feet dangled a good distance off the ground. Borik looked as terrified as his royal hostage.

"It's about to get very ugly," Kalie said into the sudden silence. "But if the right person were to take charge, and negotiate..." She looked at Riyik and smiled again.

Riyik nodded, grim resolution in his eyes. He moved fast despite his injuries.

"Kariik!" Riyik shouted as he drew close enough to command the attention of all concerned. "Tell your men to drop their weapons!"

Kariik turned what was probably intended to be a royal snarl in Riyik's direction, but his chin quivered. "Do it!" Riyik snapped, his tone brooking no dispute.

"Drop your weapons!" Kariik ordered through shut teeth. His men glanced warily at each other, but slowly complied. Kalie knew they would have to conclude this business quickly, for most of them kept knives up their sleeves, and would be looking for an opportunity to use them.

"I'll make this simple," Riyik said, his gaze somehow holding both the king and the surviving warriors who surrounded him. "Either we leave your territory safely, or you die now."

"I'm well rid of you all!" snapped Kariik, as Borik slowly lowered him to the ground at a signal from Riyik. "You, Riyik, and your followers and whichever women you've chosen are free to go. You have my word."

"Thank you," said Riyik, not relaxing in the least. "But unfortunately, your word is not worth what a king's should be. That, I'm afraid, is what began all this." Kariik and the men around him stiffened.

"Collect the horses!" Riyik shouted to his men. "Run off those who are strong enough to chase us. Leave the injured to be walked back to camp for the food and rest they need." He turned back to Kariik. "By tomorrow, you'll have regained most of your herd, and we will be well rid of each other."

As the men hurried to comply, Alessa came to stand beside Kalie and Riyik.

"Riyik, what of the wounded men?" Alessa asked. "We should leave enough horses to get them back to camp."

"Why?" asked Borik.

Riyik smiled. "Kalie, what do you think?"

She glanced at Alessa, then nodded.

Kariik's wounded were loaded on the least winded of their horses and sent on their way, over the loud objections of some of Riyik's men. But no one made a move to prevent it. They simply gathered up their own wounded and the weapons taken from their enemies. They also carried bodies, Kalie saw. Four who rode with Riyik would never see the West. Men who would have been a threat to her people? Or simply the fortunes of war?

Riyik held Kariik until Borik brought Thunder and Blossom to where he and Kalie waited. "The gods will curse you for betraying your king!" Kariik spat.

"As they will curse you for taking a crown that was not yours and allowing yourself to be ruled by evil men?" Riyik shot back. "Wake up, Kariik! The man who used you, who murdered your father and brothers, has fled—doubtless looking for another weak leader he can use. It's time for you to grow up and become the king these people need, before it's too late!"

"And how will I do that?" Kariik cried. "The

alliance is destroyed! We've stayed too long at our summer pastures! Our winter camps may well have been taken by others and we lack the strength to fight for them! And now you say the west is closed to us! So you tell me, Riyik: what are we to do?"

He sounded so desperate, so honestly lost, that Kalie almost felt sorry for him. And she could see that Riyik truly did. But no one spoke until Alessa stepped forward.

"Consider this possibility," she said, her voice carrying as easily as Kalie's had when she told her story. "Your numbers are depleted, so combine the clans—two for each winter camp. If others have occupied some of those places, then leave them! Don't start a fight you can't win. We have taken few of your animals. You will have enough to survive the winter."

Kariik stared down at her from his horse, as did the men around him.

"It is a good plan," Riyik said. His gaze locked with Kariik's. "And a good leader recognizes a good plan."

"It might help us survive the winter," Kariik conceded, but he was looking at Riyik, not Alessa. "But what then?" Despite her desperate wish to be gone from this place, Kalie began to smile.

Riyik looked at Alessa. "What do you suggest, Priestess? What will happen in the spring?"

"Spring will be hard," Alessa agreed. "The grass is drying up. There will be much fighting over water. One solution would be to kill more of your animals. It will reduce your need for water and pasture, the extra meat will strengthen your people, and you will have a surplus of leather and fur which might be used in trade for--"

"Then what do we eat next winter?" cried Kariik. "Where will the milk for cheese and kumis come from?"

"Listen to this foreign slave and we will all be dead by next winter!" shouted one of Kariik's warriors.

"That may be." Alessa shrugged as if it was no concern of hers. Then her eyes bored into those of the king. "But there is another possibility. Maylene's son is in your keeping, Kariik. If you want to try leading your people down a different path, then come next summer, bring them west. Give the boy to his mother's kin to raise. Watch him grow up and see how a man can still be a man without murder and torture for his daily fare."

"Alessa, what are you doing?" Kalie cried, but it came out a whisper.

"What I came here to do," the priestess answered softly. "This tribe will be desperate. And desperate people will try anything." She met Kariik's puzzled gaze. "It's up to you, King of Aahk. Come in friendship—and kinship—and we will help you start over." Then she turned to Kalie, who realized it was her turn to speak.

Kalie gracefully raised her arm and held a Serpent Fang before Kariik's face. "But come in haughty arrogance, thinking to take what others have built, and you will be met with these. And you will be met by people who know what life under your rule is like. We will kill every one of you before we let you harm one inch of our world." She grinned wolfishly. "And what's more, we will take your women—and make them like us!"

Kariik actually flinched at that, along with

several of his men. Alessa merely nodded her approval. "The future will involve grave risks for all of us," she said.

"But that would have been the case anyway," said Riyik. "You will have a year to decide, and a Western wife to teach you all you will need to know —"

"What!" Two shouts echoed together. Kalie looked to see who the other voice belonged to, and found herself staring at Kariik—whose confused expression mirrored her own. A ripple of laughter encircled the gathering, easing some of the tension.

Riyik explained. "Alessa is a priestess of high rank. Her words carry great weight with her people. And as the wife of the king, she will have influence here, as well. Perhaps enough to prepare our people for what you yourself have rightly called our great destiny."

"It could work," muttered one of Kariik's warriors. "He's already got a taste for Western women…"

Kalie moved closer to Alessa. "You can't stay here!"

Alessa smiled. "I have to, Kalie. It is here I will find my Goddess again. And it's here that I will atone for my part in all those deaths." She looked at Kalie with a calm certainty, greater than even what Kalie was used to from her. "You and Larren must return to our people. I must stay here, and prepare the horsemen to join them—in partnership. And perhaps, I can help poor Kestra find her way back as well."

"Alessa, I can't just leave you with them!"

"As you so recently said to me," Riyik whispered in her ear. "It is not your decision to make."

"Now I really hate it when you're right!" she snapped.

"I must return to the camp to care for the wounded—" Alessa was saying when Kalie caught a movement out of the corner of her eye. "Alessa, look out!" she screamed, as a creature from a nightmare rode into the gathering, a spear poised and ready to impale the priestess.

Riyik reacted at once, casting his own spear, injuring the intruder, and spoiling his aim. The spear missed Alessa, but only just, and clattered to the mud at their feet.

"Haraak!" Kalie shouted raising her own spear. Her old enemy bled from a dozen wounds, although none appeared fatal.

"Kalie, don't!" Riyik cried, pushing her spear down. Men and horses shifted nervously, as the threat to the fragile peace established just moments ago became apparent to all.

"We can't let him live!" Kalie hissed. "And no, this is not just about personal revenge! If he regains control of Kariik—"

"That is why we must wait. Believe me, I want Haraak dead just as much as you—and he will die today, I promise! But Kariik is on the verge of becoming his own man—but only if he can stand up to Haraak now, by himself, in front of his men…"

Kalie understood, but she didn't like the odds.

Already, Kariik's face was clouding, his newfound confidence ebbing. Haraak saw it, but instead of speaking to his puppet, turned to the men.

"These foreign witches are more dangerous than any of us supposed!" he shouted, and again, Kalie was impressed by his skill at storytelling. "You all just saw Riyik—once our brother—shed the blood of the king's own advisor, while I sought to free our king from the spell this witch has placed him under!" He raised his bloody arm, ignoring the pain he was surely in, and pointed at Alessa. "Riyik, too, is under a spell." Haraak glared at Kalie. "One I thought I had broken. But I shall do so now, before all of you…"

"Enough of your manipulations, Haraak!" Kariik said, and Kalie saw with amazement that he was angry. To a man, his assembled warriors stiffened in surprise, but none as much as Haraak. He froze, and barely recovered in time to stop his jaw from dropping. "I am king," Kariik declared, as if puzzling out the meaning of the words.

"Yes," said Haraak, turning the full force of his charm on his puppet. "You are king, and you will lead us to a glorious conquest of the lands to the West! Once these witches are dead, you will remember your great destiny! Men will sing of your deeds for—"

"I am king," Kariik repeated. "Which means that I will do what I must for the good of my people. It is not a task I sought, nor one I willingly accepted—even after you murdered my two brothers, for the sole purpose of making yourself king through me—"

An angry hiss erupted from the frightened warriors, but no one knew exactly where to point his spear. Haraak, for once, was speechless. "Oh, yes, I knew," Kariik continued. "I may lack the strength of my father, and the courage of my brothers, but I have at least as much wisdom as the gods gave a horse. I simply thought it was safer—and easier—to be the witless tool everyone thought I was. But I can't be that any longer. This tribe—what's left of it—cannot afford it." The grin that Kalie was trying to smother appeared on Kariik's face. "But you were right about one thing, Haraak: our destiny does lie in the west." He smiled at Alessa, who made no attempt to hide her grin. "Just not in the way you foresaw."

Haraak's face grew even redder than his hair. "You sniveling whelp!" he screamed. "I did not put you where you are so some foreign whore could lead to by your cock and turn our warriors into geldings!"

"That may well be," said Kariik, not sounding at all like the whining boy of just the day before. "But in case you haven't noticed, Haraak, nearly a third of our warriors are dead. The grasslands are drying and a slave girl has devised a weapon that could turn us into slaves if her Goddess was so inclined. I would say the time for conquest is over."

Kalie could no longer contain her laughter. "Come now, Haraak!" she taunted. "This is what you have wanted since the day you first came to my land! It is what you have murdered and manipulated and sold yourself for! Your entire tribe is finally moving to the west!"

"Yes!" cried Alessa. "And once there, they will swear allegiance to the Great Goddess, and atone for generations of abuse, cowardice and deceit! You're getting what you wanted—or at least what you deserve!"

When she saw the look on Haraak's face, Kalie realized she had just gotten all the revenge she needed. His face was nearly purple and he was having trouble breathing. "You will both die for those words!" he finally managed to choke out. Then he laughed, but it was forced, and there was genuine fear in his eyes. "The warriors of Aahk take what they want, and crush all who oppose them. That will not stop because of some witch's curse." Haraak turned to the men. "Watch and follow. We will each of us take these whores upon the ground right now and strip them of their powers. Then I will cut out their hearts and tongues and bury them where we stand."

"Actually," said Riyik, "we are going to conclude the business at hand, and then you are going to die where we stand, Haraak. For the rape of my wife and the murder of my king."

Kalie noticed that Riyik had placed the insult to her before the murder of a king, and despite the danger they faced, felt strangely happy.

"Please do so, Riyik" said Kariik.

Haraak whipped around to face the king, his face mottled with rage. Then he drew his dagger and with an incoherent roar, flung himself at Kariik. "You are no king!" Haraak spat. " It was always my destiny anyway! I will lead our people to—"

Whatever else Haraak might have said ended in a muffled thud as Riyik's spear slid neatly through his ribs and into his heart. Haraak was dead before his body hit the ground.

Everyone looked at each other for a moment. Then Alessa said, "My king, I really must return to care for the wounded." She slid her gaze to Riyik, then back to Kariik in silent urging.

Kariik nodded and turned to Riyik. "I owe you my life. But my only thanks will be to keep my word to you, and allow you to leave with those who would go with you."

Riyik inclined his head. "That is all the thanks I wish, my king."

From behind them, a few warriors suggested that Riyik should remain as the king's new close advisor, but Kariik shook his head. "I've had enough of strong-minded men whispering in my ear. I will do better with men who don't think much with their brains, and a woman who can actually help me become the king I want to be." Then he turned his horse and led the remains of his army back to camp.

Chapter 38

Riyik would have preferred to bypass the camp altogether and just ride west until they picked up their companions' trail. But there were injuries that had to be tended—his included—if they were to ride hard enough to catch up with the others by dark, and now, at least, they could be safely treated there.

If Kariik kept his word.

As the camp came in view, it seemed smaller, sadder and less threatening than it had before. Some of the wounded had already arrived—with news of those who would not be back—and the eerie sound of women keening their grief could be heard on the wind.

Alessa was already organizing the care of the wounded. News of her new status traveled quickly, and now Alessa had many assistants and whatever supplies she called for.

Kalie slipped away to have one last look at the tent she had lived so long as a slave. Women made the sign against evil as she passed and a few spat at her feet, but no one stopped her.

As she drew close to Maalke's tent, Kalie heard the unmistakable wails of mourning. Maalke lay dead on a blanket in front of his tent. Altia, dressed in her finest clothing was arranging his many possessions around his body, barking the occasional order to her daughters who keened their grief as they worked.

Beside Maalke lay a tiny bundle, also wrapped for burial.

"No!" screamed Kalie, rushing to open the blanket and see for herself.

"Don't you touch him!" Altia screamed back,

pushing Kalie away. "Don't touch either of them!"

Kalie stared at the dead baby. "When? How?"

It took Altia a moment to understand. Just barely, her face softened. "He is no sacrifice. He breathed his last peacefully, a few hours before my brother returned with Maalke's body. Everyone knew it was just a matter of time."

"Everyone except Cassia," Kalie said.

"If it had to happen, it's better this way. He will ride to Paradise on his father's shoulder, just as if he had lived to be a great warrior himself."

Kalie turned at the sound of the voice, raw with grief, and found Cassia staring at her. She, too, was dressed in her finest clothes, and carried bedding Kalie well remembered: soft, well-made furs, pieced together into intricate patterns of subtle colors. Altia reached out to take them, but Cassia shook her head, and began arranging them around Maalke, save for the last— a rabbit-fur blanket—which she lovingly wrapped around her infant son.

Then she turned to Kalie.

"As you can see, your work here is finished. Why do you remain?"

"I wanted to speak with you one last time," said Kalie, trying to keep the weakness she felt out of her voice. It was the first lesson she'd learned in this place: a woman must never show weakness before another woman. "To tell you I'm sorry that you and so many others had to suffer. That I wish things could have been different."

Cassia's eyes bored into Kalie's. "They could have been," she said simply.

"One of our tribes had to lose," said Kalie. "And it was yours who set those rules, not mine. So I did what you taught me to do: win at all costs. And it has cost us all a great deal."

"But it is you who will ride out of here," said Cassia. She took in Kalie's man's dress and unveiled hair knotted behind her head. "Flouting our ways to last, it seems."

"Come with me!" cried Kalie. Cassia burst out laughing. "Please, Cassia. You have skilled hands, a caring heart and a quick mind! You could be happy with my people. You have nothing left here."

Cassia looked sadly at Kalie. "I have everything here. Already my husband and child wait for me. Tomorrow, we will be together."

It took Kalie a moment to grasp what she was saying. "No!" It came out as a hoarse whisper. "You cannot. Altia is first wife. Only she…"

"She has agreed to share the honor with me. It is not often so with first wives, and I did not expect it from her. But it seems, in the end, she was a better friend to me than you, Kalie."

"I suppose we each offered what friendship we could. That is not something I expected when I came here. But I will remember it."

"Perhaps you will make a story of it."

"Perhaps."

Altia returned, carrying two knives. She gave one to Cassia.

"Now?" Kalie asked in terror, seeing, for the first time, that while they had talked, Cassia had seated herself beside Maalke, their child between them, with Altia now on his other side.

"Tomorrow," said Cassia. "But we will keep watch beside him tonight. In the morning, we will walk beside our husband's body to the grave that will be prepared." She gazed across the still half empty camp. "There will be many graves, as I hear it. We will die beside him there, after the sacrifices are complete."

"Complete?" Kalie choked. "You think your senseless deaths don't rank with the others as 'sacrifices'?"

"Leave us, Kalie," Cassia ordered quietly. "You've caused enough harm already. You can laugh with your Goddess over your victory back in your own land."

"My Goddess will never laugh at this," said Kalie, backing away. "And neither will I."

She hurried back to where Alessa was treating the wounded, wanting nothing more than ride away from this place and wash the images of Cassia and Altia from her mind. When she reached the tent, however, she saw at once that something had happened. Riyik stood with Kariik beside a body that lay on a rich fur robe, guarded by six exhausted men.

They were the last of the men who had ridden here with Nelek.

Kalie approached, slipping quietly between Riyik and Borik, and saw that the king still breathed. Alessa was examining a gory wound in his gut with far more compassion that Kalie could have mustered, had it been Maalke.

"The wound is mortal," she told him.

She tried to offer him a bowl filled with a murky liquid, but Nelek turned his head away from it. "I knew I was dying when I rode here," he whispered, seeming beyond the pain. "But I had to see you one last time, Alessa. To tell you that I forgive you. That when I am laid in my cairn, you shall lay by my side and travel with me to paradise."

He waited a moment, perhaps expecting Alessa to fall on her knees and weep with joy. Then Nelek turned to Kariik. "See to it, my brother. Let none prevent her from joining me in death. I know my warriors will think her unworthy and try to prevent it…" His voice was lost in a horrible choking sound, as blood foamed at his pale lips.

Some of Kariik's men shifted uneasily, but none dared speak. Kalie knew their dilemma: their future in the West depended on the woman to whom their king would listen. But she was still Nelek's slave, and who could interfere with a dying king's choice of companions? Certainly not Kariik, who gazed in horror at his brother king.

But Kalie herself faced no such dilemma. She drew her knife. "Rescind that order, Nelek," she said mildly. His men growled, though Kariik's were strangely silent. "If you don't, I'm afraid you will have to meet your gods with no more manhood on you than a mare has." She set her knife on the slight bulge between his legs, the blade just brushing his testicles. "And what do you think your fate in the next life will be then?"

Nelek worked his mouth, but only strangled cries emerged, along with more blood. His body seized up, and his lips drew back in a hideous grin.

Alessa pushed the knife aside, and laid a gentle hand on her former master. It seemed to help, for his body relaxed, even as the life faded from his eyes. "There will be no need for that, I promise, Nelek. You will ride to your gods just as they made you. But you will ride without me." He tried again to speak, but Alessa continued. "I will stay here, and help your people prepare for the day when deaths such as yours —and the kind you sought for me—are remembered only in legend, and your bloodthirsty gods are forgotten. It's what I came here to do. I thank you for your help, but I need it no longer. So go in peace."

Nelek gasped once more, and died.

Kalie still held her knife. "If anyone tries to follow that last order…"

"No one will," said Kariik, rising to his feet. "For to send the priestess of a foreign goddess with the king of the Wolf Tribe would surely anger his gods, and jeopardize his chance to be honored in paradise." He looked at each of Nelek's men. "Do you not agree?"

Every one of them nodded. Then they knelt, and offered their oaths to Kariik, who accepted them graciously.

"It is time for us to go," Kalie said simply. "Alessa, are you sure about this?"

Alessa hugged Kalie to her in a warm embrace. "I believe we shall meet again," was her only answer. "But in case we don't…" She stepped back to meet Kalie's gaze, a look of mischief pulling at her serene face. "Thank you for offering to geld Nelek for me. It's an image I shall savor in the years to come."

Kalie only grinned. Her friend would be just fine. But she wouldn't bet on some of the others who gathered around Kariik, jockeying for position in the new government.

Riyik reached for her, clearly planning to set her astride Thunder, but Kalie shook her head. She walked to where Blossom stood, anxious to leave the smell of blood and death that already permeated the camp. "I will leave this place on my own horse, under my own strength," she said. But she had to let Riyik help her mount.

"Will you ride beside me?" he asked when they were both astride their steeds.

"All the way to my home," she said, then corrected herself. "To our home. And forever after that."

They rode west, into a blinding sunset that seemed to paint the land the color of blood.

Soon, however, the sun sank into the grass before them, and a mellow twilight showed them where, still far in the distance, their friends were camped. No tracks betrayed the presence of enemies and no scavengers circled above the campsite.

Beside her, Riyik reached out his hand. Kalie reached out with her good arm, and put her hand in his, trusting her balance to her knees and her horse's gentle nature.

"What will we find, you think, when we reach the west?" he asked.

"That has been my greatest hope and greatest fear since I came here," she answered. "I've had nightmares: cities in flames, fields choked with bodies, a tribe of beastmen sitting on the corpse of my world while we fought here."

"But have there been good dreams as well?"

She smiled. "Yes. I have seen a land in peace for many years, because of what we did today. I've seen horses grazing beside the cattle of my country, and boys and girls learning to ride together. And weavers exclaiming with joy over the wool made by local sheep bred with these hardy eastern ones. And I've seen you, Riyik, teaching men and women how to fight. I just can't tell if that one's a dream or a nightmare."

Riyik squeezed her hand. "People can defend what they have without losing what they are, Kalie. And you and I will make certain it happens that way."

She nodded, but her thoughts were already straying to the dream she'd had last night, as she lay in Riyik's arms. The one she could not yet speak of. The one where she and Riyik lay together on a warm bed of soft sheepskins with a gurgling baby between them. In her dream, Kalie could smell the milk that dripped from her breasts; feel the soreness inside that could only come from bearing a child. Was it possible?

No fire had been lit, but they found the camp easily in the darkness. Varena was beside Kalie before she worked herself off the horse.

"Are we going home now, Mother?" she asked.

Kalie flung her good arm around the woman who would always be her firstborn child—no matter how many others the future might hold for her. "Yes, my love. We're going home."

The End

Excerpt from: In The Balance

A collection of short fiction by Sandra Saidak, including a new story in the world of Kalie's Journey Coming 2012 from Uffington Horse Press

Yuraak fought his way through the blinding snow. He had no idea how many men were still with him; no thought of anything but the horse beneath him, and the desperate search for shelter. Of the twenty warriors who had followed him from the steppes of their homeland, only seven were left. At least he hoped so. The howling wind and snow that was more like sheets of ice made Yuraak wonder if he and his mount were the only living things in the world. At least they were out of those cursed mountains.

Haraak had never mentioned mountains in his tales of the land to the west. He had only told of grain and gold and women for the taking. Of fat cattle and sheep, of fruit trees in a rich green land that never knew thirst. Haraak never told him that the winter journey would take Yuraak's wife and young son from him, along with most of this clan.

"Curse Haraak for a lying bastard!" Yuraak cried.

An answering curse made him look to his right. "Watch out!" Marek was shouting, although Yuraak caught only a muffled whisper, barely in time to keep his horse from sliding down the frozen waterfall he had mistaken for a trail. By the time Yuraak had the blown horse under control, he was having trouble seeing, but at least he was starting to feel warmer. In some corner of his mind, the warrior knew that this was not really a good thing. Then he heard Marek's voice again, from much farther away.

"There's light ahead," the younger man was shouting. "And smoke!"

Zelena stood protectively on the threshold of her home. "The Mother was awake late into the night, helping with a difficult birth," she whispered harshly. "Whatever the problem is, one of the Elders can handle it until she wakens."

"This is not something we have ever seen!" the fur-clad young man insisted. While the snow had ceased, heavy clouds made the morning barely lighter than night, and it was bitterly cold. "People—and strange animals! At the foot of the mountain—"

"No one can cross the mountain in winter—" Zelena began, but by then it seemed the entire village had erupted with voices as people shouted the news, healers gathered torches and supplies, and others argued between carrying the victims of the weather to the village, or going to offer them aid where they were.

"That is why we need the Mother," the man said quietly.

"I am here," Laniya said in her voice of practiced calm. She dressed quickly. "Zelena, please start breakfast and look after Aral. Joran, please take me to these strangers." She followed her one-time consort out of the village, and into a throng of anxious, excited, and many just plain curious villagers. Shining Mountain was small—perhaps just over one hundred souls—but it was also isolated. Even in the summer it received few visitors. In the winter, with the mountain passes buried beneath snow and the little river that nestled the village half frozen and treacherous, travelers were unheard of.

While the healers who had first heard the news and the shepherd who had brought it were already moving, Laniya was soon at their head, projecting an air of calm assurance, while inwardly fearing she would find something that was bigger than she could handle. She swatted the thought away as she always did—then soon forgot it altogether when she saw what lay before her.

Bodies lay like clay figures thrown carelessly around a potter's workshop. Although clearly human, they were like no people Laniya had ever seen: large and muscular, wearing clothing that seemed to be nothing but layers of animal skin. None of the people moved, but a small group of strange animals clustered together in the shelter of a small hill. But it was clear they would not survive long out here.

The healers and their assistants checked each body for signs of life.

"This one is dead," said Marnak, senior healer, and one of the oldest men in the village.

"These, too," said his apprentice Karya. "So sad; a mother and child, frozen together."

Laniya's voice carried above the wind. "We must bring all of them back to the village! Only when they are warm, and some time has passed will we know for certain who has passed beyond recalling."

The people nodded at the wisdom of their Mother's words. All had heard of people lost in the snow, who had appeared dead when found, yet had returned to life after hours—or even days—of warmth and care. Some had even seen it themselves. Blankets were turned into litters, strong men lifted the smaller victims, and soon all the strangers were brought into the village. The shepherd who had discovered them, and a few who shared a similar affinity to animals, led the strange beasts, who looked a bit like giant goats, away for food and shelter, and whatever care they might need.

About The Author

Sandra Saidak graduated San Francisco State University in 1985 with a B.A. in English. She is a high school English teacher by day, author by night. Her hobbies include reading, folk music, attending SF conventions, researching prehistory, and maintaining an active fantasy life (but warns that this last one could lead to dangerous habits such as writing). Sandra lives in San Jose, CA with her husband Tom, daughters Heather and Melissa, and cats, Cocu and Oreo.

Learn more at: www.sandrasaidak.com